Cynthia Harrod-Eagles is the author of the contemporary Bill Slider Mystery series as well as the Morland Dynasty novels. Her passions are music, wine, horses, architecture and the English countryside.

Visit the author's website at www.cynthiaharrodeagles.com

The Morland Dynasty series:

CYNTHIA HARROD-EAGLES

Dynasty 4:
The Oak Apple

sphere

SPHERE

First published in Great Britain in 1982 by Futura Publications
Reprinted 1983, 1984, 1990
This edition published by Warner Books in 1993
Reprinted 1993, 1994, 1997, 2000
Reprinted by Time Warner Paperbacks in 2004
Reprinted by Sphere in 2006, 2008, 2009, 2010, 2011, 2012, 2014

ISBN 978-0-7515-0641-9

Printed and bound in Great Britain by
Clays Ltd, St Ives plc

Papers used by Sphere are from well-managed forests
and other responsible sources.

MIX
Paper from
responsible sources
FSC
www.fsc.org   FSC® C104740

Sphere
An imprint of
Little, Brown Book Group
100 Victoria Embankment
London EC4Y 0DY

An Hachette UK Company
www.hachette.co.uk

www.littlebrown.co.uk

FOREWORD

The most extraordinary thing about the Civil War, apart from the fact that it happened at all, is that still, after almost three and a half centuries, it arouses such passionate partisanship that it is almost impossible for anyone, historian or layman, to discuss it without taking sides. It is necessary, therefore, to read very widely and very carefully, in order to separate fact from prejudice. It is also necessary to try to distinguish between what the people at the time said they were fighting for, what they thought they were fighting for, and what they actually were fighting for. The story as told in this book will doubtless seem wildly biased to many, but I hope that they will accept that what is presented here is the Morland family's view of the events, and that they did not have the benefit of hindsight when making their judgments.

My special thanks to the Head Librarian of the Blacksellian for much help and advice. Amongst the books I found helpful were:

The Colonial Period of American History *C. M. Andrews*
The Origins of the British Colonial System *G. L. Beer*
The Cavaliers *Mark Bence-Jones*
The Jacobeans at Home *Elizabeth Burton*
The Early Stuarts *Godfrey Davies*
The Curse of Cromwell *D. M. R. Esson*
Cromwell's Army *C. H. Firth*
History of the Great Civil War *S. R. Gardiner*
Social Life under the Stuarts *Elizabeth Godfrey*
The Yorkshire Woollen and Worsted Industry *Herbert Heaton*

To all my friends in the LSO,
especially Gillian, and Sue,
and Dennis, who was first, and
John, who knows Yorkshire, and
Martin, who has seen Tod's Knowe.

THE MORLAND FAMILY –

Descendants of Paul Morland I

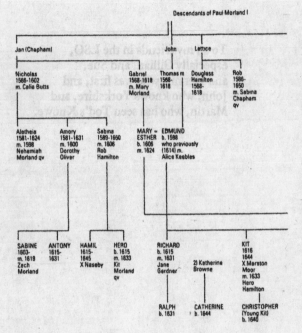

BOOK 4 – THE OAK APPLE

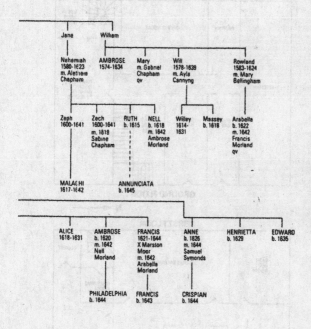

Jane — Wilham

Nehemiah 1580-1623 m. Alethiea Chapham | AMBROSE 1574-1634 | Mary m. Gabriel Chapham qv | Will 1576-1639 m. Ayla Cannyng | Rowland 1583-1624 m. Mary Bellingham

Zeph 1600-1641 | Zech 1600-1641 m. 1619 Sabine Chapham | RUTH b. 1615 | NELL b. 1618 m. 1642 Ambrose Morland | Willey 1614-1631 | Massey b. 1618 | Arabella b. 1622 m. 1642 Francis Morland qv

MALACHI 1617-1642 | ANNUNCIATA b. 1645

ALICE 1618-1631 | AMBROSE b. 1620 m. 1642 Nell Morland | FRANCIS 1621-1644 X Marston Moor m. 1642 Arabella Morland | ANNE b. 1626 m. 1644 Samuel Symonds | HENRIETTA b. 1629 | EDWARD b. 1635

PHILADELPHIA b. 1644 | FRANCIS b. 1643 | CRISPIAN b. 1644

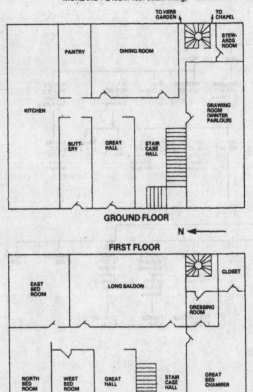

MORLAND PLACE in 1631 (Main Wing)

GROUND FLOOR

N ←

FIRST FLOOR

BOOK ONE

The Oak Tree

Her Feet beneath her petticoat,
Like Little mice, stole in and out,
  As if they feared the light:
But O she dances such a way!
No sun upon an Easter-day
  Is half so fine a sight.

Sir John Suckling: *Ballad, Upon a Wedding*

The Oak Tree

Her Feet beneath her petticoat,
Like Little mice, stole in and out,
As if they feared the Light:
But O she dances such a way!
No sun upon an Easter-day
Is half so fine a sight.

Sir John Suckling, Ballad, Upon a Wedding

CHAPTER ONE

During the night the wind changed direction, and the rain, which seemed to have been going on for ever, stopped at last. The absence of its sound woke Ambrose early to a world of dripping peace and brilliantly refracted sunshine overlaid with birdsong, and he climbed out of bed and pushed open the casement window high up under the eaves of the Hare and Heather to look out. The sky had a limpid, new-washed look, the air sparkled as if polished by the sun, and the morning smelled so good he knelt there to say his morning prayers, to which he added a plea for the harvest, that it might yet be saved. He prayed aloud, as he had been taught as a child, but quietly so as not to disturb his brother Will and sister-in-law Ayla who were still asleep in the big bed on the other side of the room. His prayers finished, he crossed himself, rose, dressed, and went quietly down to the yard to wash.

Ambrose liked to rise early, and though he was a sociable man he was always sorry if he had to share the first hour of the day with anyone. He liked to begin his day in peaceful communion with his soul, and leisure and quiet were in short supply for a man who ran the most popular inn on the Great South Road. His simple toilet finished, he let the dogs off their chains, fed the chickens, let the pigeons out and then sat down on the bench at the front of the inn and stretched out his long legs into the sunshine.

The limewashed wall at his back was already warm where the sun had been on it; not that there was much bare wall to be seen, what with the news-sheets, play-bills, and ballad-sheets that were displayed there, not to mention public notices, advertisements and religious tracts. Above his head the inn-sign creaked gently on its hinges as a pair of fantailed pigeons landed on it with a whirr and rattle of wings; at his feet an old red-brown hen had followed him and was delicately picking off the grains of meal that had caught on his breeches, croodling happily to him the while. Soon the gates of the city would open, travellers would begin to fill the road, and the sleepers in the inn would waken; but for the moment the world was his.

All his life had been lived in and around inns: in fact, he had been born in one, The Three Feathers in the village of Fulham, near London. His mother had been the innkeeper's daughter, his father Will Shawe the great actor. Later his father had revealed himself to be William Morland, had turned composer and taken them back to the family seat, Morland Place, so that he could concentrate on his great work, his *Missa Solemnis*. All William Morland's great music had been written at Morland Place, but Ambrose and his brother Will had never been entirely comfortable there, and it had not been long before they had taken themselves off to run the Hare and Heather Inn two miles away.

All that had been a long time ago. It was now 1630, and Ambrose was fifty-six, an old man, gaunt and grey. It would have been poor advertisement for an innkeeper to be thin as he was, had it not been that the Hare's eightpenny ordinary was famed from Holgate to Rufforth, and Will and Ayla were stout enough for three, while their sons Willey and Massey were a credit to the kitchens. Ambrose had never married, though there had been plenty of girls who would have taken him gladly had he asked; but somehow he had never got round to asking. He had not been lonely, though: he had had Mary Esther.

When Ambrose and Will had first bought the inn there had been a third partner with them: Gabriel Chapham, who had married their sister Mary. Gabriel was a bold, handsome, merry, wicked man, who had a saving weakness for Mary. Their marriage had been blessed by one child, a

2

daughter whom they had called Mary after her mother and for the Blessed Virgin, and Esther to distinguish her from the other Marys in the family. Ambrose had stood as godfather to the child, and when Gabriel and Mary had both been carried off within days of each other by the plague in 1612, Ambrose had taken responsibility for the six-year-old girl and had brought her up as a daughter.

'Though no father,' he sometimes said, 'ever took such tender care as I did, or was so well rewarded.' Even just thinking about her made him smile. His thoughts were pleasant, the sun was warm on his legs, the sounds of hen and doves were soothing, and his grey head began to nod gently. He didn't fall asleep – he was sure he hadn't fallen asleep, but someone was laughing, and as he murmured 'Yes, yes, I heard every word you said,' he discovered that his eyes were inexplicably closed.

'But I didn't say anything,' Mary Esther laughed. 'You must have been dreaming.'

'I wasn't asleep,' he said sternly, struggling to his feet.

'Of course not,' she agreed demurely. 'But your thoughts were so absorbing that you did not hear us ride up. I have stood here quite five minutes watching you. You kept so still your old broody hen has nested under your knees – look!'

Ambrose glanced down, and the red-brown hen's bright eye blinked up at him from the dusty hollow she had scraped for herself under the bench. He smiled, put his hands on his niece's shoulders, and bent to kiss her cheek.

'Deep thoughts are a privilege of old age,' he said. 'God bless you, my darling. And God's day to you, Leah,' he added to the serving woman who, mounted on a pony, was holding the reins of Mary Esther's chestnut mare a little way off. 'What brings you here, and so early?'

'The sun, of course,' said Mary Esther. 'I couldn't bear to waste any of it, so I dragged poor Leah from her repose so that I could take a ride before a thousand people begin clamouring for my attention. Look at the sky – did you ever see such a colour! Will it last, do you think? Edmund has been so worried about the harvest, and another of the ewes has the foot-rot, and there's been fever again in Aksham –'

'I have heard,' Ambrose said sternly, 'how you have been visiting the sick down by the bogs. You must be careful, child. It is so unhealthy there.'

'But I must do what I can,' Mary Esther protested, 'and my fever-drink has proved so valuable to them.'

'You can send it with a servant,' Ambrose said. 'You must not take such risks, especially with two small daughters dependent on you. Henrietta not a year old, and Anne only four – what would they do if their mother were to be carried off by fever?'

Mary Esther looked troubled. 'But Uncle 'Brose, I can't ask a servant to take a risk I am not willing to take myself.' She spoke gently, unwilling to seem to preach to her elder, and then added, smiling, 'Besides, you see how healthy I am, how strong. Illness never troubles me.'

'Aye, I see, you rosy, bonny thing. Well, I know I cannot turn you from your duty, and God forbid I should. Only take care, won't you, my bird? You are all the world to me.'

'I will,' she promised. 'And you must too. How are you, how is your shoulder? Did you use the salve I sent over?'

'I did, child, and it eased it a little, but the best salve is this sunshine. I only get the pains when the air is damp, and it has been such a damp summer.'

'It is a good salve,' Mary Esther said. 'It has willow-bark extract in it. The recipe came from great-grandmother's book – oh, and that reminds me! You remember that we could not find the Duke of York's Missal? Well, Edmund woke me up in the middle of last night to tell me he had suddenly remembered where it was.' She paused for effect, and Ambrose made a suitable face. 'He put it in the secret compartment in the Lady Chapel before we left Morland

4

Place,' she said, 'and then he completely forgot it because all the other treasures came with us in boxes. He was so relieved, Uncle 'Brose, you can't imagine. I think he values that old missal more than anything else.'

'It has been in the family a long time,' Ambrose said.

'Yes, and he does care so greatly about the family name and history and that sort of thing. That's why he gets so cross with Richard – "You are a Morland," he says,' she imitated her husband's voice – ' "and you must behave like a Morland".'

Ambrose shook his head. 'I'm rather afraid Richard does,' he said, 'but not like the particular Morland Edmund wants him to copy. Your husband likes to forget there have been wild characters in the family as well as good.'

'I try talking to Richard, but he pays no heed to me, and I'm only his stepmother. I'm hoping he'll come home before Edmund hears that he was out all last night. I've no idea where he was, but Clement told me his bed wasn't slept in. Clement was up even before me. Do you know, I don't think he ever goes to bed. I think he's afraid someone might steal his job while he sleeps. I say to him, "Considering that your father and grandfather before you –"'

'He was here last night,' Ambrose interrupted. Mary Esther's smooth brow wrinkled in astonishment.

'Clement?'

'No, Richard. In fact he still is – sleeping it off.' He gestured with his head towards the taproom. Mary Esther was dismayed.

'He was here? Drunk? Oh Uncle, how could you? Why didn't you send him home? How could you let him get drunk when you know perfectly well – and Edmund worries so – and he's only fifteen – it's so bad for him.'

'My darling,' Ambrose protested gently, 'he was drunk when he arrived here. I could have sent him away, but he wouldn't have gone home, you must know that. He would only have gone somewhere else, and that would have been

5

worse. At least here I could keep an eye on him, curb the worst of his excesses. Would you sooner he drank with strangers?'

'I'm sorry,' she said meekly. 'You're right. But, oh Uncle – !'

'I know, chuck. But you mustn't take it to heart so. It's Edmund's business, not yours, and he must be firmer with the boy. Besides, many men have led wild lives in their youth, and made decent men after it. Your own father, for instance.'

Mary Esther smiled. 'I don't believe a tenth part of the stories you tell about my father. You only do it to vex me.'

'You've had precious little in your life to vex you, my bird. You ought to be glad of the change.'

'Up until Edmund decided to rebuild Morland Place, I would have agreed with you,' she said. 'But since we moved out to Twelvetrees I've had a lifetime's vexing to strengthen my character. If I have to live in that dreadful old house another year I shall be fit for Bedlam.'

'How are the builders getting on?'

She pulled a face. 'They blame the weather,' she said concisely. 'Pray God they work faster now that the sun's shining, and get done before winter sets in. It's impossible to keep Twelvetrees warm – imagine, Uncle, no chimneys, nothing but braziers, and draughts everywhere, and the great hall filled with smoke all the time, and the servants always missing. Trying to run a household that's divided between three houses is impossible. I never know where anyone is, and I send messages to Shawes that should go to Micklelith, and my head goes round like a maypole. If it weren't for Clement I couldn't manage at all.'

Ambrose smiled at the idea of Mary Esther being in a muddle: as well as her father's good looks she had inherited her mother's level-headedness and memory for detail, and since becoming Edmund Morland's second wife at the age of eighteen she had managed the reins of the great house-

6

hold as easily as she managed the reins of her horse.

'Well it will all be worth it when it's done,' Ambrose said comfortingly.

'I suppose so. But if it had been my choice I would not have troubled to do so much to an old house – I'd have pulled it down and built a new one. But Edmund could not bear to think of abandoning Morland Place, so he must patch and put and make and mend, at great inconvenience to everyone. He won't even have the moat filled – but there, I say too much, I am disloyal. Now, Uncle, I had better go or I shall be missed. Shall you shake up Richard, and I'll take him back with me? I have so much to do – and I left Dog shut in one of the outhouses, and if I leave him too long he will break the door down.'

'Ah, I was wondering where he was,' Ambrose said. Mary Esther was rarely seen without her enormous grey wolfhound, Dog, who was as big as a bull-calf, one of the special Morland breed, and devoted to her. He was also perpetually in trouble, always stumbling into danger and hurting himself. 'What has he done this time?'

'A cut paw,' his mistress said. 'He did it on an old, half-buried ploughshare, but it won't heal and I'm trying to make him rest it just until it knits. The only way I can stop him following me is to shut him in somewhere, and even that stops him only for a while. So I had best get back.'

'I'll go and get your stepson. And don't let it be so long before your next visit, chuck. Now the rain has stopped you'll have no excuse for neglecting me.'

For answer Mary Esther put her arms round him, and he held her soft little body against him in a long hug, and, releasing her, kissed the crown of her head.

'Bless you, my darling,' he said, and went quickly indoors. Mary Esther watched him go. One corner of her mouth turned up more than the other when she smiled, and it made her look very young.

*

7

Mary Esther could not have hoped that Richard's absence would go unnoticed more fervently than Richard himself: he hated having to face his father. His tutor, the family chaplain, Father Michael Moyes, was a hot-tempered Frenchman, and when Richard was younger he had beaten him as hard and as frequently as he now beat Richard's younger brothers. He did not beat Richard nowadays, though his temper hung by just as frail a thread, and he raged at Richard for his wrongdoings in broken English and with a range of multilingual oaths that Richard could only admire; but Richard would sooner have been beaten raw by Father Moyes in his worst temper than have to face his father's cold contemptuous rage.

Richard had always found his father daunting. Firstly, he was so tall, so classically, coldly handsome with his silver-fair hair and Grecian profile that he made Richard by comparison feel small and plain and dull. And then his father had been brought up so strictly and laid so much emphasis on virtue, godliness and the Morland name that he scarcely seemed human. As a child Richard had always sought comfort from his mother, who adored, petted and spoiled him. Alice Keebles had been chosen to wed Edmund Morland for her family and fortune; the marriage had been determined by the parents of the couple and their consent had not been sought or required. She was not the person who could have won Edmund's heart, being uneducated, shy and rather silly, and so he had done his duty by her and no more; and she, finding her husband as terrifying and inaccessible as her son was later to do, had lavished her affections on that son until she died in childbirth when Richard was six.

For three years there was no-one to mitigate the sternness of his father, and Richard took to a secretive life of slipping away and lying about it, of playing off one relative against another and of bribing the servants to cover for him. By the time Edmund married Mary Esther, relations between him and his father were bad beyond her mending, even had Richard not regarded the usurper of his mother's place with jealous hostility. Richard's most blameless pleasure came from the companionship of his brother Christopher, always known as Kit, who was a year younger, and he had looked forward to the time when they might be sent off to school together. But two years ago Kit had been sent to Winchester alone, while Richard remained at home, to learn to be master of Morland Place. Richard had decided for himself that Kit had been sent away to punish him, Richard, and his last hope of escaping the troubles he had designed for himself was gone. Since then he had discovered the joys of ale-houses and inns and the oblivion of drunkenness. The odd thing was that when he was drinking in the company of his boon companions he could never remember how awful it was to be sober and have to face his father.

As they rode homewards Richard and Mary Esther studied each other covertly. It gave neither of them the gratification it should. Mary Esther felt exasperation as she observed how Richard slouched in the saddle, his shoulders hunched unbecomingly. He had not the good looks of his father, certainly, though he could have been attractive enough had he taken a little trouble; but his face was puckered in a scowl, his clothes were unkempt and greasy, his hair hung over his shoulders in matted, draggled locks that were so dirty it was impossible to tell what colour they might be underneath.

And his behaviour matched his appearance: he had never been good at his lessons, though Father Moyes asserted often enough that he was not stupid, only unwilling, and now he had deserted the schoolroom for a series of disreputable escapades that could only end in trouble. Something would have to be done about the boy. If only Edmund had sent him to school at the same time as Kit. She sighed, and her mare turned back an ear and quickened her pace, thinking the sigh was for her.

Richard's feelings about Mary Esther were less charitable. She was a pretty enough sight to gratify anyone, riding gracefully sidesaddle on the pretty chestnut, Psyche, who had been bred on the estate and reared by hand so that she almost read her mistress's thoughts. Mary Esther was small, neat and quick as her mother had been, but while her mother had been plain, she had inherited her father's vivid good looks, his luxuriant dark hair and bright dark eyes. Her hair was parted smoothly on top, and bunched into thick ringlets that framed her face under her feathered hat; her dress was of a dark grey silk which held just a hint of blue to complement the brightness of her complexion; her graceful shoulders were covered with a lace cape whose white was not more creamy than the skin beneath it.

But best of all was the expression of her face, bright, benign and happy. Leah, who had been with her since she was a child, had often said that Mary Esther could not see another human face without smiling. But Richard saw none of this. He saw the woman who had usurped his mother's place, the woman for whom his father had betrayed his beloved mother's memory, who had his father's ear and poured poison into it, who had persuaded his father to send Kit away and keep Richard home. He feared his father, but could not hate him, and he needed someone to blame; the fact that everyone else loved Mary Esther made it easier for him.

They were going up the track towards Twelvetrees now, and there were people around. Mary Esther wondered about the chances of getting Richard in unseen.

'Richard,' she began, but he cut her off.

'I expected you to come spying after me, but I'm surprised that Ambrose gave me away. I thought he was a good friend. I suppose it was stupid of me.'

'Very stupid,' she said.

'Considering he's your uncle. So now you can take me in to Father and enjoy seeing me in trouble.'

'I don't enjoy it,' Mary Esther said, but without hope of convincing him. 'As to spying on you, I had no idea you were there. But if you drink in the family inn you can hardly be said to be trying to avoid notice: I suppose that is in your favour. Richard why can't you just behave yourself? It would be so much easier, for you and for everyone else. Do you like upsetting your father? Do you enjoy putting thorns in Our Blessed Lord's crown?'

'Oh yes, bring religion into it,' Richard muttered gracelessly. Everything he did was made so much of, not just against the family and his father but against religion too; punishment was always weighted with penance. He had spent hours on his knees. 'I can hardly draw breath without finding it's a sin.'

Mary Esther sighed anxiously. 'Richard, you make things so hard for yourself. Well, we'll see if we can't slip you in this time without being seen. As long as Clement is out of sight –'

'What matter?' Richard said perversely. 'You'll tell my Father sooner or later. It might as well be sooner.' And with that he spurred his horse into a gallop, and charged straight at the house giving hunting cries at the top of his voice, to make sure he was discovered.

'Lieu in, lieu in, lieu-lieu-lieu. Hike à Richard, Hike!'

Mary Esther followed on more sedately; Leah came alongside her and they exchanged a glance of exasperated pity.

'What can I do, Leah?' Mary Esther sighed.

'Naught, Madam. 'At young lad will come to grief, which Heaven forfend, but there's naught anybody can do if he'll not help himself. Eh, Madam,' she added suddenly as a strange noise reached them from the direction of the house, 'hark at that blessed dog!'

The strange penetrating howls rose louder and louder as they hurried towards the house. An outside servant came running to take their horses as they came into the yard, and as he helped Mary Esther dismount on the mounting block he cried,

'Eh, Madam, it's glad we are you're back. T'dog's been at howling fit to kill this hour sin', and t'maister's runnin' mad. He broke out of shed you put 'im in, and we couldn't keep 'im in but by shuttin' 'im in cellar, and he's rampaged about and broke three dozen eggs and Lord knows what else besides –'

'Oh my poor Dog,' Mary Esther cried, hurrying towards the door to the rescue. But with Edmund already roused she had small chance now of keeping Richard out of trouble, and it was even more likely that he would blame her for it.

The house reverberated all day with the quarrel between Edmund and his son. Everyone was subdued, and servants and dogs made themselves inconspicuous for fear of attracting sympathetic rebuke. Privacy was hard enough to come by at Morland Place, harder still here at Twelvetrees with so many people crowded into a small and antiquated house, so it was not until after the second Mass of the day that Mary Esther was able to invite her husband by a look and a nod of the head to join her in a walk in the orchard. Once outside, Mary Esther tucked her hand through her husband's arm and strolled with him up and down the alleys between the fruiting pearmains. Dog came up on her other side, butted his rough head up under her free hand, and limped along beside her. Reunited with her, he was going to make sure she did not get away again.

'Well, Madam?' Edmund asked at last, looking down gravely into her sunny face. That he did not smile was no sign of displeasure. He was a man to whom smiles and emotional outbursts did not come easily, who had been bred to do his duty and did it, without ever having expected pleasure, or happiness beyond the happiness of duty faithfully carried out. He had married his first wife out of obedience to his parents' wishes when he was not quite sixteen, and though his parents had loved each other dearly he had not associated love and marriage in his mind. His own feelings for Mary Esther had therefore surprised him when at the age of twenty-six, a grave and solemn widower, he had fallen in love with her, with her bright, merry, open-hearted disposition. It had taken him a long time to get round to asking her to marry him, and he had found himself for the first time unsure of the outcome. He had felt there was no reason why she should accept him, and he found himself unable to face the thought of rejection.

But she had not rejected him, and there had followed six years of such happiness as he had not imagined could exist on earth. Loving her and being loved by her had opened a door in his soul, through which he glimpsed a bliss so intense that it frightened him, and on all but a few occasions he kept the door tightly shut. But best of all was that Mary Esther seemed to understand this, understand that he loved her far more than he was able to shew, except on rare occasions; and she gave him her love in the full, generous measure that existed for her unspoken inside him.

The light summer breeze stirred the fronds of dark hair that curled about her brow, and her face turned up to him on her long slender neck like a flower turning up to the sun. His love clenched like a fist, squeezing his heart, and 'Yes, Madam?' he said unsmilingly. 'You wanted to speak to me – about Richard, no doubt.'

'About Richard,' she concurred. 'Something has to be done about him. He is going to get into trouble. You should have been firm with him.'

Edmund raised an eyebrow. 'I am firm with him.'

Mary Esther shook her head. 'No,' she said. 'You are severe, but you are not firm. Father Moyes was the same. I wish you had sent him to school with Kit, but it's too late now.'

'Do you think that he should be sent away? To University

13

perhaps?' Edmund asked. Mary Esther looked at him steadily. She knew her husband better than anyone else, and she knew that his way was always to seek opinion, gather information from every source. But in the end he always made up his own mind, and she would never persuade him to change it. She could only present her thoughts for his consideration, and the best way was to present them unemotionally. She, and she alone, knew of the passion that was in him, shut down like a bubbling spring under rocks, waiting to burst forth.

She looked up into the beautiful, clear face: the broad brow, the high cheekbones, straight delicate nose, strong chin; the hair so fair it was almost silver, the eyes dark grey under fine fair brows; it was said he looked very like his grandmother, Mary Percy, heiress of Todsknowe. He might have been carved of crystal, his beauty was so perfect and so cold; but she knew that at the heart of the crystal was a vein of gold, liquid running fire.

She knew, but Richard never would. 'No,' she said. 'I think that he is beyond discipline now, unless he disciplines himself. He would get into more trouble at University than he does here. What he needs is to be occupied, to have some work to do that he feels is important. Could you not send him abroad, to Italy perhaps, or Venice, on some business for the family? A factor could go with him to guide him along the right way.'

Edmund considered. 'Abroad? Well, I will think on it. But I kept him here because I wanted him here, at home.'

'Then give him some occupation.'

'I think perhaps he should have someone with him all the time. A manservant of his own, but one who is reliable.'

Mary Esther despaired. 'If he thinks he is spied on, it will give him the greater pleasure to escape his jailor.'

'Spied on? Jailor? Those are his words, I think, not yours.'

Mary Esther saw her mistake, and calmed herself. 'At

14

least, he should have companions of his own age. When we move back to Morland Place, could we not find someone for him? Perhaps Malachi – ?'

'Or your Uncle Will's sons? Well, I will think about that too. And now my dear –'

He paused in his walking, and turned to face her. She looked up at him sadly, knowing already that her suggestions would not be taken up, and he looked down at her apologetically, not liking to deny her any gratification.

'I must be about my business,' he said. 'Will you come in?'

'No, I'll walk a little longer.'

'I'll send Leah to you.'

'Leah is busy – send Nerissa.' He nodded, but still hesitated as if there was something else he would say. She waited, but in the end he went away without speaking, though before he left her he put his hand up to her face for a moment and touched her cheek. It was a great deal for him, and it comforted her. She strolled a little, alone with her thoughts and Dog's company, until her little maid came hurrying to find her, bringing a light cloak and the master's instructions that she should beware the wind, which was fresher than she might think. She was not in the least cool, but she suffered herself to be draped in the cloak because it was Edmund's way of saying that he loved her and cared for her. She knew that her advice would not be taken.

The evening was like a calm after a storm. The whole family gathered in the Great Hall to pass the evening in their accustomed manners, and Mary Esther, seated near one of the windows with a piece of embroidery, taking advantage of the light, thought that it must have been rather like this in the olden days when all family life was passed in the Hall. Twelvetrees was not an unpleasant place in the summer, when there was no necessity to light the smoky fires on the raised hearth: the Morlands had long used it as their summer house, while Morland Place was being sweetened, and she had passed many long twilights like this since she first married.

Edmund and Father Moyes were playing chess, seated on low stools on either side of the beautiful Venetian chess-table of mahogany and ivory. Father Moyes, a small, swart, stubby man, was leaning forward, his face resting on his fists so that his chins lapped forward like a lace collar. His expression was fiercely concentrated, for he played, as he did everything, with fervour and determination, and though he always lost to Edmund, he never ceased to hope for a win. 'I believe in miracles,' he said once when she had laughed, gently, at him. 'I am no Jesuit, Madam, I will strive against my nature.'

Edmund, by contrast, looked almost insultingly relaxed. One knee was bent, the other long leg stretched out along-side the table, and his arms rested across his thighs. He did not look at the board – he knew the position of every piece. He knew already the move that Father Moyes would even-tually make, and what his own move would then be, but though Father Moyes sweated, Edmund did not smile. The late sunshine on his silvery hair turned it a deeper, reddish gold; it hung loose to his shoulders, brushed back from his face and curled under. He went clean-shaven, which made him look more than ever like a statue, a pale-golden statue in black silk doublet and breeches, a cascade of lace at throat, wrists, and calf, where it hung over the tops of his soft leather boots. Watching him, Mary Esther wondered for whom that elegance, that show was meant. He was not, she knew, a vain man; he must know that she loved him, could not love him more; and he wanted no other than her. Was it, she wondered, his defence against the eyes of the world? or did he simply love his own beauty as he might love a beautiful tree or flower?

Now he felt her eyes on him and turned his head. Their

16

eyes met; he did not smile, but she felt the lapping warmth flooding over her. *Tonight*, she thought, and the sweetness of anticipation made her smile quiver. Richard saw the look pass between them, and he too quivered, but with indignation and anger. He was playing, a little sullenly and reluctantly, at cards with Rob and Sabina Hamilton and their son Hamil. Rob was Edmund's uncle, and he had married Sabina Chapham, who was the daughter of Mary Esther's uncle Nicholas. They had been brought up together at Morland Place, had loved each other as children, and had married as soon as they were able, and as far as anyone could tell there had never been a cross word spoken between them. Even now, as they played at Cribbage, Rob tried to cheat himself to give Sabina a good hand, putting cards into her box that he should have kept for himself; but since Sabina did the same, to try to let him win, their efforts cancelled each other out.

Hamil, their son, was fifteen, a small, quick-moving, handsome boy with the lithe body and curly dark hair of a Pan. His attention, too, was only half on the game, and the rest was on his twin sister, Hero, who stood behind him, leaning her weight on her arms which rested on his shoulders. Hamil and Hero were inseparable, 'closer than lovers' Sabina sometimes said. Hero was pale, golden, blue-eyed and pretty, and she made a lovely picture, pink-cheeked and ringleted in a gown of sky-blue. Only when she moved was there anything ugly about her – she limped. Not a slight, romantic, interesting limp, but a horrible, ungainly, lurching limp. At the age of nine she and Hamil had gone out riding on the moors on their matching ponies. They rode like centaurs, and had no fear, daring the roughest country, and Hamil had led the way at full pelt through the heather and bracken, with Hero racing him only a head behind. His pony had swerved to avoid a boggy patch, had cannoned into Hero's mount, and her pony had caught a foot in a heather root and gone down, with Hero trapped underneath. It was a couple of hundred yards before Hamil could halt his careering horse, turn it and go back for his sister. He had never forgotten, would never forget until he died, the sight of her white staring face as she refused with bitter courage to cry out with the pain, pain that must have been made unendurable by the pony's thrashing about as it tried to regain its feet. He thought that Hero would die, and he blamed himself silently but unrelentingly for the accident. When the surgeon said that she would live, but would never walk or ride again, he had sworn that she would both walk and ride, or he would cripple himself in atonement.

It had taken years of patience and courage on Hero's part, but with Hamil supporting her, physically and spiritually, she had, step by painful step, regained her mobility. She would never dance, and her movements were so clumsy that she preferred always to ride if she could, even if it were only a few yards, so the twins almost lived on horseback. She was Hamil's constant care, and they were never apart, so that now they barely needed to speak to exchange their thoughts.

Seeing Richard's anger, Hero exchanged a quick glance with her brother, and he, understanding her, said, 'I'm tired of playing cards. When we have finished this hand, shall we have some music? Will you sing for us, Richard?'

Singing was the one thing at which Richard excelled. He brightened up at once. 'If you like,' he said.

'A good idea,' Rob said. 'Shall the children play to us while we finish this game? It would be a shame to throw the cards in when Sabina is on the point of winning.'

'Boys, fetch your instruments,' Edmund said. 'We will have your new duet.'

Ambrose and Francis, his youngest sons, who were ten and nine years old, left their toys to obey him, and accompanied by their sister Alice on the virginals, they played a duet for flageolet and flute which Mary Esther's uncle Ambrose had written for them. Then Alice, who was twelve, played the guitar and sang, and as soon as she had finished a catch, Richard, who could restrain himself no longer, took the instrument from her and played and sang to them. There was silence while he sang, the silence that comes naturally in the presence of a superior performer, and at the end everyone applauded. Richard smiled a little shyly, his ill-humour and sulkiness forgotten.

With Alice playing the virginals, he then played some part songs and everyone fell to with a will, dividing the parts between them with great gusto, until it was time for evening prayers, and Leah brought down the babies, Anne and Henrietta, to say goodnight to their parents.

And then Edmund said, 'There's just time for one more song. Richard, let's have your own song, "The Skylark". You play the accompaniment, and your mother shall sing it.'

How can he not know, Mary Esther thought in anguish as she felt his words shatter the delicate happiness that the music had built up. Richard scowled, glaring at Mary Esther, and then at the two little girls, offspring of his father's betrayal with the usurper.

'She's *their* mother, not mine,' he said savagely, with a jerk of his head towards the babies. 'Let them write songs for her – she'll not sing mine!'

And dropping the guitar on the empty hearth, he rushed from the room, leaving a moment's uneasy silence behind him. Then Alice stooped and picked up the instrument, smoothing it with her hands as if it were a sentient thing that could be hurt, and her movement broke the tableau.

'Fetch him back,' Edmund commanded quietly, catching Clement's eye, and when the steward had gone he said to Mary Esther, 'He will be punished for his disrespect. And from now on, I think he must be kept in stricter bounds. And now, Father Moyes, shall we get ready?'

But it would not help, Mary Esther thought, and though

she knew that Richard must be made to apologize to her, for his own sake and for the example to the others, she dreaded it, that it would make him hate her more.

CHAPTER TWO

Outside the new windows of Morland Place the rain streamed steadily over the green wetness of spring, filling the moat and beating ever flatter the ranks of yellow asphodels and flags that crowded the moatside. Within, the house was filled with noise and bustle as the household worked at putting the furniture back in as short a time as possible.

In the great bedchamber four maids were wrestling silently with the straw-and-wool-filled under-mattress, which seemed to have developed a desire to be anywhere other than in the base of the great Butts Bed. They weaved back and forth like a drunken eight-legged beast, much to the discomfort of the two estate carpenters who were still working on the frame.

'Look out, there! You'll have me off!' the elder of the two cried. He was up a ladder, engaged in marrying ever more tightly the joints of the frieze which carried the tester and curtains. The curtains, new ones of glorious red damask tasselled with gold, were lying in a corner on the polished oak floor, glowing like a heap of sunset clouds, awaiting their final resurrection. 'Dickon, can't you give these maids a hand, 'fore they fetches the ladder out from under me?'

'How can I?' the younger man said peevishly, snatching at his cap as the mattress whisked by above his head. He dropped his mallet for the third time and cursed, but discreetly. 'Now I been and lost the peg, darn take it. This bed 'as altogether too much blamey carving for a Christian.' He reached under the bed for the long conical peg and hammered it savagely into the side-frame. On top of the under-mattress would go three feather beds, and then the covers, and the pegs were there to stop everything sliding off onto the floor during the night.

One of the maids dropped her end of the mattress and said, panting, 'Here, you Dickon, mind what you're about! Don't you knock that bed about like that – it's very old, is that, and worth more than you'll ever see in your life, if you live to be fifty.'

This was more like it. Dickon glanced up sideways with a wicked grin. 'And don't you be saucy, my maid, or I'll come and shew you –'

'Shew me what?' the maid giggled, and darting in knocked his cap off. He started up in anticipatory rage, and made a grab for her which she evaded easily, so that he had to chase her round and round the mattress which the other three maids were holding patiently. Then the door opened and Dog pushed in, and seeing the fun bounced over to join in, barking excitedly. His lashing tail smacked against the ladder, knocking it from under the carpenter, who went flying backwards, arms and legs flailing.

Mary Esther, who had come in behind Dog, cried out in alarm, 'Catch him, someone!' but even before the words were out he had landed on the mattress, and his weight coming down on it pulled the three maids over on top of him. They went down as woodenly as ninepins, and the mattress was a confusion of muffled shrieks and waving limbs. Mary Esther burst out laughing.

'Oh dear, they do look funny! And squeaking like a nest of mice. Come, Dickon, Meggy, help them up. Gently now!'

Dickon plunged in with a will, grabbing for the most lissom waist he could see. 'Some people have all the luck,' he muttered. 'And pity of it is, Ben's too old to enjoy it.'

Meggy giggled, and helped straighten the clothing of the righted girl. In a moment Ben appeared from under the tangle, clothing all awry and a smile on his face that made Dickon recalculate his age.

Mary Esther sobered herself and said, 'Now Ben, you're not hurt, are you?'

'Nay, Mistress, but I'd as soon not have that dog to help me.'

'I'll take him away. I only came to see how you were getting on. Back to work now, all, or we'll not have this finished before supper, and the master will want to know why. Come, girls, you haven't even got the mattress on yet.'

The four maids, refreshed by the interlude, caught up the corners again, and renewed their swaying, and Mary Esther snapped her fingers in exasperation.

'Dickon, come now, leave the pegs a moment and take the middle and guide it. Up a little more! There now, that's done,' as the mattress sank obediently into the frame, conquered by organization. 'Now you girls, are the rings on those curtains yet? Well then, set to, and quickly. And Ben, when you've finished here, the door to the dining room needs attention – it sticks a little. And then you can see to the table there, and by that time the men should have got the other bed up into the east bedroom and you can go and put that together.'

'Yes, Mistress.'

'Good. No more play now – we have much to do. Come Dog.'

She went out of the bedroom and into the saloon. This was one of the new features of the rebuilt house. The Great Hall, which had originally taken up most of the house-space on both floors, had been divided in half. One half was the entrance hall and the new Great Staircase, a magnificent thing of oak, broad and fair, with pierced panels supporting the handrail which were the work of a leading York carver, and shewed acanthus leaves and fruit and ribboning. The newel posts rose up above the baluster level, and the finials were carved in the shape of heraldic beasts, those at the base being the Morland leopards sejant, their broken chains

23

hanging down over the front edge of the newels to tangle with the flowers, corn and heather carved there.

The other half of the former Great Hall had been converted by a new ceiling into two floors. On the ground floor was the new dining room, and on the upper the long saloon, where Mary Esther now stood. She regarded it with satisfaction. It would serve the function that the Great Hall had served in the olden days: the place where the family could all gather together for celebrations, or simply to talk and play and dance together in the evenings or on wet days. The room was panelled in dark oak – very different from the pale, linen-fold panelling that still lined the winter-parlour – and the ceiling was plastered in a squared pattern with deep bolection moulding and an acanthus frieze. There were sash windows all the way along the back wall with good deep window seats, but owing to the construction of the house they only looked out over the inner court with its herb garden, instead of having a fine view over the park such as great people had in their new houses. It was one of the reasons Mary Esther would have preferred knocking down the old house and building entirely anew.

But it was a lovely room, even so. The polished floorboards were covered down the centre by matting, and along the inner wall there were the new handsomely carved buffets at which the servants were now busy unpacking and displaying the family's plate, glass and porcelain. Mary Esther tucked a finger into Dog's collar to keep him by her – he would wag a fortune to shards with one swing of his tail – and walked along, seeing that the things were going into the right places. The servants had had detailed instructions, and in any case Leah was on hand to watch them, but Mary Esther looked all the same.

Above the buffets the family's paintings would be displayed along the wall, and over the fireplace in the short wall at the south end a space was reserved for the new portrait that Edmund planned, a group portrait of himself, Mary

Esther, and all seven children. It would all be most elegant and satisfactory. Mary Esther caught Leah's eye and they smiled approvingly at each other.

'It will be lovely to dance here,' Mary Esther said. 'Imagine – a group of musicians at the end there, and all the finest people in the county dancing, and the old ones sitting along the side admiring our plate – children, come away, don't interrupt the servants, or something will be broken.'

Alice, Anne and Henrietta were playing at the far end. Alice was teaching Anne to dance, and Henrietta was staggering after them, arms and legs spread wide for balance. Mary Esther reached them just as Henrietta went down again for the fourth time on her well-cushioned behind.

'Come now, lambkin, up again. You should manage better than that by now.' Dog pushed past Mary Esther and thrust his big nose into the baby's face, and Henrietta pushed it away unconcernedly. She was a good tempered baby, although she rarely talked. With her little round lace cap and her bunchy skirts she looked like a large coloured football with stumpy arms and legs sticking out at random. She looked up at her mother, and laughed, and clapped her hands together, and then as Dog's tail passed her field of vision she grabbed at it and, when Dog stopped and looked over his massive shoulder at her, she began determinedly hauling herself upright by means of it.

'Mother, look what Henrietta's doing!' Alice said in alarm. But Dog only smiled, bracing himself patiently.

'It's all right, Alice, Dog wouldn't harm her. Don't you remember how Anne used to ride on his back when she was a baby?'

'She still is a baby,' Alice said provokingly. Anne, red in the face and panting from her exertions, looked cross.

'I'm not a baby. I'm nearly five o'clock.'

Alice crowed with laughter. 'Five o'clock! You see, she

25

doesn't know the difference between her age and the time. Five o'clock! Anne's a baby!'

'Don't be provoking, Alice,' Leah said, 'or I'll find you something to do.'

'Not a baby,' Anne persisted fiercely. 'Hetta's a baby. Hetta's stupid – she can't even walk.'

'Henrietta,' Mary Esther corrected automatically. There were several words that Anne could not manage, though her mother had an idea that in the case of her little sister Anne did it deliberately. 'And she's not stupid. She's only young. She's a little love.'

'She's stupid,' Anne said, and Mary Esther could see that tears were near. Her elder daughter was a strange, stormy child, and Mary Esther could foresee all kinds of difficulties with her before she was safely married and off her hands. 'She can't walk and she can't talk and she's no use at all. Stupid Hetta, no use at all.'

It was a kind of chant, and at the sound of it Henrietta looked up and gave another gurgling laugh, and for some reason it provoked Anne even more, so that she darted forward and slapped the baby's face. Henrietta was so surprised she lost her grip of Dog's tail, poised for a moment on the point of balance, and then went down heavily on her backside again, hands out and mouth open in a perfect 'O' of a wail.

'You naughty child!' Leah cried, dashing to the rescue. She smacked Anne sharply before picking up the baby, so that in a moment two lots of wailing were competing with each other, and Alice set her hands on her hips and looked disgusted.

'Oh children!' she cried in disgust. 'I do wish the rain would stop and I could go out. I'm so bored with nothing to do but play with children.'

Mary Esther, comforting Anne, whose tears she could feel soaking through her skirt where the child had buried her face, smiled sympathetically at Alice. 'Perhaps it will

26

clear up this afternoon, and then you can ride over to Shawes for me.' Alice did not looked cheered by the prospect.

'I don't think it will ever stop raining. Hamil and Hero are so lucky, going over to Watermill when they did, just when the rain stopped for half an hour. I wish I'd gone too.'

Mary Esther smiled, remembering how scornful Alice had been at the idea of there being anything entertaining about visiting Watermill House. Just then a servant came in and delivered a murmured message to Mary Esther.

'Never mind, Alice,' she said, 'here's something new for you. Willey and Massey have brought the ale and wine over, so at least you can come and talk to them while their men unload the cart.' Alice's face brightened – she liked her cousins, and they always had some fresh news or gossip. It seemed to her that an ale-house must be the most exciting place in the world. She did not wonder her bad brother Richard spent so much time there. 'What about you, Anne?' Mary Esther went on. 'Will you come and see your cousins. Come now, chuck, be a good girl. No more tears. Let me see your face? Eh, little suck-a-thumb! You're all smeary and teary like Hetta.'

She stroked her turbulent daughter's wet red face, but Alice interrupted her with a crow of laughter.

'Mother, you called Henrietta *Hetta*!'

'Oh dear, so I did. I must be careful, or I'll forget what it really is.'

'Baby's got a new name,' Alice laughed. 'Now Anne won't need to learn to say it properly.'

'I can say it properly,' Anne began, but Mary Esther took her hand and drew her firmly towards the door.

'No more quarrelling. Come, let's go down and see Willey and Massey, and hear what they've got to tell. I want to know how Uncle Ambrose's chest is. This wet weather's bad for the coughing.'

*

Watermill House stood on a foundation of brick behind Mill Field, which flanked the River Ouse just below the great mill and just above the osier beds. It made a stark contrast of black-and-white against the lush green of the water-meadows and woods, for it was a beam-and-plaster house with a reed-thatch roof, once the mill-keeper's cottage and elevated into a gentleman's residence a hundred years ago by the addition of buildings to house kitchens and other offices. It had been the home of Jan Chapham, known as the Bear-Cub, who had wed the Queen's child Mary Seymour. Here he had brought up his two sons, Gabriel, Mary Esther's father, and Nicholas; and here now lived Nicholas's son, Amory.

The Chaphams were hereditary Wardens of Rufford Forest, a lucrative sinecure awarded to Jan Chapham's father by Queen Elizabeth. Amory was the present warden, but he had inherited something else, too – he was also known as the Bear-Cub. In his case it was not inappropriate, for he was a short, burly man whose stockiness was enhanced by plentiful indulgence at table, and whose temper was sometimes a little uncertain.

He had some excuse: his wife, Dorothy Oliver, whom he had adored, had died very young in childbirth. She had given him twins, Endymion and Sabine, and had died bringing into the world a son, Antony, who had been so damaged in the process that though he was now almost sixteen his mind was that of a four-year-old. Endymion had been lost at sea two years ago; Sabine had married her cousin Zechariah Morland of Shawes; and so the Bear-Cub was left alone and morose at Watermill House with his idiot son. His daughter Sabine often told him briskly that he ought to move into one of his city properties.

'Living in York would keep you cheerful,' she said. 'You brood too much here – and you don't go to church half often enough. If you moved into, say, the house at the top of Goodramgate, you would be right under the Minster and could go twice a day. That would comfort you.'

'But it would be so unhealthy for Antony,' Amory had said.

'Well, and if something carried him off,' Sabine said even more briskly, 'it would be a blessing.'

'Sabine!'

'I mean it, Father. I don't wish the poor child harm, but he is no use to this world, so let Our Lord have him, that made him what he is.'

'You would have me put him out of the way?'

'I don't mean that, of course not. But perhaps you preserve his life too carefully.'

But the Bear-Cub stayed where he was. Watermill House had happy memories for him. He had been brought up mainly at Morland Place with his twin Aletheia and younger sister Sabina, she who had married Rob Hamilton, but when he had married he had moved to Watermill and it was there that he had spent all his happy years with Dorothy. It was true that he brooded, and was often lonely, but he was not always alone, for his children and his nephews and nieces visited him: in fact the ride over to Watermill was a favourite one for all the Morland children.

Today, for instance, his sister Sabina's children, Hamil and Hero, had ridden over during a brief pause in the rain – too brief, for they arrived wet enough even for Amory to notice.

'What your mother would say I don't know,' he grumbled as he urged them closer to the solar fire. A servant came in with a tray bearing pewter tankards. 'Drink this, now, and put some warmth in your bodies.'

'What is it, Uncle?' Hamil asked suspiciously. 'Is it medicine?'

'Never mind what – just drink it. There's a good girl – see, your sister is drinking hers.'

Hero looked at her twin over the rim of the tankard and grinned, shewing little white teeth like a vixen. 'It's lovely,'

29

she said. Hamil took his tankard and peered in, and smiled.

'Lambs wool,' he said. He tasted. 'Mm, delicious. What's it got in it, Uncle Bear?'

Amory sometimes growled when Hamil called him that, but this time he only said in surprise, 'Surely you know how lambs wool is made? Pulped apples, milk, egg-whites, sugar –'

'Ah, but what else besides?' Hamil asked. 'It never tastes like this at home when Mother orders it for us. What have you slipped into it?'

'Nothing, nothing – well, just a little Seres wine, that's all, to warm you up.'

'Ah! Well, if that's medicine, I'm all for it. What cheer, Cousin Antony,' he added as the youth came in from the Great Hall. Antony smiled shyly, and then held out his hand for the tankard. 'Ah, no, you'll have to get yourself soaking wet before you can have any of this. There now, I've finished it.'

As Antony turned towards Hero, to see what might be going there, Amory reverted to the question of their wetness. 'I'm surprised your aunt let you come out in the rain,' he said. 'And surprised that you do not take better care of your sister than to let her get soaked to the skin like that.'

'Oh Aunt Mary was glad to be rid of us,' he said. Mary Esther was not really his aunt, but it was a convenient title. 'There's so much to be done that we were only in the way, and when the rain stopped for a little while we asked her quickly and went before she could wonder if the pause would be long enough.'

'It would have been,' Hero added, 'except that we went the long way round, by Harewood Whin, to see the badgers' setts. I do wish we could go out one night and watch for them. You can't see badgers during the day. But Aunt Mary won't let us.'

'I should think not indeed,' Amory said. 'Why did you not shelter in the wood?'

'Oh we did,' Hero said, 'but the rain didn't look as if it would ever stop, and Hamil thought I was getting cold, so we rode as fast as we could for Watermill. So you see, he does take care of me.' She looked fondly at her twin. 'None better.'

Hamil returned her look, but not with gratification. She always tried to reassure him that her accident was not his fault, and he resisted the comfort always.

'And how do you like the house now it is finished?' Amory asked.

'It's very fine,' Hamil said. 'Especially the stairs – I love the griffons and wyverns and the big grinning lions on the newels.'

'And the stairs are easier for me to manage than the spiral staircase,' Hero added, 'but I'm sorry the gallery in the chapel has gone. I liked sitting up there.'

'And is Edmund pleased? Is it what he designed?'

'Well, you know Uncle Edmund – he never says much, but I saw him standing in the new hall this morning with what looked almost like a smile on his face,' Hamil said teasingly. Amory frowned at his boldness, but he was not really displeased – he liked the twins' liveliness, only regretting that his own son made such a sad contrast. 'And Aunt Mary is pleased with the new dining room,' Hamil went on, 'because it's nearer to the kitchens so the food will arrive hot instead of half cold, and if Aunt Mary's pleased, everyone's pleased. Or at least will be when everything's in place again.'

Amory glanced out of the window at the sodden willow trees overhanging the pond. Even the ducks were sheltering. 'Well it looks as though you will be here for some time,' he said cheerfully. 'I had better give orders about dinner. You may even,' he added, brightening still further, 'have to stay the night.'

Hero and Hamil exchanged a glance, and Hero caught her uncle's hand as he passed and smiled up at him. 'May I

31

play your virginals, Uncle Bear, and sing a new song? I haven't been able to practice for days, with all the furniture being moved.'

Amory pressed her hand, and with his other stroked her glossy golden ringlets.

'Of course you may, my dear – only wait until I come back, will you? I'd like to hear.'

His walk as he went out into the hall was almost springy, and Hero watched him with a smile of satisfaction, until a stealthy hand on her hair drew her attention to Antony, who was stroking her curls in a clumsy imitation of his father, his eyes almost crossed with concentration.

They did have to stay the night, but late the next morning the rain stopped, and they all went out of doors for a walk under a fast-moving, pale wet sky. At least, the men walked, Amory and Hamil and Antony, while Hero ambled along on her pony. They walked down towards the mill to see how the river was.

'It's very swollen, with all this rain,' Hamil observed. The Ouse had cut a deep bed at this point and normally the banks went down a good long way, but now the river was so high that it was almost lapping over onto the river-path. 'Do you ever get flooded, Uncle?'

'This field has been, but the house is a little higher, and so far we have not been troubled.'

'What about the pond?'

Amory shook his head. 'It is fed and drained by a little underground beck, and I have never known its level vary, even in a drought. It's the same beck that feeds our well – that's why our water is so good. My father dug it out once to see, the time a water-diviner was in these parts, and the diviner followed the course of it right past the well-house.'

They walked on along the river-path, which was tolerably

firm even after all the rain. 'It's part of my duties to keep it up,' Amory told them, 'and I do what I can with cinders and gravel. It takes such a lot of traffic, for all that it's not really a road.'

Hero on her pony was dawdling behind the two men, and the pony was ducking its head here and there to snatch a mouthful of the lush water-meadow grazing. Antony was wandering near her, keeping a covert eye on her, fascinated by the gleam of her golden curls under her little black-cloth hood. He was walking between her and the river, looking at her and not where he was going. He was too near the edge, and just at a moment when she pulled the pony's head up and made it walk on, Antony's foot slipped on the wet mud. A piece of the bank gave way underneath him, and he gave a cry and grabbed at the nearest hand-hold, which happened to be Hero's leg.

She was almost dragged from the saddle, but in a second she had seized the hand that grabbed her with her own and cried out for help. Her pony shied, skidded on the greasy path, and as it pushed with its powerful hocks to get clear of the treacherous ground, more of the bank gave way, it went half down into the river, and Hero, with Antony's weight hanging on her, was dragged from the saddle and into the water.

The two men had turned just in time to see Hero and Antony disappear. The pony, digging its toes in frantically, managed to lurch back onto the bank and stood trembling with fright, its reins hanging. But no-one had time to catch hold of it. With a despairing cry Hamil flung himself into the river after his sister, and Amory threw himself down on the bank to reach out helpless hands.

After the first shock of the cold water, Hero had recovered her senses enough to break the surface and tread water. The current was pushing her downstream but though fast it was not violent and she could just manage to hold her position in the flood, though it took all her effort.

33

Then she remembered Antony and looked round for him. He broke the surface some way downstream from her, gave a horrible gurgling cry, and went under again.

Hero had never been in the water before, but she was not afraid. She knew that Hamil could swim, and anything he could do she was confident she could also. She let the water take her, not attempting to swim, merely holding herself up in the water by beating with her hands and feet. It seemed surprisingly easy. She saw Antony break the surface again, nearer, and found she was able to guide herself towards him. The water jumped into her mouth and she coughed and choked. *Hamil*, she thought, *where are you?* And in her mind she seemed to hear his voice, *I'm coming. Hold on.*

She reached what seemed like the place that Antony had last disappeared, and as the current pulled her onwards she saw a gleam of something under the muddy water – a red gleam. Antony had been wearing a red doublet. She guided herself towards it – and then she was caught and dragged under. The sound of the river boomed in her ears, her mouth and nose were filled with water and when she tried to breathe she choked, water pouring into her as though she were full of holes like a sieve. She struggled with Antony – it was he who had seized her of course – and tried to kick her way upwards. But though the boy's brain was weak, his body was strong, and he held her like a leech, his weight pulling her down. For a moment her head broke the surface – she knew it by the change of pressure – but before she could catch a breath she went under again, and going down, down, down, her head seeming to bulge under the pressure and the lack of air, she despaired: she knew she was drowning.

The pain in her lungs was so terrible she prayed that she might die, if only to be rid of it. Her feet touched something – she supposed it was the bottom – and then suddenly the weight was gone from her. Antony had lost consciousness. She opened her eyes, and saw the gleam of red below her now. It was that that made her realize that she was drifting upwards. *The river is helping me*, she thought, and at the same moment she heard Hamil's voice in her mind again, saying *Swim*. Her hand touched the stuff of Antony's doublet, she grasped it, and began feebly kicking for the surface.

How long does a nightmare last? It can be moments only, and yet it seems to go on for ever. Hamil, swimming towards the place where his sister had gone under, seemed to live a whole lifetime of helpless despair. A second time he had failed her. A second time! Three times he dived, hunting under the water, cheeks and eyes bulging, for some sign of her. Antony he had forgotten already; but it was Antony's red doublet that led him to her. He dived again, and saw her gripping the doublet, trying to haul her cousin upwards. He got a hand to her waist and pushed her upwards, with all the strength of his legs, and they broke the surface together.

'Breathe!' he cried. 'Cough! Breathe!' Hero choked and gasped, and he made out the words, 'It hurts.' She did not want to breathe, because it hurt worse than dying.

Beating water with his legs, holding her up by the armpits, he managed to shake her a little.

'Hero, breathe! Again! Keep breathing.' He saw that she was obeying him. The weight of the two bodies was wearing him out, pulling him down. 'Let go of Antony,' he shouted to her. He saw her eyes widen. 'No!' she cried. 'We must save him.'

So it was. Relieved of Antony's weight, and with Hamil's help, Hero could keep herself up enough to kick slowly towards the bank. Hamil supported Antony and pushed him ahead slowly, though he thought the boy must be dead for he made no movement. They had gone a long way downstream, but here was a bend in the river that slowed the current, and they were making progress. After what seemed like hours they reached the bank, and pulled themselves along to where a tough old tree grew out over the water on which they could haul themselves up.

There was no sign of Amory. Vaguely Hamil supposed he had gone for help. While Hero held on to a branch, Hamil managed to hoist Antony's limp body over the horizontal trunk of the tree so that he hung, feet in the water and head hanging just clear of the surface. Then he scrambled out of the water and pulled Hero up onto the bank, and they collapsed together, exhausted, their limbs aching and lungs burning with the terrible effort.

Perhaps they slept for a while. At any rate, it was with a sense of coming back from somewhere that Hamil became aware that Antony was groaning. He was not dead, then. With a terrible effort, Hamil got to his feet and manhandled Antony along the tree until he was clear of the river, and then onto the bank. Antony coughed, was copiously sick, and then began to groan again.

'We must get him back to the house,' Hero said weakly. Hamil turned to her and knelt beside her.

'How is it with you?'

'I'm all right. Tired to death, but all right.' She met Hamil's anguished eyes. 'It was not your fault.' He clasped her hand, unable to speak. 'Hamil, *it was not your fault*.'

'If anything had happened to you –' He could not finish. Hero pressed his hand and tried to turn his attention.

'How are we to get Antony back? And where is Uncle Amory?'

'I don't know. I suppose he has gone for help.'

'Where's Goldcrest? If you can catch him, we can get Antony onto his back somehow.'

'I'll go and find him,' Hamil said. He got to his feet and set off along the bank. He felt as though he had been savagely beaten, for every part of his body ached terribly, and he was almost numb with exhaustion, more tired than he could have believed possible. Through a haze he saw the pony Goldcrest coming towards him, having followed them downstream, grazing as it went. It did not try to avoid capture. He led it back to Hero, and with her help managed to heave Antony's inert body across the saddle, while the pony, for wonder, stood rock still. It did not even protest when asked to take a double burden, for Hero was too weary to walk through heavy going with her damaged hip.

The haze grew thicker, like fog, as Hamil stumbled homewards, less leading the pony than being supported by it. They were met a little way from Watermill House by some servants who had seen them coming. The alarm had not been given; Amory had not been there. Hamil heard their anxious questioning voices like the chatter of birds, growing more distant as the welcoming fog closed over him, and without a cry he slid to the ground and lost consciousness.

Amory's death remained a mystery for all time. His body was recovered from the river the next day, but whether he had slipped and fallen in, or had jumped in to try to save the others, or had met with some other mischance, it was impossible to say. The repercussions of his death were felt more at Shawes than anywhere else. Shawes was the home of that branch of the family called the Bible Morlands. Amory's sister Aletheia had married Nehemiah Morland, master of Shawes and captain of a ship in the East India Company. He had been killed at the massacre of Amboyna in 1623, and Aletheia had not long survived him, dying, it was said, of a broken heart.

She had left behind twin sons, Zephaniah and Zechariah, and two daughters, Ruth and Mary Eleanor. Zeph had married a York girl who had died giving him a son, Malachi. Zech had married Sabine, Amory's daughter, and they were yet childless. Zeph and Zech had both followed their father's footsteps into the East India Company and were often away on long voyages, in fact were rarely home.

Sabine had never liked Shawes, an old, dark, inconvenient house, and so when Amory died she decided to go back and live at Watermill House and take care of her brother Antony.

The problem was that it left no adult at Shawes, and Ruth, who was fifteen, Mary Eleanor, who was twelve, and Malachi, who was fourteen, could not live there unsupervised.

'You'll have to go and live at Morland Place until your brothers come home,' Sabine said coldly when the subject arose. 'If they ever do come home.'

'But what will happen to Shawes?' Malachi asked anxiously. It was, after all, his inheritance.

'A steward can run it until you are older,' Sabine said. 'Clearly you cannot take charge of it now.'

'A steward!' Malachi cried, but Ruth cut across him angrily.

'I don't want to go to Morland Place. This is my home.'

'You will have to. You cannot stay here, once I am gone.'

'Then why must you go? You never minded before.'

'I have to go and look after my brother.'

'Let *him* come *here*,' Ruth cried, her face red with passion. 'I won't go to Morland Place.'

'You will have to,' Sabine said. Of all the trials of her life at Shawes, she had found her eldest sister-in-law the worst. 'You forget, Watermill House is my home, and I assure you I feel as passionately about it as you do about Shawes. More so, in fact, for Shawes will never belong to you, while Watermill is already mine.'

Hers, entirely hers. Antony clearly could not inherit, being an idiot, and if Zech never came home, there would be nothing to come between Sabine and her inheritance. If he did come home – well, she would worry about that if and when it happened. Now with the prospect of escape she could say what she liked.

'I have never liked it here in this horrible old house. Now

I am going home, to my own place, and I shall never come here again.'

'But what will happen to us?' Mary Eleanor asked, near to tears.

'I neither know nor care. You'll go to Morland Place until your brothers come back or you're old enough to look after yourselves. You are no longer my responsibility, thank God.'

Mary Eleanor burst into weeping, and Ruth put her arms round her, fiercely protective, though she had never had much time for her younger sister. 'We'll go to Morland Place because we must. But as soon as I'm old enough I shall come back here, and then no-one shall ever take *me* away again. Don't cry, Nell, all will be well, you'll see.'

'Besides, my papa will come home,' Malachi added, but it was said in defiance, not belief, for his father had been away so long even he did not expect ever to see him again.

CHAPTER THREE

Richard woke to the powerful smell of chicken dung, and could not remember where he was. He tried to sit up and open his eyes, and both objectives made him feel so sick that he lay down again and tried to reassemble his thoughts from a horizontal position. After a while he opened his eyes again and looked up at a sloping wooden ceiling, through whose dusty gaps daylight poured in. Beneath him was extremely dirty straw, and he was itching maddeningly from what he knew from experience were new flea-bites.

Somewhere behind his head a pigeon flew down with a rattle of wings and began a deep-throated courting which, judging by the noise, was not being entirely rejected. Richard sat up again, cautiously, and remembered. He had escaped last night from the custody of the manservant, Patrick, whom his father had set to spy on him, and had spent a very enjoyable evening in an inn – or he assumed it had been enjoyable. He didn't remember very much in detail, except that the inn was the White Hart in Goodramgate – he no longer trusted the Hare and Heather.

There had been a very good fiddler, he remembered, a young man with red hair and a great tufty beard, and a little white bitch who danced on her hind legs on a command from her master, and who later got so drunk on lees that she began howling like a wolf and would not leave off, to the great merriment of the onlookers. And later, he remembered, a Puritan had come in and begun preaching at them: how they were all bound for the dark place unless they left off their sinful singing and dancing and drunkenness. They had hectored and jeered at him, and he had gone on, shrieking hoarsely until Richard and his boon companion had crept up behind him and seized him. Richard had held him while the boon companion poured a quart of ale down his throat so that the Puritan must either swallow it or drown.

After that things had got very merry. Richard scratched his head and tried to remember the boon companion's name, but in vain. At any rate, they had left the inn together and had sworn eternal brotherhood while reeling down the blackness of Patrick Pool – Richard remembered making some devastatingly witty joke about his missing servant Patrick, which he could not now recall. Then the boon companion, on being told that Richard had no desire to go home, had offered him the hospitality of his loft and had led him into one of the little yards between Jubbergate and Little Shambles. Richard remembered stumbling over a rooting pig and squelching through mess and offal before being helped tenderly up a ladder and bedded down in the loft with the care of a mother.

After that Richard supposed he must have fallen asleep, for he remembered nothing more. Presumably the companion had gone home, or else had slept beside him and got up early. A pity he could not remember his name – a most kind, amusing companion he had been. Richard scratched his head again, and felt something moving about in his hair. He grinned, thinking the boon companion had left him some company. Outside an ox was bellowing nearby – stalled behind one of the butcher shops in the Shambles, presumably, waiting to be killed – and the perpetual church bells were clamouring. Richard was both hungry and thirsty, and thought it must be getting on for dinner time. He fumbled to button up his doublet, which was hanging open, and then looked down in surprise to discover he had no buttons to do up.

He reached around himself, puzzled, but every button on his clothes had been neatly cut off with a sharp knife. Understanding came to him slowly. His hat was gone, and his purse, and even the fancy buckles off his shoes. The boon companion, then, was no companion, but a simple coney-catcher, who had had all the wealth Richard carried for the price of a pint of ale. No, he recollected, not even that, for he, Richard, had bought the drinks all evening, outbidding the other for generosity. Inns were traditionally full of such rogues, along with card-sharpers and tricksters and simple plain thieves, but Richard had always thought himself too clever to be gulled.

He scratched again and cursed feebly, and then shrugged and began to smile – after all, it *had* been a good night, and he *had* outwitted Father's spy. He climbed backwards out of the loft, down the ladder into the stinking yard, which was inhabited by a family of tough little black pigs and a few speckled hens, and made water in a corner. Then he tore a strip off his shirt to tie round his waist to hold up his breeches, squelched his way out of the yard and found himself in the Little Shambles. Judging by the light and the activity around him he guessed it was nearing noon, and the mouth-watering smell of roasting meat came strongly to him, reminding him how hungry he was.

'Mind out the way, youngster!' a man cried, and he stepped backwards as a butcher drove three terrified calves past him; then he was shoved the other way by a stout woman carrying two brace of live hens by their feet, and almost tripped by two dirty urchins with bare feet who shot past behind him cramming bread into their mouths as they ran – stolen bread, probably, to judge by their haste. He couldn't stand around here, jostled on all sides. He crossed the narrow lane, jumping the open kennel in the middle, and dodging a stream of filth flung out of an open window above, he trotted along into the Shambles proper, following the smell of cooking to a cookshop at the end of the street opposite Whipma-Whopma Gate.

Outside the shop, one above the other over the great fire, were the four huge spits, turning slowly by the efforts of the blind and bandy-legged spit-dog running frantically in his closed wheel. On the highest spit were four chickens; on the lower ones great dripping joints of beef, veal, lamb, pork, and mutton; presiding over all, and basting the meats with a huge spoon that would have held half a pint, was a fat woman in a dress that had once, probably, been red, but was now so spattered and spotted with grease that the colour shewed through only here and there like a pattern. As Richard paused before her she grinned at him invitingly, shewing a mouthful of blackened stumps for teeth, and then scratched herself where her waist would have been, awaking a sympathetic itch in Richard's own anatomy. He could smell her, even above the smell of roasting.

'Now then, young master, what dost want? Tha looks hungry enough to ate me!' And she roared with laughter.

'How much?' Richard asked wistfully, licking his lips like a dog at the dripping meat, and feeling about himself cautiously. His purse was gone, but he had had odd coins in odd pockets, and perhaps – ah yes, the front pocket of his breeches, presumably too tight for the companion to get into without waking him. There was something there – would it be enough?

'Ordinary's sixpence,' the woman said seductively. 'Sempence wi' pudden. Reet tasty pudden an' all, wi' currant jam if tha likes – or gooseberry.' She eyed Richard speculatively, and he felt suddenly light-hearted. It made life strangely simple when you had nothing, he thought – decisions became irrelevant. He grinned at her, scratched at his lice again, and imitated her speech.

'Eh, but tha needn't call me master – I 'aven't seven-pence to ma name. I were set on last naight by thieves, and they took all but –' he brought out the coins from his pocket and examined them on his palm – 'fourpence ha'penny. Will ta give me fourpence worth?'

'Poor lad,' she said, her giant bosom heaving with sympathy. 'What is thy master thinking about to let thee out

43

alone at night? Coom, sit thee down on't bench there and I'll give thee what I can.'

So a moment later Richard was seated on the bench with his back to the warm wall watching the woman carve him a plateful of meat.

'Doos ta like it fat or lean? An' well or rare-done?' The sizzling slices fell fair and fat on the platter. A little salt and a dab of mustard on the side of the plate, a good roll of half-and-half bread, and a stone bottle of small beer: an ordinary to satisfy any hunger. He ate comfortably, looking about him cheerfully, and was soon joined by other diners, 'prentices and bachelors mostly, and not a few stray dogs cringing near for scraps. He was just wiping the last grease off the platter with the end of his bread when the cookshop-woman said to him, a little disapprovingly,

'Now young master, does 'at wench want thee?' and he looked up to see a hooded figure lurking in St Crux yard and gesturing furtively to him. Richard jumped up, wiped his chin with his hand, and hurried across the street, taking the girl by the elbow and drawing her into the shadow of the narrow alley. Her dark hood fell back, revealing a head of pretty golden curls, and anxious eyes of summer blue looked up into his face.

'Oh Richard, thank heavens I've found you. I've been so worried, and I didn't know how to get a message to you.'

'Now Jane,' Richard said uneasily, glancing about him. 'How did you know I was here?'

'I didn't,' she said. 'But I was just passing the end of the street on my way home from market –' she gestured to the basket on her arm, 'and I saw you. So I told Betty I'd dropped the packet of braids I'd just bought and sent her back to look. She won't be long – oh Richard, I've been so worried.' She sought reassurance in his eyes. 'I – I think I'm with child.'

'Oh,' Richard said feebly. He could not think what to

44

say. Jane Gardner was the daughter of a stonemason who lived in St Saviourgate. They were decent enough people, though not well-to-do; Jane's mother was dead, and she kept house for her father and was attended by a maid-of-all-work called Betty who had a weakness for Geneva-water which had come more than once to Richard's aid. Jane had been persuaded by him on several occasions to let him into the house while Betty was drunk and her father was out at the Black Swan or the Red Lion; her life was lonely, and held little pleasure.

'Are you sure?' he asked at length. She nodded.

'I've counted again and again, and in any case, I can tell now: my – my breasts are swollen, and I'm beginning to get fatter. Betty hasn't noticed yet, but she soon will, and then –' She left the sentence hanging. Richard shivered, his feeling of wellbeing deserting him. Master Gardner was a violent man in his cups, and even when sober he had a tongue like a stone-rasp. Richard racked his brains.

'Can you – I mean could you – if I got money, there might be some woman you could go to –'

Jane looked puzzled. 'What do you mean?'

'To get rid of it – there are women, so I've heard, who can – do things, to make it go away.'

Jane's mouth opened but no sound came from it, and she stared at him in horrified misery, and her eyes filled with tears.

'No, no,' she whispered at last. 'I could never do that. Oh Richard, how could you ask it? You said you loved me –' The tears welled over from the blue eyes and rolled down her cheeks. Richard found himself wondering vaguely that the tears weren't blue; then he pulled himself together. He must stop her crying, or passers-by would wonder what was going on. And Betty would be back –

'All right, Jane, don't cry. I didn't mean it, not really.'

'But you do love me?'

'Of course I do,' he said hastily. She moved closer,

45

looking up at him with eyes that would have melted a stone saint.

'I know it was a sin, what we did, and perhaps we're being punished. But I did it because I loved you. You know I wouldn't have gone with anyone else – only you. And only because you said you loved me. And now I'm carrying your baby –'

His baby. Richard stared at her front and thought with sudden elation, *his* baby! That was one thing his father had not given him, that he owed to no-one but himself. He was unexpectedly touched, by her and by the situation, and a surge of warmth for her came over him, making him put out a hand to her. She clutched it and pressed it to her cheek, and as if echoing his thoughts she said, 'Oh Richard, what will your Father say? He'll never let us wed. He'll say I'm not good enough for you.'

Richard's heart swelled. He had not until that moment thought about marrying Jane – she was quite right when she said they would think her not good enough for him, and until that moment Richard himself would have acknowledged her as too far his social inferior even to speak of marriage. But at the idea of his Father forbidding him, defiance hardened in him.

'He shan't stop us,' he said. 'Don't be afraid, Jane – I shall wed you, and before the child is born. Our son shall not be a bastard. You shall be my wife, and all shall be well.'

'Oh Richard!' Smiles broke through the tears, and she hugged him in delight. 'Shall you come and tell my father? Oh do,' she urged, seeing him blanch, 'please do, for I'm so afraid of him. But he won't beat me if you tell him you will wed me. Please, darling Richard, please.'

Richard swallowed. 'He might beat me.' Jane hugged him harder.

'No, no, he won't, not when you tell him we are to be wed. He'll be too glad to be angry. Come now, while he's at

46

dinner. He's always in a good mood at dinner. Look, here comes Betty – please, please come.'

Richard allowed himself to be drawn along, but the sixpenny ordinary was lying unexpectedly heavily on his stomach, and he caught himself thinking that mutton-fat did not really agree with him, and that he must remember not to eat it in future.

'Edmund is heartbroken, of course,' Mary Esther said to Ambrose. 'Richard expected him to be angry – I suppose anyone would have expected that – but he was more shocked and hurt than angry, and that's what upsets me so much.'

She and her uncle were strolling along the neat, boxed paths of the Italian Garden in the peaceful time between Mass in the chapel and Sunday dinner. The whole family would be assembled. From the Long Walk came the sounds of voices and laughter and the whizz and thud of archery practice at the butts, and from the other side of the yew hedge, in the rose-garden, came the sound of Nerissa playing with Anne while Leah walked the baby telling her the names of flowers.

'That's heartsease, chuck, and those are pinks. No, no, don't touch the bee, lovey, it'll sting thee . . .'

'He'll get over it,' Ambrose said comfortingly, patting Mary Esther's hand, which rested on his arm. 'After all, it's only to be expected that a lively young man will sow a few wild oats –'

'Oh it isn't that that upsets him so much,' Mary Esther said. 'Of course, he deplores Richard's fall from virtue, but what really hurts him is that he cared so little about the family's standing that he promised to marry this girl.'

'Is she really so bad?' Ambrose asked gently. Mary Esther shook her head.

'She isn't bad, just ignorant; I've spoken to her, and she seems decent enough, obviously loves Richard, and bedded

47

with Richard out of a romantic urge – and probably loneliness, poor creature. But they are low and poor people, and the girl has no dowry at all.'

'It's the money then?'

'No, Uncle 'Brose, not principally. Edmund says he would have accepted a penniless girl from a good family quite happily. But if this Jane Gardner had a thousand pounds, he would not think her fit to be his son and heir's wife. But there, what's done is done. He tried to buy the father off, but the man saw where his best interest lay, and would not have it, and Richard is digging his toes in and will not be shifted.'

'That's a good sign, at least,' Ambrose said, 'a sign that he has a good heart and a tender conscience.'

Mary Esther smiled briefly. 'Like you to think so!' she said. 'But he's doing it for no better reason than to defy his father. If Edmund had ordered him to marry the girl, he would have refused indignantly.'

'Ah well,' Ambrose said as they turned at the end of their walk, 'it may turn out well at last. Richard may settle down when he has a wife and child of his own to care for.'

'But what a child!'

'You don't know,' Ambrose said, shaking his head. 'The girl seems healthy enough, and strong new blood is no bad thing. There's too much inbreeding in our family, cousins marrying cousins over and over. The child will be brought up at Morland Place under your eye – and Edmund's. He may turn out to be the best of the litter.'

'I hope you're right,' Mary Esther said. 'And particularly about Richard. If only he didn't resent his father so – and he's so suspicious of me, that when I try to be kind to the girl, he thinks I'm trying to turn her against him. Oh dear – what's to-do now?' A noise of altercation came from beyond the hedge in which Mary Esther distinguished Alice's voice raised in shrill protest. 'Will you excuse me, Uncle 'Brose? I'd better go and see what's happening.'

'I'll come with you,' he said. With Dog at her knee, she had already hurried ahead of him through the gap in the hedge. In the rose garden Alice and Ruth were red-faced and shouting at each other, Mary Eleanor was weeping, Anne was pummelling Ruth as high up as she could reach and making no impression on her many-petticoated skirts, Nerissa was trying to stop her, and Leah was vainly trying to restore order, while the baby on her hip was unconcernedly eating the petals off a pink which she held in her fat little hand, and watching the scene with round eyes.

'Hush girls, hush, all!' Mary Esther cried. 'What is the matter? Quarrelling on the Sabbath? For shame!'

'Mother, Ruth pulled my hair!' Alice cried, running to her to get her word in first. Ruth glowered sullenly.

'She hit my Nell. No-one shall hit little Nell,' she said defiantly. She seemed at last to notice the attack going on behind her, and turned to shove Anne away from her so hard that the child reeled into Nerissa and almost knocked her over.

Leah said angrily, 'For shame, Ruth, to be so rough with the little ones! A great girl like you.'

'All right, nurse,' Mary Esther said hastily, seeing Ruth gathering her forces to argue. 'Mary Eleanor, are you hurt? Come here, let me see.'

'She hit me on my arm – look,' Mary Eleanor sobbed. Mary Esther looked.

'Now, chuck, it isn't even red. Fuss for nothing. Hush your crying now. Alice, why did you hit her?'

Alice stuck out her lip. 'She came and spoiled our play. I was playing with Anne and she came and spoiled it. I don't want her playing with us.'

'Well she doesn't want to play with you,' Ruth cried quickly. 'We didn't ever want to come here, so you needn't think it.'

'Then why don't you go away again?' Alice retorted. Leah at that point was so distracted that she snatched the flower away from the baby, and the baby after a second of surprise closed her eyes and yelled, and held out her hands for her mother.

'Give her to me, nurse,' Mary Esther said, taking Henrietta and nestling the hot wet face against her neck. 'Now girls, I want no more of this quarrelling, and on the Lord's Day, too! You should all love each other, and be in peace with each other. Alice, you are a naughty girl to be so unkind to your cousins. They are welcome here, and they will live here for as long as they like. And Ruth, you mustn't be so cross and unruly, even if Alice did hit your sister. You are much too old to be hitting the little ones. Come to me if you have a complaint. Now let's go and see how they are getting on at the butts. It will soon be dinner time, and I don't want any sulky faces at dinner, so let's have no more of this.'

Still holding the baby, Mary Esther shepherded the whole group out of the rose garden towards the Long Walk, and Ambrose, following behind, wondered with a smile at the way his little girl coped with the great household and the numerous family. To him she was a little girl still – it seemed no more than an eyelid's blink ago that he had been dressing her own childhood's cuts and bruises and learning how to curl and braid her dark hair. 'I made a tolerable mother,' he thought with a private smile, 'but I could never have run a great household like this.'

Summer of 1631 brought the plague to York again. York, though a very beautiful city, was a stinking and unwholesome one, and there had been many plagues since that which had wiped out the entire Butts family sixty years ago. This was the one called the Black Death, and it came creeping up the sluggish, half-stagnant river from the rat-infested wharves and raged through the crowded, insanitary tenements with its hideous, incurable affliction. As

50

soon as the outbreak was known to be serious, guards were put on all the city gates to stop people entering or leaving, but it was already too late to stop it spreading. Along the roads it went, striking at dwellings on the way; down Blossom Street to invade St Edwards' Hospital, pausing at the Hare and Heather to snatch away Willey Morland, Will Morland's much-loved eldest son; and along the Holgate track to Rufford where it took twenty victims, after having slipped unnoticed into Morland Place.

'I don't like the look of Miss Alice, Madam,' Leah said that evening. 'Will you come and look?'

Mary Esther started up at once. 'Why, Leah, what's wrong?'

'I don't know what's amiss, Madam. Perhaps she has been too long in the sun today.' Leah avoided Mary Esther's gaze. 'Or perhaps –'

'Don't say it,' Mary Esther said quickly, crossing herself. 'I'll come. It *has* been hot today –'

In the remodelled nursery wing, Alice shared a bed in one room with Anne and Henrietta, while the nursery maid, Beatrice, slept in a truckle bed. Beatrice was standing by the bed now, wringing her hands nervously. It was she who had called Leah's attention to the state of Miss Alice, and she feared that whether or not Miss Alice was ill she was going to find herself in trouble. Mary Esther went to the bedside and leaned over, putting her hand to Alice's brow, and the child stirred at the cool touch on her hot skin. Beyond her Anne and Henrietta were asleep, Anne sprawled, all angles with her skinny arms and legs, fat Hetta rolled up like a woodlouse. Mary Esther's heart turned over – they were so vulnerable, alone in sleep for disease to creep up on.

Alice moved restlessly and muttered, and Mary Esther gently drew off the bedclothes from her and unlaced her bedgown, but there were no spots to be seen on her neck or between her budding breasts.

'We'll call the doctor in the morning,' Mary Esther said,

'if she's no better. She does feel hot, but it might just be too much sun. Beatrice, if she wakes, you may call me.'

'Yes Madam.' The maid curtseyed nervously.

She was not better in the morning. She had vomited, was feverish, complained of pains in the head, and averted her eyes painfully from the light, and when the doctor came and examined her, his face was grave as he called Mary Esther to the bedside and silently indicated the low red swelling in the child's groin. Cold terror gripped Mary Esther's heart, and she could not speak. She looked from the doctor to Leah, and saw the sweat on the latter's lip and the greasy whiteness of her face. Oh Lord God, she prayed inwardly, not that, not that!

'Will she live?' she managed to ask at last. The doctor shook his head.

'Madam, I cannot hold out any hope. Few victims of the plague survive. But we will do all we can, and there is always hope, and prayer. You must move the other children out, and no-one must come into the room except the person who is to nurse her. And nothing must leave the room – not the least rag or bowl – unless it is purified first. I will leave you instructions for that, and a receipt for a remedy, and I will come again this evening.'

Mary Esther stayed with the child while Leah saw the doctor out, and while she was waiting for the nurse to return Edmund came in. Mary Esther turned to him automatically, longing for comfort, before she remembered.

'Edmund, you must not come in, nor touch anything. It is – it is the plague. It is very infectious.'

Edmund looked across at the narrow shape of his daughter under the covers, and then at his wife. 'You must come away too, then. A servant shall nurse her.'

Mary Esther looked at him with bright eyes, knowing what it must have cost him to say that. 'No,' she said. 'I will nurse her. It is my right.'

Edmund looked puzzled. It was a strange word to use,

52

'right' instead of 'duty'. 'But you are not even her mother.'

'She calls me so. I will nurse her.'

Edmund stared a moment longer, and then, 'God bless you,' was all he could say. Leah came back with the doctor's receipt.

'I cannot read it all, Madam, but certain we haven't half these things.'

'Let me see,' Edmund took the paper from her and read out. 'Vipers fat blended with honey, to which add twenty-four woodlice, baked until crisp enough to powder and well-pounded, an ounce of dried hen's dung . . . rue and rosemary . . . yolk of egg . . . mixed with a quarter of a pint of old ale and the same of salt water . . . two pinches of pepper . . .' He looked at his wife. 'My dear, can this really help?'

Mary Esther looked helpless. 'Who knows, Edmund? If the doctor says so – but he promised nothing. Yet if we do nothing, she will surely die.'

Edmund looked down at the paper again, and then handed it back to Leah. 'Well, then, as you think best. Tell Clement, nurse, and he shall get anything you need.'

'Thank you, Edmund. But you must go, now, and make sure no-one comes near. You had better burn herbs in all the rooms, in case the infection is in them. And take Dog away.'

The hound set up a dreadful howling as he was dragged away, and all day long Mary Esther heard his crying as a background to the nightmare of the child's sickness. In the evening the doctor came again, but he did not go nearer than a yard from the bed, looking at the child over the orange stuck with cloves that he held to his nose against the sickness.

'Did you give her the remedy?' he asked.

'Yes, but she vomited it up.'

'That shews that she has the infection within her,' the doctor said. 'You must persist with it, forcing it down her if

53

she throws it up, for otherwise there is no help.'

'And if she keeps it down?'

'Then she will recover – if God wills it.'

Mary Esther looked doubtfully at him, and then at the delirious child. 'She is much weaker,' she said. 'I'm afraid the vomiting may be too much for her.'

'Turn back the covers,' the doctor said. He examined the child's body from his safe distance. The bubo was larger, hard and angry red, and the child stirred and whimpered in pain as Mary Esther touched it lightly. 'Yes, the plague-boil is bigger, it is drawing the strength from her. If it has not burst by midnight, you must apply a cautery to burst it.'

'A cautery?'

'I'll write down the recipe. Vitriol and mercury made into a paste with lambs' fat and horses' dung will be best. I will come again in the morning, if she still lives.'

Helpless frustration overcame Mary Esther as the doctor left her again to her vigil, and she sat down by the bedside and wept until Leah came back and she forced herself to be calm. Tears could not help poor little Alice, only her unremitting vigilance. Leah rolled up her sleeves and set about mixing a new batch of the remedy, and then between them they held the child in a sitting position and forced the brew down her throat; and a little while later held the bowl while she vomited it up.

At midnight she seemed weaker, her skin was dark and her pulse weak, and she had been unconscious for some time. The room stank of her infected sweat, and Mary Esther and Leah were both blind weary; but they did what had to be done, mixing the caustic poultice and spreading it on a fold of linen. Then they uncovered the wasted body, and standing one either side to hold the child still, they clapped the caustic onto the plague-boil.

Huddled together in one bed in the east bedchamber, Ruth and Nell and Anne and Hetta heard the screams, and they held on to each other and prayed desperately that Alice

54

might be spared – and that they might not fall to the horrible pest. In another bedroom, Jane wrapped her arms round her swelling belly and was too frightened even to think. Beside her Richard felt her movement and stirred. The bedcurtains were partly open because of the heat: one of the advantages, Richard had discovered, of being married was that he was no longer expected to share a bedchamber with his brothers and cousin, but had one to himself with his wife.

His wife! It still seemed strange to call Jane Gardner his wife. He did not feel particularly attached to her; he did not feel he even knew her. Now, for instance, what was in her mind? She was murmuring something under her breath – a prayer?

'What are you saying?' he asked abruptly. She was silent at once, afraid of having offended. He saw, when he troubled to, that Jane was afraid of everyone at Morland Place, not just the family but the servants too. If anyone asked her anything, however simple, she did not answer directly, but searched around desperately in her mind for the answer she thought was required. So it was in everything – she tried so hard to please she pleased no-one.

'Were you praying?' he asked. 'What's the matter with you?' She murmured something. 'What?' he prompted irritably. She repeated the murmur, and he caught the word *plague*. 'You wish you had never come to Morland Place, is that it?' He was cunning, phrasing the question to elicit what he thought was her true response.

'Yes,' she whispered. 'I wish I was at home. We shall all die.'

'You fool,' Richard said. 'You are better off here by far. Don't you know they are dying by the score in the city? In all likelihood everyone in your street is dead by now.' She began weeping, and he felt a little sorry for his words. He had meant to cheer her, not upset her. 'Come, here, stop your crying. Come kiss me, wife.' He said the last word rather shyly as he gathered her towards him. She rolled over, belly first, and the swell of the child butted him out of the way. He tried to embrace her but she pulled away.

'Not now, not with – your sister ill.'

Richard flung himself over onto his back angrily. 'It is always *not now* with you. Saints' days or fast days or washing days or some reason – I wonder you bothered to marry me at all. I was better off a bachelor – you were willing enough then. Have a care, or I might go and seek better company.'

'Oh Richard,' Jane cried, and, afraid she had offended him, sorry that she had hurt him, she moved closer and began caressing him, crying now in earnest. 'I'm sorry, Richard, I didn't mean – I do want you, really I do. And I love you. It's only that – with your sister so ill – it didn't seem right.'

Richard allowed himself to be coaxed into fondling her. 'Just you leave the worrying to me, Jane. You know that I love you – don't you?'

'Yes Richard,' she said meekly.

'Then do you think I'd have you do what was wrong? Don't you trust me?' There was no answer to that, of course. He began cautiously to make love to her. She held her body stiffly, and once again she murmured something under her breath. 'What is it now?' Richard asked, pausing.

She was more reluctant than ever to tell, but at last said, very hesitantly, 'I'm only worried that it might hurt the baby, being so near the time –'

'Oh, the baby!' Richard said indifferently, and Jane held her breath and made no more protest.

The doctor did not come until late the next morning, and by that time Alice's body, incredibly emaciated by her short, violent illness, horribly disfigured by the half-burnt bubo, was wrapped in a winding-sheet and lying in a coffin that Ben and Dickon had hastily knocked together early that morning. The house was redolent with the fume that was being burnt in every room as a precaution – a mixture of pepper, frankincense, burnt barley, and white vinegar – and the doctor seemed to approve of it, for after one sniff he lowered his protective orange for the first time, and inspected the body from a safe distance.

'She died when we applied the caustic to the plague-boil,' Mary Esther said. The doctor nodded, and made no comment. Wearily Mary Esther re-covered the corpse and turned to find the doctor's exit blocked by Edmund, whose face was white under his tan, the sole sign of his great inner turmoil.

'I think it was your cure that killed her, doctor,' he said. The doctor looked amazed and shocked.

'My receipt, sir, is an infallible cure,' he said. 'Infallible. I am asked for it wherever I go, sir.'

'It did not save her,' Edmund pointed out. 'How can you say it is infallible?'

'Evidently, you know nothing of medicine, sir,' the doctor said kindly, 'or you would not speak so simply. My receipt never fails to cure – *if God wills it.*'

Edmund stared. 'If God wills it?' he repeated dully.

'Certainly sir. If God wills otherwise, no mortal on earth can help, nor no remedy, however compounded. Good day to you, sir. I pray I may not be needed here again.'

Edmund concurred with his wishes. When the doctor had gone, Edmund turned again to his wife. She looked weary and draggled after her night of nursing, and the stoop of her shoulders was comfortless as she stood beside the coffin, looking down at the uncovered face of his daughter. He longed to reach out to her, but he could not find the way.

At last she said, 'She was so young, just beginning life.' Edmund moved a step nearer. 'I loved her like my own,' she said then, as if she heard his unspoken thought, 'and she called me mother – always, always.' The generosity of an easy heart; so different from Richard; even the younger

57

boys did not accept her as wholly as Alice had. 'So young,' she said again. Her eyes burned and she rubbed them wearily. She wished she could cry. It was as if there was a great stone in her throat and chest, stopping up the spring. It hurt her with a physical pain. Behind her Edmund reached out a hand, unseen, that stopped a little short of her bent shoulders; they were only a foot apart, but out of touch.

At last he said in a husky, uncertain voice, 'I love you.'

It was not the right thing to say, it was not the form of words he would have chosen consciously, but in the end it was what all comfort came down to. She turned slowly, as if movement pained her, and looked up into his face, and read all his sorrow and his need, read too the deep, unspoken apology: 'Shew me love, for I cannot shew you mine. Comfort me, because I cannot comfort you.' With a little shuddering sigh she took the last step towards him, and in a moment was pressed against him, with his arms enfolding her tightly, tightly.

'Hold me,' she said. 'Don't let me go.'

He pressed her harder against him, and she shuddered again as the pain in her throat swelled up, and then broke at last, and the healing flood began.

CHAPTER FOUR

In the spring of 1632 Kit came home. He had been two years at Winchester and two years at Oxford, and Richard was so excited at the prospect of seeing him again that he waited on the road at Aksham Bogs three days running in order to meet him. In the way of people who are unhappy with themselves, he pinned all his hopes on his brother's return. Everything would be all right, he told himself, when Kit was home again. So he waited, his horse hitched to a thorn, and Patrick perched on a milestone a little way away watching patiently. Richard had hoped that Patrick would get bored with waiting and want to leave him, and he dropped hints enough that Patrick need not stay. But Patrick was Clement's nephew, and knew his duty too well.

At last, a little after noon on the third day, Richard saw the far-off dust cloud of an approaching party of horsemen, and mounting and riding forward he saw Kit amongst them, and waved his hat in greeting.

'Kit! At last! I thought you'd never come. Lord, look at you! I wasn't expecting a courtier! I only recognized you by your horse. How come you're still riding old Magpie? I'd have thought you'd have got yourself a new horse to go with all the new clothes.'

'Where do you think I'd get the money for a new horse?' Kit asked, amused by the babble of greeting.

'What about all those new clothes? I can't believe they all come out of your allowance from Father.'

'Oh, it pays to be a man of fashion,' Kit said airily, turning old Magpie to fall in beside Richard. 'Cards and dice can make a reasonable income for a man who keeps sober when all about him are drunk.'

'Gambling?' Richard said, with a note of respect in his voice.

'Just a game or two between friends,' Kit said. 'One thing that the University has taught me is that vice is not vice when it is practised by gentlemen. It's only wicked when lower sort of people do it.'

'Father wouldn't agree with you,' Richard said. 'He thinks me depraved because I drink and gamble and – well – things. But what's a man to do? I wonder sometimes if he expects me to labour in the fields along with the servants.'

'Oh, the north is always far behind in fashions,' Kit said. He was more than half joking, but he soon saw that his brother was not. Richard was agog and envious: his brother had gone away a child, and had come back a gentleman. He drank in the lace-trimmed suit, the long sweeping feathers on the hat, the lace tucks falling over the folded-back tops of the riding boots, the embroidered gloves, the dark curls falling over the shoulders and down the back. Richard felt provincial and dull, a boorish clod, beside his elegant brother. He had done nothing, seen nothing, been nowhere but home, while Kit . . . but Kit was home, and everything would be all right now. Kit would shew Father how things ought to be done.

'You must be sorry to be back,' Richard said as they turned off the road towards Akcomb Moor; in daylight it was safe enough to take the cross-country route.

'Not at all,' Kit said. 'I'm glad to be home, but puzzled all the same. I had expected to be another two years at Oxford, but then came the letter from Father calling me home without any explanation.'

'That's his way – he never gives a reason for anything,' Richard said. Kit eyed him sideways.

'You're not still quarrelling with Father, are you,

60

Richard? I thought that by now you would have settled your differences, now you've been a husband and a father yourself.'

'He doesn't seem to remember that I was married,' Richard said.

'I'm sorry about your wife. I had looked forward to meeting her one day. I'm sure she was lovely.'

Richard did not look at Kit, and his face was bitter as his eyes stared unseeingly ahead. 'They say it was childbed fever, though it wouldn't surprise me if Father had had her poisoned.'

'Oh, come!' Kit protested.

'He hated her, he always hated her. You heard about the portrait, didn't you?'

'What portrait?'

'The great family portrait he had painted for the long saloon. It hangs in pride of place over the fireplace, an enormous great thing, and the whole family's on it – Father in the middle with his wife, and all us children grouped round them. You're in it – your body painted from a model who stood in for you, and your face from description. Actually, it isn't at all a bad likeness. And me, and Ambrose and Francis and that woman's children, and even her cursed dog. And our sister, Alice, she's in it – painted all shadowy and standing apart from us to shew she's dead.'

'That's a nice touch.'

'Father ordered it so. And on a cushion in the foreground my son. Everyone's there – except my wife. When I heard Father was having Alice painted in, I asked if Jane was to be painted in too, and he said no. I asked why, and he said she was not one of the family.'

Kit shook his head sadly. He saw, from the vantage point of his absence, how father and son provoked each other, and how each provoking brought on the next. Edmund wanted to punish Richard for marrying without proper care, and Richard would now seek some way to punish Edmund for

61

punishing him. Where would it end? He sought for something to change the subject.

'I'm looking forward to seeing your son.'

'I named him Ralph. Henrietta can't pronounce it, she calls him "Waif" and Leah clucks and shakes her head and says "That's about the measure of it, poor blessed infant".' His imitation of Leah was good enough to make Kit laugh. 'But he's no waif – he's a bonny bairn, fat and lusty as you could wish. Even Father can't find fault with him, though I'll wager he wishes he could; but Leah defends him like a tigress, and Father Moyes can't wait to start teaching him Latin, Greek and astronomy.'

'And you – what do you wish to teach him?'

'Oh, the usual things – to ride and handle hawk and hound, and to shoot, and dance, and –'

'This boy will have all the accomplishments. And what of the rest of the family? I heard that poor Antony had died. Of the wasting sickness?'

'Yes. He melted away like snow in June; but it's probably for the best. His life was of no use to him anyway. But old Elspeth, Uncle Amory's old servant, was so devoted to Antony that she swore Sabine had made away with him, on purpose to get her hands on Watermill House. Sabine was furious and dismissed her, and now the old woman tells the story far and wide out of revenge: how Sabine used to say it would be a mercy for Antony to die, and how she put him away. Of course she did say, often and often, that it would be a mercy, but as to the rest –' he shook his head. Kit looked surprised.

'You surely don't mean you believe there's any truth in it?'

'Not really,' Richard said slowly. 'It's only that – Sabine has become very strange recently. She shuts herself in the house, and she won't let anyone visit her. You know Hamil and Hero practically lived there and, when Uncle Amory was alive they used to visit and stay such a lot, and now

62

when they try to visit, Sabine won't let them in. She says they're trying to steal her inheritance.'

'But why should they – ?'

'Oh, because the Hamiltons haven't any property of their own, only the little houses in North Street that were Sabina's dowry, and Sabine thinks they want the Watermill estate for Hamil and Hero. But it's all nonsense – if Sabine has no children, and it seems unlikely now that she will, with Zech being away all the time, Watermill will go to the Hamiltons anyway when she dies.'

Kit shook his head. 'It all sounds unpleasantly rancorous. I was looking forward to the peace and tranquillity of life at home in the country.'

Richard grinned maliciously. 'Peace! You'll get no peace here, brother. It's everyone at each others' throats. Even when they do it politely, like Rob Hamilton and Father –'

'Surely not!'

'Oh, yes. About the Hamilton estate. They're going to go to law about it. It seems that the fifth Lord Hamilton has died with no issue, and of course Rob is the third Lord's *son*, but born after he divorced Rob's mother. So Rob wants to claim the estate on the grounds that he was conceived in wedlock and that the divorce was illegal anyway. But part of the estate is not entailed, and that part would go to Father through his mother, who was the third Lord's *daughter* born in wedlock, unless Rob's appeal succeeds. And you know what Father is like about the estate, and land, and increasing the family's wealth.'

Kit was silent, wondering if matters really were as black as Richard painted them. He glanced for guidance at the servant, Patrick, but Patrick's face was a well-trained blank. The Morland servants were not, on the whole, servile, but anyone who attended on Richard had to learn to keep his counsel. He was searching around in his mind for some new neutral subject for conversation when a sound drew his attention. It was the swift passage of a heavy body

63

through the tall bracken, and Kit, alert to danger, had reined his horse and reached for his knife, but at the same instant Dog burst out onto the path and bounded back towards them barking a greeting.

Patrick, who was ahead, called, 'It's the mistress, sir.'

'That woman's dog, curse it!' Richard muttered at the same moment.

Kit threw a curious glance at his brother, and then touched Magpie with his heels to trot forward to meet the little knot of riders as they came round the bend of the path and into view. Mary Esther was the first, Psyche carrying her ahead of the others with a showy, raking trot, and when she saw the boys she waved her hand and gave a halloo of excitement that made the mare canter on the spot.

'Kit! Kit! You're home at last! Well met, my dear,' she cried. Kit pushed Magpie forward and snatched off his hat, laughing with pleasure at the greeting.

'Mother! Madam! It's good to be home, albeit so unexpectedly; it's good to see you. Give me your blessing.'

Mary Esther held out her hands to him, but Psyche boggled at his waving curls and feathered hat and danced about so with alarm that it was minutes before she could be coaxed close enough to Magpie for the two riders to touch. Then, just when she seemed to have quietened, Dog came thrusting past, disturbing Magpie and setting the chestnut mare dancing again. Kit laughed.

'It's no good, Madam, she won't have it,' he said, and with a swift movement he jumped down from Magpie, took Psyche's reins with one firm hand, and held the other up to his stepmother, who took it in both of hers and smiled down at him affectionately.

'God bless you, my son,' she said. 'I am glad you are come home. You look every inch a *chevalier d'honneur*; it is so strange to send away a child and receive a man in return. Strange, and perhaps a little sad, for I loved that child and shall not see him again.'

Kit smiled. 'Oh, the child came back too – it's just that you can't see him.' But she could, just for a moment. He was there in the unselfconscious grin that screwed his eyes into slits and wrinkled his nose.

'Won't you greet your cousins, now?' Mary Esther said, glancing towards the rest of the party that had ridden up with her. At the rear Nerissa and Clem, Clement's son, sat patiently, talking in low voices to Patrick; before them were two young women, one on a chestnut and one on a bay pony. 'I expect you don't recognize them?'

Kit advanced a step to look up at the girl on the bay; a girl of sixteen, going on seventeen, a girl who was heart-breakingly plain and knew it. Her face was large-featured, freckled, and her reddish-brown eyes were ginger-lashed and smouldered with suppressed resentments. Her hair was reddish too, foxy-red, and stiff and straight, defying every method of curling known to woman, so that it hung straight down, its coarseness holding it a little out from her face. Her body was caught halfway between childhood and woman-hood, was large and ungainly, seeming all knuckles like a puppy's; but her long hands were very white, and rested on the reins with a touch that knew every silken movement of her pony's mouth.

'My cousin Ruth,' Kit said, holding out his hand, and when she gave him hers hesitantly, he pressed it kindly and put his lips to it. She looked at him with surprise, and some doubt, until he caught her eye and gave her a wink of complicity that started a reluctant smile. 'Of course I know her. How could I forget her? Do you still love hawking, cos?'

The minute change in the expression of the ruddy brown eyes told him that she was used to being forgotten.

'I have a merlin now,' she said abruptly. 'She's called Shadow, and she's the finest in Yorkshire.' He had remembered her: she repaid the gift in her own kind, by speaking of her merlin; but Mary Esther was speaking again.

65

'She's a deal too fond of hawking, and not fond enough of reading and studying. A woman should have many accomplishments, Ruth, not just one or two.'

Kit pressed his cousin's hand in quick sympathy and moved away, to draw attention from her, for already her face was turning a dull red with embarrassed anger, clashing with her hair. Kit moved a step away to the side of the chestnut pony and held up his hand to the rider.

'And this, of course,' he said, 'is my cousin –'

He stopped. Hero looked down at him, her head bent a little forward, her yellow ringlets slipping forward from under her black stuff hood. Everything about her was graceful, from the curve of her wrist above the rein, the straight flexible line of her back, the arch of her slender neck, to the very fall of her cloak. She moved her hand to meet his, and as their fingers touched their eyes met, and hers widened a moment with some surprise, like recognition. Her fair face was lightly flushed, like the first May rose when it begins to open, and her lips were softly parted. Kit held her hand, but his mouth was suddenly dry, and for a moment he could not speak. It seemed like a very long moment, but it could not have been more than a heartbeat long, for Mary Esther had not even time to prompt him before he concluded, a little huskily.

'My cousin Hero. God's day to you, cousin. I would have known you anywhere.'

'And I would have known you,' Hero said.

How long they would have remained thus, looking questioningly into each other's faces, Kit sometimes wondered afterwards; but Dog sat down just behind him and scratched himself noisily, breaking the spell, and Mary Esther said, 'Shall we go on? Everyone is waiting, at home, wild to see you, and Jacob had prepared some special dishes for dinner to celebrate your homecoming. I should not like to have to face him if we are late.'

Richard stared at her. 'But how did you know he was

coming today?' he asked in angry amazement. 'I have been waiting on the road for three days.'

Mary Esther looked at Richard with exasperated pity. 'It was all arranged, Dick. The party he was to come with was to arrive at York this noon.' Richard muttered something crossly, thinking about the time he had sat patiently by the bogs. 'You could have saved yourself much trouble if you had asked,' she went on. 'But I did not even know where you were these two days past. Why do you always make life so difficult for yourself?'

Richard did not answer, but kicked his horse to a canter and rode up the path. She always contrived to spoil things for him, he thought. He had devised the plan of meeting Kit on the road, and it had been his own special plan, a surprise for his brother, and a surprise for the family when the two of them rode in through the barbican together. But that woman had spoiled it, had stolen the march on him, had known all about it beforehand, and would make the occasion hers, so that there was no room for him.

Kit walked back to where Magpie was peacefully grazing amongst the bracken, caught up the reins and mounted, and falling in beside his stepmother he looked thoughtfully at the expressive back of his elder brother. He had known some people at Oxford who were like that, who seemed to take a perverse delight in making life difficult, and he hoped Richard would not make his homecoming unpleasant. Then his eye caught the slender figure of Hero, reining Goldcrest in beside Ruth's bay to let Mary Esther pass, and all thoughts of Richard flew out of his head.

It was a noisy homecoming, and the yard was so full that the grooms had difficulty in leading the horses away to their stalls. Leah wept, Father Michael roared with laughter, Clement made speeches that no-one heard, Ambrose and

Francis shrieked at the tops of their healthy young voices, Anne and Hetta babbled and chattered, and only Mary Eleanor was silent, though that was from shyness, not lack of excitement. Then after the family had been greeted, there were the servants, coming forward with beaming smiles, shy nods of the head and curtseys, hand-shakes and kisses, for Master Kit had always been a favourite, with his good looks and easy manners. Even Jacob, the cook, emerged from the kitchen, which he ruled with genius and ferocity, like a Vulcan of the sauce-pans, and set the seamed wrinkles of his face into motion in what passed, with this dour old Yorkshireman, for a smile.

'Welcome 'ome, Master Kit, Ah've fet such a feast for thee, as tha s'lt think tha's deed and gone above,' he said, and having wiped his great horny hand carefully on his apron he shook the hand Kit offered. Kit was the only one of the children that Jacob had ever appeared to care for – perhaps because only Kit was not afraid of him. However it was, he had sometimes given Kit a bit of gingerbread out of his apron pocket when the child came across him taking the air in the yard in a break from his hot labours. The other children had retreated from his growls and scowls – though it was not generally known that Hetta sometimes brought him a stone or a limp flower that had taken her fancy in one of the gardens, or that he kept them all in a box under his pillow.

When they got as far as the hall they had to stop again, for it was all new to Kit, and he had to wonder and admire, and look at the noble staircase, and allow the children to point out their favourite beasts among the carvings on the newels and finials.

They had progressed no farther when Kit at last found a pause long enough to ask Mary Esther, 'But where is my father?'

'He has gone over to Twelvetrees to see one of the mares – you know, old Queen Mab that he dotes on.'

'Lord, yes – is she still alive then?'

'Not only alive, but still producing a foal every year. Hamil is with him; but they'll be back for dinner. And there will be others here too: Rob and Sabina of course – they've been visiting in the city – and Uncle Ambrose and Uncle Will and Massey, and I hope Sabine, though I am not sure. But there is still time before dinner to look upstairs. You must see the long saloon, at least, and the portrait – you must see the portrait.'

Ambrose and Francis and Anne and Hetta accompanied them upstairs, and they stood for a long time in the saloon, admiring the paintings and the displays of plate and the fine long windows and, above all, the family portrait. As Richard had said, it was a surprisingly good likeness of Kit, and he said laughingly to his stepmother, 'I begin to believe I travelled here in spirit to be with you. I like your having Alice in the picture – poor little girl. I wish she had been here to greet me too.'

'I miss her every day,' Mary Esther said. 'She was my eldest daughter.'

Kit looked round cautiously, and seeing the children were a way off he said quietly, 'But tell me, why was my brother's wife not included in the same way?'

Mary Esther shook her head. 'I cannot speak on that head. Your father would not have it so. You cannot expect me to question his decision.'

Kit had not thought of that. He stared a while longer at the picture, and then said, 'Yet it seems a shame. The child is there, I see, and what will he think, when he is old enough to understand, that his mother was not included?' Mary Esther did not answer, and he went on, 'It must make Richard unhappy too.'

'Your father –' Mary Esther began, and paused, as if thinking better of it, and at last began again, 'Your father may sometimes act a little more harshly towards Richard than he would, for instance, towards you. They do not live

69

easily one with the other. I am afraid their tempers are too alike. That is why –'

But at that moment Francis came running back into the saloon calling, 'Madam, my father is come! Shall we go down? He is in the hall – Kit, will you come?'

They went down the great staircase, and as Kit turned the angle of the stair his father turned to look and they exchanged a long glance that spoke of mutual approval. Kit was glad to find his father no less handsome, upright, and dignified than his memory had made him; Edmund was happy to see the quiet manly assurance of his second son's carriage, so different from the surly slouch of the heir to Morland Place.

Kit completed his descent and went straight across the chequered marble floor of the hall to kneel at his father's feet, sweeping off his hat with a graceful gesture, and bending his head.

'Give me your blessing, Father,' he said.

Edmund placed his hand on the top of the dark curly hair and blessed him, and said, 'We are glad to have you safely home again.'

Kit looked up and smiled, and got to his feet, and in the exuberance of the moment he almost embraced his father; almost, but not quite. Edmund's cold dignity froze the impulse at birth, and Kit's hands dropped to his sides. He looked up into his father's grey eyes – Kit was tall, but Edmund was taller – and said instead, quietly, 'I hope you are well, Father. I am glad to be home – though to a house much changed.'

'I hope you think it changed for the better.'

'Of course, Sir. It is very fine, though I have seen little of it yet.'

'You shall see it all later – and tomorrow I will take you round the estate. We must find you a new horse, too. Old Magpie will not do for a young gentleman – he is a boy's pony. One of Mab's colts, perhaps, a two- or three-year-old that you may train to your own ways. I wish to see you well mounted.'

It was all said in a grave, almost expressionless voice, but Kit exchanged a rapid, pleased glance with Mary Esther, knowing that for Edmund to offer one of his favourite mare's colts was a gesture of love.

'Thank you, Sir,' he said, flushing a little with pleasure. 'How is the mare? Still well, I hope?'

'She is getting old, but yes, I thank you, she is still fit. Your cousin and I have just come from visiting her.'

At that mention, Kit's eyes were drawn to the figure of his cousin Hamil who was standing behind and to one side of Edmund, engaged in a private conversation with Hero, who was leaning on his shoulder in her usual way. To Kit, it was like the way he had seen young men, courtiers, lean together to whisper; it was not a womanly thing to do. But in thinking it his mind held no censure of the gesture. Even as he greeted Hamil, his eyes strayed over his cousin's shoulder to seek out the blue eyes that had been fixed on his face for some time; and as he smiled in automatic reaction, he missed the small start of surprise and indignation as Hamil glanced from one to the other.

But there was no time for more, for the rest of the family was arriving, and when the greetings were all over Edmund said, 'We shall go in to dinner. My dear, will you take my arm?' and Mary Esther put her hand through his arm and turned with him towards the dining room.

Kit gave a flourishing, half-joking bow in the twins' direction and said, 'Cousin Hero, may I escort you in?'

Hero's lips curled in a smile, but as she opened them to answer Hamil caught her free hand and pulled it through the crook of his own arm, and said, rather more sharply than the occasion warranted, 'Thank you, but she prefers to walk with me. We always go in together.'

He turned away abruptly, and Hero, with no more than a fleeting glance at Kit, went with him, her left arm on

71

Hamil's shoulder, her right hand on his right arm, and whatever surprise Kit had felt at such a sharp rejection was swamped in pity as he saw her ugly, lurching gait. He had forgotten that she limped. It wrenched at his heart that one so lovely and so graceful should be so disabled: on horseback she was like a bird in flight; on the ground, like a bird shot down and wounded.

As they passed ahead of him, Kit found another pair of eyes on him, and quickly offered his spurned arm to his cousin Ruth. She took it without a word, but with a sharp look that said she knew herself to be very much second best. As they passed through the door she murmured to him quietly, 'You have put Hamil's nose out of joint today. He and Hero are never apart, but this morning when he wanted her to go with him and my uncle to see the new foals, she said she wanted to come and meet you instead, and they had as near a quarrel as they ever can have. And now you try to take his place as her prop. It won't do, you know – you had best leave her alone if you don't want to find his dirk under your ribs.'

Kit looked down at her and saw the humour that lurked deep down in her sharp-eyed, plain face.

'You notice a lot, don't you, little cousin?'

'I notice everything,' she said. 'For some reason, being plain makes people think I'm stupid, and they say things in front of me that they would keep private if I were pretty like Hero or Alice. Sometimes I think being plain makes me invisible.'

'You are not plain,' Kit said firmly. She made a face.

'I am not pretty, so you needn't lie. But watch out for Hamil. The Hamiltons have tempers, you know, and he carries a little, wicked knife like a bee-sting under his doublet.'

'You are exaggerating, and enjoying it,' Kit said. Ruth gave him a strange look.

'You think so? Well, Hamil loves two things in the

world – Hero and horses. Uncle Edmund had almost promised to give him one of Mab's youngsters. That's two wrongs you have done him in one day.'

'Come now –' Kit said laughingly.

'Oh you will not believe me, I know – but you'll see I'm right. You may leave my arm go, now, cos – my place is at the other end.'

Disconcerted, Kit let her go, and watched her with a smile of rather perplexed amusement as she moved to her place at the foot of the table, while Edmund indicated a place near the head for his second son. After grace had been said they all sat, and Kit had time to look around him and speak the words of admiration his father wanted but would not ask for. The dining room was very handsome, panelled in dark oak, with a moulded ceiling, and made light and pleasant by the great windows in the long east wall that looked out over the herb garden with its pretty bower. The dining room occupied what had been the rear part of the great hall, and the windows were the tall lights of the old chamber. The furniture was sparse, but grand and solid – the enormous table which had replaced the old-fashioned trestles rested on six massive, elaborately carved legs, and at the head and foot were two tall-backed, armless chairs with leather-cushioned seats, though the rest of the places were supplied only with stools. There were two buffets which served as carving tables along the west wall, and in the north and south walls were two huge fireplaces whose surrounds were deeply carved with a profusion of fruit and flowers, swags and ribbons, vines and acanthus. Over the south fireplace were the old portraits of French Paul Morland and Nanette Morland, so dimmed by a hundred years of house smoke that their features were almost indistinguishable; and over the north fireplace was a much newer painting, of the stallion Prince Hal, who had sired so many of the Morland horses, including Queen Mab.

The servants were bringing in the dishes now, and Mary

Esther had taken her place at the top buffet to dress the main dishes as they came in, taking the knives from Clement as she needed them. Once dressed, the dishes were handed to the sewers, who at Clement's directions took them to the table and arranged them in the proper manner. The sewers needed no directions, but Clement could never be content to be silent on any occasion. Jacob had exerted himself to good effect: there were two full courses, each of sixteen dishes, not to mention the side dishes of lettuces, sallets, fricassees, preserved fruits, wafers, and orange and lemon slices. As well as the usual boiled meats, roasted meats, and carbonadoes, Jacob had provided those special dishes that his soul delighted in, over which he had laboured lovingly for days. There was one of Kit's favourite dishes, a Florentine, the pie-crust containing kidneys cooked with herbs, currants, caramelized breadcrumbs, cinnamon, eggs, and cream; there were giant oysters from Scarborough, which had been gently simmered in drawn butter and white wine and sprinkled with grated nutmeg, bread and thyme; a pie of anchovies and sparrow-grass; a sucket made with gooseberries boiled up in thick cream seasoned with cinnamon, mace, sugar, eggs and rose petals; and a sucking-kid stuffed with a pudding made of quinces and almonds at one end and another of spinach and pounded walnuts at the other.

It was a very leisurely dinner, and in the intervals between musical entertainments there was plenty of time for conversation. Malachi and Richard were both very eager to hear what University was like, and if they were disappointed in the restrained stories that Kit told, they comforted themselves that the details of the wilder events would have to be withheld until Father and the womenfolk were not present.

Kit knew what they were thinking, and wishing to prepare them for disappointment he said, 'I believe Oxford used to be the scene of some very unlicensed behaviour, but since Archbishop Laud became Chancellor, he has made some very strict reforms, and we must all behave most respectably now, and cap the seniors and not sing in the streets and go to chapel properly dressed.'

'Those things are insisted upon?' Uncle Ambrose asked.

Kit nodded. 'Oh yes – one man was sent down only a month ago for insolence to a senior. He was a Puritan, and therefore thought it the next thing to idolatry to call any man "Sir". He called the senior "thou" and "thee" and the senior said if he did it once more he would break his teeth for him – but instead he had him sent down.'

'There are Puritans in Oxford?' Mary Esther asked.

'No, none at all, though I believe in London and the eastern counties there are any number. But Oxford is as right-minded as you could wish, Madam, so you need have no fear I should be corrupted.'

Mary Esther smiled. 'You are too well brought up to be corrupted, I am sure,' she said, 'but they are a dangerous breed, sowers of dissent and faction, and I would the King would be harder on them.'

'Oh the King, I believe, is happy for every man to do what his conscience bids, so long as they don't trouble him with noticing it,' Kit said. 'But his ministers – they are a different matter. Presbyters to a man, though it pains me to have to say it.'

Mary Esther shook her head. 'Just when we had thought to be rid of Church courts and Church law. It is going backwards.'

'They will make nothing of it up here,' he comforted her. 'The north will never change, I firmly believe. It feels both good and safe to be back. And that brings me to another subject; why am I back? I had thought, Father, to be two more years away.'

All eyes turned to Edmund to see if he would answer. He laid down his knife precisely by his plate, reached out for a bread, and said without looking up, 'You are come to

75

supply your brother's place. Richard is to go to Oxford, and you are to take over his tasks for the time being.'

There was silence. Kit, glancing round, saw that no-one had known, except, perhaps, Mary Esther. She was looking grave but composed; Uncle Ambrose was watching her, until his eyes moved to Richard; Richard was looking stunned; and Hero, whose eyes moved away as soon as Kit glanced at her, was looking faintly pleased.

'You are sending me away?' Richard said at last. It came out in a splutter, he was so shaken and angry. Edmund still did not look up.

'You are to go to university. For two years at least, perhaps more. That depends.'

'On what?' Richard demanded. Now Edmund did look at him, coldly and hard.

'I will not have you question me in such an improper manner. Be silent or leave the room.'

Richard moved abruptly, flinging back from the table so violently that his stool was upset and rolled away a foot or two, and his knife fell with a clatter to the floor. 'You are sending me away!' he cried, leaning with his fists on the table, glaring at his father. 'I see the plan now – Kit is to supply my place, is he? Aye, I see it all – you will make him heir, and rob me of what is mine. And my son, too – you will rob him, just as you always meant to. And what of me? Will you make away with me, have me quietly poisoned one night –'

'Richard!' Mary Esther cried, fiercely enough to halt him before he said the unforgivable words. 'Enough – be silent!'

'Enough, yes – and more than enough,' Edmund said, and his quietness was shocking by contrast. 'You had best go to Father Michael's room, and speak to him. And when you have done whatever penance he gives you, go to your room.'

Richard faced him a moment longer; their faces were set, one red with anger, the other white, but their eyes did not meet. Then with an ugly movement Richard swept his hands off the table, knocking his plate and goblet to the floor, and while they still rang with the fall he walked out without another word. Edmund flicked a glance at Patrick, who left his place by the wall and followed. There was a moment more of frozen silence, and then Clement came forward to right the stool and pick up the fallen implements, and the meal went on.

CHAPTER FIVE

When dinner was over, the family removed to the new
drawing-room, and Mary Esther took the opportunity to
say quietly to her husband, 'Edmund – let me go and talk to
him.'

'Richard? For what purpose?'

'To persuade him that it is for the best, that it is not done
to spite him. I think I can make him understand.'

Edmund frowned. 'He will do what he is told, without
needing reasons.' Mary Esther looked up at him, and there
was laughter in her eyes.

'Of course, so he will. No-one doubts it, so you need not
look at me so sternly. But is there any reason why he may
not do what he must willingly?'

Edmund was silent for a moment, and then nodded and
slipped her hand from his arm. 'Very well,' he said quietly,
and Mary Esther touched his hand gratefully and in a
moment was gone. Upstairs she found Patrick, lounging
against the wall. He straightened up hastily at the sound of
her feet, and a silent exchange of glances told her that
Richard was in his bedroom.

He was lying sprawled face down on his bed, the bed he
had shared with Jane, and he did not move or look round
when Mary Esther came in, even when she sat on the edge of
the bed beside him. She looked with pity at his rigid back,
and longed to stroke the unruly hair, but she knew it was
not possible. Instead she said quietly, 'Richard, I am come
to talk to you.' He made no movement, and she went on, 'I
know that you do not love me, because I am not your
mother, and it does credit to your heart that you loved her so
much. But will you believe that I have no reason to dislike

you, or to want anything but your welfare?' This time she waited for an answer, and after a moment he turned his face so that one eye looked up at her.

'What do you want?' he growled at last.

'Will you listen to me, and do me the justice to believe I speak sincerely?' she asked quietly.

He turned his face away again, but muttered, 'Well – go on.'

'Richard,' she began, 'you are the heir to Morland Place. One day this house and all the estates, everything, will be yours, and your son's after you. What you do, then, affects everyone, and that is why your father has been more severe with you than with the younger boys. It is not because he hates you. It is because he loves you.' Richard muttered something which she could not catch, but the tone of it was disbelieving, so she went on. 'You were kept at home when Kit went to school because it was important for you to learn the management of the estate; but your father believes now that you should also have a taste of university life, and see a little more of the world than just York. That is why he is sending you to Oxford, so that you will be a better master when you come back.'

She paused, and there was no reaction from Richard, but she sensed that he was listening. After a moment she said, 'Richard, do you hear me?'

'Yes,' he said ungraciously.

'And do you believe I'm telling the truth?'

This was harder for him, and after a long pause she placed her hand very gently on his shoulder. He shrugged it off violently.

'Yes,' he snapped. 'Yes, yes, yes. Now leave me alone, will you?' He flung himself across the bed so that he was sitting on the opposite side to her, with his back to her. She got up quietly and went to the door, and there she paused for a moment to look back at him, with an ache for the lonely, brittle set of his young shoulders.

'God bless you,' she said very quietly, and went out. Richard sat unmoving for a moment after he heard the door close, but then his shoulders began to shake, and he put his face into his hands.

The Morland sheep in the West Fields were mutton sheep, and by September they were so fat on the good summer grass that they could barely bring themselves to get to their feet to get out of the way of the rider who came galloping down on them from the direction of Harewood Whin. Psyche's coat gleamed as brightly as a gold coin in the sunshine, and her small hard feet were so sure even over the rough and tussocky grazings that she seemed to fly a little above the earth without actually touching it.

Mary Esther did not attempt to check her. Psyche was not an easy mare to ride, for she never walked if she could dance, and never danced if she could gallop, while a tardy grouse rattling away from under her feet could send her a yard into the air; but she was easier to sit, especially for a sidesaddle rider, when she was going flat out. Mary Esther knew by the cock of her ears that she had seen the sheep, and her presiding devil made her lean a fraction further forward and breathe an encouragement in Psyche's ear. Their pace increased and as the nearest of the tegs, belatedly alarmed, began wriggling its fat bottom in an attempt to rise, the mare took off, clearing the startled animal and dancing her way lightheartedly through the rest of the flock.

At the far side Mary Esther managed to check her, and they waited breathlessly for the rest of the party to catch them up. Dog reached them first, swirling round and round Psyche's feet and making her dance on the spot, and then Ruth on her bay Zephyr, with Shadow bating wildly on her fist and a dozen small birds, her morning's catch, strung behind the saddle.

'That's dangerous,' Ruth said reprovingly. 'You'll break

her legs one of these days. Supposing she'd put her foot down a hole, or the teg had got up a moment sooner?'

Mary Esther laughed exuberantly, trying to check Psyche from walking backwards away from the merlin's rattling wings. 'I know, I know, but it's so hard to stop her – and she never puts a foot wrong. I don't think she touches the ground at all.'

Ruth looked enviously at the golden mare. Though she was fond of her own Zephyr, he was dull compared with Psyche. 'And it's such a bad example to the twins – they already fly about the country quite heedlessly.' They were coming up now on their matching ponies, and some way behind them, going very sedately, was Mary Eleanor, with Nerissa, and Clem carrying Mary Esther's falcon. They had all been hawking up by the Whin.

'It's lucky those aren't ewes, Aunt Mary,' Hamil called as he reached them, 'or you would be in no little trouble.'

'I wouldn't have done it if they were,' Mary Esther said reasonably. 'And besides, you wouldn't tell your uncle, would you?'

'No need to,' Hamil grinned. 'He has seen you.' And he nodded over her shoulder. Mary Esther turned her head, startled; Psyche span round three times on the spot before she managed to halt her facing in the right direction, and sure enough there, over towards the burn, was a group of horsemen amongst whom Edmund was easily distinguishable by his height and his silvery hair.

Mary Esther clapped her hand to her mouth in a comic gesture of dismay and said, 'So he has. Well, I'd better go meekly down and take my rebuke.'

'If you would appear meek, you had better walk,' Hamil advised, 'for you'll never get Psyche to hang her head.'

At a touch from Mary Esther the mare began dancing jauntily towards the other group of riders, shaking her head so that her bridle-ornaments rang and caught the sun, and her companions fell in beside her.

'He's leading a horse,' Ruth observed, narrowing her eyes against the brightness. 'Kit is with him, and the servants have a couple of colts with them – can that be Mab my uncle's leading?'

She pushed Zephyr forward into a trot in her eagerness. Hamil looked sideways at Hero, who returned his look with a quizzical raise of the eyebrow. She could not but be aware that Hamil had noticed and was jealous of Kit's regard for her, which had grown through the summer.

Edmund greeted his wife gravely as always, too careful of formality to rebuke her even had he wanted to. It was indeed Queen Mab that he was leading and on Mary Esther's enquiry he told her, 'I am bringing her up to Morland Place for the last few weeks of her gestation. I prefer to have her near, where I can keep an eye on her. She can graze in the orchard while the weather is warm.'

'She is looking very fit, Sir,' Hamil said. Queen Mab's coat had a very healthy shine, her carriage was alert and her eye bright. She was a handsome mare, a dark reddish chestnut with a lighter gold mane and tail. It was obvious that Psyche was one of her daughters.

'She's wonderful for her age,' Kit said. 'Twenty-one, isn't she, Father?'

'Rising twenty-two,' Edmund told him. 'I was given her by my father as a wedding present when I married your mother, and she was a three-year-old then. You have had a good morning, I perceive,' he added, nodding towards the string of birds on Clement's saddle.

'Enough for Jacob to make us a very handsome pie,' Mary Esther said, as the two groups joined and rode on towards Morland Place. Ruth fell in beside Kit, who moved Magpie a little to the side to make room for her on the path.

'Which colts are they?' she asked him, gesturing towards the young horses that the servants were leading on behind. 'That big red one looks like Oberon.' Oberon was Mab's three-year-old son. Kit nodded.

'The other's Firefly. My father is to let me try them both, and choose which I like the best, though I think he hopes I will choose Oberon.'

'Firefly's a fine horse,' Ruth said critically. 'What will happen to the one you do not choose?'

Kit lowered his voice discreetly. 'Hamil is to have him.'

'Oho,' Ruth said. Kit spread a hand in resignation.

'It is only reasonable that my Father should give me the choice. If Hamil cannot see that it is reasonable, he is a fool.'

'About Hero he *is* a fool,' Ruth said eliptically. Kit, aware of the presence of the twins not far behind him, changed the subject.

'The clouds are coming up,' he said. 'I think we shall have rain. It is well that you went hawking early.'

The rain persisted all afternoon, and the family was confined indoors. It was so chilly and damp in the evening that Mary Esther had the fires lit in the long saloon, and everyone gathered there to work or play quietly, listening to the gurgling of the rain in the gutters and the hideous shrieks of the peacocks that Edmund had bought to keep down the plague of frogs that came up from the moat. Everyone was a little restless; only Dog, with his mistress sitting down where he could keep an eye on her, and his belly stretched out towards the flames, was really content.

The children were still in the school room, Ambrose, Francis and Malachi with Father Michael, Mary Eleanor and Anne doing some lessons with Leah. At the far end of the saloon Hetta was playing with Ralph, whom she regarded as her own private toy, while Nerissa kept an eye on them and did some mending. Nearby Hamil was seated on a stool reading while Hero leaned on his shoulder, ostensibly reading with him, but more often finding her eyes drifting towards Kit. She often stood rather than sat, for her awkward hip made sitting for long periods uncomfortable.

Kit was sitting in one of the window seats, mending a piece of harness. Ruth sat near, sewing desultorily, and talking to him in a low voice about horses. Edmund and Rob Hamilton were playing chess, and Mary Esther and Sabina were working together, one at either end of a new altar cloth. Sabina had been telling her about the progress of their court case for, despite Richard's ideas, there was no hostility between Edmund and the Hamiltons on the subject.

'So now nothing more will be done until the Hilary term,' she concluded. 'The law is so slow, I sometimes wonder if we will ever have a judgment, but Rob says the slower the better, for a quick judgment would be sure to be against us. I don't really understand it. If it weren't for the children, it would not be worth going on with, but they must have some kind of estate. One can't expect Edmund to support them for ever.'

'He does not in the least mind,' Mary Esther said.

'I know, but Rob does. He feels it strongly that he has nothing for his own children but those four little houses in York, and that would not keep them in hose and shoe-leather.'

'Perhaps Hero will marry a rich man,' Mary Esther said, smiling. Sabina shook her head.

'Money marries money,' she said. 'Without a proper dowry, and with her crippled leg. But Hamil, now –' She paused and looked cautiously at Mary Esther, as if wondering about the wisdom of going on. Mary Esther pretended not to see the look, and made an encouraging noise without looking up from her work. 'I had wondered, just recently, what plans there were for Ruth. She and Hamil are of an age, and she is well provided for.' Mary Esther made no comment, and Sabina went on, 'Nothing has been heard from Zeph and Zech recently, I suppose?'

'Nothing,' Mary Esther said. 'Zeph is Ruth's guardian, of course, so until Malachi comes of age I suppose it is for

Edmund to say what shall happen to Ruth and Nell. I have an idea, though, that he was considering a match between Ruth and Kit –' A movement nearby caught her eye and she broke off abruptly as she looked up to see Ruth standing by the table a little way off, choosing a new piece of silk for her sewing. Had she heard? Her face did look a little red, but that could be the result of stooping, and besides, poor Ruth blushed as easily as unbecomingly. All the same, it was necessary to change the subject.

'How dull I feel,' she said. 'It is almost time for the children to finish their lessons; why should we not have some music, some dancing perhaps? A dance would liven us up, what do you say, Sabina? Clem,' she said to the young man who came in at the moment, attending the maid who had come to make up the fire, 'do you send word to Father Michael and ask him to let the boys come and play for us while we dance, and tell Leah she may bring the girls to see the fun.'

Ambrose brought his flute, Francis the flageolet, and Malachi joined in on the cornett, while Mary Esther took her place at what had been Alice's virginals. They had some of the stately old dances, until the children began to call for something more lively.

'Can't we have hoyte-cum-toyte?' Ambrose asked in a pause for breath.

'No, omnium gatherum!' Francis cried.

'Or tolly-polly!' Malachi called.

'You can't dance and play both,' Mary Esther pointed out, and Father Michael came to the rescue.

'If one of you boys will run and fetch my bagpipes from my room, I'll play and you can all dance.'

It was quickly done, and soon everyone was joining in the rumbustious country dances while the watchers clapped their hands and sang the old words to the familiar songs. Edmund and Rob continued with their game of chess as if nothing was happening, though Rob's foot could be seen to be tapping under the table. Sabina took her son's hand and obliged him to partner her. He went reluctantly, and she said, 'Don't be so simple – Hero doesn't mind in the least, do you, chuck?'

'Of course not,' Hero said, but something in her voice drew Kit's eyes to her. She would never dance, and though she must be well used to the idea by now, she was young and pretty, and it must hurt her sometimes. He smiled at her, and she smiled back and a flicker of her eyes drew his attention to Ruth, who, Kit felt, ought not to be left out of things because she was plain. He went and bowed to her and took her hand, and her ruddy eyes sparkled with pleasure, which was his reward.

He had sought her out; he had asked her to dance; he had talked to her and paid attention to her on numerous occasions; and she had overheard Aunt Mary's words about her. She was in heaven. Since she had first clapped eyes on him, she had been hopelessly, painfully in love with him, painfully because she knew that she was awkward and plain and could never win the heart of someone so handsome and lively. But over the months she had begun to think that perhaps it was not so impossible after all. He had often told her that she was not plain, had sought her out and seemed to enjoy her company. Perhaps he could see beyond her exterior to the worth inside her. She danced with him, her face transfigured with her hopes. Kit smiled at her pleasure, glad to bring a little joy into her life, wishing he could do the same for Hero. They danced, and while Ruth watched Kit and Kit watched Hero, Hamil watched them all and suffered.

When they had danced themselves breathless, the servants brought in refreshments, and Kit took the opportunity to slip away and see how the two colts were settling, and as everyone gathered round the buffet, Hamil slipped out after him unseen and caught him up in the yard. Kit started when a hard hand gripped his sleeve and pulled him round, and his heart sank when he saw Hamil's angry face close to his own.

'What is it, cos?' he said mildly, hoping to defuse the anger. 'You are hurting my arm, by the way.'

'I'll hurt more than your arm if you don't leave my sister alone,' Hamil growled.

'Leave her alone? In what way?'

'You're upsetting her, and I won't stand for it.'

'She doesn't seem upset.'

'I saw her watching you dancing with Ruth. You leave her alone!'

'Leave Ruth alone?'

Hamil made a grab for Kit's throat, but Kit caught his hand in an iron grip and the two stood locked together, near equal in strength, though Kit was the taller and older.

'Don't you laugh at me!' Hamil snarled desperately.

'I'm not, Hamil, truly, but you are confused, you don't seem to know what you want. You don't know whether I'm upsetting your sister by attending her or not attending her.'

'I know what I want, and I know what you want. You want to come between us – but I won't have it. I've looked after her since we were children, and I'll look after her for the rest of our lives.'

'Does she have no say in this?' Kit said gently. With a violent movement Hamil freed himself and stepped back.

'She says the same as me. She doesn't want you – she has always been with me and she always will be. So you stay away from her, or –' his hand moved to his doublet, where he kept his little knife.

Kit's heart burned with pity for Hamil, but he said firmly, 'Or what? Or you'll kill me? But you would need to be sure, would you not, that killing me would be what she wanted too.'

It went home, and though Kit was sorry to wound him, it had to be said. Hamil turned away without another word, and went into the house.

The last Mass was said at nine o'clock, and after it the family retired to bed, but Kit stopped his father as they were coming out of the chapel and quietly asked him for a private interview. Edmund nodded and led the way into the steward's room. Edmund had been almost the last to leave the chapel, and so no-one saw the encounter except Ruth, who had lingered in the hall in the hopes of exchanging a few words with Kit. As she saw him accost his father and turn away with him, her cheeks burned with excitement and happiness, for she was positive it was matrimony that they were going to discuss. She ran up to bed, but it was a long time before she could compose her fluttering thoughts enough to get to sleep. Indeed, she didn't want to sleep – it seemed a waste of all that happiness.

The next morning was fine, the world seeming new-washed by the rain of the day before, the sky a cool autumn blue, promising heat later on. The maid Ellen came to dress Ruth and Mary Eleanor, and found the former already up, standing by the window singing, quietly, so as not to wake Nell, and tunelessly, because she had no voice.

'Well, Miss,' Ellen said, 'you're in a good mood this morning, I'm glad to see.' Ruth had never been famed for her good temper, and she and Ellen had often quarrelled sharply.

'Why shouldn't I be?' Ruth said cheerfully. 'It's going to be a lovely day.'

'Aye, it is that, and rightly so, for what could be better,' Ellen said, nodding significantly to herself as she went round the bed to pull the clothes off the sleeping Nell. 'Come along my lamb, rise up now and say your prayers. Have you said yours, Miss Ruth? I'll warrant you've not.'

'I have, then,' Ruth said, and humming a tune she danced a little in the space before the windows. Ellen paused in hauling the sleepy child upright and regarded her.

'Eh but you're right jolly. Well at least you'll have a right

88

face to greet the news with, and that'll please some.'

'What news?' Ruth said, pausing in her dance and pressing her hands against her chest to stop her heart fluttering. Ellen smiled mysteriously and shook her head.

'That's as may be, until Master tells it. But something'll be said today, or I'm much mistaken. And if you've said your prayers you'd best be getting washed, and start getting the tugs out of your hair.'

So, there was news! Ruth thought happily. And something would be said today. What a glorious day it was! She forgot what she was doing, and drifted over to the little toilet table, picking up the ivory comb that her brothers had brought her back from the East years ago, and began to comb out her thick red hair, harsh and thick and stiff as a horse's mane. She looked at her reflection dreamily in the little polished silver mirror propped against the wall, and its muted and dimpled reflection softened her features and showed her the brightness of her eyes and the new curve of her smile. 'He's right,' she thought, pausing in her grooming, 'I'm not really plain.'

'Why, Miss, you're stood there like you was mazed. Come, stir yourself,' Ellen said sharply, breaking into her reverie. 'You'll never get tugs out with such timid strokes.'

Ruth shook herself and got to work, digging the comb well in, and making the mane of hair crackle with the vigour of her combing.

Other interviews were conducted that day. Edmund's with Rob caused no remark, for they were often closeted together on business, nor Rob's with Hero, for he managed it discreetly while she was sitting in the Long Walk watching Hamil shoot at the butts.

'I want a word with you, my hinny,' he said, sitting beside her on the stone bench. She turned such expressive eyes on her father that he smiled and touched her glowing cheek and said, 'Perhaps you've guessed already what I have to say? Aye, I think you have, by your rosy face. A young man has spoken for you, and I am to know if you will have him.'

Hero's lips parted, but she could not find any words to say. Rob smiled indulgently. 'I *was* come to say, that though it is an excellent match, better, in truth, than I had hoped for, considering your lack of dowry, yet you should not have to wed him if it was not to your liking. But I see my words are not needed. Do you love Master Kit, my hinny?'

'Yes, sir,' was all that Hero could manage, and that in a very low voice.

'Well, I'm glad of it, for he's a fine young man, and will make you an excellent husband. So I'm to tell Edmund you are all consenting, am I? So that's settled, and I'm very glad, chick. To tell the truth, he is only just good enough for you, though he married you barefooted.'

Rob prepared to leave her, when she gathered her confused thoughts and caught him back.

'Papa, wait,' she said urgently. He sat again, looking at her with surprise. Her eyes were on her brother, and as he followed the direction of her gaze he began to guess what she would say. 'Papa, please, can it be kept a secret until I have spoken to Hamil? He -- he won't like the idea, and I must tell him myself. He must not hear it from anyone else.'

Rob nodded slowly. 'As you wish. You think he may be troublesome?'

'I don't know. He will be upset.'

'When shall you tell him, then?'

Hero bit her lip. 'This afternoon, it had better be. We are riding over to Watermill. I will tell him when we are alone.'

Rob patted her hand. 'Just as you wish, my hinny. I'm sorry that there should be any shadow for you today. But Hamil is a sensible lad. He'll see it is for your best happiness. I'll leave it to you, then. Tell me when it's done.'

She told him as they rode past the Ten Thorns towards the North Fields. Their ponies walked on easy reins, their necks stretched, enjoying the sunshine, and Hero's quiet voice had no competition but the soft thud of their hooves on the turf, the occasional ring of a shoe against a stone, and the leather creak of the saddle. In the heat of the afternoon even the birds were silent. Hamil too was silent as she spoke. She saw his face turn white, saw his mouth tense as he heard her out.

'I asked Papa to say nothing until I had spoken to you – I wanted to tell you myself.'

'That was kind of you,' he said harshly. She looked at him pleadingly, but he would not meet her eyes.

'Hamil, don't be angry, please. I don't want you to be hurt, and I don't know why you should be, though I see you are.'

'You don't know? Yet you must have, or why did you think you must tell me yourself?' he said. 'So he has succeeded, then, young Master Christopher,' he went on bitterly. 'Master Morland has succeeded in taking you away from me. The Morlands are like that, aren't they? They think they have a right to anything they want. Masters of the world!'

'Hamil, how has he taken me from you? How can he? Please don't say such things. I am your sister, your twin, how can anything change that?'

'You *were* my sister,' he said, looking at her at last, and she flinched at the pain in his eyes. 'It was always enough for you, until *he* came. Now it's him that you want. He'll take my place, he'll come first with you from now on.'

'It's not true,' Hero cried. 'You will always come first –'

'Then don't marry him! Say you won't marry him!' Hero was silent, staring at him helplessly, and he made a sound of despairing anger as he turned his face from her again. 'You see! You won't give him up. You would sooner give up your brother.'

'But why must I give up either? Why must there be a choice?' Hero cried. Hamil laughed bitterly.

'Oh, has he taught you that trick already? You want everything, like a true Morland. Well this time, even if it's the last time, you can't. You've chosen him, and you must bide by it now.' And with that he kicked his startled pony into a gallop, making Goldcrest rear with surprise.

Struggling to control her pony, Hero called after him, 'Hamil! Where are you going? *Hamil*!'

'To the Devil!' he yelled over his shoulder.

The atmosphere in the house was strained that evening. Impossible though it seemed, it appeared that Hero and Hamil had quarrelled, for she came back alone and explained very awkwardly that Hamil was staying over at Watermill for the night to keep Sabine company. And no announcement was made. Ruth, restless and puzzled, wondered why not. Surely Uncle Edmund could not have objected? And yet Kit did not look at her once during the evening. She must, she *must* speak to him, and find out what had happened. Her eyes followed him every moment, and when they retired for the night, his attention caught by her, he looked at her just once, a puzzled glance that she interpreted her own way.

She lingered in the hall and on the stairs, and was rewarded at last by seeing him slip into the long saloon. She waited a moment longer, checked that there was no-one in sight, and then blew out her candle and putting it down on the floor went silently along to the other door and slipped inside. It was not quite dark in the long saloon, for at the end where Ruth stood there was still a glow from the fire, while at the other there was the soft cloudy luminosity of a shielded candle, in whose light she saw Kit's beloved profile. She started towards him, and then froze as he took his hand away from the slim candle-flame and its glow increased to shew her that he was not alone.

Hero was standing just inside the door, and Ruth watched first with perplexity and then with horror as Kit stepped towards her, hesitated, and then placed a hand on her shoulder and kissed her upturned face lightly.

'It is "yes", then?' Kit said quietly. Hero's face was tilted towards him like a flower towards the sun.

'Can you doubt it?' she said.

'But your brother – ?'

'I have told him. I wish it were otherwise for him, but I cannot help it. Do not think of it, Kit. It is my burden, not yours.'

'All your burdens are mine, from now on. Oh my darling –' and he set the candle down on the buffet behind him so that he could put both arms round her and draw her against him.

'I love you,' she said in a voice almost too low to be heard. For a long time they did not move, and their bodies in the flowing candlelight seemed made of one substance, deeply shadowed so that the unseen watcher could not tell them apart. Ruth clenched her hands together, and bit her lip, unaware of the pain, though she tasted the salt blood that trickled into her mouth. The candlelight touched the shine of the yellow hair as Hero moved her head at last to look up at Kit again, and Ruth saw his hand come out of the shadows and cup her cheek with a tenderness made her throat ache with the effort not to cry out.

'Oh my darling.' His voice, though quiet, came very clearly through the dark room. 'I love you with all my heart, with my soul. Everything I am, everything I have, is yours now – my arms to keep you, my body to warm you, my tongue to praise you, my sword to defend you – my life to serve you, Hero. Take me to you, keep me –'

His voice stopped, and his head bent towards the face he held cupped in his hands, and as the two faces met Ruth could not bear any more, but clapped her hand over her own lips and stumbled blindly from the room, not caring any more if they heard her. Outside she kicked over her candlestick in the dark, and, sobbing, felt her way down the stairs and through the hall, seeking by animal instinct some dark safe place to hide with her wounds. She did not know where she was going, but it seemed right when she found herself in the stables. Zephyr was sleeping in his stall, one hind leg cocked and his head drooping, but he did not seem to resent being woken. Ruth slipped in beside him to the head of his stall and leaned against his neck, and her tears fell hot into his mane. He shifted his balance to her weight but did not move, other than to nudge her gently from time to time with his muzzle, curious but undisturbed.

The tears stopped at last. Her face felt swollen and sore, she felt ugly, and the shame of it, of how she had deceived herself, of how her vanity had deceived her, filled her with hopelessness. How could she ever have thought he loved *her*? She was ugly, unloved, unwanted, no-one would ever want her, and Kit – Kit was to marry Hero, who was beautiful, whom everyone loved. She thought of the words she had heard, of the look on Hero's face as Kit put his arms round her, and the pain in her heart was sickening. She could only stand still, leaning against gentle, understanding Zephyr, until it passed, and there was only emptiness there.

Emptiness. Empty, vain hopes, empty longing for what she could not have. She was suddenly very aware of herself, an ungainly, ugly young woman in a rumpled gown, an ugly woman with a red, swollen face, weeping into the mane of her dozing horse. It was laughable, wasn't it? She could laugh – but at least she was spared the ridicule of others. No-one knew what her hopes had been, and no-one ever should. She would keep her pride, though she had nothing else. And never, *never* again would she be such a fool as to love. She would never court that pain again.

She talked to her pony, stroked him in gratitude for his patience, and then made her way out, back to the house. All

94

she asked now was to get to her bed undetected, and find the oblivion of sleep. Tomorrow – the vision of tomorrow and the new life it began, the life of emptiness, made her steps falter, and it took all her will to hold back another flood of weeping and to walk on steadily towards the dark house.

CHAPTER SIX

Kit and Hero were married in the spring of 1633 in a private ceremony in the chapel at Morland Place, witnessed only by their four parents. It was done thus because of Hero's disability, but the family, friends, neighbours and servants were not left out of the occasion, for the Mass took place very early in the morning and the rest of the day was given over to more public celebrations to which what seemed like the whole of Yorkshire was invited. As the day miraculously turned out to be fine, the celebrations were held mostly outdoors in the gardens and park. There was feasting of course: a whole beef was roasted in a cooking pit dug for the occasion, and Jacob's skills were exercised to such effect that the trestles set up before the house were loaded to breaking point with fantastic delicacies. There was entertainment too, of every kind: music, singing, dancing, morrissing, wrestling, games of all sorts, a may-pole, and a very pretty water-pageant on the moat. And through it all, appearing always wherever the crowd was thickest and the fun fastest, Kit took his new wife. Hero, everyone said, looked as beautiful as an angel, in her wedding gown of the palest primrose satin, lavish with lace, her long golden ringlets dressed with white and yellow flowers; and she rode everywhere on a small white pony, whose mane and tail were braided with golden ribbons and who wore about its neck a wreath of yellow and white flowers. It had been Kit's idea – he could not bear that people should see Hero limping, and perhaps pity her, and so she was led like a queen upon a white horse. Had it been necessary for the celebrations to take place indoors, he had arranged for her to be carried on a magnificently decorated litter.

Only one thing marred the wedding for Hero, and that was her estrangement from her twin. After that day when he had run away to Watermill, she had not seen him for almost a week, and it was the longest week of her life, for she had never been from him for more than an hour or two since they were born. Then at last Hamil had come back to beg her pardon and wish her happiness, but he was awkward and distant with her, and it was clear that, though he saw that it must be, he could not forgive her for preferring another man to him. He did not stay long, and when he made to go, Hero protested.

'You aren't going away again, surely?'

'I'm going back to Watermill. I shall live there with Sabine from now on. She needs me to help her run the estate.'

'But Hamil, I need you.'

'No you don't, by'r Lady,' he said savagely. 'You have someone else. I told you before, you can't have everything. You have chosen *him*, and you must bide by that.'

'But – won't you live here any more?' Hero asked, bewildered.

'I won't – I can't live near you and him. I wish you well, I hope you may be happy, but I don't want to see you together. I couldn't bear that.'

So he had gone, and she could not make him change his mind. Since then he had lived at Watermill and she had hardly ever seen him, and though he had come to the wedding celebrations, he kept his distance, and she only knew that he was there at all by catching a chance glimpse of him far off. Kit tried to comfort her, and told her that he would come round in the end, and see that there was no need for them to be apart, but though she hoped her husband was right, she had little faith in his assurances.

At the end of a long day they were seen off to bed by the cheerful crowd to the great bedchamber, which they were to occupy for their first week. Kit was attended into the dressing-room by Patrick, while Leah undressed Hero in the bedchamber and put her into her nightgown and brushed out her hair. Flowers had been arranged round the room, and the air was sweet with them and with the honey-smell of beeswax candles. Hero stood patiently while Leah brushed her hair, looking at the Unicorn tapestry which hung on the wall opposite the bed. The white of the unicorn stood out brightly against the dark background and the long black hair of the maiden who was shewing him his reflection in a glass.

Leah saw the direction of her gaze and said, 'That was a wedding-present to a Morland bride, who knows how many years ago. And she slept in this very bed, too.'

'Here? Is that her in the picture?'

'Very like. They mostly had dark hair, the Morlands.'

'Unicorns only come to virgins, don't they?' Hero said. 'She must have been sad to part with him when she married.' Leah gave her a swift glance, and touched one of her hands.

'Eh, but your hands are like ice. You're not afraid, are you, my lamb?'

'A little,' Hero said. 'But more – I'm not sure – it feels a little like sadness, and yet it can't be, for I'm so happy. I do love him, Leah, I do.'

'I know you do, lambkin, and I think I know what you feel, and it's all quite right and proper. Everything we do that makes us happy has a touch of sadness about it, and its been that way since we left the Garden of Eden. But don't be afraid. Your husband will take care of you.'

'My husband,' Hero said with wonder. 'How strange that sounds.' And she started as there was a scratching at the door. Leah gave her a questioning look, and she nodded, and the woman went to open the dressing-room door. Kit came in and paused just within the room to look at Hero, dry-mouthed, and Leah gave a smile of private satisfaction and went out, closing the door behind her.

It seemed a long time before Kit crossed the space between them, and then he only stood in front of her, looking at her silently. Then he gave a strange smile, a small, grave smile that seemed to stem not from laughter but from awe, and he reached out a hand and took up one of her silken curls and caressed it.

'You are beautiful,' he said at last. 'That was not what I meant to say, but now that it comes to it, I don't seem to have any words for what I feel inside me.'

Hero nodded slightly. 'I know,' she said.

'Do you? Do you really? Hero, do you understand, when I say I don't feel merry, though I'm more happy than I can say? I feel – rather solemn, and rather – afraid. No, not afraid, but –' he searched helplessly for the word, and could not find it.

Hero said again, 'I know.' He studied her face.

'Yes, you do,' he said at last, and it seemed to ease him. He smiled more freely and said, 'Today you are a bride. It is a beautiful word; was it always so, or have you made it beautiful? You did not dance at your wedding.'

'I have never danced at a wedding,' she said, watching his face in wonder.

'A bride should dance at her own wedding. You should dance, just once.' He put his arms round her, and she put her hands up to his shoulders, and he lifted her so that her feet were just clear of the floor, and he began to move slowly across the floor in a stately dance, carrying her, and humming, so faintly that the tune seemed lost in the soft shadows of the room. Her warm body was pressed trustingly against him, swaying when he swayed. Her eyes never left him, and when he saw the expression of them change minutely, he let his dance drift him to the side of the bed, and there he laid her tenderly down.

He looked down at her, studying her face, and then said gently, 'Don't be sad. Sadness is for endings, and this is a beginning.' He left her for a moment to blow out all the candles but the one at the bedside, and as he did so the shadows thickened and crept forward so that the room shrank to the circle of honey light in which she lay, and the unicorn was hidden in the darkness.

Shawes was an old, dark, damp and inconvenient house, built in the days when alarms were frequent and a man's life might depend on the smallness of his windows and the stoutness of his walls. It had belonged for a hundred and fifty years to the Bible Morlands, and successive masters of the house had spent so much of their time at sea and so little at home that almost nothing had been done to improve it. Aletheia Chapham, Ruth's mother, had had the windows glazed and the chimneys rebuilt, but when she and Nehemiah had died within months of each other the twins, Zeph and Zech, were already at sea, and so nothing more had been done.

The maid, Ellen, was glad enough to have left it with her young mistresses for the glamour and comfort of Morland Place, but when a letter arrived from Zephaniah containing some instructions for the steward, she was quick to offer to walk there with them. Her ladies did not need her, Ruth having gone out hawking and Nell helping Mary Esther sort out the linen for its annual washing, and it was a fine day for a walk. More compelling than either reason, however, was that she had been courting the steward, Parry, for two years and was hoping soon to bring him to the question.

Mary Esther asked her if she would go a little out of her way and take a message also to the bailey at Twelvetrees.

'It is adding to your journey, I know,' she said apologetically. 'Perhaps you had sooner ride? Will you take the mule?'

'Nay, Madam,' Ellen said quickly: the mule had a ferocious temper. 'I'm not so dainty as that comes to. It's no but a step there and back.'

It was pleasant walking. The fields were quiet, most of the men being up on the moors or out at Ten Thorn Gate where the two pens had been set up for branding the new season's sheep; but here and there she passed by a group of men working or young women watching kine, and that was excuse enough to stop and talk. Ellen had been born at Shawes and knew everyone right down as far as the city walls.

At Twelvetrees she enquired after the bailey and was told he was down in the home paddock 'with the young master', and with that clue her ears soon directed her to the right place. The rails of the paddock were thronged with grooms and other servants – anyone who was not vitally needed elsewhere, in fact, – and all eyes were directed towards the beaten, dirty centre of the enclosure where Kit was engaged in a battle royal with the colt Oberon. The horse's coat was dark with sweat and dust and his chest white with spilled foam, but he was not yet near to giving in. As Ellen approached he flung his master once again to the ground, and a sympathetic groan arose from the watchers as Kit got to his feet with a stiffness and weariness which shewed how many times before he had made close acquaintance with the hard-packed earth.

As Oberon trotted round the outside of the ring, head up and white eye rolling towards Kit, who tailed him doggedly and patiently for a chance to grab the loose rein, the groom standing next to Ellen said, 'He'll have to give in soon, he's *obliged* to.'

'Who? The horse or the master?' Ellen asked. The groom looked at her gloomily.

'I knawt which'll dee first, but nowt else 'll end it. T'master will not use whip nor goad, nor hobble horse, nor put a twitch on him, and he'll have no-one in to help him.'

Ellen stared in amazement. 'How does he propose to break him, then?' she asked. The groom looked even more gloomy.

'He says he'll fettle him without. He says he'll not break horse's spirit, but fettle him with love, and if the horse doesn't come to him willing, he'll not have him at all. Eh, but it beats all, does that. I knaw reet enough who's put such ideas into the master's head, and much comfort will it give her when she's widowed for it.'

Ellen watched Kit catch up with Oberon and stand gentling him. The horse's forelegs were trembling now, and even as she watched she saw his ears go out sideways in a tentative gesture of compromise. To win a horse by love? Well, it suited what she knew of the young master.

'Well, after all,' Ellen said, 'he won her by love and gentleness, and she'd as much spirit as any horse.'

The groom looked sceptical. 'Who dosta mean? The Haltling?' It was the local people's name for Hero – the little lame one – but it was not used unkindly. 'Aye, well, a woman's one thing, and an entire horse is another – though to my mind both are better for a touch of the whip now and then, as tha s'lt find out sooner or later. Has that man of thine bought thee thy wedding knives yet?'

Ellen grinned. 'Not yet – but then I've not told him yet he's to marry me.' She watched as Kit, having petted and soothed the big stallion, took hold of the saddle and gathered himself to mount once again, and then, feeling she did not care to see him hurt further, she asked her companion where the bailey was, so that she could deliver her message and be on her way.

She reflected as she walked on towards Shawes at the strange circumstance of Kit's marriage to Hero – Kit, who could have had anyone he wanted, and would have been expected to marry an heiress, and Hero, the Haltling, whose dowry was nothing but a parcel of shabby old houses in North Street. To be sure, her father and mother were still building their hopes on the Hamilton estate in Scotland, and were a week since gone to Scotland themselves to be at the court in person when their case came up, but no-one, least of all Hero, really believed in their hopes.

And then there was the sad business of the coldness between Hero and her brother. The twins' love of each other and their inseparability had been a legend since their early childhood for miles around, but now here was Hamil going off in that strange way, never coming near his sister, refusing to meet her or even to answer the letters that she sent so faithfully, begging for his love. And strangest of all that he should have gone to live with his cousin Sabine, who had formerly been convinced that Hamil, like all her other relatives, was conspiring to rob her of Watermill House. But then, Ellen thought as she walked briskly along, Sabine was well known to be as mad as a March hare; like her brother, God rest his soul, poor Antony who had been lacking; and even the other brother, Endymion, who had been lost at sea, he had always been strange, as folk remembered now, if you asked them. All the Chapham kind were a bit mad, and that was the truth – it was said they had bad blood, though Ellen had never heard the whole of *that* story, but she wouldn't be at all surprised; and then all that marrying of their own cousins, well, good Catholic folk should know better than that . . .

Her musing was broken off abruptly when she reached the square grey building of Shawes and saw Zephyr hitched to a ring in the wall. A moment's thought and a brief search led her to Ruth, sitting in the darkest corner of the dark, gloomy chapel, staring at nothing. Ellen noticed anew how pale and how thin her young mistress had become.

'Eh, now, Miss, what brings you to sit all alone in the dark this way?' she asked with a rough sympathy. 'It's such a bonny day, too, and how comes it you're not out flying the merlin. It does no good to brood.'

Ruth looked up at her and said only, 'Ellen, how should you like to come back to Shawes to live?'

'I shouldn't like it at all, Miss,' Ellen said stoutly. 'What, live in this damp old place, after the grand house over yonder? How can you think it?'

'I'll do more than think it,' Ruth said harshly. 'And so will you. I am going to speak to Malachi tomorrow, and we shall be back home within the week. He's old enough now, and it is *his* place after all. And as for it being a damp old place – it was good enough for you once, Ellen, before you grew too fine and dainty, but if it isn't good enough now, you can·find another mistress, for this one wants to come home, where she belongs.'

'Why, that's hard talk for a young lady,' Ellen began, but Ruth interrupted her fiercely.

'I *cannot* live there any longer. I cannot bear it. I will come home, for there's nothing more for me to hope for, but the peace home can give me, and the love of my nephew. So now, Ellen, do you come, or do you not?'

Ellen dropped any further pretence not to understand. 'I go wherever you go,' she said, and then, eyeing the girl with sympathy, asked roughly, 'eh, but, Miss, however did you come to make such a mistake about the young master? Why, any fool could see he were struck all to ruin over the other young miss.'

'Not *any* fool,' Ruth said wryly. 'There was one fool did not see it. But she'll be fool no more, no, never again.'

'Don't be bitter, Miss,' Ellen said quietly. Ruth stood up restlessly.

'I shall give my love to those that want it – my nephew and my horse and my hawk.'

'And thy servant?' Ellen asked awkwardly. She was a plain-spoken woman to whom love-words did not come easily.

Ruth eyed her sardonically, and said, to hide how the gesture had touched her, 'You need not pretend to be unwilling to come back, Ellen, for when you are living here again Parry will not be able to avoid marrying you. It is only the distance that saves him now.'

Ellen put her hands on her hips and primmed her lips.

'Eh, but you're a sharp-eyed, noticing one, and you always have been. Well, you'll have your own way in this as in all things, and I be thinking you deserve the luck of it.'

'I mean to have my own way from now on, I can tell you,' Ruth said, and standing up, led the way out of the cold darkness of the chapel and into the sunshine. She was a girl no longer, but a plain-faced, sharp-boned woman, but though she did not know it, she had gained a kind of dignity, and as she walked out to untie her pony she no longer looked awkward and ungainly. Ellen could not define the change, but she noticed it, for it was from that moment that she began to call Ruth 'The Mistress'.

Richard was not sure what he had expected to find when he went up to Oxford, for the stories he had heard conflicted with the view Kit had presented when he came home; but six months was enough to shew him that any story coming out of Oxford might be true, for all extremes of behaviour were accommodated there. The rules were very strict, both with regard to the curriculum and to the way the undergraduates comported themselves; but the person responsible for controlling the undergraduate was the tutor, and if, as was often the case, he was old, infirm, or indifferent, a young lad had no difficulty in evading him.

The younger dons tended not to live in college, but had lodgings in the town, and there was great resentment between the senior and junior dons. The preoccupation of the seniors was the governing of the colleges, while the juniors were absorbed with the problem of how to get on to one of the governing bodies and oust one of the seniors. Neither had much time for the undergraduates. Consequently, as Richard soon found, those boys who had come up very young, or who were docile by nature, or who had an active, energetic tutor, tended to be quiet and scholarly; the rest did pretty much what they pleased, and what they pleased was often drinking, gambling and whoring, but very rarely studying.

Richard's tutor was a good man, educated and well principled, but he was also very old, very short of sight, and greatly preoccupied with his own work, and Richard, used to trying to evade the discipline of a sharp-eyed, sharp-tongued Father Michael, found Master Walker easy going. Lectures were compulsory, the main study in the first year being rhetoric, and the undergraduate was tested regularly by disputation, but the curriculum was narrow and Richard, thanks to his good education at home, was already so far ahead in theology, astronomy and metaphysics that his trouble was to conceal how much he knew rather than to pass the tests.

The ages of the first year undergraduates ranged from fourteen to twenty, but most were around sixteen, and so Richard, far ahead in his studies, and already a widower with a child, found himself drawn towards a group of second-years from his own college whose principal pleasure in life was playing at cards and dice in taverns, and getting drunk every night. It seemed to him very much like home had been before his entanglement with Jane, except that there was no friction, no angry Father and uncomfortably observant Michael Moyes to lash him with their tongues. He spent his days in idleness and his nights in drunkenness and swayed back to his narrow bed on the shoulder of a boon companion, and altogether thought Oxford more homelike than home.

The main difference between Oxford life and his previous, similar life in and around the taverns of York was the lack of women. His particular group of friends was not much interested in the delights of fornication. One of them, a gentleman's son of large means, had a regular mistress, a very pretty and discreet young woman whom he kept in a lodging up by Carfax, and another sometimes slipped off very quietly, almost apologetically, to a whorehouse. But there was no talk of women or recounting of tales of sexual excess amongst them. The undergraduates lived in an entirely male world, and showed their prowess in drinking, gambling and occasional fighting. Richard, anxious to fit in with his new friends, became celibate too.

It was in his second year that Richard began to be particularly friendly with Clovis Byrne, the young man who kept a mistress. Richard's widowed status gave him some distinction amongst his companions, and Clovis once said to him, 'You and I are alike in this, Dick, that we are both half-married, both having the shadow without the substance.' In their second year Clovis and Richard became so intimate that the former invited the latter to dine one evening with him and his mistress, and Richard was too surprised and intrigued to refuse what might have been regarded as an equivocal invitation. It turned out to be a very interesting evening, and was the first of many which Richard spent in the lodgings of Mistress Lucy Sciennes.

The first surprising thing to Richard was that Lucy Sciennes was nothing like his imaginings. He had thought she would be pretty but sluttish, perhaps very young, a member of the lower orders with nothing to recommend her but her pretty face and willing body. But Lucy was none of these things. She was older than both Richard and Clovis, being in her early twenties; she was elegant, intelligent, and well-educated, and when they dined and the conversation ranged freely over many topics Lucy joined in on such equal terms that Richard often forgot, absurd as it seemed, that she was a woman. She was, however, very beautiful, with very white skin, dark eyes, dark luxuriant ringlets, and slender white hands which she used to great effect to demonstrate her points in conversation. But when they were talking Richard forgot all this, forgot the white bosom displayed above a dark silk decolletage, the soft curls nestling against a slender neck, and noticed only what was being said. It was his first lesson in recognizing another person as an individual.

Their talk was fascinating too, particularly when it covered religion and politics, for it was Richard's first taste of the world outside his own small, local concerns. Both Lucy and Clovis had connections at court, and it was through them that Richard learned of the conflict that was growing in the south, the dissatisfaction of the middle sort with the government.

'It is hard to see how it can be resolved,' Lucy said thoughtfully one evening. 'The King cannot govern without money, and he cannot get money without taxes.'

'Equally,' Clovis added, 'the middling people – the merchant kind particularly – don't want to pay taxes if they have no say in how they are spent.'

'But it is the King and his ministers who decide how it will be spent,' Richard said, puzzled.

'Quite,' said Clovis. 'But the merchant kind think this way: if the King cannot do without our money, then he should not be allowed to do without our advice.'

This sounded shocking to Richard, but he tried to appear unconcerned. 'And what would they advise the King to do?' he asked.

'I dare say,' Lucy said, 'nothing very much that the King would not advise himself, except when it comes to religion.'

'Aye, and there's the breaking point,' Clovis said. He gave a dark, sardonic smile. 'I speak as an interested party – as a second son I am destined for the church, and our family are all old catholics. Not Papists, I hasten to assure you, my dear Richard, but catholics in the sense that Great King Harry was.'

'And King Charles still is,' Lucy added. 'The people of London, it is said, hate and fear the Queen because she is a Papist, and they fear she will corrupt the King, but between his religion and hers there is little but a name. The Puritans hate Anglicanism as much as Papism. They would have us all work together in the fields and worship in a hovel with no more respect than one shews towards a close-stool –'

Clovis smiled and said, 'Lucy has a particular grievance against the Puritans, for they think that women should be silent and obedient to their masters and should not be educated, not even taught to read and write.'

Richard was now thoroughly confused. 'So the merchants are Puritans?' he asked.

'Ah no, you must be clear about this, dear Richard, for it is a subject that will arise again and again. The Puritans are mostly low sort of people; the merchants are mostly Presbyters, and want to rule the whole country through the church, and since they are the ones who have a great deal of the money, they are the ones the King has to deal with. Lord knows how it will all end.'

A little while later Richard got up to go, and Clovis, with a sardonic smile, saw him out, watching him from the door with his hand on Lucy's shoulder. It occurred to Richard that they were like a husband and wife, and the thought embarrassed him a little. Clovis evidently loved her like a wife, and the fact that he could never marry her accounted for that dark sharpness in him. So in his second year Richard lived a quieter life, often dining with Clovis and Lucy, and frequently meeting other friends there. The conversation was serious and profound, and gradually Richard was learning to use his mind, and to think about things he had never considered before. Oxford was proving very different from his expectations.

The winter of '33 was very cold, and the snow was so deep during January and February of '34 that the family were confined to the house for almost six weeks. It was particularly bad for Hero, for she could only move about with freedom when she was out of doors and she was little accustomed to being indoors, but she bore it with patience.

'I only hope that the weather breaks before I am too large to ride any more,' she said to Kit, putting her hands over her belly. She was pregnant, and her child was due to be born in June.

'Of course it will, my hinny,' Kit said, for he could not bear to deny her anything. 'You shall ride again soon if I have to take a brand and melt all the snow myself.'

The thaw began on the last day of February, and by the third of March the ground was clear enough for a lady to ride, though it was still heavy going.

'Still, if the mud had been five fathoms deep, we are all still wild to get out,' Mary Esther said that morning as they came out of the chapel after first Mass. 'And look how bright the sun is, Kit. Take that poor child out, won't you, and get some colour back into her cheeks. I can't bear to see her so pale.'

'You are going out yourself?' Kit said, smiling.

'Of course,' she said gaily. 'I am going to ride over to the Hare and Heather and see how my uncles do this long while, and then I shall call in at the school and the hospital to make sure all is well there, and then there are two sick tenants I must call on at Hob Moor, and then –'

'Madam, you will need a day as long as a week for all you have to do,' Kit said, interrupting the flow. 'I had best not delay you.'

'No, indeed. Nerissa, make sure Miss Anne and Mary Eleanor are ready right away, and be sure to put on your thick cloak – I don't want you catching another rheum. And, Leah, if the ground should not be too wet, take Hetta and Ralph out in the gardens this morning, so that they can see the sunshine. Now, Sir, have you any messages this morning?'

'None that I will not perform myself, my dear,' Edmund said, his eyes bright with amusement. 'What will you take to your uncles? I am sure you do not go empty handed.'

'A crock of honey, I think – their hives did not do so well

last year. And may I take them some of that veal we killed yesterday? For who knows when they last had fresh meat?'

'Take whatever you wish,' Edmund said. 'Now I must be about my business. God bless you, wife.' He kissed her, distributed a blessing amongst his children, and went away.

'Now, Leah,' Mary Esther said when she had watched him turn the corner, 'I must give you your instructions –'

'Madam,' Leah interrupted. She had been fidgeting for some minutes. 'I must protest – surely the young master will not take Miss Hero out a-riding in all this mud, and she five months with child?'

Hero laughed and hugged Leah, and said, 'No, Leah, it is I who will take him out. You can't imagine how I long for the fresh air and the sunshine. But Kit will take care of me. No harm can come to me while Kit is here.'

'You see, Leah, how could I possibly prevent her? Go children, don't delay. God bless you. Come Leah, we had best decide what to do with that veal –'

The fresh air was almost intoxicating after being indoors for so long. Kit did not ask where she wanted to go, but turned automatically onto the path towards Harewood Whin. It had always been a favourite ride of hers, and to add to its attraction was the memory of all the times she had gone there with Hamil to watch the foxes or the badgers, or to fly their birds. If she hoped that she might get a sight of him there today, she did not say so, and Kit did not ask, but when they had reached the Whin and rested their horses on the north side, the side facing towards Watermill, he said gently, 'Perhaps another day? Now that the weather has broken, you can ride up here every day. He is bound to come sooner or later.'

She looked at him quickly and away again, and he saw the brightness of her eyes. She shook her head. 'No, I don't expect it. It is not reason that makes me hope to see him, but foolishness.'

'Is love foolishness?'

'It may be,' she said, and then looked at him and smiled. 'Not when it is love of you, though. That is the greatest wisdom.'

He had dismounted, and he came now to lean against Goldcrest's shoulder and took his wife's hand, looking up with concern into her face and noting that it was thinner and paler, and that some of the fresh bloom had gone from it.

'I wanted you to be happy, and in my arrogance I thought I could make you so. I did not want you to lose anything by marrying me. It is fitting that I should be punished for my pride, but not you. I wish –'

Hero stopped him, and pressed his hand. 'Another moment, and you will be wishing you had not married me. I am content, Kit – more than content. I love you, and I would not have anything different.'

'Not even Hamil?' Kit asked. Hero put his hand to her lips, and her eyes were bright and steady.

'I miss him – how could I not? – but if that is the price, I pay it willingly.' Kit sighed and moved away and went to lean against the ancient oak that marked one of the boundaries of the Whin, resting his hand against the lowest branch. There was a silence broken only by the jingling of the bits as Goldcrest and Oberon snatched eagerly at the thin, bitter March grass which was so delicious to them after a winter of dry feed.

'That's the trouble,' Kit said at last, with his back to her, looking out across the flat lands towards Watermill. 'I don't want you to have to pay. If anyone has to pay, it should be me. I want you to have everything.'

Hero smiled, knowing he could not see it. It was what Hamil had called the Morland trick, wanting everything. 'But we can never have everything, my Kit,' she said. 'Life is never so generous.'

'*I* have everything,' he said in a low voice. 'Sometimes I am afraid, I am so happy.'

There was nothing to say to that. In silence they watched

a cloud shadow sweep across the fields, and Oberon paused in his grazing for a moment, pricking his ears towards some movement in the distance. Then as he put his head down again, Kit turned, determinedly cheerful, and came back to Hero with something in his hand, something he had broken from the tree.

'Look what I have found,' he said, holding it out to her. She looked.

'It's only an oak apple,' she said, smiling quizzically.

'Ah, yes, but look, only look here. You see? If I break off the twig, here and here, and then, you see the marks here could be the eyes. Wait, I'll make them deeper.' He pulled out his knife from his belt and worked a moment with the point of it. 'There, now,' he said, holding it out on his palm. Hero took it, and laughed.

'It's a rabbit,' she said delightedly. Kit looked affronted. 'No such thing,' he said, 'It's a hare, a Morland hare. It must be a good omen, that we found it here, when you have a new young leveret in your belly.'

'And there's a hole through the top of its head, look, to thread it on,' Hero said. Now Kit was laughing.

'You wouldn't really wear it? Ah, Hero, you wouldn't!'

'Of course. You gave it to me – no, no, you can't have it back. It's mine now. I shall make a plait of silk and wear it round my neck for a talisman. It will bring me good luck.'

'Nay, Mistress, you shall have a chain of gold to hang it from if you *will* wear it,' Kit said cheerfully. 'And now we had best move on, or you will catch cold. It is too cold to be lingering, even though the sun is so bright.' He caught Oberon and mounted and they rode on, and Hero stowed the oak apple inside her bodice for safety.

Leah always claimed afterwards it was riding that did it, though Mary Esther said it was the effect of the long cold winter, lack of air and sunshine, and bad food. But Kit knew, privately and unreasonably in his heart, that it was his fault, that he was somehow doomed to bring sorrow to the one he loved most in life. Whatever it was, less than a week later Hero miscarried, slipping her child one dark night. It was unformed, naked, blind: much like a dead leveret had anyone been in a condition to make the comparison; but it had been a boy, that much was known. Hero wanted to be brave in front of Kit, but she was too weak to hold back her tears, and at last she wept herself to sleep in his arms. When at last he laid her down on the pillows and smoothed the wet curls from her flushed cheeks, his own tears started, and he had to turn his head aside so as not to wake her with them.

CHAPTER SEVEN

Hero was ill for a long time after her miscarriage, and everyone discovered how much they missed her about the house and found reasons to be passing through the West Bedroom on their way elsewhere. It was not Edmund's way to find an excuse: he simply called formally every morning before beginning the day's business and sat with her for a quarter of an hour or so. Hero found herself, unexpectedly, looking forward to his visits. Edmund had no fund of chat or gossip at his command, and could only talk to her as he would talk to a man, but lying unoccupied as she was she found his conversation stimulating to her mind. As for Edmund, what had begun as a duty rapidly became a pleasure, and his talking soon took on a quality of thinking aloud. His time with Hero in the mornings became a chance for him to reflect quietly and assemble his thoughts and talk through his problems. Mary Esther soon saw what was happening, and stifled a pang of jealousy. If Hero could give something Edmund needed, she must not be angry because it was not herself that was giving it.

Mary Esther, of course, bustled in and out many times a day, squeezing in visits between all the other things she had to do, bringing the invalid scraps of gossip and amusing stories of the things she had seen on her rapid travels. She wished more than anything she could bring Hero the one thing she longed for – but she never saw Hamil, or heard anything about him. Other gifts filled the bedroom however, from family and friends and even servants. Old Jacob made a special batch of little cinnamon cakes, coloured them pink with a few drops of his precious cochineal, arranged them in a basket, and then when little Hetta wandered in to see him, bribed her with a sweetmeat to take them up 'To little halt maistress' for him.

Hetta toiled up the stairs and along the passage to the west bedroom and found Hero, for a change, alone, lying back on her pillows and staring at the window blankly. She roused herself quickly to a smile when Hetta came in.

'Have you come to see me, chuck? Do you want to come up on the bed? Give me the basket then, and I'll hold it while you climb up.'

'It's for you,' Hetta said, a little breathlessly, when she had arranged herself on the broad bed, her short legs sticking out at right angles from under her bunchy skirts. 'Jacob gave me them and bid me bring them. He gave me this for it.' She took the remains of the sweetmeat out of her mouth, inspected it, and put it back in. 'It's nearly gone now, though.' She swallowed. 'It's quite gone now.' And she eyed the basket of cakes appreciatively.

'Would you like one?' Hero asked gravely.

'Thank you,' Hetta said promptly, selected a pink cake, and began to nibble it. 'Jacob says you don't eat enough. Won't you eat one? He says you're pining. What does pining mean? Will you always be in bed? I don't like to be in bed when it's daytime.'

'Nor do I,' Hero said, looking again towards the window.

'Why don't you get up then? If you get up, I'll shew you my garding. Papa said I could have a garding for myself, and Abel gave me a bit in the corner of the Talinan Garding, but there isn't anything in it yet, except some shells Jacob gave me. But Abel says he'll give me some seeds by and by. What does by and by mean? Does it mean soon?' She didn't wait for an answer but reached over and uncurled the fingers of Hero's left hand. 'What have you got in your hand? Is it the hare? Can I see?' Hero relinquished the oak apple, already growing shiny with being held, and Hetta examined it critically. 'It doesn't look very much like a hare,' she said. 'Is it magic?'

'No, not really. It's just an oak apple,' Hero said, but her voice took on a warmth even as she said it.

'O-kapple,' Hetta said musingly. 'If I planted it in my garding would it grow into an apple tree? If it's magic it might grow into a hare-tree.'

Hero smiled. 'That would look funny, wouldn't it. Give it me again, please. What is the weather like outside?'

'I don't know,' Hetta said vaguely. She wasn't interested in the weather. She wriggled down off the high bed, and, hearing footsteps, went to the door and looked out. 'It's Kit!' she cried jubilantly, and ran out, reappearing a moment later high up against Kit's shoulder: she adored her older brother. Hero looked up at him and they exchanged a tender smile.

Kit kissed Hetta and said, 'Will you run away now, chuck? I want to talk to Hero privately.'

Hetta like the good little girl she was, wriggled to be put down, and said, 'I want to see if Beetriss has finished bathing Waif, and then if she has he can come and see my garding. I wonder if he would grow into a Waif-tree if I planted him.'

Left alone, Kit sat down on the edge of the bed and leaned over to kiss Hero. 'What a sunny child she is. Did she bring you these?' touching the basket of cakes. Hero nodded.

'From Jacob. She was telling me about her garden. How I long to be up!'

'My darling, I have to talk to you,' Kit said abruptly. He held out his hand, and she transferred the oak apple from the left to the right to free her left hand for him. He watched the manoeuvre and smiled quizzically.

'You really mean to keep that thing?'

'It's my talisman,' Hero said defensively. Kit's face darkened.

'It has not protected you yet. Oh Hero —'

'Kit, don't! What comes to us, comes. It's God's will.'

117

'I can't accept things as easily as you.' He pressed her hand, not meeting her eyes. 'I have had less practice, I suppose. Darling, the doctor has spoken to me about you.' He looked up now, steadily into her eyes, and Hero caught her breath, seeing that hurt was to come. 'He said that it was very dangerous for you to try to have a child. He said that you must not try to have another, not for a long time. Perhaps –' He swallowed. 'Perhaps never.'

Hero's hand tightened on his, and he returned the pressure, gripping her slight fingers as if to help her bear a physical pain. She said nothing for a long time, and when she spoke at last her voice was husky.

'Does that mean – ?'

Kit lifted her hand to his lips, and then laid it against his cheek. 'We must not risk your getting with child. We must not risk it, Hero.' He could feel her trembling, and he saw her make the great effort it took to calm her body and her voice. She turned her face towards the window again, and said hopelessly, 'Does that mean – do you wish us to sleep apart?'

'No, no, my darling,' Kit cried. 'I don't, of course I don't – unless you feel it would be too difficult –'

She turned back to him, her face lighting up. 'Oh no! Oh Kit, please let us go on sleeping together. Oh Kit, I want you near me – I can bear anything as long as you are near. Hold me – please hold me.'

He took her in his arms and held her close, and she put her arms round him and snuggled in against him, burrowing her face into his shoulder and pressing tight against him where it was warm and dark and safe.

'I'll hold you,' Kit said, laying his cheek down on her smooth hair. 'I won't ever let you go.'

After some time she drew her head back to look up at him earnestly and say, 'Kit, if we can't – I mean, if you want – if you should feel –'

He knew what it was she couldn't say. He pulled her close

again, and said, 'Hush, don't say it. I know what you mean, and I thank you, but do you think I could bear to take that pleasure you were denied? And how would it be pleasure, with anyone but you? No, my hinny, we will share all things, good and bad.' He stroked her hair, and she pressed harder against him. 'Oh Hero, I love you so,' he said quietly.

Hamil was woken by a stealthy noise in his bedchamber, and was alert at once, sitting up in bed and cautiously drawing back the bedcurtain. It was a dark night with no moon, and the room outside the curtains was as dark as inside, except for the very slightly paler square of the window. In a moment, something moved across this, and he heard the slight noise again, the noise of a long garment brushing over the reed-matting.

'Who's there?' he said sharply. 'Speak, or I'll wake the house!'

'Shh!' came back a voice, and then a whisper, 'hush, where are you?' Relief flooded over him – it was Sabine's voice. The sounds of movement continued as she groped her way towards the bed, and he felt the soft bump as her knees found it, and the clambering of her hands over the bedclothes looking for him.

'What's the matter?' Hamil asked, instinctively keeping his voice low.

'Don't make a noise,' she whispered. 'They'll hear us.'

'Who will? What's the matter? Wait, I'll light the candle.'

'No! Here, give me your hand.' The patting, groping on the bedclothes continued. Hamil reached around, and a thin hand caught his wrist and fumbled something into his palm, warm and hard – the hilt of a knife. He swallowed, suddenly nervous; a naked blade in the dark, the shortest way to heaven. Even so, his mind was working now. Sabine had been growing stranger over the months – did this portend some new fantasy? 'There,' she whispered. 'It's all right, I have another. We'll just wait here until they come, and then –'

'Until who comes?' Hamil asked in a normal voice. Sabine clutched him tighter.

'Hush! Don't give us away!'

He reached away from her towards the shelf where his candle and flint were, and she obviously understood the movement, for she began climbing up onto the bed, trying to restrain him. He thought of the other knife, imagining its dark silent burning – where? Chest or neck or groin? Sweat broke out all over him as he tried gently to wrestle his way free.

'No no! No light!' she cried, abandoning her whisper. 'They'll see, they'll find us. You're on their side – you want them to find us! You're one of them!'

'No, Sabine, of course not. I'm on your side,' Hamil said, feeling stronger now. The voices would wake the servants. He would not be long alone.

'They'll come and find us, and then they'll take it away from us. No light, no light! Antony! Don't let them take it away! Hamil no, don't!'

He had managed to get both her wrists in one hand, while with the other he reached for the flint, and she was shrieking now. Take it away? he wondered vaguely. Her old fantasy about losing Watermill to some other claimant, perhaps? He had dropped the knife she had given him, and now as she struggled one thin wrist out of her grasp she was reaching for it. Where was help? There were sounds of voices outside in the house, and now a gleam of a candle lighting the bottom of the door.

He shouted out. 'Holloa – help there!' just as the blade whistled past his ear and struck the pillow behind his head. She was on top of him now, and he grabbed her loose arm and was wrestling her, trying to keep her from his face. Madness indeed, to strike at his face with a knife – a sane person would go for throat or heart – and now she was trying to savage him, like a dog. But the door had opened, candlelight billowed in, and there were servants there, armed with whatever they had grabbed.

'Help me,' Hamil cried. 'The mistress is taken ill. Gently now – have a care! Watch for the knife!'

Even with many hands to help, even after the knife had been dropped, it was hard to subdue her. Sabine fought like a wild thing, shrieking madly. No-one wanted to hurt her, which made it harder to contain her wild movements. At last, however, one of the women thought to take off the shawl she had flung round her shoulders when she jumped from her bed, and this was wrapped around Sabine and tied, pinning her arms to her body. After that she was soon quiet, and fell into a heartbreaking sobbing, collapsing to the floor and rocking from side to side. Everyone else fell silent, looking anywhere but at her, awkward with embarrassment and pity.

Hamil had to speak, and said at last, 'She is unwell, and fancies things. Let her be taken to her room, and given all care. She must not be left alone. Two of you must sit with her at all times. Take it in turns. And give her a sleeping-draught in some warm wine, and secure her in her bed with a sheet. I dare say it will not be necessary, but we must take care of her for her own sake. In the morning all may be well.'

But he said it without conviction, and the servants took the sobbing woman away with sad and sober faces, leaving Hamil to wonder what should be done. He felt that he should have realized before the direction her strangeness was taking. Was it true that there was madness in the family, as people said? The same blood, the Chapham blood, ran in his veins, through his mother, though she seemed as normal as anyone could be. But there had been Antony, the idiot; and Zeph and Zech were strange too, with their determined travelling and refusal to come home;

and Ruth and Malachi, living alone together at Shawes, almost recluses; and Mary Eleanor, more quiet and subdued than a normal child – was she hiding the seeds of madness too? Thank God, at least, that Sabine and Zechariah had never had children. He slept but little the rest of the night, tossing and turning, and when he did sleep, his dreams were haunted with monsters.

Autumn was a particularly busy time for Mary Esther, for as well as all the other perennial tasks there was the harvest to deal with. Apples and pears had to be sorted and stored; other fruits had to be dried or bottled or made into jam according to their nature; the winter killing had to be prepared for, fish dried, cured, salted or pickled; eggs pickled and stored away; vegetables cleaned and stored; fuel for the winter gathered and stacked, and the stacks arranged in the best way so that the fuel would stay dry and the stack not collapse as the fuel was drawn and used. Store cupboards must be emptied, cleaned, and filled again. Winter clothes must be looked out, cleaned and mended, bed-hangings and shutters changed, chimneys swept, dry stores replenished against isolation.

Yet a crisp and sunny morning in October found her riding Psyche across the Stray towards the Hare and Heather to visit Uncle Ambrose. Psyche danced and pranced even higher in the sparkling air, and the new bridle-ornaments on her browband trembled with every toss of her head. They were a present from Edmund – dark pink coral beads, strung on gold chains and hanging from a gold boss, they looked like bunches of redcurrants. Edmund had a genius for choosing pretty things for his wife, but he dismissed her thanks almost curtly, and Mary Esther learned not to trouble him with her gratitude. Dog ran ahead of her, tail up and nose down, and Nerissa rode behind more sedately, carrying a basket full of good things that Mary Esther was bringing to comfort her uncle's sickness.

'You need bring only yourself,' Uncle Ambrose said when she was admitted to his little room under the eaves, 'for that is the best medicine of all. Come nearer, chuck, till I see you.' His eyes had been failing all year, and he could see things only as blurs now, unless they were under his nose. 'What's this you're wearing? Ah, but you're pretty! What do you call this colour?'

'It's called musk-rose,' Mary Esther said distractedly. 'Uncle 'Brose, I'm sure you haven't been eating – you're thinner than you were last week. You must take care of yourself. I have brought you some good things, but what use is it to bring them if you won't eat?'

'Sit down on the bed here, my little bird, and hold my hand. That's better. Now, I swear I will eat everything you have brought.'

'Good – you may begin with the honeycomb, then. We harvested the honey yesterday, and it has been an excellent one. There is a jar of honey there, too, and some of my own lemon cheese, and some blackcurrant jam – that is good for rheums and chills, Uncle 'Brose, so eat plenty. And some good goose dripping, and one of Jacob's brawn pies which he made specially for you, and some of the apricots you like so much and some dried figs – and half a ham, and three smoked trout which you must have tonight, for I know you like them – and a lardy cake and – what can this be? I don't remember it – oh yes, of course! Hetta sent you this, and I should be in mortal trouble if I forgot it. It's a cake she made herself, though Jacob must have helped her. You can see she made it by the finger-marks. Can you imagine, Uncle 'Brose, Jacob allowing a child to morris around in his precious kitchen?'

'Hetta is such a little plump brown sparrow of a child, I could believe anything,' Ambrose said. 'She never stops chirping all day long, and she goes so fearlessly up to people

123

and demands love with so little expectation of disappointment, that it is not surprising she finds it wherever she goes. She reminds me of you when you were that age.' He reached up a gnarled, chalky hand and pulled gently at one of the dark ringlets. 'And how is the mother sparrow? How is it you can find time to visit a sick old man with all you have to do? And bring all these good things. You are looking pale, my hinny. I'm sure you do too much.'

'And I'm sure you are trying to distract me from your ills by reminding me of mine,' Mary Esther smiled.

'Have you ills, child? What are they?' Ambrose asked anxiously.

'Oh, do not fret, Uncle, I have as little to vex me as ever. In fact, the house seems too quiet now, with little Ambrose away at Winchester, and Hero and Kit gone to live at Watermill.'

'Ah, yes, I had forgotten that. They are settled in now?'

'Quite happily, I believe, though Hero still frets about Hamil. She is afraid he will be killed, and worries that he might have gone to be a mercenary for that very reason, to get himself killed. I tell her it's nonsense, but the fact that he went without saying goodbye to her makes her feel that he has not forgiven her, and strengthens her conviction.'

'And why did he go?' Ambrose asked.

'To get away, I think. Watermill held too many unhappy memories, and he still felt too close to Hero and Kit. When he has seen something of the world and fought a few battles he will be glad enough to come home – though not to Watermill, I think. It will always be haunted for him now. He blames himself for Sabine's death, though I told him that it is impossible to watch lunatics closely enough, unless you tie them up like animals. They are cunning, and will find ways of doing what they want.'

'That young man takes too much blame to himself, it seems. He is greedy for it.'

Mary Esther nodded. 'It is so sad. He was happy once,

before all this happened – but he makes his own sadness out of whole cloth.'

'And how is your good husband? Does he miss Ambrose?'

'Oddly, I think he misses Hero more,' Mary Esther smiled. 'He had taken quite a fancy to her, even used to sit with her of an evening. Now he has to make do with me.'

Ambrose laughed and patted her cheek. 'Make do, indeed! What other news have you for me?'

'Well, you have heard, no doubt, that Rob and Sabina won their case and are to move into Aberlady House in time for Christmas. They wanted Hamil to come up to them, but he had gone by the time their letter arrived, and so it will be some time before the news catches up with him. But it means he is provided for, and Kit and Hero can have Watermill, which is all very satisfactory. Now Edmund can give his whole mind to worrying about Ambrose and Francis.'

'He is worrying?'

Mary Esther nodded. 'He worries what they will do for land. There is Tod's Knowe, of course, for one of them – but at least one more estate will be needed, if the Morland Place estate is not to be broken up – and Edmund would sooner cut off his limbs and distribute them than break pieces off Morland Place. I often think how lucky it is that my children were girls. More sons would only add to his troubles. Where to come by land – that is the sum of it.'

'And what of the future master of Morland Place? Have you news of him?'

'He writes to Kit quite regularly, and Kit, in his kindness, brings his letters for his father to read. Richard seems to be behaving so well it makes me quite nervous – I wonder in which direction he will break out next. But Edmund is pleased, and suspects nothing. Richard is in with a very gentlemanlike young man called Byrne, who has friends at court, and their circle, for a wonder, does nothing more wicked than smoking tobacco, talking, and singing part-songs. Richard's letters are all full of what is going on in the south, court gossip and politics, and very little about himself.'

'He was always one to go to extremes,' Ambrose said. 'We must all pray that when his head stops spinning he is facing the right way.'

'Amen to that,' Mary Esther said. 'These young people he is with now seem to have the right influence over him, at all events, and Edmund is delighted. He has written to Richard to tell him so, and to say that when he has finished at Oxford he will send him to Norwich to learn all the new methods that are being used there in the wool trade, against the time when he will take over the reins. I only hope Richard recognizes the compliment for what it is, and does not think he is being kept from home for some secret purpose.'

'Well, all in all, it seems as though you do have very little to vex you, my child,' Ambrose said, and Mary Esther squeezed his hand.

'Very little, Uncle, except your health. We must have you fit and well again, before the cold weather starts. I have been wondering, in fact, if you would not consider coming to Morland Place, so that I can nurse you better. I'm sure Ayla does her best, but an inn is not the perfect place for an invalid. And Morland Place is much warmer and more comfortable –'

Her voice trailed off as she saw the expression on her uncle's face, tender and regretful, and a cold hand seemed to clutch at her heart.

'Mary, my hinny,' he began, and the cold hand squeezed tighter.

'No, Uncle, don't say it, please.'

'Mary, dearest, you have to face the truth sooner or later. All creatures lose their parents some time. I am very old, loveling –'

'No, not so old! You have many years left to you yet. You have been ill, but we will get you well again, and in the spring –'

'I won't be here in the spring,' he said simply. 'Ah, Mary, love, don't cry. Don't be sad. I am old, and have had a good life, and am content. I shall regret nothing, except leaving you. You have been the sunshine in my life, you know that.' She could not speak, and he pressed her hand. 'Don't make it hard for me.'

'I can't do without you,' she whispered.

'You can, you can. You are a grown woman now, well able to manage without a dry old husk that has finished his life. Come, little bird, no more tears. I will not go just yet – we shall have plenty more talks together, and then, one day . . .'

Mary Esther silenced him with a shake of her head, and leaned down and rested her cheek against his for a moment, while she controlled her tears. When at last she spoke it was in her normal, cheerful voice, with only the hint of shakiness about it.

'Shall you come back to Morland Place, then?'

'No, my darling, I won't. I am happier here. I've lived all my life in taverns. Leave me be happy here – but come and visit me often?'

A convulsive hug was his answer.

The voices and the candlelight only made Mary Esther stir, but the coldness in the bed when Edmund had got up and left her woke her. She lay wondering drowsily. Some trouble, to get him out of bed in the middle of a cold January night; but then not trouble bad enough for her to be called. They had fetched him without meaning to wake her. Who had fetched him? She sorted through her memory and found the voice of Clement – of course – and then at last of Gideon, the head groom. Her mind was not long after that in coming to a conclusion, and she sat up quickly and reached for the candle.

She knew better than not to dress, but she put her gown on over her nightdress for quickness' sake, wrapped her warmest shawl around her, and went downstairs. The great door was still locked and bolted, and she guessed that they had gone out through the pantry. Sure enough, the little door which the servants used to go into the kitchen from the yard was unlocked, and she stepped out into a brilliantly cold night, bathed in blue light from a frozen moon. Her candle flame flattened violently in the cold wind, and she let it go out. One could not take a lighted candle into a stable, and in any case she could see across the yard that a lamp was alight in there, looking very yellow by contrast to the moonlight.

Clement was holding the lantern at the doorway to Queen Mab's stall, and within the old mare was stretched on her side, her eyes wide, and her nostrils flaring with her laboured breathing. Edmund and Gideon knelt in the straw with her.

'Is she in labour?' Mary Esther asked. Clement turned, startled, but neither of the other two seemed surprised at her presence.

'She's not getting on with it,' Gideon said. 'She's too old.'

'She's weak, that's all,' Edmund said defensively. He was at the mare's head, and her great pain-filled eyes were on him. Mary Esther touched Clement's hand.

'Give me the lantern, and get you back to bed,' she said.

'Nay, Madam,' he began, but she was firm.

'You have enough to do, and need your sleep. I will hold the lantern. I would not sleep as long as the master is here.'

Clement bowed and backed out reluctantly, too good a servant to protest more. Edmund looked up at the movement of the light, and his eyes touched her vaguely and moved away again.

'She is weak, she would not feed properly. Was I wrong to put her to the stallion again? She seemed so fit in the summer,' he said. Gideon looked at his master, and then at Mary Esther, not knowing who the question was meant for. Mary Esther knew.

'She would not have taken if she had not been fit,' she said. 'All may yet be well. She has great spirit.'

Edmund nodded, and then said to Gideon, 'Go and mix a hot mash, and put some ale into it. But wait – first run after Clement, and tell him to give you a bottle of aquavit, and bring it here. Quickly now.' When Gideon had gone, Mary Esther found the lantern-hook, and hung up the lantern, and moved closer to Edmund, kneeling down in the straw beside him. He caressed the mare's cheeks and pulled her ears, and spoke soothingly to her, and while he did Mary Esther saw her flanks heave in a prolonged spasmodic effort that ended in a jerking of her hind legs. Edmund's face mirrored the effort and the pain; there were already blue shadows under his eyes, and in the high lamplight his face was all planes and angles, skull-like.

He said, 'We will have to try to bring the foal ourselves.' His wife answered the unspoken question.

'I will stay and help you.' He looked up at her face, and she saw the further question there. 'I have helped with the birth of countless babies, Edmund. I can help you.' He nodded, and looked relieved, and she longed to touch him, but knew she must not.

'In the tack-room,' he said, 'there should be several coils of rope. Bring the finest and softest, and some rags, if you see any. And there should be more lamps. Take this one, and light another and bring it back.'

He did not need to tell her to be quick. Kneeling in the darkness, he knew a distant and muted feeling of relief, which anxiety could not quite blot out, that she was there with her quick mind and light feet. She came back with the light and the rope at the same moment as Gideon came in

129

with the aquavit, and he made her take a swallow of the fiery spirit before she helped him to pour some down the mare's unresisting throat, while Gideon went away to make the mash.

The aquavit seemed to help the mare, for shortly afterwards she began to labour again, and with the help of the two humans she got over onto her chest, and began to try to struggle to her feet. Edmund kept up a stream of gentle encouragement, while setting his weight against her shoulder to help her, while Mary Esther pulled at her head collar; and at last, with a long groan of effort, the old mare got her hocks under her and managed to stand, though she swayed wearily before bracing herself against the birth-pains.

When Gideon came back, Edmund stripped off his jacket and rolled up his linen sleeves, and while Mary Esther held the mare's head and stroked her sweating neck and encouraged her, Edmund and Gideon got the ropes, padded with rags, round the foal's pasterns, and prepared to help by pulling as the mare pushed. It was a long, hard business, and several times it was only a sharp cry from Edmund that kept Mab from collapsing again. Mary Esther found herself sweating and straining in sympathetic effort, and the glimpses she caught of Edmund's face shewed her that he felt everything too. But at last the efforts were repaid, and the foal came slithering out onto the straw, and Edmund, kneeling to untie the ropes and clear the creature's nostrils said, 'A filly – and alive.'

In a moment the foal sneezed, wriggled, flapped its wet ears, and let out a bleating cry, and Queen Mab, turning her head wearily, knuckered in reply, though she was too weak to move. 'Help me bring the foal to her,' Edmund cried to Gideon, and together they carried the filly round to where Queen Mab could lick her dry. Under the slow rough caress of the mother's tongue, the filly blinked her long eyelashes and sneezed again, and soon was trying to stand, unfolding the endless, brittle-looking legs until, awkwardly as a stiltwalker, she would be able to seek out her mother's udder and the life-giving milk.

But Queen Mab was almost beyond it; her legs were buckling, and Edmund left the foal to Gideon's charge while he grabbed at the head collar, jerking the mare's head up and crying, 'Hold up, mare! Come Mab, come, hold up! You must not give in now! The mash – give me the mash. She might be persuaded to eat some. It would give her strength.'

Mary Esther held the bucket while Edmund fed the mare from his own palms, though she was too weary to take more than a mouthful or two. But somehow he managed to pour his strength into her so that she stayed on her feet while her small daughter suckled, and though she swayed, and though her head hung heavier and heavier on Edmund's shoulder, she let down her milk to the urgent butting of the small hard muzzle, and it was only when the filly had filled her belly that the mare with a long sigh went down into the straw again.

'Good mare,' Edmund crooned, kneeling beside her and stroking her face. 'Oh good mare. That was well done. The little one sleeps now, and you can rest.'

Gideon brought a rug to fling over the mare, and Edmund nodded him away, but as long as he would not leave his horse, Mary Esther would not leave him. He spoke quietly, and at first Mary Esther thought he spoke to himself, but he knew she was there, and was grateful.

'The best mare I ever had, the best horse, the best dam. Her colts are the best in the county. And such a heart! You were never afraid of anything, were you, Mab? Anything I rode you at, you would take in your stride – a heart as big as a house. You would not go down until you had fed your youngling, would you, sweet Mab? Good mare, oh good mare.'

He held the horse's head on his lap, stroking her and talking in a low voice, and the mare breathed quietly; now and then her eyelids would flicker, or her ear twitch, as if responding to his voice, for she could make no other movement. Mary Esther crouched near in silent sympathy; under the warmth of the flank, the new foal slept. Edmund looked at his wife wearily.

'We were young together, she and I. My father bred her, raised her by hand as they do in the Borderlands, and she never knew a harsh word or a blow in all her life. She had no fear of human hands. How many thousand rides have we had together? Twice ten thousand perhaps, from first to last. I was riding her when I first noticed you – do you remember?' Mary Esther nodded. 'She carried me when I came to visit you, and when I brought you back to Morland Place, she carried us both – you rode before me on the saddle. You were so small and light she barely noticed. And now –' He looked down at his hands as they pulled the silken ears, and his voice was uncertain. 'Animals' lives are too short.'

'She has had a happy life,' Mary Ester said. Edmund did not speak again. The night was beginning to lighten when at last he laid the heavy head in the straw and got stiffly to his feet. Mary Esther, swaying with weariness, stood too, and Edmund looked down and said only, 'My youth dies with her.' Then he turned and walked away, but at the door he stopped, and after a long hesitation he turned back. He did not quite meet Mary Esther's eyes, and his voice was stilted and shy, but he made the great effort and said, 'Thank you – for staying with me.'

Warmth spread through her, and she went forward and took his arm and looked up at him, and slowly, slowly, his eyes met hers, and he allowed her to draw his arm around her shoulders.

'Will you go in to bed? There is still a little of the night left.'

'Yes,' he said. He cleared his throat, and said awkwardly, 'Will you come too? I need you, Mary.'

Together they crossed the quiet yard and passed through the sleeping house to the bedchamber. In the dark safety of the curtained bed, he was bolder.

'You are cold, my dearest. Come closer, and let me warm you.' She snuggled in to him, and he held her and stroked her head.

'You do warm me, Edmund,' she said. 'You are the warmth of the sun to me.' She felt him quiver under her words, and in a moment turned her face up for his kisses. The tension of the long night, the pain and sadness of loss, broke through his restraint, and he kissed her passionately, her brow and eyes and lips, lifting her fingers to his mouth, drawing her long curls again and again through his fingers. He did not need to ask permission, nor she to give it, nor did their garments hinder them; flesh to flesh they found again the freedom that their lives and his nature had so rarely granted. To give himself as completely as she gave herself was so nearly impossible that now when it happened it seemed to open his soul and turn it inside out like a ripening fig; a joy so intense, so piercing, that he felt he might die of it, that a wrong word could kill him.

But she said only, 'I love you –' and shuddering he yielded the last bastion of his spirit, and their joy was accomplished.

They drifted together in the darkness for a long time, and then he roused himself enough to say, in a voice unlike his own it was so warm and so easy, 'Mary – my own love.'

The warm darkness claimed them; cheek to cheek, breast to breast, they slept. Mary Esther was still wrapped blissfully in his arms when in the grey of the January morning she was woken, dragged unwillingly from the sweet dark sleep by a voice she wanted to ignore. Never had she so little wanted to wake.

'Madam, Madam.' It was Leah's voice. 'Wake, Mistress, wake up.'

'Oh Leah – what is it?' she mumbled sleepily. 'It can't be important.'

'Oh Mistress – oh Mistress, I'm so sorry.' The words pierced the delicious fog – ah, painful, painful to be woken! 'A messenger has come – from The Hare and Heather – your Uncle Ambrose, Madam. Oh Madam, I'm so sorry.'

Edmund's body was quite naked, as was her own: their warm flesh was pressed together the whole length of their bodies, and it was like tearing the heart from her body to drag herself away from him. 'Very well, Leah, I'll come,' she said.

134

BOOK TWO

The Apple Tree

For I must go where lazy Peace
Will hide her drowsy head;
And for the sport of kings increase
The number of the dead.

Sir William Davenant: *The Soldier Going to the Field*

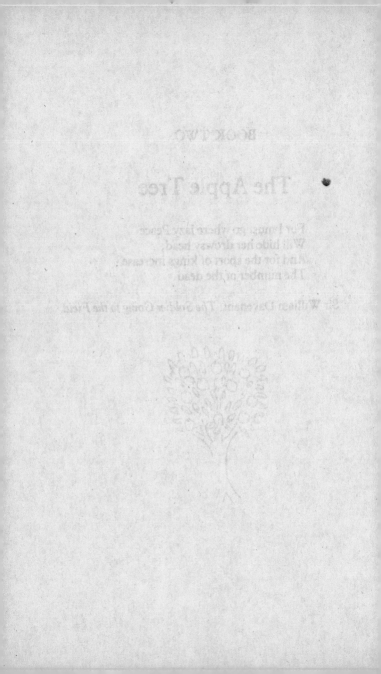

these rooms, won't you? It has brought you to walk tonight, I hope; your house is not far off.'

'Why, no,' Richard said. Lucy sat on a chair by the fireside, and Richard remained standing, leaning against the chimney-piece, so that he could look down at her face. Most of his reform had been necessitaten for the sake of Lucy. [Bout]

CHAPTER EIGHT

The maid who opened the door of the lodgings in Carfax looked with no disfavour at Richard as she let him in and lit his way up the stairs. He was not really handsome, to be sure, she thought, but he was a gentleman, and there was such an improvement in him since he first came visiting that you would hardly believe; so she said civilly, 'Very mild tonight, for October, Sir,' and smiled at him as she turned the stair ahead and the light of her candle brightened his face. It was a broad, high cheekboned face, fair-skinned, with a short, broad nose and a rather attractively crooked mouth; clean-shaven but for the fine, red-blonde moustache and the fashionable tuft under the lower lip. Richard had that gingery-fair hair that is fuzzy and wavy without actually being curly; now he kept it clean and combed, and wore it just to his shoulders. His clothes were clean, too, and smart, and though he did not attain to the fashionable dandyism of his friend there was a lace edging to his deep linen collar and cuffs, and black silk rosettes fastened his shoes. The most noticeable change of all, however, was that he no longer slouched and scowled, and the expression of his face was intelligent and alert.

Lucy Sciennes noticed it too, and received him each time he called with more pleasure.

'My dear Richard,' she said now as she came forward to greet him, 'you are a little early – Clovis has not yet arrived.'

Richard bowed over her extended hand. 'I'm sorry – I walked up, and misjudged how long it would take me.'

'Oh, don't apologize – I am glad of your company. I have been very dull today. Meggie, bring some wine. You will take some, won't you? What brought you to walk tonight? I hope your horse is not lame?'

'Oh no,' Richard said. Lucy sat on a chair by the fireside, and Richard remained standing, leaning against the chimney-piece so that he could look down at her face. Most of his reform had been undertaken for the sake of Lucy, though he hardly knew it himself; he only knew that she was half a goddess to him. 'No, he is fit enough. I wanted to walk to give myself time to think. I have had a letter from home.'

'Not bad news, I hope?' Lucy said. Richard stared reflectively into the fire. 'No-one is ill, pray God?'

'No – but it is bad news all the same. My – my father's wife has had another child. A son. Born on St Edward's day, and they have called him Edward.'

Lucy studied his averted face and smiled. 'But that is good news! Come, Richard, my dear, you are not such a simpleton as still to resent your father's marriage?' Richard gave a grunt which she interpreted easily. 'You who are a widower yourself? Come now!'

'What has that to do with it?' Richard asked resentfully.

'If you fell in love with a woman tomorrow, would you think it a betrayal of your Jane to marry her?'

'That's different.'

'No it is not. Your mother was not set aside, but died naturally, albeit a tragedy. How then did your father offend by marrying again? Is no-one to marry a second time in your world, though they live widowed for fifty years? Be reasonable, Richard.' She laughed coaxingly, and Richard smiled reluctantly, not wanting to seem ungracious.

'It seems, all the same, as if my father does not want me to come home,' he said. 'The letter says that when I finish at Oxford I am to be sent to Norwich.'

At this moment Clovis arrived, and when the greetings had been exchanged and three cups of wine distributed, Clovis said, 'Who is going to Norwich? I heard the words as I came in.'

'Richard, next year when he finishes at University,' Lucy said. 'I have not yet heard the purpose of his visit.'

'My father is sending me,' Richard explained, 'to study the new methods in the clothiers' industry – or so he says.'

Clovis raised an eyebrow questioningly, and Lucy said, 'Richard seems to imagine there must be some conspiracy to keep him from home.' Clovis smiled.

'I have not seen my home for six years, and may not see it for six more. All the better, as far as I am concerned – I live much more comfortably anywhere but there. So you are to go to Norwich – well, you should be comfortable there at least for it is one of the richest cities in the land, though you will have some to-do to find your pleasure.'

'How so?' Richard asked.

'Because, my dear Richard, Norwich is the centre of the east country, and the east country is the breeding ground of every Brownist sect that human ingenuity can devise. If you stay a year they will make a Puritan of you yet!'

'Nonsense,' Lucy said cheerfully. 'Richard is a Catholic like you.'

'Not quite like me,' Clovis said thoughtfully. 'But he will have to convert, or he will go quite mad. Every man there is a preacher, and every street corner a pulpit. Ah, poor Richard, you are lost indeed!'

'It cannot be as bad as you say,' Richard said stoutly. 'My father would never send me if there was a chance of my becoming a sectary. Imagine, one of the great Morland family a Puritan!' He laughed at the very idea. Lucy and Clovis exchanged a glance, and Clovis felt it necessary to change the subject.

'And how is that boy of yours? Thriving still, I pray God?'

'Yes, he is well, and doing well at his lessons, so the letter says.' Richard frowned, and added, 'He will be half way to manhood before I see him again. He won't remember me at all. He is already four years old.'

139

'All the better,' Clovis said lightly. 'It is no good thing to be brought up under a father's eye. Parents are too partial to be good masters.'

Richard's attention was drawn by that from his own troubles to Clovis's. 'Is there any word what is to happen to you?' he asked. Clovis, being a year ahead of Richard, was nearing the end of his stay at Oxford, and Richard knew that leaving Oxford was what Clovis dreaded, for it would almost certainly mean leaving Lucy.

'I am to take orders, of course,' he said neutrally, 'and then a living will be bought for me. In the meantime, until a suitable living arises, it is more than likely that I shall be found a position at Court.'

'Oh,' said Richard. 'How shall you like that?'

'How should a man like to be attached to the most elegant, sophisticated, witty, charming Court in the world? The balls, the masques, the banquets, the fine paintings, exquisite porcelain, delightful gardens, amusing fountains, charming women –'

'The Papist Queen,' Lucy interrupted, 'the servile, flattering ministers, the violent populace and dissaffected Parliament.'

'Is it like that?' Richard asked.

'It is like that,' Clovis said. 'Richard, my friend, I go to seek my own destruction. The King, I believe, is a good, sober, virtuous, pious prince. He rules the country so badly that he could not do it worse if he tried a-purpose; trouble is brewing in London, and at every step the King makes matters worse, partly from his own short-sightedness and partly from the bad advice of his ministers; and yet everyone who comes into contact with him, loves him. So you see, I shall go and fall in love with him like everyone else, and once I have eaten his bread and kissed his hand I shall be a King's man for good or evil, and be bound to live and die for him, although my good sense tells me otherwise. Oh yes, I am doomed. I am a lost cause, Dick.'

Richard was silent a moment, wondering. 'And Lucy?' he dared to ask at last. Lucy and Clovis exchanged a painful glance.

'Lucy comes with me,' Clovis said abruptly. 'I will find some place for her nearby, and visit her when I can, which I expect will not be often.' Lucy's eyes were fixed on Clovis's face, and he tried to laugh. 'She, you see, is doomed as I am. I have begged her, but she will not leave me and marry someone else, though I have offered her a dowry –'

'Clovis – !' Lucy began, half rising, and he turned to her and took her hand and pushed her gently back down.

'I know, dearest, I know. God knows, I wish I had your courage and then I might say Fig! to my father and my position and go and earn an honest living in some trade. Should you like to be a tradesman's wife, and live in a room over a pigsty, and sweep your own floors and wash your own clothes?'

'I would go anywhere, do anything, if it was with you,' Lucy said with quiet intensity. Clovis smiled sardonically.

'Aye, I know you would. It was never *your* courage that was in doubt. I am not worthy of you, Lucy, and that's the truth.'

There was a silence, and Richard, looking from one to the other, felt suddenly how petty his own selfish concerns were; and he felt, also, strangely lonely, that he had never experienced a love like that. Though it gave them pain, they had each other. Whatever happened, they were not alone, as he was, and had always been.

It was late when he left to go back to his own lodgings, and Lucy was worried for his safety.

'There are footpads everywhere – I'm sure it is not safe. Let me send for a link-boy. You should not have come afoot, Richard, indeed you shouldn't.'

But Richard insisted. 'I have my sword,' he said, patting its hilt. 'My own right arm must keep me safe.' Lucy would have argued further, but Clovis stilled her with a glance.

'Keep away from the walls, then, Dick, and do not go down any narrow alleys, lest your right arm be unable to draw your sword. At least you have been well taught – I can vouch for that, Lucy. I have seen him in action.'

'In play,' Lucy pointed out, but she said no more. Her anxiety had at least made Richard cautious, and he walked briskly and alertly, keeping his hand on his sword-hilt and his eyes about him. As he turned the corner into Catte Street he saw two figures some way ahead of him, and froze for a moment, only to relax as he saw that they were not ruffians but a man and a woman, obviously decent folk, hurrying home themselves. A second later he was running down the street towards them, his hand already drawing his sword from its sheath. As they passed the mouth of an alley, two dark shapes had jumped out on them.

It was all over in a moment in a flurry of noise and movement. Two footpads who had been willing enough to attack an unarmed elderly man and a young woman were less willing to face a healthy young man with a drawn and very sharp sword. They took to their heels and fled off into the dark safety of the warren of alleys, leaving Richard panting and victorious, without a scratch on him. He turned to his protégés. The man was on the ground, already trying to raise himself on one arm, and the girl had knelt beside him and was anxiously trying to assist him.

'Are you all right, sir?' Richard asked.

The man felt his head cautiously, and said, 'My hat – where's my hat?'

'Here it is, Father,' said the girl, reaching for it and putting it in his hand. The man clapped it on, and seized the girl's arm firmly.

'Help me up, Kate, That's right. Yes, yes, I'm all right, young man, thanks to you – and thanks to my hat. One of those damned villains hit me with a club of some sort, but my hat took the blow. Good stout felt it is, and the brim wired. A man's hat tells the world what he is. Now young sir, to whom do I have the honour of being indebted?'

On his feet, the man proved to be small, wiry, and around fifty years old, silver-haired but firm of face and alert of eye. His clothes were of good plain stuff, fine quality cloth but unfashionably cut. His accent was so strange that Richard had to concentrate to understand what he was saying, and he took him therefore to be a foreigner – a Dutchman perhaps.

'Richard Morland, of York, Sir, at your service,' he said, bowing, and then again to the young woman. 'And Madam.' The old man's eyes swept Richard's face keenly.

'You came along most timely, Sir – but wait! Morland of York? Morland of York? Bless my soul – not related to the Morlands of York, the wool family? Morlands of Morland fine cloth?'

Richard was surprised. 'Yes Sir. My father is Edmund Morland, of Morland Place. I am his eldest son.'

'Why, bless me, who would have thought it!' The old man seemed delighted. 'I have heard of your family, Sir, as you can tell. We are in the same business, you and I. Allow me to introduce myself – Geoffrey Browne, Sir, Clothier of the City of Norwich – at your service Sir. And my daughter Katherine.'

Richard made another bow, and the girl curtseyed deeply. She was well wrapped up in a thick dark cloak and hood, so that her face and body were all but concealed, but as she rose from her curtsey, she turned her face up to him, and even in the darkness he could see that she was young, no more than sixteen, and that her eyes were very bright. The old man was talking on.

'Who in the cloth trade has not heard of the Morland family? Well well, who would have thought it. It is very agreeable to be indebted to someone who is, if I may put it so, one of the same family. I would like to do you some service, Sir, in return, though I do not know what service can repay saving a man's life.'

'It was nothing Sir,' Richard said, embarrassed. 'But will you allow me to walk with you to your lodgings? I must see you safely indoors.'

'Certainly Sir, certainly. We are staying at the White Hart — and when we are within, you must allow us to offer you some supper at least. Bless me, I would like very much to talk to you, young man. Morland of York eh?'

He chuckled delightedly as he took his daughter's arm and began walking on. Richard fell in beside them, still somewhat bewildered, still trying to catch the tune of the strange East Anglian accent, amused at the coincidence that had brought the name of Norwich to his ears twice in the same evening, and not at all averse to having the chance to prise the young girl's modest eyes from their study of the ground to his face.

The trouble that had been brewing in the south had not been felt at all in the north. There life went on peacefully as it had for the last fifty years or more, and it was all the more shocking therefore when the trouble finally erupted. It began in 1638 when the King, as part of his policy to enforce a uniform religion in his lands, ordered that the Anglican Book of Common Prayer should be used in Scotland. Scotland had been too long Presbyterian to accept such an abomination: the Scottish Assembly rejected it out of hand, and early in 1639 a Scottish army began to muster under the command of the veteran Leslie.

Edmund himself brought the news to Morland Place, seeking out Mary Esther in the long saloon where she was overseeing the first-quarter cleaning. On the hearth stood a large bucket of wheat-straw ash and another of fresh urine: these mixed in the right quantities would clean almost everything, but there was also a small pot of alum and another of whiting. Two of the servants had spread the Turkey carpet that normally covered the long table on the floor and were brushing ash into it while the rest were engaged in cleaning the silver and the paintwork. Mary Esther herself was divided between overseeing, talking to Hero who had come to visit, and keeping small Edward from putting his fingers into things. Leah hovered restively near, itching to take the baby away, but Mary Esther adored Edward, who was three now and beginning to be amusing, and she also missed the presence of Anne and Hetta who now spent much of their day doing lessons.

When Edmund appeared, Edward ran to him at once, and Mary Esther turned with a loving smile and said, 'Ah, Edmund, I am glad you are come. I have been wondering what we might do to clean those old portraits –' She stopped as she realized that her husband's face was more than usually grim. 'Why, what is the matter? Edmund, has something happened?'

'The King has called out the militia of the northern counties. I am afraid – it is war.'

The word fell with a leaden ring into the sudden silence. War with the Scots – the ancient enemy. Though there had been two generations of peace, the inherited memory made the skin prickle with fear. It was that fear the King had depended on in calling out the northern counties. Now Mary Esther instinctively glanced at Hero, who said in a small voice, 'My father and mother, Sir – ?'

Edmund shook his head. 'I don't know. I hope they will not be affected, but so close to Edinburgh as they are – I pray God it may not come about that a Morland is brought to fight a Hamilton.'

Mary Esther drew in her breath in exasperation. It was like Edmund to be so tactless! The Hamiltons would be in a very difficult position whether they fought or whether they did not, as Hero must be aware. She said quickly,

'What of Tod's Knowe, Sir? If the Scots come, they will surely come down Redesdale.'

'It is likely, unless they march by the coast. The steward

is a good man, and the Tod's Knowe people will be quick to arm, but it is in my mind that there should be a Morland there. I cannot go myself, and Richard and Ambrose are away, and so –'

Mary Esther was there before him. 'Edmund – oh not Francis! He is too young!' she cried. Edmund frowned warningly. 'He is barely eighteen!'

'Madam,' he said coldly, 'the decision is already made. And if it is danger you fear, let me remind you that we will all have our share in that. If the Scots come, they will come here; and if they are held back, it will be our men that do the holding.' With that he turned and left them. Mary Esther swept Edward up in her arms and looked towards Hero anxiously, seeing her own apprehension mirrored there. In time of war, they all had so much to lose.

Through the spring uneasiness reigned in the north. The Scots had gathered a mighty army, but though the men of the north responded to the call and left their fields, there were but few of them in comparison, and they were largely unarmed, and had no experienced officers. By summer the King saw that a battle was impossible, and he was forced to treat with the Scots to gain time. The Treaty of Berwick, signed on 18th June, disbanded both armies and referred the matter of the prayer book to the Scottish Assembly and Parliament.

It was only a respite; it could not be otherwise. The Assembly abolished the prayer book and the episcopal system in Scotland, and made it obligatory for every Scots subject to sign the Covenant, the document of Presbyterian faith; while the Scottish Parliament confirmed Presbyterian rule and removed the power of the King to elect ministers, officers or army commanders in Scotland. As they laboured to get the harvest in, the men of the north knew that the next spring would bring war in earnest.

'The King has yet other worries,' Kit said one evening when he and Hero were supping at Morland Place. 'After the muster of this spring, he must know that he will have to raise money and arm us properly. We cannot fight the Scots with stones and flail-handles. And to raise money he will have to call Parliament again.'

Mary Esther, who was holding Edward on her lap and overlooking a piece of Hetta's work, glanced from Kit to Edmund. Kit was their source of information from the south, for he still had letters from Richard; and Mary Esther knew that it still hurt Edmund that Richard would not write to him. The source of the information was rarely openly acknowledged, but now on the eve of danger Edmund said,

'Does Richard think there will be opposition from Parliament?'

'He has it from his friend Clovis,' Kit said, 'that the elections will return a separatist Commons of the ilk of Master Pym; and that the Commons will not lose the opportunity to demand the reforms they want in return for a grant of money. All will depend on how much the King is forced to cede.'

'The old religion – ?' Hero said anxiously. Kit shook his head.

'Who can tell? There are those who will doubtless want every show of worship swept away, while others may only want some of the outward trappings removed. In London they fear and hate Popery so much that they that consider any outward show of respect is the short way to Rome. They would have men enter a church with as much awe as a fiddler and his bitch enter a tavern.'

'Aside from religion, what does Parliament demand?' Edmund asked.

'Restoration of old rights and liberties,' Kit said. 'The power to choose the King's ministers, to call out the army and place their own men as officers. The abolition of all courts of privilege –'

'Choose the King's ministers?' Mary Esther interrupted.

'But that has never been their right. That is the King's prerogative!'

Kit smiled bleakly. 'There you have it, Madam. As Richard's friend said, Parliament begins to feel its strength, and is no longer able to distinguish between old privileges and new. It is hard to know what the King can do.'

'I do not like the situation,' Edmund said gravely. 'Men should know their masters.'

'And masters their men,' Kit added. 'I would agree with you Sir, but the new spirit is that every man should seize what he can for himself.'

There was a silence, and the atmosphere was so tense that Dog lifted his head from his paws, looked at his mistress and whined, and then shivered convulsively. Hero, too, was looking at Mary Esther, and at Edward who had fallen asleep with his thumb in his mouth and his curly head against his mother's neck, and her face was thoughtful.

Kit noticed, and broke the silence by saying briskly, 'We must go home soon, but first, shall we have some music? Will you sing for us all, Hero?'

Later they rode home to Watermill in silence, but Kit knew that as soon as they were alone Hero would voice her thoughts, and so he did not trouble her. When they were in bed together and the thick curtains were drawn round, sealing them in in darkness and privacy, Hero put herself into his arms and sighed, and he asked her gently, 'What is it, hinny? The talk of war upset you, I could see.'

He felt her nod in the darkness, assembling her thoughts. At last she said, 'Oh Kit, I am so worried. Everything points to war with the Scots – and then what of my parents? Suddenly they are become the enemy. They will be forced to sign the Covenant and fight against us.'

Kit did not attempt to deny it – no useless comforting for her, for though he longed to protect her, he acknowledged that she was as able and as clearsighted as he was, and he could only offer her the support that one soldier offers another – a shoulder to lean on.

'And then, what of Hamil?' she said, and the quiver of her voice shewed this was the deeper wound. 'I wish I knew where he was. Will he come back and fight?' Kit did not need to hear her say it to know that the rest of her thought was that perhaps he was already dead in some battle in a foreign land. Nothing had been heard from him since he went to be a soldier. But there was more yet, and he waited for it. It came at last in a very low voice, dragged out from the heart of pain.

'And what of you? Oh Kit, what of us? If you have to fight, what if you should be killed?' And she pushed herself against him convulsively, as a foal nudges into its dam's flank, hearing the singing of wolves. He could only offer her her own philosophy.

'Hero, what comes to us, will come. We are all in God's hand.' He folded his arms around her, and her own hands crept up in the darkness and felt for his face, marking out his features, seeing for her in the dark. She turned her face upwards and her lips followed her fingers, brushing lightly over his chin and mouth and cheeks and eyes, and he felt her body grow soft and yielding. His own reaction was instant, and through long habit he tried to arch himself back from her, to control his longing, but her tender mouth crept round to his ear and she whispered, 'Not this time – don't hold back this time.'

Warm passion flooded him, but he said, his voice trembling, 'My hinny bird – what if – you may get with child –'

'Oh my heart's heart, let it be!' she cried. 'I love you, my Kit. Let me bear your child. If I should lose you –' She could not even say it. Still Kit hesitated.

'But the doctor said –'

'The doctor does not know everything. I know. It is time – oh Kit, love me!'

Tears filled his eyes involuntarily. 'I do – I do.' He

turned over, his whole body aching and trembling as he stretched against her, and in the dark their hands met and twined. Love and death are close kin, and in the dark share one soul; their lips were salt with tears, though they met in joy. Long afterwards, it seemed, they rested together in peace, Kit's head on her breast, Hero's fingers stroking his hair, and her lips curved into an unseen smile of accomplishment. Time bore them always on towards the grave, but the spark of life passed between them to make it immortal that once, somewhere in the universe, Hero and Kit had loved.

The events of spring 1640 were confusing and unhappy. Parliament sat, and at once came into direct conflict with the King. Parliament demanded that its requirements over religion and privileges were met before they discussed the matter of money for the war; the King said there could be no discussion until money for the war had been granted. Neither side would budge, and the King dissolved Parliament only weeks after it had been called. He did not, as was traditional, also dissolve Convocation, which continued to sit and not only made the King a grant of money but also passed seventeen canons concerning church observation. The most offensive to the Puritans were those which ordered that all altars should be placed in the east end of the church and railed in; and that obeisance must be made towards the altar on entering and leaving church. To the Puritans this was Popery and tantamount to Devil worship.

In late spring the militia of the southern counties was called out, but many men refused the call. Others mustered, but expended their energies in protests against the new canons. In some places the soldiers attacked churches, threw down altars and burned the hated altar-rails. Meanwhile the King was trying to raise private loans to supplement Convocation's grant, and to persuade the wealthy to make up private armies to supplement the inadequate militia; and all the while Scotland's well-equipped, well-drilled army was gathering on the Border.

So far Edmund had watched passively, though anticipating that the King would eventually come to him, too, for a loan, once he had worked his way through the great families. His own sympathies were divided: though no separatist, he did not entirely agree with some of the high-church ritual, and felt that unless checked Laud and the King would lead them within a stone's throw of Rome. His mother had been half Scottish, and there was in him a streak of Calvinistic reserve over the ostentatiousness of Catholic ritual. In addition, like all men of substance, he disliked being taxed, and the King's demands for money had grown every year. It would be well to know that the Commons, made up of men like him, were to control the King's demands for taxation.

But it was his personal reserve that eventually drove the estate servants to petition Mary Esther instead of him. Edmund was known as a just master, but a cold man; it was easier for the frightened people to approach his wife, whom they all knew and had invited into their homes, who had played with their babies and cured their sicknesses and settled their disputes and scolded them into economy and virtue. Mary Esther took their troubles to Edmund, seeking him out in the steward's room, where he was seated at his desk. He looked up as she came in and said, 'Clement tells me that he heard from one of the men from the Hare and Heather that there is great resistance to the muster in the eastern counties. I think it is time that Richard came home. I am afraid that he may be in danger from the Brownists and Levellers there.'

'He has been away long enough in any case,' Mary Esther agreed. 'If we have war, he should be here.' In case, was the unspoken reason, anything should happen to his father or

151

his brothers. 'And Ambrose too – will you not bring him home?'

'I have been thinking about Ambrose,' Edmund said. 'Times are troubled, and I cannot see an end to the troubles, and we stand to lose a great deal. Land, we need land. If we should lose Tod's Knowe – if the Scots should reach us here – but where is land to be had?'

Mary Esther tried to think with him. 'I don't know, Edmund. Not here at any rate.'

'No, not in this country.'

'In Ireland?' Mary Esther hazarded. He shook his head.

'More troublesome than Scotland, even. No, my thoughts are going further afield. Where is there land to be had for the asking – land in plenty, empty, uninhabited land?' Mary Esther's eyes widened. 'Aye, I see you have it. The New World, Madam. The Americas. Look at this.' He handed her a bill that had been lying on the desk between his hands. She took it and pushed away Dog's enquiring muzzle. 'Clement was given it by the man from the tavern. They are circulating by the hundred, coming up the South Road from London.'

It was a call to men of all degrees to join an expedition to the New World, to settle in Virginia, promising land to all who went. Land! What every man hungered for. Each man was to contribute to the cost of the journey according to his means, and would receive land in accordance with the amount he paid.

'Think how much land could be purchased there!' Edmund cried. He sounded almost delirious at the thought. 'A whole estate – hundreds of acres!'

'You mean – you wish to send Ambrose?' Mary Esther said slowly. Edmund nodded.

'He shall found a Morland Estate in the New World. We shall furnish him with money at first, but in a few years he will be sending back produce enough to repay the invest-

152

ment a hundredfold. He will be able to expand. We will be able to send others from the family to him. A whole new world – a Morland world.'

She had never seen him so excited. All she could say was, 'It is a long way. Ambrose – will be lonely.'

Edmund did not even hear her. He was poring over the bill which she had handed back to him. She drew her anxious mind back to the purpose of her interview.

'Edmund, I must speak to you – the servants and the tenants are all nervous about this news of the altar-rails in St Nicholas' church being torn out and burnt. They have asked me to speak to you, they want you to assure them they will be protected from the Puritans, and not forced to abandon their religion.'

Edmund frowned. 'Protected? From a few necessary reforms? The rabble may perhaps have gone a little too far, but –'

Mary Esther, for once, interrupted him. 'Husband, consider, Morland Place has a responsibility to all those people on this side of York. The chapel is the place where they worship, they look to us for guidance. They are your loyal servants, and you must protect them.'

He frowned. 'Must?' he said ominously. She forced him to meet her eyes.

'You know it, Edmund,' she said quietly. 'If the servant must give loyalty and obedience, the master must give protection and justice.'

The grey eyes looked long and steadily into hers. 'You are right,' he said at last. 'And yet – to fight the Scots is one thing. Pray God it will not come to fighting our own people. If an army of Puritans should come here –'

Mary Esther dismissed the idea briskly. 'It could not come to that. If soldiers come it will only be a few, a rabble, the undisciplined and disorderly, not an army. You may oppose them as wholeheartedly as you would oppose any thief or footpad. Will you speak to the people after Mass tomorrow morning? They will all be assembled, and it will be a convenient time.'

Kit led the Morland men north in early summer. Edmund had not been entirely happy about marshalling and equipping a troop at his own expense for the King, but since Tod's Knowe was in danger he could hardly do less, and Mary Esther was persuasive on the score of loyalty to the King. It was right and fitting that Kit should take command, but leaving was hard for him. As he rode out from Morland Place, all were assembled there to see him go, and the women watched from the upper windows until the scarlet of his cloak and the bright copper of Oberon's coat were quite out of sight. Mary Esther and Mary Eleanor watched with the ordinary feelings of pride and apprehension that could be expected from any woman on such an occasion. But at another window, Ruth, who had come to see off Malachi, who was accompanying them with four men from Shawes, watched him go with deeper, and well-hidden feelings; and at yet another Hero watched long after he had disappeared from sight, her lip caught between her teeth and her hands folded over her swollen belly. In her turmoil of feelings two fears were uppermost: that Kit would be forced to fight against her parents; and that Kit would not come back.

The English army was small, undrilled, and lacking in arms. One or two small private troops, like the Morland men, were properly equipped, but even they lacked experience and leadership. The Scottish army crossed the Tweed unopposed at Coldstream in June, and from then the news that flew back swiftly to Morland Place was all bad. The two armies faced each other at Newburn-on-Tyne, but the English ranks broke after the first fusilade, and the would-be battle became a rout. The army fell back on Newcastle, but could not hold it. The news that Newcastle had fallen reached Morland Place on the night of the 29th August, and shortly afterwards, perhaps brought on by the shock, Hero's labour started.

She had been living at Morland Place since Kit left, so she had the best of attention, but her labour was very hard. A few days later the English army had fallen back on York, which it looked likely to be able to hold, and Kit was able to come home to reassure his wife that he was unhurt. He found his home prepared for a siege, for now that the Scots held all of northern England, they lived in daily terror of an attack; and he found his wife desperately ill, too ill even to know he was there, and in the cradle beside her bed a feeble, wailing boy-child.

It was while he was sitting beside Hero's bed, holding her hand and trying to infuse some of his strength into her that a distant commotion drew Mary Esther, with an apologetic glance, to leave him and go down to investigate.

As she came into the hall she saw Clement hurrying out of the great door and Leah ran across to her.

'It's Master Richard, Madam, come home.' Mary Esther shook her head.

'How like him to choose the most inconvenient time. However he must be met – has someone gone for the Master?'

'The Master's there, Madam – he was crossing the hall when the horses were heard.'

As she went out into the yard, Mary Esther saw Richard just dismounting from his horse. There were five horses in the yard, three of them ridden by three strange servants, two men and a woman. A fourth was mounted sidesaddle by a young woman in a sober cloak and hood. A sudden sinking conviction sent Mary Esther hurrying to Edmund's side to slip her hand under his arm in mute support. He glanced at her, and then looked back in puzzlement at the woman that Richard was lifting down from her horse. The couple approached Edmund and Mary Esther. Richard was looking amazingly well, much grown, much more mature, but his air was both guilty and defiant, like Dog's when he had been stealing eggs.

'Sir,' he said, bowing to Edmund, 'I would like to present to you Katherine Browne – my wife.'

Whether or not it was what Richard had planned, his arrival and his astonishing announcement threw the house into uproar for the rest of the day. Mary Esther found herself wondering at times whether she was asleep and dreaming; Kit was desperately anxious lest the noise woke Hero, who was sleeping what he hoped was a healing sleep. After Edmund's first, terse questions, Father Michael had been sent for, and he, Edmund, Mary Esther, and the young couple had retired to the steward's room for a very uncomfortable interview, whose intention was to discover whether the marriage was legal and whether it could be annulled. Mary Esther would have felt sorry for the young woman, had she not shewn a most immodest self-assurance, and a tendency to preach to her elders.

'Now, Richard,' Edmund said icily as soon as the door was shut, 'tell Father Michael exactly how this – *marriage* – of yours came about. Father Michael, I require you to listen carefully, and tell me if this can be lawful. Madam –' turning a cold eye on Mary Esther, 'have the kindness to send that dog out.' Poor Dog had in his excitement wagged a clutch of papers from the desk, and Mary Esther could only obey. 'Richard, begin.'

'There's nothing much to tell,' he said sulkily. 'We were married before a justice of the peace, in Norwich. That's all.'

'Was there no priest present?' Mary Esther asked, shocked.

'It is the new way,' Katherine said kindly, 'you will perhaps not have come to it yet, up here. But then your ways are shockingly barbarous, so far from civilization. Your talk of *priests*, for example – priests were the creatures

157

who sacrificed live animals on pagan altars. We talk of ministers in the new religion.'

'Be silent,' Edmund said, not loudly, but firmly, and his cold eye was enough to quell even that bold young woman, at least temporarily. Mary Esther studied her and wondered what Richard loved in her. She was not ugly, but was certainly plain, with a sharp, freckled face and slightly protruding teeth, and her clothes did nothing to enhance her appearance. Divested of her cloak, she was seen to be wearing a dark brown woollen dress with a broad starched white collar and cuffs, devoid of any decoration, and covering her from chin to wrist and ankle. Her hair was completely concealed under a stiff linen coif which did nothing to soften the bony harshness of her features or the downrightness of her expression. Mary Esther became acutely aware of the soft bunches of curls that brushed her own naked neck and shoulders and of the lace that fell over her bare forearms, and felt suddenly and strangely wanton by comparison. That the young woman thought her so was evident from the severe, disapproving glance she had given Mary Esther on entering.

'This young woman's father, I presume, is Master Browne the clothier with whom you have been staying,' Edmund went on. Richard nodded assent. 'I had thought him a respectable man. How came he to allow his daughter's marriage without my consent?' Richard reddened.

'Master Browne thought I had your consent. He wrote to you on the subject, but –' he hesitated, and was unable to continue under his father's penetrating gaze. Katherine took up the story for him.

'We intercepted the letter,' she said calmly, 'and after a suitable period Richard wrote one purporting to come from you and had it delivered to my father, saying that you consented to the match but would not attend the ceremony.'

The unabashed admission took everyone's speech from

them for a moment. Even when Edmund could speak, he could only say in a tone of amazement, 'You presented your father with a forgery?'

'It was necessary,' Katherine said indifferently. 'I knew that Richard and I had to wed, just as I knew we had to come here to save you all. It is our mission, from God. When we were wed, Richard wanted us to take ship for the New World, where truth prevails and the Whore of Babylon holds no sway, but God spoke to me in a dream and I told him we must come back here, as your letter bid. Richard always heeds my dreams, and when I told him you were all in danger –'

'In danger?' Edmund managed to say.

'Your immortal souls, Sir, are in grave danger from Popery and prelacy and false gospels. We have come to free you from the chains of recusancy, ritual, and idolatry.'

'Be silent!' This time Edmund roared it. 'Have you no shame, girl, to speak so in the presence of your elders and betters, and in the presence of a priest of Holy Church? Father Michael, does not this forgery make their marriage unlawful? May it not be set aside?'

'Allow me to question the boy, Edmund,' Father Michael said. 'Richard, can you remember the words of the – service?'

Richard repeated the simple form of declaration each had made before the justice.

'And were there witnesses present?' the chaplain went on.

'Oh yes,' Richard said. 'Any number – all the servants, as well as the family, and some friends of my fa – of Master Browne's.'

'The girl's father consented, then?'

'Of course. He was well pleased and thought it a good match. He was not so pleased when we said we were coming here, but Katherine told him of her dream and so of course he said we must go.'

Father Michael shook his head and said to Edmund, 'I'm afraid it seems unlikely that we could get an annulment. The girl's father consented, and Richard is of age and therefore does not need your consent.'

'What if the girl's father is told of the forgery? He will then surely withdraw his consent.'

Before Michael Moyes could answer, Katherine said, 'Oh no, even if you told him he would still think it a good match.'

Edmund stared from one face to another, and his frustration shewed in his struggle to remain calm. At last he said tersely, 'Get you gone, all but Master Michael. And Madam, see that those children are kept quiet. I will speak to you later, Richard.'

The other three walked out into the staircase hall where the younger children, Anne, Hetta, Ralph and Edward, were playing on the stairs with Dog and making a cheerful noise because of their unexpected release from the chaplain's tyranny. As soon as Mary Esther appeared they came running down to meet her, and in his haste small Edward tripped and fell and set up a bellowing that his mother hastened to smother for fear of enraging Edmund still more.

'Hush there, hush my bairn! There, now, it is all better. Children, please do stop making such a noise – Papa will be angry.' She hurried them through into the great hall, carrying Edward on her hip, and Anne said loudly, 'But we want to see Richard's new wife. Is it true she's a monster, as Beatrice says?'

'Hush, Anne, for shame! This is she,' Mary Esther said distractedly, though Katherine did not seem put out, but was looking round her with appraisal and disapproval in equal proportions. Anne was not abashed either.

'It's not, then!'

'It is, I told you so,' Hetta whispered, but Anne continued to stare.

'Then why is she dressed like a servant?' she asked, and her whisper was no less audible than her full voice.

'That's how Puritans dress,' Hetta said.

Anne's next remark was forestalled by Richard, who using his wits, had worked out who Ralph must be, and now stepped forward and said, 'Ralph, my son, how you have grown. Come forward and receive a father's blessing, and be presented to your new mother.'

Ralph stared in horror at the words, and, reddening with embarrassment, remained rooted to the spot.

'Come here, child,' Richard insisted, 'you have forgotten me, I see. Have they never spoken of me to you?' And he flicked an angry look at his stepmother.

'Of course we have spoken of you, Richard,' Mary Esther said, trying to sound natural. 'The child is shy, that's all. He was no more than a bairn when you went away. Kneel to your father, Ralph, for his blessing.'

Whatever Richard had done, and whatever the situation with regard to Katherine, he was Ralph's father, and it was right for Ralph to ask his blessing. So urged, Ralph went unwillingly forward and knelt before Richard, but his eye swivelled back appealingly to Mary Esther. She had brought him up, and as far as he regarded anyone as his mother, it was she, and when Richard bid him again to greet his 'new mother' he burst into tears, and Mary Esther, to avoid further strife, bid them all run out into the garden.

'I can see it is not before time that I returned,' Richard said, frowning at Mary Esther. 'Now I must go and see Kit – where is he? Katherine, you must meet my brother.'

'I feel I know him already from his letters,' she said.

'Kit is above, in the west bedroom with Hero. But she is ill – Richard, go softly and do not disturb her.' Mary Esther watched the ill-assorted pair climb the stairs, and then, with Dog at her heels and Edward in her arms walked

161

out of doors to try to clear her head and settle her spirits in the peace of the gardens.

It was not the end of the uproar. Firstly Jacob refused to cook dinner for anyone, and even when threatened with dismissal he would not relent, nor allow anyone else to use his kitchen for the purpose. He had never liked Richard, and was outraged that he had brought a Puritan into the house and claimed, what was more, to have married her by some damned heathenish ceremony, upsetting the master and bringing shame on the house. Kit begged, Mary Esther begged, but he was not moved. In the end, though thinking it rather shameful, Mary Esther persuaded Hetta to go and talk to him, and after a long siege the old man finally gave in to her wheedling.

Then when everything seemed to be settling down again, a group of servants headed by Clement himself demanded audience with the mistress, since the master was still closeted with the chaplain. Leah brought them to Mary Esther in the Long Saloon, and a glance at Leah's face told Mary Esther that her waiting-woman was in agreement with whatever the complaint was to be.

'Not you too, Leah? Clement, what *is* the matter? Surely it is something you can handle yourself?'

'I wish I could, Madam,' Clement said resentfully, 'but it's those servants the young master has brought with him. Are they to stay, Madam? What is their position in the house?'

Mary Esther was surprised and annoyed at being questioned. 'You will be told in due course, Clement. What gives you the right to hector me in this way?'

'I'm sorry Madam, but we all feel – they have asked me to speak on their behalf, all the servants – those three Brownists – those damned heretics –'

Clement, perhaps for the first time in his life, was at a loss for words, speechless with rage, and Leah took over for him.

'The new servants, Madam, they're Puritans, terrible heretics, Madam, and we don't want them in the same house with us.'

'Why Leah, I'm surprised at you,' Mary Esther said. '*You don't want?* What sort of language is that?'

Leah was unrepentant. 'It isn't lucky, Madam,' she said stubbornly. 'Happen you haven't seen them yet, but the things they're saying, Madam – we couldn't make it out, like, at first, they speak so strange, but when we could – blasphemies, Madam, falling from their lips like poison from a snake!' The others murmured an agreement. 'And then they wandered into the chapel, Madam, and – Lord, what they were saying! And one of them, Madam, he – he *spat*! On the chapel floor!'

The others nodded, wide-eyed with shock, and some of the older ones crossed themselves or made the sign against evil. Mary Esther sighed.

'Very well, Leah, I shall speak to them and make sure nothing like that happens again. But until the master says what's to be done with them, they will have to stay, and you must make the best of it. Keep from them if you cannot tolerate their company, and do not listen to them if their speech offends you. I rely on you all for the peaceful running of the house. The master has enough trouble at the moment – we must not add to it.'

In discontented silence they left, but it was not long before Mary Esther was disturbed again, this time by Hetta, who ran in, her normally cheerful face red with anger and wet with tears.

'Mama! Mama!' she cried, and buried her face in her mother's dress.

'Now, chuck, what is it? You are too old for such a passion. Tell me what's wrong?' Mary Esther soothed her, but her heart misgave. Hetta was such a cheery, even-tempered, sunny little soul that it must be something bad to have upset her so.

'My garden – they've trampled my garden!' she wailed brokenheartedly. Mary Esther was appalled, and understood at once what must have happened. Hetta's garden was the pride of her life. Edmund had granted her a little piece of land in the sunny corner of the Italian Garden and with the help of Abel the gardener, she had laboured over it lovingly for years, shewing a tenacity of purpose and a patience unusual in such a young child. She had planted it mostly with red and yellow flowers, warm colours, the colour of life and of the sun; but Hetta was also a deeply religious child in her own quiet way, and at the back of the garden she had built a small grotto with stones and shells, planted it with ferns and the little flowers that liked rocks and fissures, and Ben, the carpenter, had carved her a little wooden statue of The Lady to stand in it.

It had all come about quite naturally out of the characters of the people involved, but many of the servants were superstitious about Hetta's grotto. She was so beloved of them, and they admired her piety so much, that they had endowed the place in their own minds with great power, and it was a rare day when someone did not pause to lay an offering of flowers there, or say a prayer, or touch the stones for luck. It was the kind of thing that was anathema to Puritans – superstition, idolatory, Popery. One of Richard's strange servants had evidently interrupted something at the grotto, and had taken his revenge in the cruellest way. Mary Esther's heart burned with anger as she soothed her daughter's sobbing.

'We'll go and speak to Papa about it,' she said, taking Hetta's hand and leading her towards the door. Nothing less than the child's tears would have made her disturb her husband that day.

*

It was all settled. The master had given his edicts, and the household must abide by them. The marriage between the young master and the Puritan woman was deemed valid; they were to have the East bedroom and to be treated with respect, though it was doubtful if anything would stop the servants referring to her as 'the foreigner' everywhere but in the master's presence. Mary Esther was more surprised over Edmund's leniency about the servants. Richard's three servants – or rather Katherine's, for they came from her father's household – struck a most discorndant note at Morland Place. They were all, as was every Browne servant, tried and tested Puritans, as could be told, if nothing else, from their names. Their accents were so strong that it was at first hard to understand what their names were, and when it was understood, the Yorkshire servants curled their lips in disdain. The footman Wrastle, short for Wrastle-with-the-Devil, and the waiting woman Fear, short for Fear-of-the-Lord, were bad enough, but when it was known that the other footman's name, If, was short for If-Christ-had-not-died-thou-hadst-been-damned, the Morland Place servants' scorn knew no bounds.

Yet the master said they were to stay, though on condition of their good behaviour, to serve the young master and the foreigner; and more surprising still, they were to be allowed to worship their own way, provided it was done privately, and were not to be forced to go to Mass. Edmund never discussed his decisions and no-one would have dreamed of asking him why he was being so lenient, not even his wife; but when Mary Esther caught him once or twice looking wistfully at his eldest son when he thought no-one noticed, she guessed that he was still hoping to win Richard's trust and love.

Edmund was lonely, lonely for the love of his sons. Kit had gone back to Watermill now with Hero and the sickly child; Francis was in Tod's Knowe; and Ambrose was soon to be wed to Mary Eleanor and sent off to the New World, perhaps never to return. There was only Richard, and with war at their doorstep with the Scots and trouble brewing in the south, Edmund had felt at last the cold wind of time passing him by. Death was close to them all: he had no time to waste in courting his son's love.

So Richard and Katherine stayed, and the three alien servants stayed, and the household must put up with it. But nothing could stop the truculent Yorkshire servants from speaking their minds as often as they felt like it, nor stop the older ones crossing themselves whenever Fear or Wrastle or If passed them; and there was also an upsurge in piety, even in those servants who had had previously to be hauled out of bed for early Mass; and if any of the Puritans stepped out of doors, it would always somehow come about that a member of the outdoor staff would have some urgent and time-consuming duty to perform in the close vicinity of Hetta's garden.

The north was ashamed. The Scots occupied their lands, and there was nothing any of them could do about it, and moreover the King had been forced in October to sign the Treaty of Ripon by which the Scots were to be paid £850 a day occupation expenses until their dispute with England was settled. To pay the enemy to sit on their doorsteps! Never had the King and his ministers been so unpopular. Parliament had to be called to settle matters, and when it met in November it knew its power. This time there would be no helping the King until its demands were met.

The north had to endure the Scottish occupation for a year – it was not until August 1641 that the armies were paid off and dispersed, and by that time the country was beginning to dislike the present Parliament as much as it had disliked the King before. It had done some good things – it had rid them of the King's unpopular ministers, Strafford and Windebank and Archbishop Laud; and abolished the Star Chamber and other courts of precedent; but it had also done away with the Council of the North, and the northerners had never liked the idea of being ruled from distant London. It had abolished some of the King's more unpopular methods of raising money, such as ship-money and enforced knighthoods and forestry fines, and had decreed that other forms of taxation, such as tunnage and poundage, could henceforth only be used with Parliament's permission; but it had also raised a heavy tax in order to pay off the Scots, and those on whom the tax fell most heavily were convinced that the Scots and Parliament had been in league together in order to line their pockets.

Worst of all, when Parliament turned its attention to the reform of religion, it went very much further than most men wanted it to go. It was all very well to free them from the secular tyranny of Bishops and church courts; and some folk hadn't liked the slant towards Rome that Archbishop Laud seemed to be giving them; but Parliament was going to the other extreme, and trying to abolish all forms of religious service altogether, as well as doing away with pleasant things like singing in church and playing games on the Sabbath, and extremist sects were arising everywhere and preaching against the good old religion. People began to feel that at least the Lord King had protected their own English church, and let them alone to do as they pleased. They had had enough of this Parliament.

Then came the shocking news of the massacre in Ireland. Irish Papists had risen up and slaughtered English Protestants in cold blood. The news flew around the country, handbills following hot upon each other adding more detail, describing new atrocity after new atrocity. Thousands had been butchered, many thousands more left to die of their wounds. Children had been ravished, babies burnt alive before their mothers' eyes, old people tortured to death – no horror was bad enough to be disbelieved. An Irish army was gathering across the sea to invade England and perpetrate the same horrors and lead the country back to Rome. It was all a plot instigated by the Queen, that well known Papist and Frenchwoman!

Parliament's power returned. An army must be raised to subdue the Irish, but before Parliament would grant a tax to raise the army, it demanded the power to appoint its officers. The King refused indignantly. Parliament planned to impeach the Queen over her responsibility for the Irish Massacre, and the King, to protect her, attempted to arrest Master Pym and four other leading members of the lower house and impeach *them*. Parliament would not give them up, and in January 1642 the King defied all tradition and marched into the lower house with an armed guard to arrest the five men by force.

London, already in a state of hysteria over the Irish massacre and the supposed Papist plot, erupted into arms, and the City militia, the best trained and armed in the country, marched out to defend Parliament and Protestantism. The situation was so dangerous that the King hastened out of London, and sent the Queen to Holland for safety while he himself began to travel northwards, for the greater the distance from London and the influence of the new religions, the safer he felt himself to be.

By March the King was in York, settled at the King's Manor, old home of the Council of the North, and the bewildered people of the north, having so recently been at war with the Scots, found themselves facing talk of war with the south. The peace of fifty years seemed to have crumbled almost overnight and at a touch, and no-one was really sure how it had come about.

The solar at Shawes was pleasant in summer, for its stone walls and floor kept it cool, and its windows overlooked the old rose garden, so that in June the air that came in through them was so scented you could almost have filled a vial with it. Ruth sat in the windowseat sewing in the company of Ellen. Time had reconciled her even to that hated occupation, which was as well since she had a great deal of it to do. She had been happy since she came back to Shawes. As mistress of the house she had authority and freedom, and with her household duties, and overseeing the estate, and hunting and hawking, she was never lacking something to occupy her. Running the estate was really Malachi's job, but though quiet and dependable, he was not by nature inventive or quick thinking. Nature had fitted him to be an able lieutenant, provided he received the right guidance.

Ruth had watched his growing friendship with wry amusement: of all the people Malachi could have chosen to hero-worship, it had to be Kit! she thought. But time had eased even that ache. She heard the news of Hero's pregnancy with little more than a calm concern for her cousin's health, and now, though she would still prefer not to see Hero and Kit together, she could honestly wish them well. Her heart was quiet: she thought it was dead, and was glad to think she would be saved any anguish in the future. She could love her nephew safely, for he could never hurt her, except by getting himself killed in battle following after Kit. But then no-one seriously believed it would come to war. Parliament had called out the militia on its own authority, but Mal told her Kit said it was only a show of strength, to try to force the King to accede to their demands. They could never actually come to battle – it would solve nothing, for if they fought until the world's end the King would still be king, and all his posterity after him, and they would be traitors and like to hang for it.

'Madam –' Ellen said quietly, drawing Ruth's attention from her work and her musings to the sound of hooves outside. The two women listened.

'Three,' Ruth said after a moment. 'Two gentlemen's horses and a mule. Who could my nephew have with him? I will go down.' She put down her work eagerly and ran down to the great door where Parry, Ellen's husband who had been raised from bailey to steward, was already greeting the visitors. Ruth's heart jumped when she saw that the second horse in the yard was Oberon. Kit looked grave, Malachi both excited and upset, and they came towards her followed by the rider of the mule, a little, stocky, salt-weathered man who, by his gait, was evidently a sailor and had not enjoyed his long journey on muleback.

'Ruth – !' Malachi cried, but was too tongue-tied by his emotions to go on. Kit took over.

'It is news,' he said. 'This man brings news – of your brothers. Shall we go inside, cos?'

'Bad news, then,' Ruth said calmly. She looked at the sailor, and saw his fatigue. 'Parry, bring wine and food for this man. We shall be in the solar.' She could not, as she led the way indoors, miss Kit's glance of admiration at her self-possession and quick thinking, but she tried not to let it affect her. He was too attractive, his dark lean face beginning to be marked now with lines of authority. Kit was a boy no longer, but if he smiled less often, his smiles were by that much the more dazzling. She forced herself to speak.

'How is Hero, and the bairn?' she asked him.

'They do as well as can be expected. Hero should never have had the child, but she is recovering slowly, and the bairn – they are all sanguine that it will live, the women-folk, though I hold my breath when I see it, it is so little and shrunken.'

They came into the solar, and Ruth directed the sailor to a stool, and seated herself on the windowseat again. Parry came in with the food and wine, and the sailor drank a deep draught and then checked himself as he was about to savage a hunk of bread, and Ruth divined his trouble.

'I would not keep you from what you so evidently need. If you can eat and talk, do so. If not, I can wait until you have eaten.'

'No, Mistress, I can do both,' he said, and sank his teeth gratefully into the dark rye bread.

'You have news of my brothers?' Ruth said. He nodded, his eyes eloquent. 'They are dead?' she said quietly. 'Both?' He nodded again, and she let out her breath in a long sigh. It was a long time since she had expected to see either of them again, and yet the knowledge of death was so final, she had not been prepared for it. 'Mal, I am sorry,' she said. Malachi met her eyes.

'I hardly remember my father,' he said, and his voice was shaky, 'but still it is a shock. When I heard at first, I cried. I still cannot quite take it in.'

'How do you come by this news, Sir?' Ruth asked the sailor.

'I was with them at the end, Mistress, and can tell you how it was. We were off the coast of Sicily, four sail of us, all English – your brothers' ships, *Mary Fortune* and *Little Hare*, and my ship, the *Endeavour*, and a pinnace. Then a storm comes up – you get some terrible gales, come summer turns to autumn –'

'Autumn?' Ruth asked.

'This was last autumn, Mistress, September time, around the equinox. I disremember as to the exact date. Well, this was a storm such as I have never seen the like of. The pinnace, she went down to leeward so fast that she was on the rocks before we could blink, and we never see her more. Not that we had time to look – we were clawing our way up to windward, trying to get some searoom, for the rocks and little islands there about, Miss, would take the bottom out of you before you knew it.'

He paused apologetically to take some more wine and another mouthful of food, and went on, his grizzled beard wagging as he chewed and spoke together.

'Well, Miss, Cap'n send us up aloft to goosewing the mains'l, for to try and get a bit of way on, but I hadn't but got my hand to the line when a gust came, and my foot

171

slipped off the foot-rope and over I went. Well, I thought I was done for, but I hadn't been in the water more than five minutes when I was washed right down onto the *Mary Fortune*, and someone gets a line down to me, and somehow or other they got me aboard.'

'And you saw my brother then?' The man nodded.

'A gentleman, Miss, a true gentleman, He took off his own cloak and put it round me, and ordered them to give me wine. Well, Miss, to cut a long story short, we beat about in that storm for three days, and when dawn came on the fourth day we found ourselves off a rocky shore, and the first thing we see is the *Little Hare* down to lee of us, her spars gone and leaping onto the rocks like a horse.' He paused out of a natural instinct for dramatic effect, and saw his audience's wide eyes and wrapt attention. He went on, his voice quiet but tense. 'Cap'n Zeph gives a great cry, like the rocks were tearing his own heart, and he orders the wheel over, and we flies down towards her. It warn't no use – we heard her strike, and then we struck too, on a sandbar. We was thrown all aback, the spars snapped, and she went down.

'The sea was boiling like a cauldron, but some of us got ashore, Lord knows how. Cap'n Zeph was one of them, and the first thing he did was to make his way up the shore to where the *Little Hare* struck. I went with him – didn't seem much else to do. Half a dozen of 'em had come ashore, and amongst 'em Cap'n Zech, but –' He shook his head sadly. 'He died in Cap'n Zeph's arms within the hour. The rest of us – well, the natives in those parts were decent folk, and they took us in. I stuck with the Cap'n. He took the fever – all of us did. I was mortal sick, Miss, and when I recovered my hair had gone grey, same as you see it now. But I could hear Cap'n Zeph raving in his fever, talking about his brother. He died the third day. It's my belief he didn't want to live, knowing his brother was dead.'

There was a silence as his words ended, and after a

moment he continued, apologetically, to eat. At last Ruth roused herself to say,

'It is good of you to bring us the news.'

'Why, Miss, I couldn't do less, the Cap'n having saved my life, though I know those that bring bad news are not welcome.'

'We do not blame you for the news,' Malachi said, prompted by a glance from Ruth, 'and we shall shew ourselves grateful. There will be gold for you, and a place here if you want it.'

The sailor wiped his mouth on his wrist. 'Well, Sir, I do thank you for that, but if it's all the same to you I think I'll make my way to Hull-port and find myself a ship. I've been at sea since I was ten year old, and it's all I know.'

Later, when Parry had taken the man away to shew him quarters for the night, Ruth said to Malachi, 'Well, Mal, you are master in truth now.'

'And Warden of Rufford,' Kit reminded them. 'I will take the news to the rest of the family – I know you will not wish to talk of it yourselves, and my father should be told. You will have to think about marrying now, Mal, I suppose.'

'And my uncle will no doubt want me to marry one of his daughters,' Malachi said with a rueful smile.

'You could do worse,' Kit said. 'My sisters are good girls. Once this trouble with Parliament is settled, and we have time to think –'

'But you do not think it will come to war?' Ruth said. Kit shook his head.

'And yet, if it did,' he said, and looked hard at her, trying to meet her eye, 'Mal and I would have to go and fight, and I would want to ask you, cousin Ruth, to look after Hero and the bairn for me. You are so strong and capable, and she is so frail. I would need to know that you would take care of her.'

Ruth met him with a level gaze, her face flat and express-

173

ionless. Hero, she believed, was as strong as an oak, despite her frail appearance. But, whether or not he knew what he was asking, he insisted.

'Would you take care of them? For me, cos?'

'I would not see harm come to them,' she said at last, with a sigh, and he was content.

'But it will not come to war,' Kit said again. 'The King will be reasonable, and Parliament will stand down. All will be settled by Christmas.'

CHAPTER TEN

The young man who picked his way along the docks at the Hague could be seen by anyone to be a soldier of fortune, even if it had not been for the pack on his back. His hard, lean body, his jaunty walk, his alert look, his weather-beaten, keen, lined face all proclaimed his trade, as did his hard-worn clothes. The casual observer would have noted his long leather boots, his clean-shaven face, and his curly-brimmed, feather hat, and would have guessed him to be a soldier of horse rather than foot, and the guess would have been confirmed for him had he seen the man stripped, by the long seams of healed wounds on his forearms and thighs.

Hamil had come to the Hague because the Dutch court was there and it was around the court that the professional soldier was most likely to pick up employment. Hamil needed a job. He had not done badly out of his last campaign, but he had drunk and caroused his plunder away, and then his horse had died under him, and he had been walking for a week to get here, and that was a week too long on his own two feet. As soon as he arrived in town he headed for the docks, for it was there that the cheapest lodgings and food were to be found, and it was there that luck found him. He came across the tail end of a crowd, and began, with the lithe ease of a small, compact man, to ease his way forward to see what was going on.

The centre of the crowd, and the instigator of the inci-dent, was easily seen and easily recognized – a tall young man, well over six feet, with a magnificent physique, elegant clothes, long waving dark hair, and the kind of lean, dark, saturnine good looks that struck even the boldest women dumb with admiration. He was in a furious temper, and was gesticulating and shouting in a mixture of at least three languages. The crowd around Hamil was enjoying the scene, and adding its own comments, but Hamil's Dutch was not of the best, so he tried asking his nearest companion in French what the commotion was about.

The man shrugged, not understanding him, but at the sound of Hamil's voice another man further forward in the crowd turned to look, and at once pushed his way to him, exclaiming in delight, 'Hamil Hamilton! Why, you old fox, what are you doing here?'

'Daniel O'Niel, by all that's holy!' Hamil cried, and in a moment they were embracing, hard and affectionately. O'Neil was a short, stout, gingery, balding, swaggering, foul-mouthed adventurer, who was also a professional soldier and a genius at warfare.

'Holy God,' he said, standing back to look at Hamil, clapping him by the shoulders so hard that it brought involuntary tears to Hamil's eyes, 'but if you haven't been sent a-purpose then I'll never take the Mass again, turn Protestant and sign the Covenant! Come on, come on and I'll take you to the Prince, for he's sore in need of comfort this minute, I'll tell you.' And O'Neil without further ceremony began dragging Hamil through the crowd to where the irate figure of Prince Rupert of the Rhine, King Charles' nephew, was still drawing all eyes.

'But what has happened?' Hamil asked. 'Why is he so angry?'

'Ah,' said O'Neil, 'wasn't he sorely provoked by that devil of a ship-captain that's as crooked as a pig's hind leg? Captain Fox, I'm meaning – we were all aboard the *Lyon* and bound for England for to fight for the King, when up comes a storm, and the captain he says it's all ashore we must go, and he'd pick us up again when the storm bated. But this day comes the word that this same captain has dropped off all our baggage and run for it, like the hell-bent son of a Flanders whore he is, and the Prince paying him in advance for our passage and all!'

'To England? To fight for the King? Why, what's happening, Daniel?'

'God bless us, haven't you heard?' O'Neil actually stopped still to stare at Hamil. 'Hasn't the Parliament called up the army and declared against the King, and he up in Yorkshire trying to raise an army to put them down. But come on, and the Prince'll tell you all –'

In a moment they had broken through into the circle around the Prince, and he had turned, looked enquiringly, and halted in mid-trilingual flow, and his dark angry face had lit in a smile of welcome that would melt one's bones.

'Hamilton! Well met, my friend!' he cried.

'Highness,' Hamil said, dropping to his knee and pressing his lips fervently to the outstretched hand.

'No, no, rise up, my friend, rise up. Why, man, where has fortune taken you this long while? We haven't met since –'

'Breda, Highness, the siege of Breda. We charged together, the time –'

'Jesu, yes, that charge! O'Neil, you were there –'

'Aye, was I! And didn't his highness of Orange put himself in a terrible taking over you risking your royal person, after him forbidding you with his own tongue to go!'

Rupert sighed. 'Ah, but it was a famous charge!'

'I heard that your Highness had been imprisoned since then, and was right sorry for it,' Hamil said.

'Three years,' Rupert said, his face darkening for a moment, before he added, 'but I put them to good use, reading and studying. And I was not all alone, I had Boye to cheer me – did I have my white poodle when I last saw you?'

177

'No, Highness.'

'– And Seline, my pet hare, and –'

'And sundry divers maidens, fear you not Hamil,' O'Neil added sagely. 'The Prince will outstrip you yet, my young stoat, though you'll need a score of years to the both of you to catch me up.'

Rupert wisely ignored this. 'But, Hamilton, you have come at the right time. There is a venture afoot, a grave and glorious task before us. You have heard of the trouble in England?'

'I had not, Sir, until Daniel mentioned it just now.'

'Treasonable stirrings, and my uncle the King in grave need of loyal and experienced soldiers. My aunt the Queen has sold her jewels to buy arms, and we were to take them across until we were cheated by that devil-spawn of a captain –'

'So Daniel was saying, Sir. But there are other ships in the world. Perhaps the Prince of Orange – of his great friendship to you –'

'Aye, he will give us a ship, surely, and we will gather together our good friends and go with all speed. Come, now, Hamilton, are you with us?'

Hamil knelt again, taking the long strong hand and bending his head to it. 'Highness, with all my heart. I came here looking for employment; I hardly expected such a cause to present itself. But if you will have me, I am your man, heart and body.'

Rupert stood looking down at him, his great dark eyes shining. Loyalty was the closest thing to his own heart, and he knew how to value it.

'God bless you,' he said. 'I knew you would.'

'He's the cut of man we want, Sir,' O'Neil said. 'Hard men we can trust, cavalry men, gentlemen.'

'Gentlemen?' Hamil queried, straight-faced. 'Ah, but we need you too, Daniel.' And Daniel cuffed him on the side of the head with a hand the size and weight of a bear's paw.

'Have you a horse?' Rupert asked Hamil.

'No Sir – my good sorrell dropped dead under me this week since.'

'Well, we'll get you one. I know you Englishmen, particularly from the north, ride like Centaurs. Give me a regiment of such men, and I'll conquer any country you care to name.' He looked around the group nearest him, and saw his own elation mirrored in every face. A good campaign in the company of one's friends, that was the life for a man! With Rupert to think was to act. 'Let us to the palace! We'll be in England in two weeks!'

England, Hamil thought. Home! He had not set foot on his native soil for almost ten years; he had not had word of, nor sent word to, his sister in all that time. She came before his mind's eye, clear and unsullied as new-minted gold, though common sense told him she must have changed in that time. What changes would he find at home, if he dared to go there? The pain that he fought down in his heart was half longing and half apprehension.

A month later they landed at Scarborough in a Dutch ship of forty-six guns, accompanied by another, a small galliot, into which were packed the arms and supplies the English Queen had sold her jewels for. They landed after dark, but as soon as the horses were swayed off, Rupert, unable to bear any more delay, decided to ride straight for Nottingham where the King was last reported to have been, taking with him his close companions and leaving the rest, and the baggage, to come on at their own speed.

With him went his younger brother, Prince Maurice, O'Neil and Hamil and one or two others, and the white poodle Boye riding the front of Rupert's saddle with a fold of the scarlet cloak around him. Their impetuous ride took them within a mile of Morland land, but Hamil said nothing, and kept his eyes fixed firmly ahead between his horse's ears. His thoughts were not so well under control, but he managed to concentrate them mainly with longing on the fiery sure-footed Morland-bred horses, like Oberon and Psyche and Queen Mab. A horse like that would be a fine horse to ride into battle. The first thing he would do, he decided, when they reached a base, was to buy an English horse, and persuade the Prince to do likewise.

They reached Nottingham on the night of the twentieth of August, only to find that the King was at Leicester, so they took a night's sleep and set out the next day, meeting with the King and his entourage on their way back to Nottingham. It was the first time Hamil had seen King Charles, and he was both surprised and impressed: surprised that the King was such a small man, and impressed that despite his stature he was so impressive. It was not so much that he was short, but made smaller, like a different species, delicate like porcelain. It was a moving sight to see the great, strong, godlike figure of Prince Rupert kneel to him, to kiss the small slender hand and lay his service at his feet. The King's eyes filled with tears as he embraced his nephew – large dark eyes, they were, Stuart eyes, the only point of similarity in the two men. When Hamil, in his turn, was presented to the King, the King greeted him briefly but kindly, and Hamil was contented.

They rode back into Nottingham where the King was to raise his standard on the following day, the 22nd, and Rupert was to meet with the eight-hundred-strong cavalry that had already gathered, and which he was to command.

'They are volunteers all,' O'Neil reported to Hamil as they rode into Nottingham Castle. 'Gentlemen and their tenants and servants, and a goodly number of them from the north, which will please our Prince, for isn't it these same northerners he sets such store by?'

Hamil heard and agreed vaguely, but his mind and heart were sleeping, for it did not occur to him that there might be anyone from his own family, or even from his own neighbourhood, amongst the volunteers. The Princes supped with the King that night, but later came back to their own men to report on the state of the recruits gathered so far. Rupert was particularly pleased with what he had heard of his own command.

'Untrained men,' he told his friends, 'but well mounted and fine riders – they could ride a pack of wolves through a forest fire, I firmly believe. We shall make a fine cavalry of them. And you, Hamil, my friend, how should you like to be a captain of horse? Shall I give you a troop of your own Yorkshiremen to command?'

Hamil's eyes shone as he stammered his gratitude, but still his senses slept. It was not until the next day when the foot and horse were drawn up before the castle for the raising of the standard that Hamil, riding out behind the royal party, found his eyes drawn irrisistibly to one group amongst the assembled horsemen. The gleam of a bright chestnut coat and the magnificent curve of a stallion's neck attracted his attention; he saw a band of well mounted men, he saw their russet cloaks and the black-and-white Morland arms; he saw the stallion fret and his rider check him. It was Oberon, of course: and as Hamil's eyes met Kit's, his lips curved in a bitter, ironic smile.

After the dismissal, Hamil waited, knowing Kit would seek him out. Kit rode up to him, his smile wavering uncertainly as Hamil, stony-faced, ignored his outstretched hand.

'Hamil – I hardly recognized you, you have been so long away. But well met, cousin. I see you are with Prince Palgrave – how came you here? You see, I have brought a good band of Morland men. Malachi is here too – he will be pleased to see you.'

'How is my sister?' Hamil asked when Kit's kindly greeting stopped for want of encouragement.

'She is well,' Kit said, hesitating before adding, 'there is a bairn now – a boy.'

Hamil's lip curled. 'And you have left her alone with a bairn? Do you not consider it a husband's part, then, to protect his wife?'

Kit's brows contracted at that, but he answered calmly enough, 'That is what I am doing here. I come to fight to protect my wife and my child and my home and my family. You have been long away –'

'Aye, long enough for you to see to it that I am forgotten, I doubt not.'

'You are not forgotten. Hero mentions you in every prayer, morning and evening. It was your own choice that you went, none of hers – or mine,' Kit said, trying to remain steady.

'And now I am come back, and Prince Rupert has offered me command of a troop of Yorkshire horse. But no doubt you will want to go home again, now you know I am to be your commander?'

'I have no quarrel with you,' Kit said quietly. 'I am come to fight for my King, as no doubt you are, and what he commands for me I am content with. Is not the cause we both fight for more important than your own feelings? I would have thought ten years' soldiering would have taught you that at least.'

Hamil stared at him. When he was unsmiling, there was something about Kit that reminded Hamil of Prince Rupert; but Hamil did not want to recognize such a likeness.

'You will accept me as your commander?' he said abruptly.

'If it is so ordered – of course,' Kit said.

'It is so ordered,' Hamil said. He put his heels to his horse's flank so sharply that the animal jumped, and Oberon bared his teeth at the movement and snapped sideways at him. 'You still have Oberon, I see,' Hamil said as he turned away. Kit thought it worth one more effort to reach his brother-in-law.

'Malachi has Firefly,' he said. 'I'm sure he would give him to you, if you wanted. We have spare horses with us.'

Hamil merely nodded, and rode away. Inwardly he burned – the very thing he had been wanting, a Morland horse – but to be received at those hands, the hands that had stolen Hero from him: it was a dark irony.

October found the royal army on the march for London. They had moved westwards during August and September to Shrewsbury where the recruiting ground was better, and the Parliamentary army under Lord Essex had followed, leaving its strong position in Northampton and setting up base in Worcester. Prince Rupert had spent the time hammering his cavalry into shape and teaching it the new art of mounted warfare, the cavalry charge. In this he was much aided by those professional soldiers, like Hamil, who had fought with him in Europe where modern methods of warfare were better understood.

Hamil's troop was fast becoming the flower of Rupert's regiment, having at its heart the twenty-five Morland men, well-mounted, excellent horsemen, loyal and obedient, led by Kit and Malachi who could command both respect and trust. Hamil was an excellent captain, and his coldness towards Kit passed unnoticed, for Captain Hamilton was known as a hard-bitten, stern disciplinarian who was cold towards everyone. Only when carousing with his old companions such as Daniel O'Neil did the other side of his nature reveal itself.

In mid-October the King decided the time was right to march on London, hoping by setting off without warning and marching quickly with a minimum of baggage to take Lord Essex's army by surprise. The two armies were about equally distant from London, the King's a little further north; if the King could get ahead of Essex on the road he could either fall on London and take it by surprise, or else lie in wait for Essex and fall on him as he marched towards the capital.

After ten days on the march the King's army reached Edgecott, near Warwick, and on the evening of 22nd October they stopped there to rest. Nothing had been heard of the Parliamentary army, though there were scouts out all round the main force, and it was assumed that either they were still back in Worcester, or some way ahead towards London. In either case, the army needed rest, and they decided to stop for a day or two.

The cavalry had been travelling a few miles to the south of the main body, keeping between it and where the enemy was most likely to be. When they halted, the Prince called for anyone who knew the area to come forward.

'If we are to stop awhile, we may as well be comfortable,' he said to Hamil and Daniel who, along with another friend, had gathered round him at the halt. A very nervous-looking trooper was being ushered forward, and the Prince, to make himself less formidable, dismounted and seated himself on a tree stump, handing his reins to his servant. Boye at once bounded up and danced on his hind legs before his master for a moment before ducking his head under Rupert's caressing hands. 'Well now – your name?' he said to the trooper, who was bowing so low before him that he did not at once hear. 'Your name, trooper – speak up!'

'Davy, Sir – Davy Smith,' the young man stammered. He was no more than eighteen at most, a handsome, fair-skinned, blond boy with the long love-locks that all the cavalry were copying from their officers, and two pheasant tail-feathers in his hat. Flamboyance in appearance was becoming the pride of Rupert's Horse, from the highest to the lowest.

'And you know this area?'

'Yes Sir. Well, Sir, my family comes from Stratford, Sir, but my mother's sister lives in Kineton, Sir, just over that way, four or five miles off, and I was sent to stay with her and my uncle Sir, when my mother died.'

Rupert listened patiently to all this, and then said, 'Well now, Davy, think hard and tell us what big houses there are hereabouts. Is there a big house, a gentleman's house, where we might billet for a night or two?'

'Oh yes Sir,' Davy said quickly. 'Just by Kineton, Sir, there's Lord Spencer's house at Wormleighton, Sir. You could go there, I doubt not.'

'You shall shew us the way. Quartermaster!'

'Yes, Highness?'

'Go with this trooper and arrange a billet for us. You'll need to take a patrol with you – twenty men should be enough.' He looked around the group of officers with him and his eye met Hamil's. 'You want to go?'

'Our horses are fresh, Highness,' Hamil said.

'And you feel the need of some action,' Rupert hazarded with a smile. Ever since the unexpected fight at Powick Bridge back in September, when a Parliamentary patrol and one of Rupert's had bumped into each other, everyone had been longing for a chance to draw blood again. 'Well, who knows, you may be lucky and meet with some resistance to the idea of billeting. Quartermaster, go with Captain Hamilton and whatever men he chooses. Trooper Smith, shew them the way.'

It was growing dark as the patrol rode into Wormleighton. Hamil had deliberately avoided choosing any of the saffron-cloaked Morland contingent for his twenty men, and consequently he was more relaxed and easy in his manner. The men were enjoying themselves, looking about them alertly as they trotted along the quiet streets, only discipline keeping them from chattering.

'It's down this way, Captain, Sir,' Davy Smith said, about to turn his horse down a narrow green track, but at that moment Hamil heard something and abruptly gave the signal to halt.

'Silence,' he commanded sharply. The men drew rein and listened. 'Horses,' he said.

'A large number, by the sound of it,' the Quartermaster said. He and Hamil exchanged a glance. A large number of horses could only mean soldiers – their own, or the enemy's? Hamil singled out one of his men, a bright young Yorkshire volunteer. 'Raglan,' he said quietly, 'dismount and slip along the hedge there, try to see what's coming and get back here fast. The rest of you, form up behind me here. Keep quiet – not a sound. If it is not our own men, we want to surprise them.'

Silently as a stoat, Raglan darted up the lane on foot, and he had only just disappeared round the curve of the hedge when he reappeared, running hard.

'It's the enemy, Sir,' he exlaimed, even as his foot was jabbing for the stirrup and his hands snatching back the reins from the trooper who held them. 'A patrol – thirty or more, I should think, coming this way.'

Hamil thought quickly – if it was only a patrol, their best bet was to fall on them at once, and take them by surprise. If it was the vanguard of a larger force, they would be cut to pieces, but it was necessary to take prisoners in order to find out where the enemy was. He had to take the chance.

'Sabres out!' he cried. 'We'll take them, men.' The sound of hooves was closer, almost on top of them. 'Charge!'

As the leading file came round the curve of the road, Hamil's patrol flung themselves into the charge, swords out and ready, yelling their battle-cry. They took the enemy patrol completely by surprise, and their horses reared and screamed in panic, trying desperately to turn tail and run, while their riders attempted to control them and at the same time to draw their swords. It was evident they had had no idea any royalist troops were in the area, or they would have had their swords out. In a moment the lane was filled with the dust beaten up by hooves and the cries of wounded men. To Hamil it was the world he knew. The feeling of his lithe, powerful mount beneath him, the hard tautness of the reins in his left hand, the warmth of his sword hilt in his right. Drive forward, slash, strike, and parry. Firefly, driven forward by his spurs, half-reared and locked breasts with the leading-file horse opposing him. Hamil killed the rider, and whirled Firefly on the spot, looking for the next.

The enemy had had no chance, and were already falling back, preparing to flee. Hamil's own men were new to killing, and their blood was up, but catching the Quartermaster's eye Hamil remembered the need to take prisoners.

'Call 'em off!' the Quartermaster yelled above the noise. Some of the Parliamentary horse at the rear of the group were turning tail and running. Hamil yelled to his own men, pitching his voice to carry through the din.

'Don't kill'em all, boys! We want prisoners – disarm 'em!'

Gradually order prevailed. The Parliamentarians were only too pleased to surrender, and once the haze of killing passed from their eyes, Hamil's men realized these were their own countrymen they were fighting. The noise subsided, the dust began to settle, and something akin to embarrassment spread over the group of men in the little lane.

Hamil acted quickly, knowing his men must not have time to feel shame. They had disarmed and held eleven of the opposition, killed four, and the rest had scattered. Of Hamil's men, several had received superficial wounds, and one was dead. Hamil dismounted and went to look: it was Davy Smith. He lay crumpled, his face to the earth, his neck almost severed by a sideways blow that had landed between neck and shoulder. Someone knew what he was doing, Hamil thought. The boy's eyes were open, and he looked mildly surprised, as if death were not at all as he had imagined. Hamil had seen too many dead men to react, but he always found it hard when they were as young as this. He picked up the boy's hat from the dust and laid it over his face so that he couldn't see those wide eyes. The pheasant's feathers were draggled with blood.

'Right,' he said harshly as he turned away, 'let's take these men back to the Prince. And bring the horses – even if they're not fit to ride, we can always eat 'em!'

The joke brought forth a bellow of laughter, the result more of tension relaxing than amusement, and soon they were riding back to camp through the gathering dusk, the prisoners in front, on foot, surrounded by Hamil's men, and their horses led in a string behind, the reins of each looped round the stirrup of the one in front.

From the prisoners it was learnt that Lord Essex's army was less than ten miles away, on the other side of Kineton, and that it had no idea that the royal force was anywhere near. The patrol Hamil had surprised had been on the same errand as himself, to secure billets at Wormleighton for the officers. Rupert called a meeting of his senior officers, and advised that they should ride at once and fall on the Essex army in the dark, trusting to surprise to offset the lack of numbers. But a consensus eventually decided to send a message to the King for his commands, suggesting that the army should take up a position of Edgehill and tempt the Parliamentarians to attack it. The message was sent directly, and well before dawn the King's reply came, agreeing to the suggestion. By sunrise the royal army was drawn up in battle array on the ridge of Edgehill, and Essex's army was drawn up on the level ground below them and to the north. The royal army now stood between Essex and London, giving him no choice. He had to give battle.

The sun came slowly up behind and to the right of the Morland men as they watched the cold shadow of Edgehill shorten on the broad meadows before them. Oberon shifted his forefeet and mouthed his bit impatiently, and Kit leaned forward to smoothe a lock of his mane back onto the right side, and looked around him. Prince Rupert's regiment was on the right wing. Immediately to Kit's left was Prince Maurice's regiment, and beyond them the five regiments of foot, their pikes grounded, the forest of poles hiding the cavalry away on the left wing, Lord Wilmot's wing. When a pikeman moved, the head of his pike would catch the sun and throw it like a white-hot coin across the cold grass of the scarp.

Beyond Kit's regiment to the right were two more, the Prince of Wales regiment and the King's Lifeguard, and leaning forward Kit could just see beyond them again Usher's dragoons, mounted on their little hairy ponies and tough Welsh cobs. The whole army was evenly deployed along the ridge, but Kit couldn't help feeling that here where he sat, in Prince Rupert's own regiment in the heart of the cavalry wing, was the centre of the force. He glanced at Malachi, seeing him test for the tenth time that morning that his sword was loose in its sheath, and Mal caught his eye and grinned in sudden exuberance. Around and behind were the other men of the Morland contingent, their saffron cloaks flung back, their breastplates gleaming dully. They wore the cavalry pot-helmets which made them all look curiously alike, so that Kit had to stare to tell one from the other. Round their arms they wore the black sashes on which the white leaping hare stood out startlingly – the women at Morland Place had laboured lovingly over those, and Mary Esther herself had tied Kit's on before he left, as if that way she could send her love and care along with him, to keep him safe. One of the men had tucked a sprig of heather into his cloak-pin for luck. The hare and heather. Kit had never felt less alone in his life.

Down in the low land, about a mile away, the enemy was drawn up in much the same formation. Kit stared at them, seeing only a mass of multi-coloured shapes; not individuals, but lumps of people, seeming to sway slightly as they moved. Only here and there where the elongated dot of a horseman cantered along the lines with a message were they recognizable as people. The regiments were many-legged lumps. He thought of his own men, how alike they looked. Would the enemy look like them too? How would he feel when it came to killing them? He shivered slightly at the thought: they were Englishmen, farmers and labourers like his own men, husbands and fathers leaving behind them wives they loved perhaps as much as he loved Hero, and bairns like Young Kit. He glanced behind and to his left, looking for Prince Rupert, and his eye fell instead on the King's standard over behind the infantry, uncurling that moment as the breeze strengthened a little. It comforted him, for whatever the rights and wrongs they were not his to question. He was fighting for the King, and that was right. He was a Morland, and the Morlands generation after generation had fought for their kings. The men down there in the valley were rebels, and their task would be the harder because they would know themselves to be doing what was against God's ordinances. The lifting breeze brought the sound of church bells, tunable and plangently sweet, from the village of Radway up on the hill, reminding Kit that it was Sunday morning.

Malachi caught his eye again and said, 'They'll all be going into York for the service. I wonder if they know we'll be in battle?'

'They'll be praying for us anyway,' Kit said, thinking it unlikely. 'Maybe they'll go into the Minster.'

'And later they'll have Mass in the chapel, with Father Moyes. And he'll shout at the servants for not attending.' Malachi grinned at the thought of the chaplain's loud voice and hasty temper. Kit could see he was remembering it all, that he liked the thought of the chapel better than the Minster. Kit could only think of Hero: her face was etched on the back of his eyes, laughing and pink-cheeked the way she was after a gallop, with her yellow curls tumbled and disarrayed. She would be with him throughout this day, as she was through every night he was away from her. And as if he heard the thought, Hamil turned in his saddle at that moment to look at Kit with a thoughtful, questioning eye, before turning back again, the feathers in his hat quivering in the breeze. It occurred to Kit suddenly that there was every chance one or both of them would never see Hero again. This day might be the last on earth for either of them. In his mind he prayed, 'Lord, you know I never hated him; forgive him if he hates me. And take care of Hero and the child.'

All day they stood-to. Time seemed frozen: it was only by the movement of the shadows that they could tell the day was passing. The horses were all dozing, their ears out sideways, cocking one hind foot and then the other. Then suddenly in the middle of the afternoon there was a flurry of movement, and everyone woke, startled, from a daydream and looked about them, wondering what had disturbed them. The King with his little group of followers rode out in front of the main body of the army, a small man on a very big dun stallion: his black armour gleamed, and his blue sash with the garter star was bright against it, and he swept off his great feathered hat from his long dark curls and spoke. Kit was too far away to hear what he said. Behind the King he could see the figures of the two young Princes, the Prince of Wales and the Duke of York, and to one side the unmistakable figure of Prince Rupert on his white stallion. The Radway bells began to ring again. It was three o'clock.

Now the word was hurrying back, passed from man to man: they were going to advance. The King had said he was their Captain and their cause. Movement ran like flickers of flame through stubble through the ranks of soldiers. Down in the valley the enemy must see that ripple, must know what was coming. Now Rupert was back, galloping along the ranks of his cavalry, reining his horse in here and there to speak to them. He passed in front of his own regiment, his horse half rearing, and Oberon caught the excitement

191

and gave a little half rear, his forelegs stiff, and whinneyed shrilly, and at once was answered by a dozen other horses, all fretting against the restraining hands.

'This is it, lads,' the Prince said, and his dark face was tense and alight with excitement, so that it made Kit think of a drawn sword. 'Don't forget what I've taught you. We walk, trot, and gallop on the command, swords out; go at them hell for leather, yelling. Break them with the charge. Forget your pistols, or you'll have an enemy sword through your guts while you're still trying to take aim. When and if we get to close quarters, that's the time to use them: stick a pistol up against his ribs before you fire it; that way you can't miss.'

The men laughed exuberantly at this, and the Prince grinned suddenly.

'They won't stand against our charge, lads. We're already famous – the King's Life Guards have asked permission to ride with us, that's how famous we are!'

The Life Guards were legendary – a group of noblemen whose horses and equipment were so fine that it was said that if they were sold the proceeds of each could furnish a whole troop. The King's cousin, Lord Bernard Stuart, commanded them.

'So ready your swords, my lads, and wait for the commands. Victory will be ours this day.'

A rousing cheer sent him on his way to the next regiment. Now the horses were all eager and nervous, and their riders were adjusting their armour, settling their hats or helmets, checking their girths and stirrups. Rupert came back, took up his position, and then the artillery of both sides began firing almost simultaneously, and the trumpets sounded the *walk*. The lines of cavalry surged forward violently with the released excitement, but were soon back in control. The slope from the edge of the scarp was so steep just at first that it was impossible to go fast. Once they reached more level ground, the trumpets sounded the *trot*, and soon after that

Kit saw the knife-edge flash of Rupert's sword being raised, the signal for the charge. Even before the trumpet sounded the command, the excitement had communicated itself through the men to the horses. Hamil's troop was in the front line – the fastest horses were always put in front – and as Rupert spurred his white horse into a canter Oberon almost leapt out from under Kit. Then they were galloping. Kit leaned forward, his sword at the ready, his eyes fixed on the shape of Rupert up ahead on Hamil, his captain, riding Firefly ahead and to his left. All around him was the thrilling thunder of ten thousand hooves, and the eery shrilling of battle cries; the smell of horse sweat and man sweat and bruised grass; the flickering of colours, bay necks and grey necks and wide eyes and laid-back ears, sashes and armour and cloaks and standards and feathered hats; and the light like white fire flashing off three thousand drawn swords. Who could resist them? Yelling in fierce exuberance, Kit dug his heels into Oberon's flanks, and the stallion bared his teeth and surged forward, leaping the scrubby furze effortlessly, his fair round hooves seeming hardly to touch the rough ground.

Now the enemy was closer, closing the gap with their own charge, and there was the sparkle of musket fire from between their ranks, the sound of it coming afterwards like the cracking of dry twigs on a fire. Kit heard a high-pitched whine like an insect flying past his ear, and he jerked his head away from it instinctively. At the same moment out of the corner of his eye he saw a saffron cloak tumble sideways out of the saddle. That was Jamie, son of one of the tenants. His horse, lightened of its burden, leapt ahead, reins and stirrups flapping, and then swerved across the ranks before falling in again with the charge.

A group of horsemen had come out in front of the enemy, and were firing their pistols into the ground as they cantered forward. They wore orange sashes, bright and conspicuous, and now their leader was pulling his sash off, awkwardly with one hand as he held the reins with the other. It caught for a moment under his ear before he tugged it impatiently free and let the wind flip it away from him. The others were following suit – what could it mean? But there was no time to wonder more – they had reached the enemy. Yelling fiercely, Kit followed his Prince and his Captain, sword held high. The lines opposing them wavered. A frightened face, sickly white, appeared before Kit and its mouth opened in a quivering O; Kit saw the gleam of a sword, and brought his own crashing down between neck and shoulder. He felt the shock and the yield, saw vivid, shocking redness come suddenly from nowhere, spouting over his arm and hand, felt the impact of Oberon's shoulder with the other horse. Then the other man was gone, and there was a gap ahead into which Oberon leapt, his nostrils wide with disgust and rage at the smell of blood.

Another face, this time twisted with furious yelling, another sword, this time raised to strike. Kit brought his own sword up, feeling the clashing jar run down his arm as the two blades struck. Oberon reared, striking out his forelegs with a stallion's instinct. The other horse jerked backwards away from him, and from his position of vantage Kit drew his sword up again and struck. The arm and sword seemed leaden; surely the other man would run him through before he had completed the movement. The roaring in his ears became a silence as he watched his own sword-blade go up into the sun and down, smashing into flesh. The man went sideways off his horse, but his face did not change from snarling anger, as if he had not felt the blow. The silence in his head burst into noise again, and Oberon lept forward under him.

Ahead the enemy had wavered, hesitated, and now, with the weight of the great horses bearing down on them, they were turning tail and fleeing. It seemed both slow and sudden, like a dam breaking – first the wood moves and then there is the fractional pause before the whole crumples and the water bursts outwards. Victory! They had broken the lines. Kit saw Malchi out of the corner of his eye, his face distorted with yelling, his eyes wild, and he kicked Oberon forward to keep up with him. They were fast, faster than the wind, their maddened horses galloping as if the hounds of hell were after them. The enemy's horses were too slow. They were overtaken, their riders cut down. Everywhere now there were loose horses, galloping with the charge until the opportunity came to run out at one side or the other.

The enemy were spreading out as they fled, scattering outwards fanwise, and the royal cavalry was spreading in pursuit. The Morland men were still together, those that were left. Hamil was beside Kit now, yelling something; ahead Prince Rupert had his sword up, his head turned back to his own men. Now the hooves rang on hardened earth, now on cobbles, there were houses to either side. They had reached Kineton, two miles from the battlefield, the fleeing Parliamentarians were slipping away between houses and down side-lanes. Hamil was urging them to stop. Kit took a haul on Oberon's reins, and the horse slowed. Prince Rupert had wheeled his stallion in the road ahead, unmistakably trying to halt the charge. Kit hauled Oberon to a stand, and all around him horses stopped and stood panting, their flanks heaving and nostrils stretched red, and a sudden quiet seemed to fill Kit's head, so loud after the noise of the charge that it hurt his ears.

His arm and hand were red and sticky. Mal's face was speckled with rusty spots like freckles, and Kit could see he had a sword-gash on his thigh, though it appeared he had not yet noticed it himself: he grinned at Kit, and pushed away the hair that was sticking to his sweating forehead with the back of a hand as red as Kit's own. Kit felt suddenly sick with violent anticlimax; the air smelled of blood and his face was coated with dust.

'Captain Hamilton – round up your troop and form them

up here to stop anyone coming through. Then follow me. We must round up the rest and get back to the battle,' Rupert commanded harshly. The battle? Kit stared, and then slowly the noise in the background that he had ceased to notice resolved itself – behind him on the plain below Edgehill the two infantries were engaged; men were fighting and dying under the westering sun. It was a strange clamour, a single sound made up of many, of human voices and inhuman screams, of clashing metal and gunfire. It was a sound he had never heard before, but he knew it now with a knowledge that went deeper than the brain and he knew he would never forget it, the voice of battle.

CHAPTER ELEVEN

It would not have occurred to Edmund to ask Ambrose and Mary Eleanor for their approval before he married them to each other and sent them off to the other end of the world; but that did not necessarily mean they would have withheld it. Ambrose had always been aware of his position as a younger son; and with two older brothers, both of whom already had a male heir, there was little chance of his inheriting an estate. There was, of course, Tod's Knowe, but that Edmund considered it unimportant was shewn by the fact that he sent Francis there instead of Ambrose.

Land was in short supply in England; but in the New World there was land in plenty to be had for the taking, and over there Ambrose had the opportunity to become a great landowner, something he could never hope for if he stayed at home. As for Mary Eleanor, her choice was simpler still. Unless she was to remain a useless dependant for the rest of her life, she must marry, and her marriage would depend on her dowry. For the size of the dowry Malachi was likely to be able to provide for her, she would certainly not get a landowner. Ambrose was a better match than she could have expected otherwise, and she would have been simple to refuse it.

As a couple they were well matched, for they were both of a temperament to make the best of things, and so, once married to each other, they were quite prepared to fall in love with each other. Mary Eleanor, while no great beauty, was not as plain as her sister Ruth: she was a tiny, pale, frail-looking girl with dark hair and shy blue eyes and a way of nervously twisting her hands together. She rarely spoke in company, and preferred always to efface herself passively; but Ambrose, on making the effort to get to know her, found that she had a lively imagination and a fund of quiet, steady piety that he greatly admired.

For Mary Eleanor the task was easier: Ambrose was handsome, charming, and a gentleman. He was the likest to him of Edmund's children, though not so tall, but with the clear-cut face, the silver-fair hair and level grey eyes. He was cheerful, good-humoured, and if he was also lightsome, easily led, unsteady, everyone's rook, she could persuade herself that it was because of his sweetness of temper; and when she was forced to admit to herself that it was a fault in him, she could still comfort herself that he was as likely to be led by her as by anyone else.

Having little imagination, Ambrose was not disposed to foresee difficulties in their venture. In this he was very like his grandfather, Thomas Morland; he never expected trouble, and when it came an animal instinct for comfort often enabled him to evade it. Now when Mary Eleanor hesitantly expressed her fears to him, he waved them aside cheerfully.

'I have heard all those tales about Virginia, how the planters starved and were killed by wild Indians and all the rest of it. But that was years ago, Nell, in the beginning. Things are very different there now – why, there are proper towns and shops where you can buy everything you need, and ships come in to trade every week. You'll want for nothing.'

'I know things are better now,' Nell persisted quietly, 'but still it is a wild land, Ambrose, and not like England. There will be hard work and hardship and great danger, for us as for everyone. I wish you would prepare your mind against it.'

But Ambrose only laughed and pulled her onto his knee and kissed her cheek. 'Cautious little Nell! It would not do if both of us were like thee – it needs me to keep us cheerful! But don't worry, hinny, my father would not send us all that way at such expense to labour and die like oxen.

He means me to be a great landlord, and you a great lady. Why, over there we can have an estate twice – three times – the size of Morland Place. Thou shalt live in a great house, and wear silk, and ride in a fine carriage, I promise thee.'

She could not make him see otherwise, and when Edmund talked to them about his plans, it did nothing to disabuse him.

'You shall go,' Edmund told them, 'to that part of Virginia called Maryland. It lies to the north and the land there is very fertile and good. It is a palatinate and friendly to Catholics and Protestants alike, so you will not be threatened by separatists there. And the land grant, though it is less than it was, is still very good.'

'How good, Father?' Ambrose asked.

'Two hundred acres per head if you take five able-bodied men at your own expense,' Edmund said. 'That means you will have a thousand acres, my son, to begin with – and if you do well it will be easy to buy more.'

Ambrose's eyes shone, and he turned impulsively to Mary Eleanor. 'There, Nell, you see? I said you should be a great lady.'

Mary Eleanor refused to be moved. 'Where shall we find the five men, Sir?' she asked her father-in-law.

'It will not be difficult,' he said. 'I shall advertise that we are ready to pay the passage of five sturdy yeomen and choose the best. There are many good men who want land. They will be indentured to you for seven years, and at the end of that time you should be in a position to hire more servants for wages if necessary.'

Edmund's optimism was only partly justified. There were many who came forward willing to have their passage paid to the New World, but not many of them were decent, godfearing, hard-working yeomen. Mostly they were people who had good reason for wanting to flee England, or who hoped it might be easier to live comfortably without working in a place where they were not known. With patience, however, he eventually found seven men to sign up for the venture. The best of them was a yeoman, Joseph Hammond, and his wife Betty, and his brother-in-law Josiah Pulman, who had farmed a small holding as tenants-at-will in north Yorkshire, and who had recently been put out by their landlord. There were three labourers, Will Brewer, Pen Huster, and Robert Updike, a young herdsman, John Hogg, and a carpenter called Samuel Goodman, and his wife Hester. Though it was a matter which would concern them nearly, Ambrose and Nell were not required to give their approval of the seven; if they had been, Nell would have objected to the Goodmans, for as soon as she did meet them, she disliked and distrusted them on sight.

But they did not meet them until they took ship together at Hull for the journey by sea to London, and by then it was much too late. Their baggage was already aboard, all the things they expected to need: chests full of clothes and household linen, axes and other tools, guns and knives, household equipment such as cooking utensils, needles, bowls, pans, and supplies such as candles, salt, soap, herbs, and of course food. In this respect they were lucky, for one of Zeph and Zech's friends had captained a ship on the Virginia trading run, and was able to advise them on what they should take, and Edmund invited him to dine at Morland Place, consulted him, and had comprehensive lists drawn up. On the captain's advice they also took seeds for planting, some sapling trees, and some livestock – sheep, chickens, goats, and an in-calf heifer.

There were a few concessions to luxury, though had Ambrose thought about it their very paucity would have warned him of the kind of life he was going to: a box of books, a chess-set, and a small guitar. At the last moment before the chests had been roped and sent away, Mary Esther had sought out Nell and given her one other treasure to take with her: a beautiful ivory crucifix on a rosewood stand.

'It belonged to your grandmother,' Mary Esther said, 'but when she died she left it to me. It had been given to her, you see, by *my* great-grandmother, Nanette Morland, and she felt it should come back into my family.'

'Is that Nanette Morland whose picture hangs in the dining room?'

Mary Esther nodded. 'Yes, the same. So now I return the compliment and give it to you, my dear. I know you will treasure it, and it will remind you that our love and prayers go with you. Trust in God, Nell, and cling to your Faith, whatever happens.'

The two women regarded each other gravely, both well aware what the hazards of the venture were. 'I shall miss you, Madam,' Nell said at last. She would miss them all, all the family she had grown up with. It was against all likelihood that she would ever see any of them again.

But when they embarked at London Dock on the good ship *Grenvelle* bound for Jamestown, Virginia – Ambrose and Nell, the seven indentured men and two women, and the three personal servants, Rachel and Phoebe and Austin – Nell knew that she and Mary Esther were the only people who had any apprehensions about what was ahead. Ambrose, like his father, imagined that he would live in Maryland as he lived in Yorkshire, and if the servants hadn't thought as he thought they would never have consented to accompany them

Christmas did not seem like Christmas that year of 1642. To the normal privation of winter was added that of the war: though York and most of the north was Royalist, Hull-port was still in Parliamentary hands, and roads to the ports of the south ran through the Parliamentary midlands, so that the extra imported goods that were normally available could not be got this year.

'Oranges and lemons and ginger and sweet wine,' Anne

grumbled to Hetta as they sat in the windowseat in the drawing room. 'When shall we see them again? And silk and ribbons – when I asked Papa about a new gown for the Christmas season he didn't even answer.' She leaned forward and rubbed a clear patch in the frosty window and stared out at the frozen landscape. Even the moat was frozen, and the swans were standing on its bank looking disconcerted. Every now and then one of them would jump down and skid a little on the ice before jumping back onto the bank. 'Stupid creatures,' she muttered. They had been doing it for half an hour. 'You'd think they would learn.'

Hetta looked up calmly from her task. She was threading holly berries onto a twist of silk to make a necklace, and they made a bright splash in her pale blue lap, like drops of blood. 'You won't need a new dress,' she said. 'There won't be any great balls this year, and even if there were, Papa would not let any of us attend them, not with the Parliamentarians being so close.'

'Oh it's all right for you,' Anne said crossly. 'You're only thirteen – it doesn't matter to you. But I'm sixteen, and if I don't meet any young men, how shall I ever be wed?'

'Papa will see to it,' Hetta said peacefully, pushing her needle through another berry. Anne stared at her in exasperation, and suddenly reached out and slapped the chain of glowing berries from her sister's hand. It flew across the room and hit the polished floor, scattering half its scarlet drops in all directions. Hetta's hands jerked out involuntarily to save them, and then she looked at Anne and her lip quivered. 'Why did you do that?' she asked. Anne clenched her fists.

'To wake you up! To wake you and shake you, you pudding! I can't bear it when you sit and sit and don't care about anything! "Papa will see to it." Pah! You don't even care that Christmas will be dull and dreadful, with no parties or dances or anything nice! Sometimes I think nothing will ever be nice, ever again.'

'It will,' Hetta protested, forgetting her necklace and wanting instead to comfort her sister. 'The war won't go on for ever. Everything will be nice again when it's over.'

'When it's over – I shall be an old woman,' Anne said crossly, and Hetta laughed. 'If you laugh I shall slap you!' Anne cried.

'Well then, slap me, if it will make you any happier,' Hetta said peacefully, and Anne's hands slowly unclenched and her face slid into an unwilling smile.

'Oh Hetta, it's just that –'

'I know. It seems so quiet, with Ambrose and Nell gone, and Kit and Mal away with the army in Oxford, and Frank in Northumberland. But we've got Richard home –'

Anne snorted in contempt. 'Richard! What use is he, when he and that dreadful wife of his think everything in the least pleasant is a sin? If you ask me, we'd be better off without him home. It's my belief Papa wouldn't be half so worried about the Fairfaxes and the rebel army if Richard weren't here.'

'It puts him in a sensitive position,' Hetta said solemnly. Anne pushed her.

'Baby! You don't even know what that means – you just heard Mother saying it.

'Heard me say what?' Mary Esther asked, coming in at that moment. Dog pushed ahead of her and ran to the girls, thrusting his great head into one lap and then other, his tail thrashing. 'Why are your beads on the floor, Hetta? I thought you were making a necklace. Who is it for, chuck?'

'For Hero,' Hetta said, getting up quickly and going to pick them up. Anne half rose to help, and then sank down again ungracefully on the windowseat, scowling.

'That's nice. She'll be coming over tomorrow, with the baby, so we must get a bed ready for her. Anne, sit up straight, and don't frown so. You will never get a husband if you look so unpleasantly.'

'How will I ever get a husband when I never meet any

203

men?' Anne asked, reverting at once to her old grievance. 'Mother, why won't Father invite people this year? We always have lots of people at Christmas.'

'Darling, he doesn't want to draw attention to ourselves, when there are so many Parliamentarians all around us. You know we are very close to Fairfax country, and with so many men gone to the war –'

'Oh bother the war! And the damned Puritans!'

'The war will soon be over,' Mary Esther said soothingly. 'And remember that your own brother, who will one day be master of this house –'

'*Half*-brother,' Anne corrected. 'And I don't believe he will ever be master. Papa would never let a Puritan have Morland Place.'

'That's enough, Anne. I can see you need something to do. Help Hetta pick up those berries, and then you can both come and help me look over your gowns, and see what we can do about turning them. We must be thrifty, until the war's over.'

Though Edmund had made more concessions to Richard and his wife and servants than pleased him or anyone else at Morland Place, Katherine and Richard were very unhappy with their progress. At night, when they had retired behind the curtains of their bed and their three servants were reassuringly snoring on the other side of the room, they would pray and talk over their situation, before going to sleep. Though they slept in the same bed, their bodies never came into contact, for Katherine slept under the sheet and Richard on top of it, so that there was always a fold of the linen between them. It was Katherine who had taught Richard that the pure in heart never had carnal relations, and that carnal thoughts were sent by the Devil.

'Our marriage is ordained by God for a higher purpose,' she had said often and often, and she praised Richard for resisting his base nature until Richard, not liking always to be the inferior member of the partnership, denied any more having any urges to resist. It was largely true. He had fallen in love with Katherine for her mental qualities rather than her physical ones, and if he sometimes felt hot and uncomfortable and had strange dreams, he did not trouble to seek out the reason. Feeling uncomfortable and unhappy was so much a part of his life by now that he would have missed the feelings had they changed.

'Husband,' Katherine said on this particular night, 'we are not drawing this household any closer to God. All the months we have been here, not one single soul has seen the light of the true religion. Not one soul saved, Richard!'

Richard shifted restlessly. 'Well I don't see what we can do about it,' he said. 'The servants all hate me – they hardly even speak if I ask them a direct question.'

'You are starting at the wrong end,' Katherine said severely. 'The servants in a house will do pretty much what the master does. Your father, Richard, must be persuaded to close the chapel. You must save him! Once he has been reborn, we can begin on the others. The children – that heathen priest must be got rid of. And your stepmother – though,' she added thoughtfully, 'I'm not sure that she might not be more difficult than your father.'

'Well, I still don't see what more I can do,' Richard muttered. 'I try to talk to Father, but he never listens to me. It's as much as I can do to get a moment with him – it's always "Not now, I'm busy" when I go to him.'

'I know,' Katherine said more kindly, 'and I have been thinking about the problem. I know that you do your best, but the truth is you do not have much influence with your father.'

'It isn't my fault,' Richard began to protest, and in the dark Katherine reached out a hand and patted his shoulder.

'I know, husband. That is why I have been thinking how we can increase your influence. And it seems to me –' There was a long pause, so long that Richard had almost decided she had fallen asleep. Then she went on. 'The time has come when we must consummate our marriage.'

Richard's mouth went dry. They had been at great pains to conceal from everyone that their marriage had never been consummated, because if it were known it would be grounds for the annulment Edmund so dearly wanted; but as long as no-one knew, they were safe.

'But – but why?' he stammered at last. 'It is a denial of all you have ever said, and our marriage does not need it. No-one can prove we have never –'

'It is nothing to do with that,' Katherine said. 'We must have children. Richard, you must have a son.'

'But I have one. Ralph –'

'That child has been brought up a Papist, or as near to one as makes no difference. No, Richard, *we* must have a son, one that we can bring up in the true religion. You must have seen how your father dotes on Ralph. If we have a child it will make our position secure, and will increase your influence with your father. Soon Ralph will be sent away to school. Once he is gone, we shall have a clear field for our child. And who knows – a way may be found to discredit your first marriage. We may find a way to oust Ralph.'

Richard was silent, struggling with himself. His wife's words seemed so callous, for in spite of everything, Richard adored Ralph, and only wished that the boy would shew him some affection. And yet he knew that she was right, that a child would help his cause; he knew, too, that Edmund had often cast speculative eyes on Katherine, wondering why she did not conceive. Yet after all this time, after their long celibacy –

As if she read his thoughts, Katherine said more gently, 'I know that it will be difficult and repugnant, dear husband, but remember for Whose sake we do it. We should not flinch from our duty, most especially when the task is hard to do. Come, I am ready: draw back the sheet.'

'Katherine –' He swallowed. 'Are you sure?'

'Yes. I am not afraid. It is for the true, the glorious, the pure faith!'

With a trembling hand Richard drew away the sheet and climbed under it, and, grateful for the dark, reached out for her. A roaring waterfall of memories pounded in his brain, and the struggle between his old self and his new self, between his flesh and his reborn soul, between his present purpose and his dark sweet memories, made him tremble. Only Katherine was calm, her body still and firm, not flinching as his hands touched her cool slender limbs. But then, she had no doubts, and above all, no memories. Shaking, Richard unlaced her bedgown, and when he put his hands inside and cupped them over her small, unripe breasts he heard her at last give a small gasp, and unseen in the dark he smiled his satisfaction.

A warm September day was drawing to a close; the kind of sweet, drowsy day painted in all the glowing colours of late summer, the golds and tawnys and reds; the kind of day, Kit thought, on which he and Hero would have ridden leisurely up to Popple Height and sat or reclined in the grass – not talking much, just looking out across the landscape, or up at the sky, feeling the warm, wheaten air of September brush their cheeks, chewing a grass-blade idly, smelling the hot earth and the first, distant blue tang of autumn.

Well, he had spent all day sitting on the grass, holding his horse, but it had been for a very different reason. Winter and spring and summer had been spent vigorously consolidating the King's hold on the west country. August had gone in a long siege of Gloucester, and when at last the situation there had brought Essex's great army scurrying from London to its relief, the King had decided to leave Essex in Gloucester and withdraw the Royalist army to get between the Parliamentary army and London. To Kit it seemed as if they were back exactly where they had been a year ago – the two armies racing for London, nothing gained on either side to shew for a year of his life lost.

There were good memories, of course, things that he was glad to look back on. They had wintered in Oxford, and it had been strange to Kit to be back there in so different circumstances. By chance Prince Rupert had billeted at Kit's old college, Christchurch, and Kit had spent a lot of time there with the Prince and his close companions. The Prince had taken to Kit, for they were just the kind of young men to like each other, and he had been promoted to Lieutenant of his troop. Whether Hamil had liked it or not, he had been too good a soldier to protest or to stand in the way of Kit's advancement, and when they were in a group together he behaved so circumspectly that no-one would have guessed that the cousins were not good friends; sometimes even Kit had felt that his enmity was lessened.

That was one of the good things. There was, too, the excitement of the campaign, the hard rides and the wild charges, the heady thrill of success; and there was the companionship, the evenings around the fire, drinking with friends, the laughter, the mocking toasts to Robert le Diable and Sergeant-Major-General Boye, the singing, the crack of weary muscles relaxing, and the quiet afterwards, when he might be invited to do a last round with the Prince, and see that fine profile etched against the summer stars, feel the weight of his arm across his shoulders and the warmth of Boye's friendly nose in his hand.

But mostly what Kit remembered was not pleasant. The more he saw of the war, the more it made him bitter, as if his life were being wasted without cause. What were they fighting for? What were any of them fighting for? What good would it do them? He never voiced his feelings, for he knew the others did not feel like him, Rupert and Maurice and Hamil and Daniel and even Malachi. But then, it was very different for Rupert – to him it was glory and honour, and his own kin to defend, and Maurice followed Rupert unquestioningly, loving him too much to need any other reason. For Hamil and Daniel it was a way of life, and the cause was immaterial, and Mal simply found it exciting. But none of them had left behind a wife whom they loved more than glory, or a young child who was growing up unseen, with whom those lost months could never be recaptured. Please God this new move would be decisive, and they could all go home. The Prince as always was sanguine, but Kit had ceased to believe it – he only hoped and prayed.

They stood-to until it began to grow dark, awaiting the order from the King to march. They had almost been out-manoeuvred by Essex, for they had expected him to pass along one road and he had gone a different way all together. The Prince had expected immediate action, and had mustered the cavalry here on Broadway Down, and now at last, when it has begun to get dark and no word had come, he had called his page Seb and Hamil and Daniel and ridden off to look for the King, to demand orders.

It grew chilly as the sun went off the land, and Kit unpinned his cloak and let it fall gratefully round him. Its saffron was dark and soiled now, but the cloth was good Morland cloth, heavy and weatherproof. There were not so many saffron cloaks now when they formed up. Two had fallen at Bristol, one at Lichfield and one had been wounded at Chalgrove and had died of a fever two days later. That had been little Davy Cullen: Kit was with him when he died, had held him in his arms, for he cried pitifully and called for his mother, but he was only sixteen, and the fever made him delirious. Two musket balls had smashed his hip, so perhaps it was as well the wound-fever got him, for he would not have been able to walk again. Most of them had honourable wounds by now. Malachi had three scars to exhibit, and Kit had had his left forearm laid open, but Hamil had not received so much as a scratch. That was the way of it, Daniel had said – the veterans knew how to take care of themselves, it was always the rawest youngsters who took it first.

But now at last something was happening. Rupert was back. His big white stallion gleamed eerily in the darkness as he cantered onto the field, though Kit could not see the mounts of his companions at all. Word filtered back before the official orders. Rupert had found the King in his billet, playing picquet with Lord Percy, and had so moved him with his eloquence that he had got the order to march at once, and the King was to follow with the main force. The trumpets were sounding the *mount* and the horses, woken abruptly from their dozing by the sound, were milling restively. Kit held Oberon short while he cinched up the girth, and the stallion swung in circles, eager to move after the long day's inactivity. Watching his chance, Kit got a toe in the stirrup and was up halfway round one of the circles, and as his body settled into the saddle, his memories fell away from him and the habit of a soldier took over, and before he had even found his other stirrup he was rounding up his troop.

They marched all night and reached Faringdon by dawn, to learn from a scout that Essex was ahead of them, cutting across country for Newbury. Once he reached Newbury, there would be nothing to stop him marching back into London. They paused only to bait the horses and eat a cold breakfast, and then they were in the saddle again and hot on the enemy's tail, catching up on them outside Hungerford. Without pause Rupert ordered the attack, passing the order by word of mouth so that the enemy rearguard should not hear the trumpets and have warning. They fell on them fiercely, and there was a short but sharp battle. It began to drizzle, and the light was failing, and Essex's troops were weary, having marched without stopping all day. At length he drew his men back into Hungerford. Rupert harried them, and holed them up there until the King's main force could come up with them and march into Newbury. Their position was strong now – Essex was cut off from the capital and must attack, while the King need only sit it out. But for once the King was the impetuous one, and that evening, the evening of 19th September, Rupert brought the word back to his regiment that they would fight the next day.

Kit was with Hamil when Daniel brought him the news. There was a brief silence, and Daniel and Hamil looked at each other significantly. At last Hamil said, 'He pointed out, of course, that we are short of ammunition, and supplies from Oxford are still on the road?'

'He did.'

'And the King still wanted to fight tomorrow?'

Daniel scratched slowly and thoughtfully at a louse-bite. 'God knows,' he said, 'the King should pay heed when it is the Palgrave that's advocating caution; but it seems he so stirred the royal blood back at Broadway with the need to be doin' that there's no holding our little King. He's all fire and haste and our Prince reining him back! It would make a cat laugh to see it!'

Hamil made a noise of disgust, and Daniel slapped him on the back. 'Ah, don't be fretting now, there's nothing the likes of you and me can do about it. And it would not be a right world to live in if all men were good at the same thing. You and me – we *three* –' he changed it out of courtesy, picking up Kit with a glance –' we three are soldiers, and a soldier's business is to obey, to fight when he's told and to go on until he's told to stop. So come and let's find a bit o' fire to warm our breeches, and some ale to warm our guts. Come on, Kit, and help me cheer this gloomy cousin of yours.'

Kit remembered that evening a long time afterwards. The night was cold, perhaps nearing the first of the frost, and the heart of the fire was deep red with it, burning bright and fierce as if with some urgent purpose of its own. They sat round it, and the deep glow struck upwards in their faces, throwing strange devil-sharp shadows from nose and eyebrow, making the familiar friends seem fantastical; it glowed on the pewter tankard that Daniel drank out of, picked out the gold gleam of the crucifix he wore round his tough dark neck under his beard; it threw the darkness surrounding them into deeper blackness, so that they seemed cut off from everything, from the world and time and tomorrow, in a magic circle of frost-red fire, bitter ale, and smoky, laughing voices. Then Boye came thrusting in amongst them, and the fire changed his white coat to rose-pink. Kit looked up for his master, and the Prince seemed to tower away into the darkness like a mountain, his head so far above the fireglow that when he spoke, his words were lost to Kit, who could never afterwards remember them. He could only remember the spray of golden sparks that floated upwards from the smoky tip of the fire and ringed the Prince's head with tiny stars.

It was bloody, and bitter. All day they fought, charging and reforming and charging again, against the stubborn lines of the London militia and their musketmen, and when darkness came they fought on until they had struggled to a standstill, and neither side had gained a yard of ground. The King ordered a withdrawal towards Oxford, and as soon as they were off the field, the Roundheads dropped where they stood and slept where they had fought. The royal cavalry rode a little way and then slipped off their weary horses and unsaddled them and slept with their heads on the saddles. Kit was blind-weary and confused, for he had been struck in the temple by a musket-ball, and though it had not done much more than graze his scalp, the blow had dazed him, and his memories of the day were imperfect. He recalled only the noise, the screaming, and the terrible effort of staying in the saddle and fighting on, hour after hour. As he lay down, he seemed to fall effortlessly into that bright still circle of firelight from the night before: that was real, more real than the battle. The day slid away from him and he slept.

He dreamed, and woke crying, and for some time he did not know where he was or what had happened. He was looking up at a grey, drizzling, pre-dawn sky; then the shape of Oberon's head cut into his vision as the horse turned to look at something, and he remembered and sat up. All around him were the sleeping humps of men and the dark shapes of dozing horses; but on the edge of the field was movement, mounted men. Rupert was there. The grief from his dream had lingered over into wakefulness, and he wanted the comfort of being with friends. He was afraid of the strange loneliness of his waking; he wanted to warm himself at the fire of Rupert's energy and sureness.

The fire! The circle of firelight, and the strangely sha-dowed faces, laughing and talking, though the sound was missing from his memory, as if they were behind glass, as if he were outside and looking in at them through a window. And one face more than another – as he struggled to his feet, reaching already for his saddle to saddle up, the memory his mind had tried to shut out had come back to him. The smiling face was Malachi, laughing in the firelight on the other side of that invisible barrier which was yester-day. Malachi had not come back: Kit had seen Malachi fall, not in the first charge or the second, he did not know when, but Malachi had not come back.

He saddled Oberon, his fingers numb with damp and cold, struggling and fumbling with the buckles, but Oberon was too weary to move about. He led the horse over to Rupert, picking his way through the sleeping men, too sound asleep to notice even when he stumbled over them. Rupert's face was grave, but he did not look tired: he was as strong as a rock, invincible. Kit's eyes drank him in greed-ily, needing the reassurance.

'We are going over the battlefield,' Rupert said. 'The scavengers will be there soon, as soon as it's light, and they will kill anything that moves. There may be wounded men out there who need help. Will you come?'

Kit nodded. He looked round the group – not a troop, but a number of individuals, perhaps drawn to Rupert, like himself, out of a need stronger than sleep.

'Mount up, then,' the Prince said. 'I have another task, too – I must find Falkland. He hated the war, and yet when his life was needed, he gave it without hesitation. I must bring back his body.' No-one said, Lord Falkland hated you too. To die for a great cause is glorious, but to die for a cause in which you do not believe is tragedy.

They rode slowly back to the battlefield. The mist was deeper there, clinging in threads like smoke to the dew-dark shapes huddled everywhere, gathering like milk in hollows; an unearthly, unreal scene, the more nightmarish because of the beauty of the mist. They picked their way slowly, looking for survivors. One could tell at a touch – the dead were already stiffening, and cold, so cold. Kit found Malachi, a long time afterwards, it seemed, a little apart, on his own, where he had fallen. His face was to the earth, and when Kit turned him over, he saw that he could not have suffered long, for his expression was calm, as though death had come to him while he slept.

CHAPTER TWELVE

The land Ambrose and Nell were given was on the north bank of the Patuxent River, fine, fertile land of tall handsome trees and swift-running creeks, along with four hundred acres of marshy land along the Little Choptank River. It was not for some time that they discovered that this latter was on the eastern shore of Chesapeake Bay, the opposite shore to the rest of their holding; and it was more than a year before they actually saw it, for first of all they had to clear their principal holding of trees, and build a house, and fence it.

They had been nine weeks crossing the Atlantic – a good crossing, the seamen had told them, in terms of speed. It was impossible for the migrants to think in terms of speed: they could only think in terms of foul weather, violent seas, seasickness, discomfort and monotony. Cramped for days at a time in a dark, vile-smelling hold, eating nothing but cheese, weevilly ship's bread, and salt fish, with small beer to drink, tortured by seasickness and later by vermin and illness too, there were few of them who did not wish they had never heard of the New World. Nell and Ambrose managed to keep relatively cheerful: Ambrose by amusing himself forming the passengers into choirs and giving musical entertainments; and Nell through her prayers and her hopes for the future. It was while they were still on board that she discovered she was pregnant, and it gave her something to look forward to. It also gave extra force to her prayers, which she performed mostly under cover of darkness, for a great many of those on board were Puritans of one sort or another, and as always amongst the lower classes there was great suspicion of anything that even remotely resembled Popery. She was careful never to reveal the existence of Mary Esther's gift, hidden deep in one of the chests.

Before the journey was done she knew a great deal more about their indentured servants, and on the whole was glad to have had the opportunity, before they were cast away together in a strange land. The Hammonds and Josiah Pulman, she discovered, were stupid, apathetic people, hard-working but lacking in any educaton or spirit or thought for the future. They had farmed their land just as it had always been farmed, time out of mind, suffering when bad times came, but never making use of good times to lay up some store against the future. Their old landlord had died, and the new landlord, a younger more vigorous man, had wanted greater profit from his property, and had put up their rent. They had not been able to pay the extra, and so had been put out, to wander the country until chance swept them into Edmund's net. Nell knew their use: they would do what they were told to do, provided it were simple enough, and do it well, though slowly; but any emergency or even change of circumstance would flummox them, and they would stand and gawp at it until someone rescued them, or told them how to deal with it.

Of the labourers, Robert Updike was a quiet, steady man, older than the rest at thirty-eight, seeming likable enough, the kind to be a capable and intelligent worker. Nell had a strange kind of talent with people – her sister Ruth had the same thing with animals – the ability to sense things about them, whether they were good or evil, or what use they were; and from the first she knew there was something about Robert, some faultiness in him, not quite evil, but weakness at least. It revealed itself when they had been at sea for a few days: he was a drunkard, the sort that stayed sober sometimes for months at a time, and then went on a bout of wild drinking that left him incapable for days, and ill for days after that. It accounted for his quietness, and also for the fact that, despite being a good worker, he had been put off farm after farm.

Will Brewer was an enormous man of giant strength and tiny brain. He had a broad, red face, always wreathed in grins, and stiff, dry whitish hair that stood up round his head like the bristles on a broom. There was no harm in him: he was simply unfinished, sent into the world only half made up. Pen Huster, Nell soon discovered, was also incomplete: he had been sent into the world with no moral sense. He travelled with Will, and it was apparent that wherever they went Pen used Will's great muscles and childlike good nature to create comforts for Pen. He was a small, weaselly, ill-favoured creature with some animal cunning when it came to sniffing out food and shelter; sly, mean, cowardly, idle, and incapable of telling right from wrong.

John Hogg, the herdsman, was the youngest of the indentured men, being just twenty. He certainly had a way with animals, seeming to know by instinct how to get the best out of them: it was solely through his efforts that the heifer survived the journey. When the weather was really bad he sat in her tiny stall and cradled her head in his arms for nearly two days. But with humans he was surly, ill-mannered, even violent. Nell guessed he had some grudge, but she could not know what it was.

That only left the Goodmans, the carpenter and his wife. Sam was thirty-two, Hester five or six years younger, and Nell was afraid of them, smelling some evil about them. There was nothing overt – they were polite, intelligent, friendly and diligent. Sam was evidently a good carpenter, Hester had been a weaver, and both had good reports from their masters; but Nell knew they were not right. Before the end of the voyage she suspected Hester was a thief, several small things having gone missing, but she could not prove anything. She was only wary. Her fears she did not confide to anyone. Ambrose would have laughed, and though her woman Rachel and the maid Phoebe were sympathetic, it would not be right to speak to them of it. She must just wait, and watch.

Mary Eleanor and the other women stayed in St Mary's City for a month, until the men had built a house on the holding for their shelter, and in that month she heard enough stories about the hardships of the planters' lives to have made a weaker woman give up and die. But she also learnt a lot that would help her. The woman they lodged with was a clothier's wife who had been in Virginia for twenty years. They were wealthy, for planters, and much respected, and her husband had been a member of the General Assembly until they moved to St Mary's City shortly after its founding.

'The first thing you'll need, my dear,' Mrs Colbert said, 'is a boat and a landing stage, otherwise you'll never be able to leave your home at all. We live beside the water, and by it. And you'll want to lay in plenty of stuff for the winter – it can be very hard here, very hard indeed, and you won't get a harvest this year, arriving so late. Of course,' she went on, 'you'll have fish and crabs and oysters, and duck and geese if your men are any good with their guns, but you'll have to buy in your corn and wheat, and that will cost you enough.'

'We haven't much money,' Nell said, a little anxiously. Mrs Colbert laughed.

'Why, child, who has? I doubt if there are a hundred coins in the whole of Maryland. But you have plenty of things of value to trade. And if I were you,' she added shrewdly, 'I'd sell that heifer of yours. You've less chance of keeping her through the winter than someone who's already settled, and it would be a crime to waste her, after bringing her so far. And you'd get a good price for her. Cattle are rare enough, even yet. You sell her, and if you want something for milk and cheese, you can get yourself a goat next spring.'

'I'll speak to my husband about it,' Nell murmured, and

Mrs Colbert patted her arm good-naturedly.

'You are right to be loyal. But I know and you know that in your little family, it will always be you that makes the decisions. Now, what else can I tell you?'

'Perhaps – what I need to beware of,' Nell said. Mrs Colbert's face became serious.

'Sickness and death – what else? It's a long time since I came from England, but I still remember how hard it was in the first few years, when I was used to being able to send out for things, when you could order what you needed from the town, and hire a man or woman to do anything you didn't want to do yourself. Here, you must do everything. There are no ladies here, nor fine gentlemen. We are men and women, that's all. I know that you have brought your maidservants with you –'

'It was not my own idea,' Nell said quickly, 'but my husband's parents. I did not expect to live here the way I lived at home.'

Mrs Colbert nodded approvingly. 'I'm glad you know it – it will make the shock less great. Well now, the dangers? In particular, shut all your beasts in at night, and keep them by the house in winter, for the wolves are on the increase, and as bold as two-legged thieves. And the Indians – never trust the Indians.'

'I had heard that the Indians in this part of the world were friendly?' Nell said, puzzled. It had been one of the inducements. Mrs Colbert's mouth was a grim line.

'Never trust an Indian,' she said again. 'We thought, back in '22, that they were friendly. We'd lived in peace with them for years, even started making Christians of them, and then, one day, without warning, they attacked. Massacred near four hundred of us, and as many more died of starvation because we couldn't get the crops in. I won't tell you the things I saw, child, or it would give you nightmares. I'll say this and no more – no-one ever could tell what went on in the mind of an Indian. If you see one, close enough to shoot at, shoot him. Don't wait to ask him questions.'

Nell was shocked, but she held her tongue. It was not for her to judge other people; but it made home and Morland Place seem very far away.

Edmund was not best pleased when Francis came back to York in the early months of 1643 in the company of half-a-dozen Tod's Knowe men, for he came as an officer in the Marquess of Newcastle's own regiment, the Borderers, known affectionately as Newcastle's Lambs because their uniform jackets were of white undyed wool. He received Francis coldly when he came to pay a visit to Morland Place, but Francis did not at first notice, for his father had always been undemonstrative, and Francis, having an easy temper, had always taken his affection and approval for granted.

Besides, his greeting from the rest of the family was warm. Anne hung on his arm, staring at him with wrapt admiration. He had always been a favourite of hers, for he had been nearest her in age and good-natured enough to pay her attentions at an age when the other boys had ignored her as a nuisance. Hetta and Mary Esther sat near with their work – everlasting sewing seemed more than ever a woman's lot in time of war – and asked him questions with flattering interest, and Ralph and Edward examined his sword and pistol and water-flask and spurs and fought silently behind his stool for the privilege of trying on his hat.

When he was able to speak without competition, Edmund said coldly, 'I sent you to Tod's Knowe to defend it. Had I wanted you here in York I should not have sent you away.'

Francis smiled charmingly. He was in looks a softer-featured version of Kit, a true Morland in colouring, with the dark hair and blue eyes, and high cheekbones that made his blue eyes slant a little and gave him a strangely feline look.

'Of course, sir,' he said respectfully. 'But when my Lord of Newcastle came to ask for recruits, and some of the men said that very thing, that they were needed at home to defend their own walls, he said "Defend them from whom?" And when they said, from the enemy, he said, "Why lads, the best place to beat the enemy is in battle; and the only way to be in the battle is to be in the army." So of course after that we had to go.'

'*Had* to?' Edmund said.

Francis did not notice the tone of his voice, and went on, 'He is right of course – there are times when one must go forward to meet a danger, rather than sit at home and wait for it. Even Arabella saw that in the end.'

'Was she very upset at your going?' Mary Esther asked. Francis had married his cousin Arabella Morland only a few months ago.

'At first, of course, but after a while she got to looking forward to it rather, being the master you know. And then, there was our good fortune to cheer her – I have saved the news until now. Father, Madam, Arabella is with child!'

'Oh Francis, that is wonderful news indeed! But how sad for her that you have to be away,' Mary Esther said.

Francis said lightly, 'Yes, but I hope to be back by the time the bairn is born. The war cannot last much longer. It will be over by harvest-time.'

Edmund stood up. 'I doubt whether even your presence in the army will hasten the war to its conclusion by that time,' he said with cold anger. 'I am most displeased at your action in volunteering to fight. Your place is at home on the estate I entrusted to you. If I had known how little you valued that trust, I would have bestowed it more carefully.'

Francis stared, aghast. 'Sir,' he protested, 'you don't understand –'

'I understand perfectly well. I sent you to Tod's Knowe because there was danger and I considered your presence was needed to defend it. You have left it in the charge of a pregnant woman and a number of servants. So I must consider that either you doubt my judgment, or you care nothing for my trust.'

Francis reddened with anger and distress. 'No Sir, neither,' he said vehemently. 'I thought that as I was of a man's good years, I was able to make my own judgment where my duty best lay.'

'You talk to me of duty? Do you not know that a son's first duty is to obey his father? All you have, you have received at my hands. Perhaps you are of a mind to make your own way in the world, since you trust your own judgment so much, and mine so little?'

Francis was about to retort angrily when a sudden, violent movement and cry distracted his attention. Hetta had run her needle into her finger, and had jumped to her feet, holding her hand out away from her to avoid bloodying her sewing. It looked like the merest accident, but as he glanced across at her, she caught his eye pleadingly and shook her head, a gesture none saw but him; and so he bit his lip and muttered only, 'No, Sir.'

Edmund turned away. 'I will speak to you later. Do not go back to York without seeing me – I may have some commission for you to do in the city.'

And he left them. After a brief silence Mary Esther said gently, 'That was not well done, Francis.'

'He accused me of ingratitude,' Francis said angrily. Mary Esther shook her head.

'And what did you almost accuse him of? Treason? I could see the words trembling on your lips. If Hetta had not stopped you, you would have told him your views on a man's duty to his King.' She looked at Hetta, who was

222

sucking her finger. 'Poor lambkin – did it hurt?'

'Not much,' Hetta said. Anne, not understanding what was going on, jumped up and began marching around the room.

'I think Father's hateful to speak to poor Frank so. I would join the King's army if I were a man. And I think Frank looks beautiful in his officer's ribbon.' She flung back to her brother, and hung lovingly about his neck. 'Oh darling Frank, won't you bring some of your friends here, your brother officers? Bring them to visit, oh do, do! We see no-one now, and Father is so disagreeable we have no parties and I shall never be wed if I don't meet some young men.'

'Stop, Anne, it isn't seemly,' Mary Esther said sharply. Anne was unabashed.

'Well, I hear tell that Lord Newcastle is a very elegant gentleman, a true courtier, and if he makes his headquarters here perhaps he will give entertainments, and then, you know, Francis can take me with him.'

'Oh, Anne is so stupid with her fuss about dances and parties,' Ralph said. 'Soldiers don't have time for dancing with silly girls. Soldiers march and fight battles and have glorious victories, don't they, Frank? Will you get me into your regiment, Frank? I know you could.'

'You're too young yet awhile,' Francis said. 'You must wait a few more years.'

'Oh pish! By then the war will be over,' Ralph said crossly.

Later, after Francis had gone back to the city, Mary Esther went to Edmund where he sat in the steward's room. She expected to find him working, but he was only sitting staring into the fire. The fire-glow turned his hair to rose-gold, and the flames reflected in his eyes so that they looked bright and pale gold like the first stars on midsummer eve. He did not look up when she came in, and she thought he was angry, but when Dog went to him he stroked his great, grey head absently and pulled his ears, and Dog butted his head under Edmund's hand with pleasure.

'Well,' Edmund said at last, 'have you come to reproach me too?'

Mary Esther did not quite know what to say. His words were not what she had expected. 'You were severe with him,' she said hesitantly.

'Should I not be severe with disobedience?'

'He was only doing as his conscience dictated,' she said. Now he looked up, and she was quelled by the hostility in his look. She wanted suddenly to turn on her heels and run – but that was absurd. Where could she run to? And how could she run from him, her own husband?

'That comes strangely from your lips, Madam,' he said. 'If all men were to do their own conscience, without obedience to authority, what would happen to us all? I thought the first thing a Papist learnt was that obedience is all. A man who obeys needs no conscience.'

'Edmund –' she protested.

'You speak like a Separatist, Madam. Are we to have as many rules as there are men in the world? I would have expected you of all people to have thought otherwise.'

'Edmund,' she cried softly, not understanding his venom, 'you know that I am not a Papist. You know –'

'What do I know? It seems no different to me. You spend half your life in the chapel there, on your knees, genuflecting, crossing yourself, adoring the host. Who renews the flowers in the Lady Chapel? And your daughter – you encourage her with that idolatrous nonsense over the garden. I've seen the servants taking offerings there, as if it were a heathen altar.'

'Edmund, what is it? Why are you attacking me? What have I done?'

He stood up, his fists clenching and unclenching, and she forced herself not to shrink away from him. She was suddenly aware of how very big and how powerful he was. His sheer size and strength made her shiver with a mixture of terror and desire, and it was only by great will that she made herself stand still.

'You have endangered everyone here,' he said. He did not raise his voice – she knew he never would – but it quivered with intensity. 'Don't you realize the position we are in? We are outside the city, undefended. There are large Parliamentary forces to the west and south. It is bad enough that my son and your cousins are fighting in the King's army, but now that Newcastle is here, and Francis is with him, we shall be drawn in. They will ask, and how can we refuse? There will be meetings, and dinners, and they will ask for money and men – who knows what else besides?'

Mary Esther was appalled. 'But Edmund – husband – what would you do? You would not refuse? You would not side with the rebels?'

'Rebels? I don't know any rebels. There are men fighting for what they believe in. For freedom from tyranny –'

'Against the *King*?' she cried. 'It is *treason*!' He turned on her so suddenly and fiercely that Dog flattened his ears and growled, but neither of them noticed.

'Be silent!' he cried. 'Do not dare to use that word to me! Remember who you are!'

She forced herself to speak quietly. 'I remember that I am a Morland, and that Morland blood has been spent generation after generation fighting for the King.'

There was a silence, and then his voice came like a sigh. 'Then it is time to stop.' They stared at each other for a moment, and then he went on more gently, 'I don't know who is right and wrong in this war. I cannot begin to judge. I know that there were many things that the King did that I felt were wrong. I know that Parliament's powers were being limited in a way I did not like. I am an Englishman, and freedom is our heritage. But I am a Morland too – don't you remember that, Mary?' The use of her name was an appeal, and it made her tremble, though she did not know whether it was with wrath or fear or love – perhaps all three. 'Before anything, I believe in myself, in my family, in Morland Place. I care nothing, in the balance, for King or Parliament. I only care that what is mine is preserved for my children and my children's children. And whichever wins, King or Parliament, I want neither to be able to take what is mine away from me. Now do you understand?'

Mary Esther stared at him, appalled. 'I understand,' she said. She was shaking with the things she could not say, with the words she could not use, because he was her husband, because she loved him, because of twenty years' habit. To her there was no question of right and wrong: the King was the King, the chosen and annointed of God, and everyone's duty, and especially every Morland's duty, was to defend the King. To do otherwise . . . The word *treason* described not only a crime, but a sin against everything decent in mankind, a sin against loyalty, gratitude, love, piety, faith. It was a word that described the worst that man could do. God, the King, and the Church were one, and her life belonged to all three as absolutely as to one. 'I understand,' she said, 'that I never knew you until now, though I have been your wife near twenty years.'

Edmund had appealed for understanding, and she had flung it in his face. He grew cold and forbidding in his turn. 'At least then, as my wife, you must know that you owe me loyalty and obedience,' he said. She straightened a little, like a soldier facing reprimand.

'Yes,' she said. 'I know that.' Erect and proud she took Dog by the collar and walked from the room and shut the door behind her. Erect and proud she walked along the passage and through the door into the chapel, and there her control gave way and sitting in her usual seat with her hands folded in her lap she wept heartbrokenly, her tears running freely down her cheeks, for she was too proud to hide her face in her hands.

*

The scene at the King's Manor was brilliant: the thousands of candles making the Great Hall almost as bright as in daylight, the colours, the beautiful women and gallant men, the music, the dancing, the laughter, the very correct, elegant gaiety. Between them Lord Newcastle and Queen Henrietta Maria had succeeded in recreating in York the evanescent brilliance of Whitehall before the war.

The Queen had come back from Holland with a load of arms and supplies for the King, and as Parliament held all the ports in the south, and Hull-port, she had landed at Bridlington where Newcastle had been waiting for her with a thousand men to escort her back to York. There she must stay until the King could send an army to fetch her, for the way between York and Oxford lay through Parliament-held country, and Newcastle could not leave York with the Fairfaxes still so close.

Tonight there was a masque and ball in honour of the Earl of Montrose, the leader of the King's party in Scotland, who had come to consult with Newcastle and pay his respects to the Queen. Newcastle was using the occasion to consolidate support, and had particularly asked all those gentlemen of whom he was not secure. Warned obliquely by Francis that his father might refuse an invitation from him, Newcastle had made it an invitation from the Queen, and emphasized the fact that a royal invitation is the same as a royal command by sending it with an armed guard. So Edmund Morland with his wife and two daughters arrived early at the King's Manor to pay their respects to the Queen. The fact that his eldest son and daughter-in-law were present also was a puzzle to everyone, including Richard.

Richard's reaction to the invitation had at first been indignantion that he should even be asked to pay homage to a Popish Queen, but Katherine had cut short his outburst with a gesture of one hand, and after a brief, thoughtful silence she had accepted the invitation for them both. When they were alone, Richard had demanded an explanation.

'We must be cautious, husband,' she said. 'Our position here is delicate, and if we oppose your father too openly we may be forced to leave.'

'Well then, let us leave,' Richard said stoutly. 'We will find friends of our own persuasion who will take us in. We could go to Hull – or back to Norwich even. We must not compromise our child.' For Katherine was pregnant. She nodded.

'Exactly,' she said. 'We must not endanger the child. A long journey, the strain of hostility and flight, might make me miscarry. No, Richard, we must stay and make ourselves inconspicuous for the time being. Our chance will come – the chance to complete the work we were sent here for. You would not wish us to leave now, with that task undone?'

'But surely – we are endangering our own souls?' Richard said, much puzzled. Katherine smiled mysteriously.

'You must trust me, husband. Have I not always led you along the right path?'

Richard did not answer, but his expression was uncertain. He did not understand what Katherine was about. Everything had seemed clear, plain and easy at first when Katherine converted him to the true faith and enlisted him as a soldier in God's cause. But since then everything had been growing more and more confused. First there was their marriage – necessary, she had said, and after the first confusion their celibacy had seemed to confirm her words. Then they had come to Morland Place, and he had understood nothing since. They did not seem to be getting on with their job of saving souls at all; then Katherine had insisted on consummating the marriage after all, and since then they had been a torment to each other. Richard had coped very well with complete celibacy, but he could not cope with the dichotomy between his mental revulsion for the act and his physical enjoyment of it. And Katherine –

228

what did she feel about it? Was she struggling too? It made Richard uneasy and miserable all day, knowing the conflict he would have to face at night; so much so that he avoided his dear wife's company when he could and spent long hours riding and hunting out on the moors and in the woods.

And now, to confuse him even more, she was insisting that they go to the Romish Queen's assembly, the Queen who was responsible for all the sufferings of decent men in England, for everyone knew the King was completely under her spell and was forced by her witchcraft to try to take the church in England back to Rome. Richard was not a subtle person, and had always gone straight for what he wanted, however wrong-headedly. That Katherine had some deep purpose he had simply to trust, but he did not understand it, and it made him very unhappy.

That his father and stepmother were unhappy was obvious to no-one but themselves. The coldness that had existed between them since the day Francis came home was hidden by the determination of both to behave correctly in front of family and servants. For Edmund it was easier since he had never shewn his affection for her publicly in any way that anyone but she would notice; with Mary Esther it was a fierce sense of loyalty and a fiercer pride that made her hide her misery and appear almost as gay as ever. But it was a great strain. Already her face was thinner and her eyes less bright. She had always spent a good deal of time refreshing her spirit in the chapel and in the garden, so no-one noticed that she slipped away more often than before to be alone, and if faithful Dog had often to lick the tears from her face, he was not in a position to tell.

The worst times for both of them were when they were in bed, for then there was no audience to play to, and the awareness of the gulf between them grew more painfully acute. It was natural for Mary Esther to think that she felt their estrangement more than Edmund, because he shewed all his feelings less; but he knew that it was worse for him, for she had so many outlets for her emotion, while he had never trusted himself to anyone but her, and he resented her callousness in not understanding that. They both sought to avoid the forced proximity of the curtained bed; Mary Esther would hurry to bed early so that she could pretend to be asleep when Edmund came up; Edmund would sit up in the steward's room late into the night, sometimes falling asleep at his desk to wake stiff and cold in the morning. He took to spending the odd night away from home, at Twelvetress or one of the other houses, and when they did sleep together, they lay rigidly as far apart as the bed would allow, slept little and woke unrefreshed.

For Anne and Henrietta, however, the occasion was one of unshadowed pleasure. Anne was almost beside herself with delight that she should at last be going to a masque and ball – and such a ball! – in the presence of the Queen and her ladies in their dazzling dresses, the courtiers, and so many handsome, gallant chevaliers, and one of them her own brother, who must therefore introduce her and get her partners. She was pleased with her dress of pale lilac silk, and her head, daintily dressed with ribbons and fresh flowers, and Hetta was only worried that she would make herself ill with excitement, or expect so much that she would be disappointed. As for Hetta, she was thrilled and excited too, but she shewed it only by smiling even more than usual. Plump and brown like a sparrow, her good-natured expression made her pretty enough not to want for partners, though her dress was not new, but one of her mother's turned, and its green did not suit her half so well as Anne's lilac suited her.

After the masque, when the dancing began, Francis, well aware of Anne's expectations, good-naturedly introduced to her two companion officers from his regiment, Ensign Symonds and Ensign Ruddock. Symonds, being the senior, bowed low and asked for the honour of the first set, and

Anne flutteringly agreed. As they walked off to take their places, Ruddock caught Hetta's amused eye, and offered her his arm and they took their place two couples below where they could watch. It was plain that Anne was being very charming, and that Symonds was not unwilling to be charmed.

'Your sister is very pretty,' Ruddock said to Hetta. 'She has already made a great impression on my friend'.

Hetta thought the ensign had the bemused expression of a moth dancing before a candle-flame, but she said only, 'Is he a good friend of yours?'

Ruddock grinned. 'I understand you,' he said. 'Yes, he is perfectly respectable and certainly a person you need have no fear in trusting your sister to.'

Hetta laughed. 'How well you understand me.'

'Whereas I,' he said, pressing her hand as they touched fingers for a turn, 'am not at all respectable, and your reputation will be ruined for ever now that you have been seen dancing with me.'

'I do not think Francis would introduce to me anyone of whom he did not approve,' Hetta said imperturbably.

'Ah, but Frank is so good-natured he would never discover a villain until he was hanged. Whereas you, Madam, if I may be so impertinent, have, in spite of the sweetness of your expression, a very sharp and penetrating eye.'

'Sharp enough, Sir, to recognize your impertinence for what it is,' she smiled, and they danced on in perfect accord.

While the girls were dancing with a succession of young gentlemen, amongst whom their first two partners recurred with pleasant frequency, Edmund was having a very uncomfortable interview with Lord Newcastle, who seemed to be extraordinarily well informed about the Morland family, past and present.

'I was delighted to have your son with me when I left Northumberland,' he said to Edmund as they strolled along the edge of the dance sets. 'Your father, I believe, was a

231

Redesdale man, and his mother was Mary Percy, of whom songs are still sung the length of the Border.'

'Your lordship's information is impeccable,' Edmund said stiffly.

'As famed for her courage in battle as for her beauty,' Newcastle said smoothly. 'Your son took me to see her grave when I visited Tod's Knowe. I was glad to have the services of the great-grandson of so loyal a Borderer so freely offered.'

The emphasis of certain words in the compliment made Edmund extremely uncomfortable, but he said only, 'Your lorship is too kind.'

'You have other sons, I believe, who are serving at present with our dashing Prince in the cavalry? It is good to see the Morlands living so thoroughly up to their motto.'

'One son, my lord, my second son,' Edmund said with slow emphasis. 'There are two cousins also, of collateral lines.'

'No matter,' Newcastle said, unmoved. 'It reflects very well on you, Sir, very well indeed. Your horses, I hear, are famous in these parts. I should like to see your stud.'

It sounded like an abrupt change of subject, but it was not. Edmund, struggling, could only say, 'Your lordship does me honour.'

'Not at all, Morland, not at all. The King is fortunate in the loyalty and love of his great subjects, though the meaner sort may not know their duty so well. And as the King's General in the North, I do no more than my duty in expressing His Majesty's appreciation of the sacrifices you are making on his behalf. He will not, believe me, prove himself ungenerous when the present crisis is past; any more than he will be lenient to those treasonable subjects who rebel against his just authority.'

It was a speech to make Edmund sweat, it was so full of veiled hints, threats, and promises. For the first time Newcastle paused in his measured stroll and met Edmund's eye with a sardonic and unpleasantly shrewd look.

'It is a pleasure to talk to you, Master Morland,' he said smoothly. 'We understand each other well. And if I find matters of State so pressing that I have no time to visit your stud, will you forgive me for sending one of my subalterns instead?'

Edmund was roused to one last, futile retort. 'Your lordship's expertize in matters of horseflesh is so renowned, I have no fear that you would have about you anyone who did not know the worth of a good horse.'

Newcastle smiled, and dismissed Edmund with a courteous nod. Edmund moved away, seething inwardly. So Newcastle was to send a commissioning officer to commandeer his best horses! And what else would he be forced to give besides – money, plate, men? It was all very well for Newcastle to talk about *when* the King was victorious over the rebels – but what if he was not? Then the man who had aided him would bring down on his head all the wrath of the Parliamentary party, and it would not help him then to point out that his co-operation had been forced from him. Why could they not leave him alone? If they wanted to fight, let them fight – he wanted no part of it. All he wanted was to get on with his own life in his own way.

CHAPTER THIRTEEN

It was crippling, gruelling work, clearing the land. The men laboured under the hot sun, bitten almost to hysteria by the clouds of mosquitoes, lopping the branches, then cutting down the trees, then digging out the stumps. The women had to share in the labour too, dragging the branches away and trimming them, and cutting up the waste wood for fires. Rachel was at first indignant that she was expected to work in the fields but Nell silenced her with a look. Phoebe made no murmur at all, like the good child she was, though Nell watched her carefully for she was not strong, and directed her when it was possible to the lighter tasks and to work in the shade. Betty Hammond, of course, expected it, and to Nell's surprise Hester Goodman did her share without more complaint than anyone else.

But after two weeks Ambrose protested as firmly as it was in his nature to protest.

'You must rest,' he said to Nell. 'I cannot bear to see you labour so – and look at your poor hands.'

He turned them over. They had been as white and flawless as porcelain, a lady's hands. Now they were blistered and abraded, with callouses at the base of each finger, and dirt engrained in the thumb and along the side of the forefinger. Nell surveyed the ruin unmoved. She remembered Mrs Colbert's words – here there are no ladies or fine gentlemen, just men and women.

'My dear,' she said, 'I have to do my share. All must work here.'

'Not in the fields. You will have enough to do in the house, I warrant. You must not always be bending and stooping in the hot sun. Think of the child.'

'Very well,' she said. 'But Phoebe must come in too – she is not strong enough for such work.'

Ambrose agreed eagerly, thinking that with Phoebe to help her Nell might be spared the hardest tasks indoors. Soon his work force was still further reduced. Nell had not forgotten Mrs Colbert's advice about the boat, and when the men had cut down enough trees they set about building a landing-stage at the most convenient place on the bank near the house. They did it by trial and error. The first attempt simply collapsed into the river, as did the second, for they had not driven the piles of the frame deeply enough. But at the third attempt they got a framework strong enough to withstand even a freak tidal wave, and the rest was easy. Nell and Phoebe came down every day at dinner time to bring them food and a bucket of water, and the men, lying exhausted in whatever shade they could find, took great comfort from the women's enthusiasm.

Then came the matter of the boat. Ambrose, who had studied boats a great deal simply out of interest, had an idea of what he wanted; Nell, being the daughter of a long line of sailors, and having had access all her childhood to books about boats, also knew what was wanted and roughly how it should be done; but only Sam Goodman had the practical skills to put their ideas into practice. If it had not been for him, they would have ended up with either a raft or a canoe: as it was, he knocked himself up a crude shelter near the jetty, got out the tools of his trade, and began.

It was a joy to watch him, in the brief moments when anyone had the time. He worked slowly, and when asked he said that with a boat everything had to be perfect. Everyone else would have been content with something less perfect but finished sooner, but with the Englishman's natural deference towards a craftsman they let him be. He needed an assistant, and there was much truth in his argument that Hester was already accustomed to helping him at home, and knew his ways, and that she was the least useful person in the field, and therefore would be the least loss to them. But Nell could not help being struck by the contrast in their lives from that time forward, the two Goodmans working at an easy, comfortable pace under the shelter of their boat-shed, and the rest labouring hard under the sun to clear the fields and build the fences.

Ambrose was right that Nell would find enough to do at the house. Apart from the basic tasks of preparing food for everyone, and fetching water – she and Phoebe spent a good deal of time going back and forth with heavy buckets – there were the animals to tend and the kitchen garden to plant. Nell took the garden very seriously. She began to see now difficult it would be to feed them all in the winter, how unlikely it was that they would be able to plant any field crops that year, and determined that they should at least have some vegetables. She and Phoebe between them cleared a small area behind the house, taking turns to drag the small hand plough. They worked slowly, Phoebe because she was small and frail, Nell because she was large with child, but slowly and perseveringly they did it, and planted a variety of the vegetable seeds they had brought with them.

'They should do well,' Nell said to Phoebe as they went along the rows, bending double to plant the precious seeds one at a time. 'The soil is virgin, so it will be very fertile, and the climate is warm and moist. I think we should have something to shew them before very long.'

'The trees seem to have taken, too, Madam,' Phoebe said, straightening a moment to ease her aching back, and looking across the cleared patch to where the little saplings had stopped drooping and were putting out new growth. It was the first thing Nell had seen to when they arrived, when she had come up with the others to see the site of their new home. The trees had been planted before even the house was built: two apples, an eater and a cider-apple, a peartree, a Morland apricot, and, as a piece of sheer luxury, one rose tree. It was shooting wonderfully already, and would plainly bloom before the season was over. Nell thought it a good omen. The blooms would be white – it was the white rose of York.

When Ambrose had had to register his new plantation they had discussed for some time what name to register it in, and it was the sight of the rose-tree that had finally inspired Nell to say, 'Ambrose, why do we not just call it York?' And so it was decided.

Feeding them all, though not yet a problem, was time consuming. Their stock of grain was small, and Nell's vegetables not yet ready, so they must live mainly on meat and fruit. There was plenty of wild fruit out in the fields – blackberries, strawberries, sweet little wild plums – and there was fish in the river, and the big, strange-tasting oysters, not at all like English oysters, and crabs, and there were duck in plenty, and in the uncleared wood deer and wild turkeys. They had also eggs from their own fowl, and milk from the milch-goat that Nell had brought with her on Mrs Colbert's advice, and there was a family of pigs fattening on the rich grass.

Nell and Phoebe collected eggs and gathered fruit; they soon learnt how to catch crabs with a scrap of stinking meat on a string, and Nell became quite adept at shooting squirrels and pigeons, and sometimes got a turkey, though she could never get a duck. But it all took a long time, and shooting larger game was a matter for one of the men. Even if Nell had been able to stalk and shoot a deer, she would not have been able to get it home afterwards. So from time to time she would tell Ambrose firmly that he must go hunting, glad in her heart that by doing so she was taking him from the fields for a while. Though he never complained, and worked as hard as anyone, he was not used to it as were Robert and Will and even Pen, and it tired him terribly. John Hogg would go with him, and a day quietly stalking deer in the cool of the woods did them both a great deal of good.

For the harsh conditions were taking their toll. Several of them had a recurrent low fever, which Nell treated with camomile and sassafras tea, without great success. Griping of the bowels was common, too. Blackberry leaves were the cure for that; and for the constipation which frequently alternated with the other condition, an infusion of rhubarb and treacle. Josiah got a terrible wound in the foot with an axe which laid him up for days, and it would not heal. It began to go bad, and he was in terror of gangrene. Nell treated it as best she could, re-opening the wound and cauterizing it when the tell-tale heat and redness shewed it was turning again. She tried everything on it that she could think of, and Josiah bore with everything in silence, his face cheese-coloured and shiny with sweat, his eyes enormous, following her with a mixture of terror and trust that struck her to the heart. In the end, failing any new idea, she tried an old remedy which she remembered Mary Esther telling her of – spider-web and mouldy bread. The mouldy bread was impossible to achieve, since they had too little bread ever to let it go mouldy, but the spider-web was easy enough, though it took her some time and patience to collect. Josiah was more apprehensive about that than about anything else she had tried on him, but soon afterwards the wound began to heal, and in a week was completely sound.

Soon after Josiah had gone back to the fields, Phoebe fell ill with a fever. She had had the low fever several times before and had recovered, but this seemed to be something different, a fever so high that she seemed to burn up like a scrap of paper falling on a fire. Nell dared not leave her, and had to bring Rachel in from the fields to help with her other tasks so that she could have time to nurse Phoebe. In a matter of days Phoebe shrank away to nothing.

'She's dying,' Rachel said quietly on the morning of the third day as Nell gently mopped the girl's forehead with a cool cloth. Nell looked up in anguish, but she knew it was true. The bones of Phoebe's skull seemed to be pressing outwards through her thin skin, her flesh had fallen away so. Under her lips one could see the shape of her teeth, her nose was suddenly sharp, her cheeks and forehead bulges and hollows, as if her body were rehearsing its final change.

'I wish we had a priest here,' Nell whispered. 'I cannot bear for her to go like this, so far from home, without a priest.'

'Poor child,' Rachel said. 'The master should never have sent her.'

'He did not know what it would be like,' Nell defended Edmund, though with no particular reason. She had confided her own fears to no-one, but now she said, 'He should not have sent any of us. How shall we survive the winter, Rachel? We may have cause to envy poor Phoebe.'

'Nay, Madam,' Rachel said, shocked. 'You must not say so. We'll be right once the men've cleared the fields and the crops are in. Why, Madam, what should you fear! It's your condition, that's all.'

'Yes, you are right,' Nell said, agreeing for the sake of peace. It was not fair on Rachel to burden her with her own troubles, and the less everyone foresaw the hardship that was to come, the less they would suffer. 'Rachel, I've a mind to have my crucifix in my hand. I think it would comfort Phoebe too, if she wakes. Would you fetch it for me?'

All morning she sat so, praying for the soul of shrunken, dying child whose face she continually mopped of sweat. Phoebe was not yet fifteen, and it seemed so hard that she should die in a strange land with her life untasted. Then towards noon there was a change; the girl stirred, moved restlessly, and opened her eyes. They focused with difficulty on Nell's face, and Nell smiled tenderly. Phoebe's lips moved, though they made no sound. 'She is saying good-bye,' Nell thought, and she lifted the crucifix so that Phoebe could see it, and then brought it down to her face, and

Phoebe kissed it, and sighed, and closed her eyes.

Tears started to Nell's eyes, and she laid the cross down on the girl's breast and prayed silently, 'Lord, you see how she died: take her to you, though we had no priest on hand. It was so easy, I would not bring her back to suffer more.'

She bowed her head in prayer, aware only then how tired she was. She swayed a little as she sat, but she did not leave the bedside. A little while later Ambrose came in. She did not hear him until he touched her shoulder, and she started and looked up. Ambrose was smiling.

'Nell, my hinny, look what I have for you – it is a sign, I am sure.' He brought his hand from behind his back, and lying on the palm was a white rose, half open. 'The first, Nell, the first to grow in our new land.'

Nell stared up at him, uncomprehending. 'Phoebe –' she said at last, all she could manage. Ambrose turned his head and looked swiftly and his face broke into an even wider smile. 'Why, she is better!' he cried. Nell looked, wondering how to disabuse him, and saw, wonder of wonders, that the crucifix lying on the child's breast was moving gently and rhythmically with her breathing: normal breathing – the fever had broken.

'Oh Ambrose,' she said, and trying to stand she swayed and only his arms prevented her from falling.

'Why, Nell, you are ill yourself,' he cried anxiously. She shook her head.

'Only tired, my dear, so very tired.'

By evening Phoebe had taken her first nourishment, some broth prepared by Rachel, for Nell at Ambrose's insistence, had retired to bed. That night Nell went into labour, and after great suffering she bore her first child. It was a boy, and it was dead.

The summer of '43 was the happiest in Anne's life, as she frequently told Hetta when the girls were in bed together.

With the Royalist army based in York and Father forced to co-operate with them, there were ample opportunities of meeting with young officers. To be sure, Father never invited any of them to the house, and gave no parties or balls, but there was a great deal of to-ing and fro-ing despite him. Commissioning officers came to discuss horses and money, and always brought a subaltern or two with them, who would be free to wander in the gardens while their senior wrangled with Edmund. Francis paid frequent visits home, always mindful to bring a few friends with him, and when there were social gatherings in the city, Edmund and his wife and family were frequently obliged to go.

Best of all, Anne liked the hunting parties that were got up that summer, partly for pleasure and partly for the perennial necessity of supplying fresh meat. Anne was a fine horsewoman, as were all the Morlands, and she knew she shewed to great advantage on horseback. When Mary Esther did not ride out, she sometimes let Anne have Psyche, and though the mare was now rising fifteen, she was still faster than any other horse that trod the earth, and Anne knew that in her hunting green and the feathered, broad-brimmed Cavalier hat she now affected she was irresistible when mounted on the elegant, dancing chestnut.

There was some competition amongst Francis' companions for the privilege of visiting Morland Place or joining one of the hunting expeditions, and some if not all of it could be put down to the attractions of Frank Morland's two sisters. Hetta had her own ring of admirers, and though their admiration was quieter it was no less sincere than the more flamboyant homage paid to Mistress Anne. Anne was never happier than when surrounded by a group of handsome, dashing young men, vying with each other to frame outrageous compliments and express undying devotion. She had the unsuspecting Ensign – now promoted Lieutenant – Symonds half out of his head for her, but while he was her semi-official escort, she was carrying on a much more violent and dangerous intrigue with his younger brother, Reynold.

Reynold had only recently joined as an ensign, following in the wake of his brother mainly from boredom. Left at home, he had been forced to do all his brother's tasks, and thought that life was bound to be easier and more to his taste in the Royalist army. He had heard good accounts of the courteous life lived in York under Lord Newcastle, and once arrived he hastened to attach himself to Frank Morland's pleasant, elegant little parties.

He was a handsome young man, red-gold hair and blue eyes and light freckled skin, and he wore, unusually for the time, a curly, close-clipped beard. It gave him a rather dangerous, piratical look which most women found irresistible. Anne was no exception. When he bent over her hand on first being presented, and looked up under his golden eyelashes with a challenging, inviting stare, she felt herself trembling. He treated her in public no differently from any of the other young men, with extravagant courtesy and elegant compliments, but they were accompanied always by sidelong, cynical looks and a certain smile that seemed to say, 'Come, Madam, when shall we stop playing and come to the heart of the matter?' It made Anne tremble with delightful apprehension.

When they hunted, it was easy for Anne and Reynold to get separated from the rest of the company, for, apart from Psyche who was fast and hard to hold, Reynold Symonds had the best horse, and it needed only for Anne to take a bold line across country that no-one else dared, and for Reynold to follow her, and they would soon find themselves in some convenient wood or coppice, deliciously alone.

At first they merely conversed, Anne remaining mounted while Reynold stood holding both horses and leaning against Psyche's shoulder looking up at her with his light, dangerous eyes. But soon he persuaded her to dismount too, so that they could talk in comfort, and from there it was a short step from conversing to exchanging passionate kisses. But when he would go further, Anne always drew away, saying, 'No, no, I cannot. We must go back – the others will wonder where we are.'

And then one day when she said this, he did not let her go, but held her tighter, looking down into her face with his fierce smile, and said,

'You have teased me long enough, Mistress Anne. This time I will not let you go.'

'You must, you must – I cannot! Please, Reynold!'

'Why, Anne, don't you love me? Come, admit – I know that you do.'

Blushing, Anne could only nod.

'Well, then – why deny me what both of us want? Don't you know that the fortune of war is hostile to lovers? At any time we may be ordered out to give battle, and then who knows if I will ever come back? I could be dead tomorrow, Nan, think of that!'

'Oh no! Don't say it!' she cried. He tightened his grip at her reaction.

'Supposing I were to be killed tomorrow,' he went on, tormenting her, 'and you were to live the rest of your life, knowing that this was the last time we had spent together. Come,' he kissed her brow and eyes and moved down to her lips, punctuating his words with kisses, 'you love me too much to say me nay. Give me your love, Nan.' His lips moved down to her throat and breast, and she found she could hardly speak for the tightness in her chest, as if her heart were beating too strongly and choking her.

She felt weak and dizzy with longing, but she managed to whisper, 'But Reynold – what if I should – ' It was hard to say it, for she had been brought up modestly. 'If I should get with child?'

He felt the yielding limpness of her body in his arms, and knew her resistance was over. He had thought about this

243

already. 'Then we should be wed,' he said easily. She would have a good enough dowry, he calculated, to be tempting to him, for he was a younger son and his brother Sam would inherit the small estate – there would be little enough for him. And she was stupid enough not to confine his life after they were married. As long as she believed he loved her, he would be able to do anything he wanted, and it would be a simple task to fool her. He had little to lose: if she should get with child, he would have a wife with a good dowry and wealthy connections, and if she should not, the fortunes of war would soon take him far from this place.

'But –' Anne still hesitated, though his hands were already slipping into her bodice, 'but my father would never consent – he would not let us marry –' Reynold, the younger son of a small landowner, with no estate of his own? She could not put it into words, but she knew Edmund would scorn such a match. But it was too late now, far too late to try to resist. Her blood was flowing fast and hot in her veins, and Reynold's powerful arms were lowering her gently to the ground.

'I will make him let us,' he said. 'Trust me, it will be well. Kiss me, Nan, give me your love –'

The horses browsed on the sweet young leaves of the hawthorns, and the only sound was the rustling of the bushes and the ringing of their bits as they tugged the leaves free.

In January 1644, in the depths of the worst winter in memory, the Scots crossed the frozen Tweed in a psalm-singing army twenty-two thousand strong. After the battle at Newbury, Parliament had signed a covenant with the Assembly of Scotland, agreeing to convert the whole of England to Presbyterianism after the Scottish model, if the Scots would help them defeat the King. Newcastle marched out of York to confront the Scots as far from York as possible, hoping to hold them at the town of Newcastle and prevent them from joining up with Fairfax's army, still holding Hull.

Further south, the town of Newark was in danger. It was a vital point in the supply line between north and south, and was held by the Royalists under Sir John Henderson, but in March it was heavily besieged by Parliamentary forces under Sir John Meldrum, and Henderson sent out a cry for help to the King at Oxford. The King sent for Rupert, who was then at Shrewsbury attending the matters of State in his new capacity of President of Wales, and Rupert set off at once to march to Newark. He had with him only a small force, part of his own regiment of cavalry and some of the Prince of Wales' regiment, but he gathered an army as he marched by drawing men from each Royalist garrison he passed.

At the core of this scratch force were the hard-bitten, now famous Rupert Horse, people like Daniel O'Neil and Hamil and Kit who had been with him from the start. They were still dashing, fierce fighters, but they were no longer carefree and gay as they had been two years ago. They took their mood from their general, and the Prince was bitterly disillusioned. He had fought, he and his men, harder than anyone, yet he saw everything they had achieved thrown away by the amateur behaviour of the court party.

Since the Queen had joined them, bringing with her her own brand of decorous frivolity, things had degenerated until, in the Prince's view, the King and the courtiers seemed to regard the war as a series of dangerous interludes to the real life of court. Intrigue was the breath of life to the court, and the war amused them where it gave scope for intrigue. Rupert, downright, free-spoken, never tactful, made so many enemies that no-one was short of material for their plots and gossipings; while he marched and fought, they postured, posed, and awarded each other titles.

His close companions could not but see how Rupert felt,

and were affected by it. They no longer believed the war was theirs; they began seriously to doubt if they could win it at all; but still their loyalty and sense of honour drove them on, less gaily, more grimly, but as determinedly as ever.

On 20th March they arrived before the town of Newark and made a brief stop twelve miles from its walls to rest. Rupert called his officers together.

'We'll rest here,' he said. 'Bait the horses and see that the men eat. It'll have to be cold food. We want to take the rebels by surprise, and in this dark they would see any fires we lit for miles around. The moon should rise just before two: we'll move on then, and circle round to the north. Danny, have you a good, quiet, reliable man? I want to try to get a message to Henderson. If we can get him to break out as soon as we engage the enemy, it will be of the greatest help.'

'I'll find you someone, Sir,' Daniel said, nodding composedly. 'But, Sir, it will be dangerous I'm thinking. These parts are as live with rebels as a cur-dog with fleas. Suppose the man is captured – our plan will be known.'

'It's well thought,' Rupert said. 'We'll couch it in terms Henderson will understand, but the enemy will not. Find your man and bring him to me. The rest of you, see to your men. I'll be round as soon as I've dealt with this matter.'

They went back to their troops. The men were all dismounted, and now slacked off their girths and got out the horses' nosebags. The horses were grouped in sixes, in circles heads inward, so that one man could comfortably hold all six, and the riders took it in turn to hold them while the rest unpacked their bread and cheese and dried meat and sat on the damp grass nearby. In this way, if there was a sudden emergency, the men could tighten girths and mount up in the shortest time and with the least possible confusion.

Having seen to his men and checked that Oberon was comfortable, Kit found himself a quiet place on a little rise by some bushes where the ground was dry, and stretched himself out, propped on his elbows, to rest. He had taken a bad wound in the thigh during the winter, which ached after long exertion, and twinged in damp weather. His leg was aching now – a sign, he knew, that rain was coming. He had food by him, but could not eat. He felt sick at heart, and almost without knowing it he pulled from his breast the last letter he had received from Hero. He did not unfold it to read it – he had read it so often he knew it by heart – but simply held it, stroking it with his fingers. It was a kind of talisman to him, absurd as it seemed.

In a moment Daniel came over to join him, accompanied by another of the mercenary brotherhood, a Frenchman, Mortaigne, whose name the English rendered Morton. They squatted down with Kit in companionable silence and took out their own food.

'Well,' said Daniel after a while, 'that's done – I sent young Hoxton. Pray God the game little dog makes it.'

Morton savaged his hard bread with his sharp little teeth, and then cocking an eye at Kit said, 'What, my friend, no appetite? Are you sick?'

Kit shook the question off like a cat shaking off an unwelcome caress. 'I do not feel like eating.'

'Eating his heart out,' Daniel said, not unkindly. He jerked his head towards the letter in Kit's hand and said, almost as if he had read Kit's thoughts, 'That there is a letter from his wife. He regards it as a talisman, and if the rebels catch him they'll hang him for an idolater, as surely as they'll hang me for this.' And he tugged out the gold cross from his shirt-neck.

Kit looked up and said slowly, 'I gave her a thing once, an oak apple, the shape of a hare's head. She wouldn't part with it, said it was her talisman, that it would keep her safe.' He realized that he did not know why he was telling them this, except that he wanted to speak of her. He finished vaguely, 'The hare is a family symbol, you see.'

'Sure, Kit,' Morton said, scratching his dark beard. 'I've seen it on your men's coats. *Le lièvre courant, n'est-ce pas?* The white running hare. Is she well, your wife?' He gestured towards the letter.

'It's an old letter,' Kit said. 'She says in it that she is well, she and the child.'

'There is a child.' Morton nodded his head sympathetically.

'One son. He will be four in August.' That frail, sickly babe had grown, had survived the terrible hazards of babyhood, and had reached the age of four. Now there were new hazards to be faced – and the Scots were marching slowly but surely towards York. His son might be snatched away by disease, his home might be attacked by frenzied barbarian soldiers, and he was here, far away, unable to help them or be with them – and for what?

Daniel glanced at him, and said gruffly, through a mouthful of the toughest dried meat he had ever chewed at, 'You should not be here, friend Kit, and that's the truth.'

'But how can I leave?' Kit said simply, and they were silent, knowing that he, as they were, was bound by honour, a stronger bond than zeal for the cause or even professionalism.

To ease the tension, Daniel said fiercely as he spat out the intractible meat, 'Sweet Saint Mary, this beast was never a Christian while it lived, or it wouldn't try to break an honest Catholic's teeth now it's dead. Jesus, Mary and Joseph, what wouldn't I give for a nice fricassee of chicken now?'

At two the moon rose, sailing clear of the swift spring clouds, and between light showers it shewed them their way. The plan was surprise, and when they came round to the north of the city, they saw the reason for the manoeuvre, for there was a ridge here which would hide their approach from the besieging army until the last moment. The wind was in their favour, too, blowing towards them from the enemy – 'God, how the Puritans stink!' said Daniel, typically – so that the noise of their approach would not betray them. At about nine in the morning they reached the ridge, and as soon as they crested it, Rupert's hand went up, the trumpets sounded, and the cavalry thundered down on the astonished rebels.

The little group of friends as always was out in front – Rupert on his grey stallion, so easy to pick out in his scarlet coat; Kit, carried forward by Oberon's great stride; Hamil on Firefly, Daniel, Morton, all yelling fiercely, swords at the ready, too fast for the enemy musketmen, who would just be getting into position when they came upon them. Rupert was a couple of lengths ahead, galloping so hard and yelling so fiercely that the enemy line which had turned to face him wavered. But three of them stood firm, bunched together, swords up.

Kit saw his Prince set on by three men at once, and tried to wheel Oberon towards him, but others now, emboldened by the first three, had turned back, and Kit had to fight his way forward. He saw the Prince run one of the soldiers through, but even as he struggled to pull back his sword the other two were on him. There was a sharp crack from behind Kit's right shoulder, and the swordsman whose blade was in the act of descending tumbled backwards off his horse, his hands to his chest, his sword falling harmlessly away. Kit risked a swift glance and saw Morton, with a smoking pistol in his hand, open his mouth to yell, 'Queek, Danny, *le Prince*!'

The third of the trio of rebels, a huge man, had seized Rupert's collar and was trying to haul him bodily off his horse, evidently hoping to take him prisoner rather than kill him. Kit parried a sword thrust, and then saw, to his relief, that Daniel had broken through, and was leaping to the Prince's aid. The Irishman's sword went up, flashing in the sun, and came smashing down on the rebel's wrist. Screaming wildly, the man lost his balance and fell from his horse, blood spouting in a high fountain from the stump of his wrist; and Kit saw, with sick horror, that the fingers of the severed hand maintained their grip on the Prince's collar for a few moments before he knocked the twitching thing away.

In that moment of inattention, Kit felt the cold burning of a sword-wound in his bridle arm, and turned only just in time to save his own life. His arm was laid open and bleeding freely, but he could still hold the reins. By now the main body of the cavalry had caught up with them, and the enemy was backing off, turning and fleeing. Then came the thrilling sound of trumpets from beyond the rebel army, and a shout went up that Henderson's men were making a sortie from the besieged town; the Prince's message had got through, and had been understood.

The fighting went on for half an hour more, and then Meldrum, seeing his position was hopeless, sent to parley. The soldiers of both sides fell back panting, resting their aching sword-arms, while their leaders met in the middle of a clear space between the forces. Little Hoxton came riding over from Henderson's side, grinning fit to split his face in half, to be reunited with his Captain, Daniel, who thumped the boy so hard on the back in his joy at having him safe, that Hoxton went red and choked.

'You did it, you little game-cock, by all the saints! Mary bless you, child, you saved the day, that's what you did,' Daniel yelled, loud enough to be heard above the din and bring a grin to many a tired face. 'Hullo, but that was quick, be God! The parley's finished, me lads – and look at the old Drum rumbling away. Our Prince Robber's let him go.'

The rebels were to be allowed to leave, provided they abandoned their arms and baggage; but as soon as they began to march off, some of the cavalry, their blood still up, attacked the unarmed men to plunder them of their personal possessions, and, more importantly, their armour – Roundhead armour was better than their own. For a moment there was confusion, and then Rupert appeared amongst the looters, beating them off with the flat of his

250

sword, yelling in fury. Other officers joined in, and in a moment peace was restored and the looters had slunk back to their ranks, muttering. One passed the Prince still clutching an enemy standard. Rupert caught him by the collar as he passed.

'Where did you get that?' he said, his voice dangerously quiet. The man paled and stammered.

'Off that officer there, Sir – my lord –'

'Give it to me.' He took it from the man so roughly that he almost jerked him from his horse. 'What right do you think you have to that – to take a standard from an unarmed man? You coward! I expect better manners from my enemy than that. Get back to your rank! When you have captured a standard in battle, then you may keep it. Get back, you cur!'

The man escaped to his rank, pale and trembling, and Rupert, riding over to the rebel officer, handed him back his standard with a courtly bow. The officer responded with like grave courtesy, and the Parliamentarians marched off unhindered, and in silence.

Kit watched them, pressing the edges of his wound together with his fingers, resting his aching sword-arm, feeling Oberon shift his weight wearily from foot to foot. The horse was no longer young, and this kind of life took the stamina out of even the best animal. How much longer could he go on? Another fight, another siege raised, another victory, he thought. Soon it would be summer, and then harvest time, and then they would be fighting in the snow, seeing it redden with their blood. He was weary, and his longing for home was not as strong as his longing simply to lie down and stop fighting. He could well understand why Falkland had flung his life away in the battle at Newbury. He tried to think of Hero and the child, but they were misty and far away in his mind, and he could not remember what Hero looked like.

Tomorrow they would march back to Wales, and after

that – who knew? Kit watched his blood well slowly over
his fingers and drip from the side of his hand into the dust,
and wondered if he would ever see his home again.

BOOK THREE

The Bay Tree

What then remains, but th'only spring
Of all our loves and joys, the KING.

Richard Lovelace: *From Prison*

BOOK THREE

The Bay Tree

What then remains, but that we still should sing
Of all our loves and joys, the KING.

Richard Lovelace: From Prison

CHAPTER FOURTEEN

Vastly outnumbered, Newcastle had gradually to fall back, and in April, when the news came that Lord Manchester's Eastern Association army was moving up to join Fairfax in Yorkshire, there was no choice but to hurry back to save York, the key point in the north. He was only just in time, for no sooner had he reached the city than it was surrounded by the three armies, the great mass of Scots to the north and west, the Fairfaxes to the south, and Manchester to the east, and the long siege began.

Hero made no attempt to defend Watermill House – it would have been useless to try against the Scottish cannon, even if she had had more than a handful of servants. As soon as word came that the Scots were coming, she packed the family's belongings and valuables onto ox-carts, put the servants on top, mounted her horse with her boy before the saddle, and fled.

'Where are we going, Mama?' Young Kit asked. 'Are we going to stay with grandfather?'

Hero had given it some thought. 'No,' she said, 'we are going to ask Cousin Ruth if she will take us in until Papa comes home.'

'When will Papa be coming home?'

'I don't know, lamb. Soon I hope.'

Young Kit said no more. He knew what 'soon' meant in a grown-up's vocabulary. Hero could not have endured to live in Morland Place with Richard and Katherine and their heretic servants so much to the fore, even if it were not doubtful which side Edmund would finally come down on. Ruth, she knew, was fiercely loyal, the more so since Malachi had been killed; and Shawes was such an old-fashioned house, stone-built and with tiny windows, that it might be possible to hold out there against all but the heaviest cannon. It had been built at a time when men in the north still needed fortresses rather than houses, and it had never been modernized.

When the little cavalcade arrived, it was to find Shawes already prepared against possible attack. They were espied from a distance and the heavy gate was opened for them to pass through and quickly shut behind them. In the yard Hero saw servants armed with ancient pikes and wooden cudgels, and a wagon-load of stores being unloaded. Ruth herself came forward to meet them, and stood, unsmiling and unspeaking, to hear what Hero had to say.

Hero had not seen Ruth since she rode over on hearing of Mal's death, to offer her sympathy. She was aware, and had been for years, that Ruth was not entirely friendly towards her, though she did not know the cause; but she had faith in Ruth's Christian pity, and in her sense of justice, and so she said simply, 'Cousin Ruth, we are fleeing from the Scots. Will you take us in?'

The tall, thin woman before her studied her expressionlessly. Ruth was almost thirty, and, as sometimes happens with plain girls, she had grown into a kind of austere beauty. The sharp planes of her face became her better in middle life, as did the clear, level glance of her eyes. Her thick red hair was softer now, and she wore it piled up on her head to keep it out of the way, which gave her a look of dignity, as if she were a crowned queen. She moved with more ease, and the fall of her simple gown was graceful.

She looked at Hero, and saw with a fresh pang of anguish how lovely Hero still was, and how beautiful was the child – Kit's child – who rode on her saddle tree. *'I shall never have a child,'* she thought bitterly. *'There is his child, that I should have borne.'*

'Why do you not go home to Morland Place?' she asked eventually. Hero spread a hand in a charming gesture.

'Ruth, how could I? Would you go with Richard there?'

Ruth shrugged and turned her head away. Hero said, 'Please, Ruth, take us in. We can hold out together, if the rebels should come here.'

'Oh, they will come,' Ruth said shortly. 'It is only a question of whether it will be the Scots or the Fairfaxes or both.'

'Well, we can hold out against them, and comfort each other. We both have had men in the army – my brother, as well as my husband, is fighting. You have lost a man, you know what it is like.'

Ruth looked at her again, and thought how strange it was that Hero should present as an argument in her own favour the very thing that was chiefly against her in Ruth's eyes. 'You have a brother, and a husband, and a child. You have everything, and I have nothing. Why should *I* help *you*?' she thought, but she did not say the words. She sighed, exasperated by the situation, but she knew she had no choice. This was Kit's child, Kit's wife, and what was dear to him must be dear to her too. Though it cut her heart like a lash, she must take in the Haltling and the bairn.

'You can stay,' she said. 'I will send Ellen to you. She will shew you where you can sleep. Have any of your servants arms? Did you bring any food?'

'We brought all the food we had, though it is not much. As to arms –' Hero shook her head.

'As I expected,' Ruth said. 'Well, we must do what we can. Perhaps they will leave us alone, when they know we are naught but women and bairns and old folk.'

Ellen, coming up to them at that moment, sucked her teeth in derision.

'You must hope that it's the Fairfax army that comes here, then, Madam, for the Scots are savages that know no pity, anybody knows that.'

'Hold you tongue, Ellen,' Ruth said sharply. 'And tell

257

Parry that he must see to the Watermill servants and see if any of them are fit to bear arms.'

'I can shoot a gun,' Young Kit said proudly. Ellen looked at him witheringly.

'Aye, but dost have a gun to shoot, my young cockerel? Nay, I thought not, so you must do as we do, and bide quiet when the rebels come.'

Hero had not left Watermill too soon, for the next day the Scots reached the Ouse, and with their great expertise in engineering built a bridge of boats to span it on the bend just above Watermill House. The house itself was obviously very convenient as a shelter for the men who would have to be left to guard the bridge; they forced the door and stabled their horses on the ground floor while the soldiers quartered themselves upstairs. The news came quickly to Morland Place and threw the servants into a panic. Morland Place was stoutly walled, and moated, and for that very reason the Scots were bound to attack them. Would they be able to hold out? And what of the young master's heretic wife and servants? Most of them would have liked to ask the master to send them out of the house right away, before it was too late, but they did not dare. They no longer even dared ask the mistress, for she could be middling savage these days.

Then came the terrible day when Edmund and the family were at dinner and were interrupted by an uproar outside, and the distinct sound of the portcullis being lowered at full speed. Edmund jumped to his feet, and headed for the door just as it burst open and a young maidservant came in, beside herself with panic, crying, 'Master, Master they're coming!'

Edmund pushed her aside without ceremony, and hurried out, and Mary Esther ran after him, Dog leaping at her heels and barking at the tension in the air. In the yard they were met by Clement, who had been to see what was going on.

'An army coming Sir,' he said, panting from the exertion of running, something he had not done in fifteen dignified years. 'Armed men, thirty or forty they say.'

'Who lowered the portcullis?' Edmund demanded fiercely, ignoring his statement.

'I don't know Sir. One of the servants, I suppose.'

'Who gave the order?'

'Why – no-one Sir.' Clement was clearly puzzled. 'I suppose when they saw the army coming –'

At that moment there came a cry from someone up in the barbican, which was passed down from man to man until it reached them.

'It's not the Scots! It's the Yorkshire militia, and Sir Thomas Fairfax on his white horse at the head.'

Mary Esther felt a quick flush of relief, and glanced at Edmund. Not the Scots – the old enemy, whom they had feared for hundreds of years – but Yorkshiremen like themselves, and Sir Thomas an old friend, a civilized man, a humane man. There would be no atrocities at least. But Edmund's face was inscrutable.

'Open the portcullis,' he commanded Clement quietly. Clement's jaw sagged.

'But Sir – !'

'Open the portcullis, damn you, or do I have to do it myself? Open it, I say!'

He had never had to repeat an order in all his life, but it was only his furious anger that made Clement at last go to do his bidding. Mary Esther, rigid with disbelieving horror, waited until Clement had gone before saying to her husband, 'Edmund – are you not going to resist?'

He turned on her so quickly and fiercely that she flinched in spite of herself.

'Against cannon?' he said.

Still she did not understand. 'We don't know that they

259

have cannon. Clement said thirty or forty –'

'If they had no cannon this time, they would have them next time.'

'But just to give in –'

'Woman, be silent!' he cried, goaded beyond endurance. 'Do you dare to question me in my own house?'

But Mary Esther was beyond silence. 'Yes! I do – it is my home too! Am I to stand by and watch you give away my home without raising even a finger to save it?' The word *coward* was quivering in her heart, just below the level of speech, and, as if he had heard it, Edmund looked down at her with an expression of desperate bitterness.

He said, his voice low with passion, 'You forget the position we are in. You forget the presence in this house of my son. It has to be known that I was forced to help Newcastle, just as I am now forced to help Fairfax. I do not care for their damned cause, not one way or the other – do you not understand that, even yet? I care for nothing – *nothing* – but Morland Place. And do you dare to call it yours, and do you dare to suggest I do not love it as much as you? You cannot know the tenth part of what I feel! Morland Place is mine, and I will keep it, whoever wins this hellish war – I keep what is mine, and you, you who would have it destroyed by cannon for a whimsical cause, you, Madam, may keep silent, or you may go back to the tavern where you were born and hold *that* against three armies.'

Burning with shame and anger, Mary Esther watched him walk away towards the barbican, and then, afraid that she might fall, her legs trembled so, she turned and went back to the house. She was waiting in the hall when her husband came back, but when she saw him accompanied by Sir Thomas Fairfax – Black Tom, they called him, because he was so dark – she was so afraid of her own rage she hurried away before the soldiers poured into the house behind him.

Fairfax was courteous to Edmund, though a little curious. 'Your house is conveniently situated here for our headquarters, and I must ask you to allow us to use it for that purpose, and not to resist us with arms.' Edmund nodded coldly, and Fairfax said, 'You have no objection?'

Edmund said levelly, 'My objections are not to the point, Sir Thomas. You have the means to force my co-operation, and I would prefer not to be forced.'

'And yet,' Fairfax persisted, 'you have, I know, given substantial aid to Lord Newcastle, and have several sons serving for the King's cause.'

'Two sons, Sir, and a cousin. They serve without my consent. And as for Lord Newcastle, he had the means to force me, just as you have.'

'Then you do not favour the King's cause?' Fairfax asked, curious still.

'I have no desire to aid either party. I do not wish to impose my wishes on anyone – I wish merely to be left alone to persue my lawful business, and to leave others alone in the same way.'

A faint expression of distaste crossed Fairfax's long dark face. 'If all men thought like you, Sir, there would be no progress,' he said.

'If all men thought like me,' Edmund replied quietly, 'there would be no war.'

More might have been said, but at that moment there came a sound of commotion from within the house and a piercing scream, and both men started at once, running towards the passageway that led to the chapel. There they thrust their way through a mill of soldiers to see Leah flattened against the closed chapel door, and Mary Esther standing in front of her, her teeth bared in fury and her arms spread to protect her servant.

'What is happening here?' Fairfax demanded sharply.

'It's a chapel, Sir, a Popish chapel – altar and everything!' one of the soldiers cried in great excitement, and another took it up.

'We was trying to do our duty, Sir, and pull down the altar and rails, only these women got in the way, Sir.'

Mary Esther's eyes glittered, so that she looked like a maddened, wild animal; behind her Leah sobbed quietly with fear, but held her station at the door.

'Before any one of you enters this chapel,' Mary Esther said, 'I shall be dead.'

From the back of the crowd a soldier's voice yelled, 'Kill the Papist whore!'

'Silence!' thundered Fairfax. His face black with fury he turned on the soldiers. 'Sergeant, who said that? Take that man outside – I'll deal with him later.' He turned back to Mary Esther, and his expression softened. Here was a kind of courage he could understand. He bowed to her courteously. 'Madam, I honour you; and you need have no fear for your chapel or your life. Burton, come here.' A middle-aged, stolid looking soldier came forward and looked silently up at his general. Fairfax went on, 'As long as my soldiers are in this house, Madam, there will be a guard on this door; you need not fear. Burton has my complete trust. Burton, keep your station here, and allow no-one to enter except members of the family. I will arrange for you to be relieved later.'

The man came forward and very gently pushed Leah out of the way, and took up a stance before the door with his pike at the present, his face impassive. Mary Esther looked from him to Fairfax and back again, and then gave a little sigh, her shoulders relaxing. Fairfax and Edmund moved away, and Mary Esther put her arm round Leah's shaking shoulders and followed. In the hall Hetta ran to her, her face white with fear, and ducked under her other arm, and Anne and Ralph and Edward came after and gathered behind her like chicks around a hen. Edmund and Fairfax walked into the dining room, and the rest, as if bemused, followed.

'We shall have to quarter our officers here,' Fairfax said, 'so perhaps you would consider which rooms we shall have.

It will be best, I think, for your household to be kept apart from my men. And we will need cooking facilities, and stabling for our horses. We will bring what food we can, but we will have to trouble you for the rest.'

'You need not ask,' Mary Esther said bitterly, before Edmund could speak. 'You can take what you want without asking.'

He raised an eyebrow. 'If I were the Scottish commander, I would do so. You should be grateful, Madam, that your house is within my territory, and not a little further north. Your chapel would not now be safe under guard if it had been the Scottish army that came here.'

'And am I meant to be grateful that my chapel is not desecrated?' Mary Esther asked.

Fairfax did not reply, seeing the justice of this. Instead, looking about him, he said, 'This room is of a good size, and it would suit us to bring our wounded here. If you will have the furniture cleared away, we will lay them on the floor. We will not trouble you for anything else for them.'

Mary Esther met his eyes squarely. 'Wounded men cannot lie on the floor. We will find mattresses at least for them. I and my daughters and women will tend them.'

Fairfax was surprised, 'Madam, you need not –'

'A wounded man is a Christian in need of my help,' Mary Esther said, 'and a Christian is my brother – even though he call me a Papist whore.'

Fairfax bowed, and was opening his mouth to speak when Richard and Katherine came in, and Richard hurried up to Fairfax with a smile of welcome on his face.

'Sir Thomas, we are glad to see you,' he said earnestly. 'My wife and I are of the true faith, Sir, and we are of one mind with you. My wife is from Norwich, Sir, daughter of Geoffrey Browne the clothier, of whom you may have heard. We have looked forward to this moment, Sir, you may believe.'

Fairfax looked at Richard in astonishment, and then at

Edmund as if he suddenly understood a great deal more than before.

One of the wounded men brought in to Morland Place was a youngster from the Eastern Association army who had been shot in the leg by a musketman on the walls of York as he was taking a message to one of Fairfax's officers. Hetta took charge of him, and thought at first that he could be no older than her, for he had a smooth, brown, childlike face and very soft, silky curls, with barely any moustache. He was feverish from his wound for the first few days, and as she bathed his flushed face she thought how sad it was that someone so young could be fighting for the wrong side, and wounded while doing so. His mouth was gentle and curling, and when he opened his eyes, though he did not seem to see her, she saw that they were large and warm and brown, and fringed with very long lashes. He looked too gentle to want to kill anyone.

On the fourth day his fever went and he woke as she was bathing his face and put his hand up to touch hers, looking at her with a puzzled expression.

'It's all right,' she said gently. 'You are quite safe. You were wounded and took a fever, but you will soon be well again.'

'Where am I? Who are you?' he asked. His voice was hoarse, and she offered him water before she replied, slipping her hand under his head to support it while he sipped.

'You are at Morland Place, not far from York. It is my home. I am Henrietta Morland.'

'Henrietta. The same name as the Queen,' he said.

'What is your name?' she asked.

'Charles Hobart,' he said, and then smiled faintly. 'The same name as the King.'

Hetta frowned. 'How can you fight against the King?' she

asked. 'Don't you know how wrong it is?'

'I'm not fighting against the King,' he said. 'I've never even seen him. My father is the member of Parliament for our town, and I'm fighting for him, for the freedom of Parliament.' He looked at her with innocent brown eyes. 'Why, are you a Royalist?'

'Of course,' Hetta said, equally simply. 'He is our sovereign lord, and God's anointed. It is everyone's duty to obey and serve him.'

Charles tried to look lofty. 'Why, you are a child, and cannot know anything about the matter,' he said.

'I'll bet I am as old as you. How old do you think I am?'

'Thirteen – or fourteen,' he added cautiously.

'I am fifteen,' she said with quiet dignity.

'Well I am seventeen, so I know a great deal more about the world than you. For instance –' he began to lift himself in his vehemence, and fell back, wincing with pain. Hetta pressed him down gently and said,

'Hush, you will make yourself feverish again. It's all right – there will be plenty of time for talking.'

'Yes, of course,' Charles said, looking as if he liked the idea, and Hetta smiled at him, wondering why the notion of discussing the matter with him made her feel so happy.

When the Royalist army had first been penned up in York, Anne had complained bitterly and to anyone that would listen that now they would not see any of Francis's friends again – or Francis, she had added, as an afterthought. In fact she did not expect the siege to stop Reynold Symonds coming to visit her: she was so confident of his daring that she was sure he would find a way to slip out and ride over, perhaps in the depths of night, and she lived in daily expectation of a message. She did as little as possible in the sickroom, and that little she did unwillingly, making sure everyone knew that she thought it wrong for a Royalist to help rebels, even when wounded. The fact that her sister and mother laboured long and patiently did not impress her at all, and she went on with her tactless comments until Leah threatened to slap her.

But when the siege had endured for a few weeks, and there was no word for her from her lover, she grew quieter, and then as more weeks passed, she grew pale and sick. Leah noticed it, but she was busy and distracted enough to put it down to sulking; Hetta noticed, but she had always been wary of Anne's sharp tongue, and preferred to wait until Anne confided in her, rather than ask her what was wrong.

Hetta had plenty of other things to occupy her mind as April turned into a sweet, sparkling May. Apart from her work with the wounded – and there were always one or two coming in – she was absorbed with her growing friendship with Charles Hobart. While he was bedridden she spent all her free time sitting beside him, lightening the tediousness and pain of his condition with conversation; and once he was able to get up, she spent as much time as she could helping him to walk. They had grown to know each other's minds very well by now, and Hetta was amazed that they could be so alike when they were on opposing sides. On one of his first attempts to hobble, she had supported him on her shoulder from the dining room into the drawing room to shew him the Morland achievement of arms over the fireplace.

'Our motto, you see, is *Fidelitas*,' she said as he leaned on the chimney piece and admired the old painting. 'It would be shame to a Morland not to be faithful.'

Charles nodded. 'I, too, believe that a man must be faithful – but faithful to what?'

'Why, to one's lord,' Hetta said.

'And to what else? To God?'

'Of course.'

'Ah – then one must follow the true faith, and avoid false

266

prophets. One must seek for the truth, and abide by it.'

Hetta was puzzled. 'But so I do.' She did not add, 'It is you who have been led astray by false prophets,' for she was too polite.

Charles said vehemently, 'No, no, you follow the old religion, which is fogged and cluttered by ritual, which by imperceptable steps, has gone far from the original truth. The only truth is that which is written in the Bible, the words of Our Lord himself, and of the prophets who spoke with God. That is where we must seek the truth.'

'But how shall we understand it?' Hetta asked.

'Why, the ministers will help us, they will translate it for us. That is their task.'

'But then, that is what the priests do for us. It is no different.'

And they would look at each other in earnest bewilderment, and by tacit consent change the subject, for each was very anxious not to quarrel, or to let the differences between them push them apart.

One day she helped him out into the inner garden, to enjoy the sunshine.

'I'm lucky I was wounded in the leg,' he said suddenly. 'If it was the arm, they'd have sent me back by now, but as it's my leg they have to leave me here until I can walk properly.'

'Don't you want to go back?' Hetta asked, knowing the answer. He grinned.

'I'd sooner stay here. Shall we sit under the bower there? No-one will see us.' They sat, and he stretched out his legs comfortably, and then looked at her and smiled in a way that made her cheeks feel very hot. 'It is good to be alone here with you, Henrietta. You don't mind me calling you Henrietta, do you?'

'Of course not,' she said, looking down in confusion and then, to change the subject, 'tell me about your home.'

'It's not so grand as this,' he said, 'but I like it. The country seems much more closed in where I live, the lanes are deep and narrow and there are a great many trees. Yorkshire seems very open and bare after Kent. Kent is so pretty – particularly in May. On our estate we have miles and miles of orchards, and in May it is one great sheet of blossom, like snow, some white and some pink. Oh, you can't imagine it!'

Hetta's eyes were on his face now, her lips slightly parted as she tried to see what he saw in his mind. 'I know,' she said. 'I can imagine – we have an orchard too. When the apple trees are in blossom –'

'Yes,' he said, looking at her, and he took her hand, and for a long time they did not speak; and when he went on again, he somehow forgot to let go of her hand.

He told her about his home, and about his old nurse who had a jackdaw so tame it would sit on her wrist and drink ale out of her cup, and how when it got drunk it would dance and recite rhymes in a human voice. He told her about his goshawk that came all the way from Ireland, and his hound bitch, who was in whelp when he came away – 'I wish I could have word how she does!' – and about his little brother who was just two years old, and his sister who had died five years ago, who had been the dearest little girl, and about his mother.

'She's not my real mother, my mother died when I was born, but my father married her when I was so small that I always think of her as my mother. She's so pretty, and she sings like a robin while she works. I wish you could meet her, Henrietta – you'd love her!'

Henrietta's face grew sad, and she gently drew her hand away. 'But she would not love me, Charles. She would think me an ignorant Papist.'

Charles stared at her in dismay, realizing only then how far they had gone in their friendship. 'Oh Hetta,' he said helplessly, falling without knowing into the pet name he had heard her called by. 'What are we to do?'

'There is nothing we can do,' she said. 'Your parents and

mine would never approve of each other. And you are a soldier. In a little while, when your leg is well again, you will go back to your regiment, and one day you will march away and I will never hear of you again. You may fight in a battle, and though it might be only five miles from here, I would never even known if you lived or died.'

He seized her hand again. 'No, don't speak like that. Henrietta – if – *if* our parents could be brought to approve, would you – would you –'

'Marry you? Yes, of course, I would. You know that.'

Charles looked shyly at her, and then said, as if the words were newly invented by him, and he was not sure she would understand them, 'I love you.'

'I love you too,' Hetta said. 'But you know that it's no good.'

They were silent awhile, and were only roused from their reverie by the sound of Anne calling: 'Hetta, where are you? I want to talk to you.'

Hetta got up at once, and Anne did not appear to notice that she had been sitting in the bower with the wounded rebel. 'Come with me,' she said. 'I want to talk to you privately.'

'Where?' Hetta asked.

'In the orchard.'

'Oh Anne, you know we aren't allowed out of the house.'

'I don't propose to be made a prisoner in my house by Black Fairfax or his men,' Anne said angrily. 'We'll go out of the back door. The guard there will let us by.'

'How do you know?' Hetta asked anxiously, trotting along beside her.

'Because I've bribed him,' Anne said grandly. Sure enough, the guard let them by with a lewd wink and a knowing laugh, and Anne, nose in the air, marched past him and as soon as they were outside grabbed Hetta's hand and scuttled for the safety of the orchard. Hetta thought at once of what Charles had been saying – the apple trees were

269

in blossom, and the grass was white with the drifts of falling petals. Anne stopped under a tree and rounded on Hetta.

'Hetta, I'm in trouble.'

'I guessed that you were,' Hetta said, 'but I did not like to ask.'

'It's well that you did not,' she said with a grimace. 'Het, I am with child.'

Hetta's hand flew to her mouth and her eyes grew perfectly round with horror. 'Are you sure?' she whispered.

'Of course I'm sure,' Anne said irritably. 'I can count as well as anyone. I'm in terror of Leah finding out. It's only because she's got her mind full of those damned rebels in the dining room that she hasn't noticed yet. And I've waited and waited for a message or some word from Ensign Symonds, and I'm at my wits' end wondering what to do. He said if I should get with child we should be married, but who knows if Father will agree to it? And how is he even to ask if I cannot get word to him?'

'Ensign Symonds?' Hetta said, puzzled. 'But he was made Lieutenant, long ago.'

'I talk of the ensign, not the lieutenant,' Anne said, and seeing Hetta still did not understand, 'Ensign Reynold Symonds, the lieutenant's brother.'

Hetta's eyes widened. 'Oh, but Anne –' she cried, shocked. 'I thought –'

'You were meant to think, as was everyone,' Anne said impatiently. 'Oh Het, don't look like that. You're such a child! You know nothing of love – how could you? The question is, what am I to do? How can I get word to Reynold? Even if I could get away from the house unseen, I'd never get as far as the city walls, through all these rebel soldiers.'

'You mustn't think of it!' Hetta cried anxiously.

'But you are friendly with some of the wounded men, aren't you? Could you persuade one or bribe one to take a message? They could pass through to the city without hindrance.'

'But Anne, even if they could be persuaded, how would they get the message into the city? And how would your – friend get out?'

Anne was sunk in gloom. 'I don't know,' she said savagely. 'I don't know what to do.'

'You will have to tell Mother,' Hetta said at last. Anne rounded on her.

'No! Never! Can't you imagine what she would say? No – she mustn't find out, not until I've found a way to get a message to Reynold. Hetta, promise you won't tell – promise!'

'All right, I promise,' Hetta said soothingly, 'but she's bound to find out sooner or later.'

'She won't. I'll run away before I let her find out. Reynold must marry me. I'll find a way of getting to him.'

'Anne, we must go in. We will be missed.'

'Yes, I suppose so. Hetta, you'll keep my secret.'

'Of course,' Hetta said sadly. 'Oh, if only it weren't for the war –'

Anne had nothing to say to that. The two girls slipped quietly back into the shadowy house, out of the bright May sunshine.

The morning of 29th June was like any other since the siege began, except that Hetta was beginning to worry that any day now Charles might be sent back to his regiment. His leg was almost completely sound, and when they were together they were very quiet, as if to talk might be to draw attention to the fact, and hasten his departure. Then, as suddenly as lightning, the news struck their fragile peace and shattered it.

271

'Rupert is come!' the cry went up as the messenger galloped in. 'Prince Rupert and his army are at Knaresborough!'

It was little more than a dozen miles away. As the messenger was led into Sir Thomas Fairfax, Hetta and Charles looked at each other questioningly. Hetta felt a thrill of excitement at the name of Rupert; Charles felt a thrill of apprehension. He was known to be well-nigh invincible in battle. They held hands tightly and waited for the word to come. They had not long to wait. The messenger was on his way again in ten minutes, and the orders came to move out.

'We are all marching out to block the Knaresborough Road,' the officer said who came to tell Charles. 'We are moving at once, so you had better come along with us, Hobart – no time to get back to your own company. Your leg will bear you?'

'Yes sir,' Charles said. There was no other possible answer.

'Move quickly then, lad. You know how fast Rupert is. We must catch him before he reaches York.'

He left them, and Charles turned to Hetta and took both her hands and they looked into each other's faces, as if trying to memorize their features.

'I have to go,' he said. She nodded. He pressed her hands urgently. 'Hetta, one day, when the war is over – it won't matter then who is Royalist and who is Roundhead. When that time comes, I'll come back for you. Will you wait for me?'

'Oh Charles –'

'Hetta, tell me. I shall die if you don't.'

'I'll wait for you,' she said sadly. 'I love you.'

He flung his arms around her and hugged her tightly for a moment, and then dashed away to join the rest of the soldiers gathering their belongings and forming up. She was in the yard as they marched out, and when he reached her, he had only time to say quietly and quickly, 'I'll come back for you!' before he passed by.

Within half an hour, the house was deserted again, left to its owners, almost as if the two-month-long occupation had never happened. Hetta went up the stairs to the barbican roof and watched the column march away with the westering sun in her eyes.

CHAPTER FIFTEEN

The most direct and obvious road from Knaresborough to
York ran through Tockwith and Long Marston, skirting
the south side of Marston Moor and the northern boundary
of the Morland Place estate, to the south gate of the city.
Rupert knew this as well as did the Parliamentary generals.
He waited in Knaresborough until his scout came in to say
that the enemy were marching out towards Marston Moor,
where they evidently planned to mass and tackle him. Then
he sent out a troop of cavalry along the Knaresborough road
to deceive any enemy scouts into thinking he was coming
that way, and with the rest of his force swung to the north
towards Boroughbridge.

They marched all night and the next day, making a long,
twenty-mile loop to the north, crossing two rivers, and
finally coming down to York from the north, arriving at the
abandoned Scots camp outside Clifton on the north side of
the city on the evening of 1st July. The enemy was completely taken by surprise; the siege was lifted and York was
saved.

As soon as they came into sight of the long white walls of
York, the bridge of boats that the Scots had built could be
seen spanning the Ouse, and the Prince ordered a troop of
cavalry to go and secure it and make sure no enemy guards
had been left there. Kit, white in the face, sought the Prince
and asked to be assigned the task.

'Why, what is wrong? You look sick, Morland,' the
Prince said. Kit drew a breath, controlling his trembling.

'General, the house you can see there, just below the
bridge – that is my home.' Rupert looked. A wisp of smoke
could be seen rising from it – but not from the right place.

274

He bit his lip. 'My wife and child –' Kit began, but could say no more.

'Go then,' Rupert said. 'Secure the bridge first. It is likely they may have set up a guard post at the house, so approach it with care. Report back to me when it's done.'

'Thank you Sir,' Kit said, and wheeled Oberon about. He took his own troop, pistols at the ready, and crossed the bridge, beating the bushes on either side in case any enemy guard should be hiding there, but it was soon obvious that they had withdrawn. Then Kit divided his troop, and told half, 'You go round the house that way, the rest of you come with me. If there's any sign of the enemy, or any firing, we'll charge and get in against the walls where we'll be covered. Look for my signal.'

Oberon flung his head up and down nervously, sensing his rider's tension, as Kit led his men round the north side of the house to approach the front door. As soon as he rounded the house he saw that there was no need for caution. The front door was gone, the wall around it partly broken down, and one end of the house was a smoking ruin.

'Oh God,' he whispered pleadingly. His knuckles were white on the hand that gripped the pistol, and he slowed Oberon without realizing it, loath to go on, for fear of what he would find. His men looked at him sympathetically; most who had not already known it now guessed the truth. He stopped on the beaten earth before the ruined door, and the rest of his troop came up with him from the other direction.

'No sign of anyone, Sir,' a trooper reported.

Kit did not reply; if anyone was alive inside, they would surely have come out, or called for help. He licked his dry lips and said, 'Smith, Harcourt, come with me. We'll look inside. The rest of you wait here.' He dismounted, flinging Oberon's reins to a trooper, and walked forward. It seemed like a dream, to come home to this ruin that looked so much like his home. The fire that had destroyed one end of the house had burnt out, and it was not possible to tell if it had been fired deliberately, or if it had merely been carelessness on the part of the enemy. There was ample evidence, however, of the Parliamentarians' occupation, the smell of horses downstairs and the heaps of dung, and upstairs the stronger smell of humans: human ordure, human waste. Kit walked, wide-eyed and rigid with fear; waiting for the cry from a companion or for his own stumbling foot to discover the bodies. They searched the house completely, and when no mutilated corpse came to light, his relief was such that he thought his legs would give way.

'Whose house was it, Sir?' Harcourt asked as they made their way back out into the fresh air. Smith kicked him and by gesture indicated it was the Captain's wife they had failed to find, and whose fate was still unknown.

Smith said, 'Now the city's relieved, Sir, we might get news of your lady from there. She might have sheltered in the city when the Scots came.'

Kit nodded brusquely, back in control of himself. 'We must get back and report,' he said. He left half his troop at the bridge to guard it, and rode back to the Prince. When the Prince finally had time to admit him, Kit gave his report and said, 'There was no sign of my family or servants, Sir. I wondered if it would be possible to send a message into the city, to ask if they are there?'

Rupert looked thoughful, tapping a letter he held against his fist. 'You must be worried, of course,' he said. 'I have here a letter from Lord Newcastle in the city, and the men who brought it are still in the camp, waiting for a reply. I'll send for them, and you can question them. It is possible they might know something.'

When the two men were brought into Rupert's tent, at first they shook their heads, but then one of them asked, 'Captain, Sir, would you be Ensign Frank Morland's brother, Sir?'

'That's right,' Kit said. 'Do you know him? Is he here?'

'He's serving with the Whitecoats, Sir, Lord Newcastle's regiment. I did hear tell what happened to his home, Sir, a big moated house to the south –'

'Morland Place?' Kit said eagerly. The man nodded.

'That's right, Sir – that would be your father's house, I guess? Well, Sir, Sir Thomas Fairfax took it over for his headquarters, and the wounded were taken there to be safe.'

'They took Morland Place? Was it much damaged?' Kit asked, thinking of the great cannon. How else could they have got in?

'Oh no Sir – there wasn't any fighting. The gates was opened to them and they just walked in.'

Kit stared, aghast, and Rupert shot him a keen glance.

'It's as well to know these things,' he said, not without sympathy. 'It is good to know what places are friendly to us.'

The messenger noted the distress on Kit's face and said, 'Ensign Morland was rare upset, Sir, when he heard. But the next day there came news about another house of your family, Sir – would it be called Shaw House?'

'Shawes – aye, what of it?'

'Well Sir, it cheered the Ensign when he heard that this house had not given in, and held out against Sir Thomas's men, though it was held only by two women – ladies I should say, Sir – and servants, Sir, and one of the ladies a cripple, begging your pardon Sir.'

'A cripple? A lame woman? Was there mention of a child, a boy?' Kit cried.

'I couldn't say, Sir. Seemingly Sir Thomas himself went up to the house, and come away again. The story is that when he found 'twas only two ladies there, he said he honoured their courage, Sir, and would not molest them further. Well Sir, that was the story – you know how these things are told.'

Kit thanked the men, and Rupert dismissed them.

'What house is this, Kit?' he asked when they had gone.

'Shawes belongs to another branch of the family, Sir, and lies a little to the north of the main estate. My wife's cousin, Ruth, owns it – it was my cousin Malachi's home.' Rupert nodded. 'It's an old-fashioned place, stone walls and small windows high in the outer walls, fit to be held. Perhaps my wife heard about Morland Place and went there.'

Rupert nodded again, and then raised an eyebrow as he anticipated Kit's next question. 'You want to go and find out, of course.'

'It isn't far, Sir. If I could but know she and the boy were safe and well.'

'Yes, you have been from them a long time,' Rupert said. He stood up abruptly and walked a few paces up and down the tent, and then turned to face Kit. Boye got up from his bit of blanket in the corner and jumped up onto the Prince's chair to paw his arm, and the Prince caressed him absently as he spoke.

'You know that the letter I had from the King that sent us here to relieve York enjoined me to defeat the forces in the north. It impressed upon me the need for the greatest dispatch. The enemy are all massed out at Marston. God knows, for myself I would sooner wait a while before we attack them – we all need the rest. But I dare not delay. We shall march out before first light tomorrow and fall on them at dawn.' He met Kit's eyes, and a hint of a smile relieved the grimness of his dark face. 'You may go to this Shawes of yours, my Kit. You'll fight better for knowing your family are safe. But you must be back at midnight without fail.'

'Yes, Sir, of course Sir. Oh, God bless your Highness,' Kit said, quick with relief.

'Go then, waste no time. And for God's sake go carefully, the enemy are not far off. Keep your eyes open, and report to me when you get back anything you see or hear that might be useful.'

He watched Kit dash away, and for a moment almost

envied him that close concern. Then he sighed, lifted Boye off his chair, and sat down to compose his letter to Lord Newcastle.

Kit pushed Oberon as hard as he could, though he felt the big stallion's weariness. They had both had little rest since they began the march from Lancashire to rescue York; and there would be another battle tomorrow, at dawn, and then, who knew, another march perhaps. He dared not look ahead, for it was only by living each day as it came that he could keep his heart from failing him. He cantered Oberon down the long stretch of the North Field, wondering if the stallion recognized it, knew he was on home ground. It was strange to Kit to be riding over these familiar fields again, fields he had hunted over since he was a child. Strange, and disconcerting; he felt like a ghost come back to a place it had loved in life, but unable to repossess it. He felt lonely, bereft.

Through Ten Thorn Gap, and up the rutted path, and there at last the grey bulk of Shawes came into sight, its windows black and sightless in the shadow of the setting sun. He slowed Oberon to a walk to give them time to see him and recognize him – he did not want at this late stage to be shot for a Roundhead. He took off his hat so that his face might be seen, and rode towards the main gate, and before he reached it it opened, and a tall figure of a woman came out, a thin woman, graceful and upright in her carriage, like a queen. She carried a musket, but it pointed at the ground as she waited for him to ride up. Her expression was unfathomable, but as he halted beside her she looked up at him with brown eyes filled with pain.

'Aye, they're here,' was all she said. Kit felt himself sagging with relief.

'God bless you, Cousin Ruth,' he said. 'I knew you would take care of them.' She turned her face away, moving carefully as if movement woke the pain to sharpness, and put her hand to Oberon's bridle. The stallion dipped his head and nuzzled at her hand. Horses had always loved her.

'Go on in,' she said. 'I will take care of the horse. Go in to them. They are in the great hall, waiting for you.'

Kit swung down from the saddle without another word, though he looked gratitude at her. She evaded the look with her eyes. She watched him walk in through the gate, seeing the defeated stoop of his shoulders, the weariness of his gait, and the pain in her heart was a double-edged blade, for she could see that Hero's husband had not come back. She chucked to Oberon and led him forward.

'Lord God, but you're tired,' she said. 'Come, I'll get you some good mash, poor fellow, and some green beans. I'd give you corn if we had any.' Oberon walked with her willingly, his great head nodding with his weariness, his ears moving to the sound of her voice as she encouraged him along. 'Poor old man,' she said to him. 'If men would be fools, would to God they did not make you horses suffer for it.'

He came through the door into the great hall, and with a small broken cry Hero was in his arms, and he strained her body against him, pressing his face down onto the top of her head, closing his eyes against the flood of tears that threatened to overwhelm him. Hero held him, and felt him shaking, felt the hot wetness soak into her hair, and her heart ached because her hands did not know the shape of him, because he felt like a stranger to her. After a little while she pulled back from him, drew away to the length of his arms, and said, 'Let me look at you.'

He freed one hand quickly to wipe his eyes, and then gave it back to her wet. She looked at him, and could not speak. She felt suddenly shy, embarrassed, as if she had mistakenly hugged a complete stranger; he looked at her, but would not meet her eyes. A silence ensued, which she felt at last obliged to break.

'You are well?' she said. 'You are not wounded?'

He shook his head.

'How long have you got?' she asked.

'I must be back before midnight,' he said. Was that his voice? How strange it sounded to him. He felt remote, unreal. The woman before him was like someone on the other side of a glass, he could barely feel her hands, though he held them, though his body trembled, knowing what it lacked. He felt sudden, piercing despair, and longed to be anywhere but here. To be here, and not here, was too subtle a torture.

'Four hours then,' she said awkwardly. She looked over her shoulder, and he looked too, and saw the boy, standing by the fireplace, watching him with brilliant shining eyes. 'Your son,' she said softly.

Kit dropped her hands and looked, his eyes devouring the boy hungrily. God, how tall he was, this baby of his, going on four now, tall and thin, with stooping brittle shoulders like a bird, and a frail, brilliant face, bright as a sword-blade, staring at him as if the eyes were fingers and tongue too. Kit held out his hand, and Young Kit came forward.

'Father,' he said, and there was a question in it. Kit nodded. The boy came forward and knelt for his blessing, as Kit had always done to his father, and Kit laid his hand on the boy's head. The hair was very dark and curly – good God, how silken, how soft the hair was – and under it the skull felt hot and thin and fragile, like a fledgling bird's, as if he could have crushed it between finger and thumb.

'God bless you,' Kit heard his own voice, faint and hoarse, and the boy stood up again, bringing Kit's hand with him, and looked up from very close, the brilliant, dark-blue eyes surveying his father's face with wonder and pride. Kit wanted to cry out, for his heart felt swollen fit to burst, he wanted to cry out and tremble and run with this desperate, aching love that had no expression. He reached down through a mist and lifted the boy up – so light, lighter than he had expected – so that he was on a level with his face, and then, helplessly, hugged him, burying his face in the child's hair. Young Kit put his hands round his father, and to Kit they felt as tiny and light as the touch of sparrow's feet, unreal, unreal! This frail child, his own, and none of his, beyond his possession, grown while he was away. Life had continued here while he was gone, his own life had ended when he left them, his wife and child, and now he was come back like a ghost, and he had no right here, the dead had no right to impose upon the living.

He set the boy down gently and looked at Hero and saw the same dark blue eyes looking at him with too much intelligence and too much pain. She knew, he thought. He should not have come.

'Are you hungry?' she said, and the words were an acknowledgment. Their life together had ended; he was a soldier, they were two separate people; only when he was no longer a soldier could their life together begin again. 'There is some food.'

'Yes,' he said. Let there be food. It was something to do. She moved away to fetch it, and he saw with a savage wrench of the heart the ugly limp that he had forgotten. He followed her and sat by the hearth, and she brought him bread and meat on a platter, and sent the boy to pour him wine. Young Kit came back, carrying the overfull goblet carefully in both hands, his face shining with pride when he got it to his father without spilling any. Kit took it clumsily, and the wine lipped over the edge and a heavy splash, bright as blood, hit the floor, scattering drops like beads on the grey stone. They looked at each other, aghast: it was somehow too much. 'Ah no,' Hero breathed in protest, and went down clumsily on her knees, trying futilely to wipe up the drops with her bare fingers. In a moment she desisted, hung her head, hunched her shoulders. Kit saw her shaking with silent sobs, the tears running over her face in an astonishing, extravagant flood, and she put up her wine-stained fingers and pressed them against her cheeks as if she could stem the flood that way.

Kit looked, and looked away. He could not touch her, or reach her, or comfort her, He turned his face away, and ate bread and meat, though he could not taste it. Young Kit bit his lip, not understanding his mother's pain, and then went to her, standing behind her uncertainly, and put a tentative hand on her head. Kit saw out of the corner of his eye, relived in his mind the too-light feeling of that unhuman, frail hand. Savagely he chewed bread. After a while Hero's sobs stopped, and she said in a muffled voice, 'Give me your kerchief.' It was her son she addressed, and he pushed the linen into her groping hand. In a moment, her face dried, Hero took the child's shoulder and got to her feet and limped to a stool on the other side of the fireplace. Kit saw without wanting to see how the child's shoulder had already become an accustomed leaning-place, how the child stationed himself beside her where she sat. He remembered, abruptly, like dark countryside seen for a moment in a lightning flash, the Hero of ten – no twelve – years ago, leaning on Hamil's shoulder like a courtier.

He put down the bread on his platter. To that Hero he could have said 'I love you'. Instead he said, 'You will want to know that Hamil is well.'

'I am glad,' she said. Her voice was amazingly calm.

'He is the only one of us who has never been wounded. He leads a charmed life.'

'Is he happy?' Hero asked. Kit considered. It seemed an irrelevant question, and he did not know how to answer it. Instead he said, 'He is a good officer, and highly thought of.' He thought for something else to say. 'I'm glad Ruth took you in. I heard that you and she held out against Fairfax.'

283

'He was very courteous. We were lucky it was he and not the Scots. We saw them marching past yesterday, and so we guessed that Prince Rupert had come. The siege is lifted?'

'Yes, they have all gone.'

'Then we can go home tomorrow.'

Kit looked up in surprise. Of course, she had no way of knowing. 'The house is destroyed,' he said. 'Burnt. You cannot go home. You must stay here.'

She was shocked. 'Burnt?' she whispered. She met his eyes, and he saw that this was real to her, that until now the war had not been a matter of reality. 'Kit, our home?'

'Who burnt it, Father?' Young Kit asked.

'The Roundheads,' he replied automatically.

'I hate the Roundheads,' Young Kit cried. 'When I am old enough I shall join the army and fight them like you.'

'The war will be over by then,' Kit said, but he barely heard the child's words.

'Will it soon be over?' Hero asked.

'God knows,' he said, and then roused himself, for her sake, for the child's sake. 'Yes, I suppose so. It must be over soon.'

'When the war is over,' Hero said, 'shall we build a new house? Watermill was too small really.'

'Yes,' he said. She had not lived the war – the war was the other place where he lived, the place that made him a ghost in her country. He could not tell her about the war, or of his fears; and he could not imagine a place where the war was over and he was free to come home. It didn't matter what he said – it was a game for her to comfort herself with. 'We'll build a bigger and better house.'

'A gentleman's house, for Young Kit to inherit,' she said. The door opened and Ruth came in, still carrying the gun. She said, 'I've fed Oberon, though I had no corn for him. I gave him beans. You're overworking him, you know. His off-fore is very warm. He's going to be lame if you don't rest him tomorrow.'

Kit looked at her. 'Tomorrow we fight a battle.' There was a cry, quickly stifled, from Hero; it was to Ruth that Kit addressed himself. He felt that he could talk to her. Somehow the gun made her more real, as if she was a go-between for the two worlds, his and Hero's.

'The enemy is massed on Marston Moor. We march out before dawn tomorrow to engage them. The Prince has orders – they must be defeated, so that we can get back to the King.'

Ruth's eyes were clear and intelligent. 'It will be no easy task,' she said. 'The Scots are a fine fighting force. And we have heard that the Eastern Association cavalry are as good as Rupert's, now that Cromwell has taken them over.'

Kit said, 'We have no choice but to fight. But we have never been beaten yet. The Puritans think the Prince is a devil and his dog is his familiar. We have that on our side.'

Ruth read in his eyes the despair and defeat, the loneliness of a man shut out for ever from his own feelings. She knew it for what it was, for she had closed a door in her own mind in the same way, long ago when she had left Morland Place and come home to Shawes. She longed to comfort him, to say, 'I understand'; she longed, absurdly, to say goodbye, but that was impossible too, because Kit had gone long ago. It was not Kit who sat here by her empty grate, this tall, stooping man with the tired face. She saw as he moved his head the light gleaming briefly on a spray of grey hairs amongst the dark curls, and it moved her deeply. It seemed so unfair; she had loved a gay, debonair young man, a laughing, dancing, handsome, ever-young, young man. How absurd was human love! They had all loved him, she and Hero and this greying, defeated man, all loved that handsome chevalier. Only Young Kit, who had never known him, admired the soldier without shadow.

Abruptly she said, 'Perhaps you would like to rest? Hero, you could show him your room – he could lie down there.'

She saw them exchange a quick glance of question and

affirmative. That was one thing that they could still do, and each hoped they might make some contact that way. For Ruth, it was a perverse pleasure, like the pleasure of probing a sore, to invite Hero's gratitude for helping them. Hero limped to the door, and Kit followed her, with one backward glance of complicity at Ruth. Young Kit made to follow them, but Ruth caught him by the shoulder and stopped him with a firm look. When they had gone, he said, 'Why can't I go too?'

'They want to be alone for a while,' Ruth said.

'Why?' he said.

'There are private things they want to say to each other,' Ruth said briskly. It had been easy to keep Kit out of her heart, but she had to defend herself all the time against the child that should have been hers. 'They want to say goodbye.'

'Oh,' said Young Kit, and she felt his shoulder relax under her hand as he accepted the ban on his presence, though he did not understand it. 'He's going to fight another battle tomorrow,' he said, his face shining at the thought. 'Is that really my father?'

It was not a question – he merely said it in wonder; but Ruth, with a grim little smile as she remembered the Kit she had fallen in love with, said, 'Oh yes, that really is your father.'

In the darkness, in bed, in each other's embrace, they could find safety and anonymity. With her eyes closed, Hero could pretend it was the husband she remembered in her arms. To Kit, she was a female body, warm and willing, wonderfully soft and sweet-smelling to a man who had lived with soldiers for so long. Their bodies understood each other at least. Afterwards they felt comforted, and the sense of accomplishment cheered them. It was possible to forget how much of themselves they had shut away.

286

In the dark they talked a little. Kit told her something of his life, of the battles they had fought, of the glorious charges, of Rupert's leadership and courage, of the companionship of other soldiers, the pleasant nights around a camp-fire singing and drinking. He could have been any soldier talking to any girl. Curled small and warm in the crook of his arm, she was any girl listening to the voice of her lover, her first lover, whom she did not yet know, but already adored. For a little while, they were almost happy.

But in a while he grew restless, and pushed her away and sat up.

'I must go. I must not be late back. I have the General's trust for that. Light the candle again so that I can dress.'

Hero sat up, reached out for the flint, and in a moment the candle grew a yellow flame and the world crowded in again out of the dark corners. She looked at him, and was embarrassed and looked away. He got out of bed and began to pull on his breeches with rapid, impatient movements. Silently she slipped out of the other side of the bed and pulled her gown on over her head, moving quietly and sparely, as if she did not want to draw attention to herself. When he was dressed she was already waiting by the door. He took up the candle, and she held out her hand, closed into a fist, to stay him.

'Kit,' she said, and she felt shy using his name, like a young girl again. 'Will you take this?'

'What is it?' he said, stiffly, impatiently. She pushed her closed hand at him again.

'Please, take it.' He held out his palm, and she placed upon it the oak apple charm. He stared at it in the candle-light, watching the leather thong on which she had strung it uncurling like a live thing, slowly. 'I would like you to wear it, to keep you safe,' she said. He thought suddenly of the gleam of the gold cross round Daniel's neck, and it seemed absurd, the contrast, the gold cross and this crudely shaped bit of worthless gall. But it was a bridge, a bridge from her

287

world into his. A talisman – a soldier understood that. He looked up at her quizzically, and she saw the change, saw that it puzzled him, but that he was *there*, at last; at the very last, and for a moment only, but she was grateful for it.

'Yes,' he said, 'thank you.'

She looked into his eyes, smiling. She wanted to touch him, to say goodbye, to tell him she loved him, she was so glad that she had reached him at last; but she knew she could not. Already the moment was passing, he was going from her again, he was a soldier and she was remote to him, merely something delaying his departure. She turned from him without a word, and as he lifted the candle to light the way, she limped down the stairs before him.

When he went out into the yard – alone, he would not let Hero or the boy come with him – Ruth was there, holding Oberon for him. She was brisk and businesslike, and he was grateful for it.

'Here,' she said, 'I've packed some bread and meat in a bag for you. You may not have time to get anything else before dawn.'

'Thank you,' he said, taking it and tying its lash through one of the dees. She was still holding the reins, and so he took the opportunity to put the charm on its leather thong over his head and stow it away inside his shirt. Looking up, he caught Ruth's amused, cynical glance. Let that keep you safe, it said, if anything can. 'It will please Hero,' he said.

'Oh yes, of course,' she said, and her lips curled with a hard amusement. Suddenly, unexpectedly, he wanted her, and it angered him. He seized her chin in his hand and holding her head still he kissed her violently, forcing her lips apart with his tongue. She did not struggle or respond, merely endured, never ceasing to smile that cruel smile; and yet her mouth was very sweet. He let her go at last, and she rocked to her balance, her eyes unfathomable.

'Look after Hero and the boy,' he said. He could not bear that knowing smile. 'Until I come again.'

'Until you come back,' she said. He put his foot in the stirrup and swung up, and she released the reins to him. It occurred to him suddenly that she had not asked him about Malachi, and he honoured her. She was like a soldier. The dead were dead, and should be left in peace. He raised a hand to her in salute, swung Oberon on his haunches, and rode out through the gate.

Ruth stepped forward to close it after him, disdaining to watch him ride away. Her mouth burned with the imprint of his angry lips, her mind echoed maddeningly with his final words. He had put on her a burden he knew to be intolerable – to look after his wife and child until he came back. He knew, and she knew, and he knew she knew, that he would never come back. The mark of death was on him, the despair that would find its way out. The next battle, or the one after, or the one after that, it made no difference when. But he would not come back.

CHAPTER SIXTEEN

Rupert's men were assembled on the Marston road in the grey of the morning of 2nd July, but Newcastle and his men did not come. Orders had been given, as usual, for scouting patrols to go out. It was a lieutenant's command, but when Hamil came to tell off his men, he took Kit to one side and said, 'I want to take your patrol, and leave you here in charge.'

He looked, unusually for Hamil, uneasy, and Kit raised his eyebrows in mute enquiry. It was not for him to question, of course – if his captain wanted to take his patrol, he could not stop him – but it was an odd thing to do. Firefly pawed the ground, and Hamil checked him sharply, and then looked around him as if he scented danger. 'I can't bear just waiting here,' he said abruptly. 'We are on Morland land, and –' He looked away in the direction of Shawes, and then back, meeting Kit's eyes for the first time. 'You saw her?' he said. 'How is she? The Prince told me what the messenger said. They were not harmed? Was Shawes attacked? For God's sake, tell me if she is all right.'

'They are both safe,' Kit said, a little stiffly. 'Hero went to Shawes when the Scots came and she and Ruth prepared for a siege. But Shawes was in the area occupied by Fairfax, and he would not trouble them when he learned they were but two women. All is well with them.'

'Thank God,' Hamil said, and then, with difficulty, 'Did she – did she ask about me?'

'I did not put her to the trouble,' Kit said coldly. 'I told her that you were unharmed.'

Hamil smiled cynically. 'And would have, I doubt not, if I had been all but hacked in pieces.'

Kit flared up. 'I would not have her worry more on your account, since you cared so little about her that you left her without a word for near ten years.'

Hamil went white with rage, and for a moment Kit thought he would strike him. But Hamil was a soldier, and he pressed down his anger, biting his lips until he had control of his voice, and could say in a low, steady tone, 'You will be sorry that you ever took her from me, I promise you yet. You are in charge until my return. I shall take your patrol.'

At eight in the morning they were still waiting for the York garrison when Hamil's patrol came galloping hurriedly back and word went round that they had come up with the rearguard of the Parliamentary infantry, marching away towards Tadcaster. For a while everyone was very excited, expecting the order to mount up and go after them, but nothing happened, and when Hamil came back to his troop his report was depressing.

'I told the Prince they were all in disarray, trying to turn about and get back to the moor with the rest of the force, and I could see he would have liked to give the order to fall on them. But he has to wait for my lord Newcastle – who, no doubt, is still in front of his mirror having his hair dressed. By this time they will have got back into order, and the chance is lost.'

It was not until nine o'clock, five hours late, that Newcastle arrived at the rendezvous, and it was seen at once that he had not brought the whole garrison with him, but only a couple of thousand horse. It seemed that there had been trouble during the night, and the major part of the garrison had refused to form up and march out without their pay. Word came that the Prince had urged an immediate attack on the enemy with what force they had, but that Newcastle had declined to move without the rest of his army, which was coming up under his second-in-command, Lord Eythin.

'Newcastle will not stir without his Lambs,' Hamil said bitterly. 'And so we must all wait.'

They waited all day, at first alert, then bored, and then lethargic. Kit's mind went back again and again to the events of the night before, and they seemed so remote to him now that it was only by reaching into his shirt to touch the oak apple that he could convince himself that it had not all been a dream. The remaining three Morland men sat their horses near him, and talked of old times. It was subtle torture to them all to be on home ground, and unable to go home. One of them had gone so far as to ask Kit for permission to ride quickly and see if his wife and bairn were all right, but even before Kit had framed the negative, his voice trailed away, and he said, 'No, of course Sir, I see it is impossible. Sorry, Sir.'

It was at that moment that one of the others cried out, 'Look Sir, over there, by the trees – there are three ladies Sir, a-horseback. Isn't that the mistress, Sir?'

They were too far away to recognize faces, but as Kit turned to stare at the three cloaked and hooded figures, there was no mistaking the showy gait of Psyche.

'I think you're right, Dick. I'll go and see.'

He put his heels to Oberon's flanks, and cantered over, and when they saw him coming, the three riders halted and waited, a little way off from the body of the army. It was Psyche, tossing her head up and down so that her gold and coral ornaments shook and rang, and as Kit approached, Mary Esther put back her hood so that he could recognize her. Involuntarily he slowed, devouring her with his eyes, seeing the marks of age and sorrow that had not been there when he went away, and when he halted beside her he looked at her for a long time without being able to speak.

'Mother,' he said at last. 'It is good to see you again. How goes it with you?'

'Oh Kit,' Mary Esther said. She held out a hand, and he gripped it hard; they had no other words.

'Hetta, Anne, you are looking well,' Kit made a great effort.

'We heard the army was drawn up here,' Hetta said. 'A shepherd boy came in to tell us. We thought we'd ride out to try to see you. Are you well, Kit? You are not wounded?'

'No, I'm not wounded. How is my father?'

He saw Mary Esther's quick, silencing glance at the girls, and looked at her questioningly. What did she want to prevent them from telling him?

'He is ill? Mother –'

'No, no, he is quite well, I promise thee, Kit. Only much troubled. But what do you all here? You will not fight here?'

'We are waiting for the rest of the York garrison, and then we march to Marston – the enemy is drawn up on the moor.'

'The York garrison is not here, then?' Anne cried eagerly. 'Do you expect them?'

'Every hour,' Kit said, looking at her curiously. 'Why –'

'You know that Francis is with them?' Mary Esther said. 'He joined Lord Newcastle's Borderers.'

'I had heard. I have not seen him yet.'

'I hoped to have a sight of him. Anne and Hetta were anxious to see him again. He has been quite a favourite with them since the army garrisoned York.'

Kit looked at Anne's pink cheeks and excited eyes and wondered. 'You have been seeing much of Francis – and the other officers?' he asked her, gently teasing. Hetta spoke quickly, defending her.

'We have had many meetings with Francis and his friends. We hoped perhaps to see them before –' Her mouth dried, and she looked down and asked very quietly, 'You think to fight a battle on the moor?'

Kit shot her a look of quick compassion. She sounded troubled, apprehensive.

'Don't worry, little Hetta, we shall beat them. We have never been beaten yet. Why, look how they fled from the city when they knew we were coming.'

Hetta looked up, and for a brief moment her eyes, disconcertingly clear, met his with some denial, some information, which just as quickly she suppressed.

'We brought some food,' she said instead. 'Some hard-boiled eggs, and some pasties Jacob made for you especially. We were not sure you were getting enough to eat. Jacob said to give them to you with his best wishes, and to say when you come home, he'll make you an oyster pie, just as you like them.'

They reached into their saddle-bags for the food, and Kit said, 'I must share these things with the rest – I cannot eat when they do not. Mother, will you speak to Dick and Jack and Con? They will like to pay their respects.'

'Of course,' Mary Esther said, looking past him to where the three men sat their horses at a respectful distance, their eyes fixed on her like hopeful dogs at the kitchen door. 'But, Kit – where – ?'

Kit's eyes were compassionate. 'They are all that's left, Mother,' he said. Mary Esther opened and shut her mouth without being able to speak. Kit beckoned to the three men, and they rode up eagerly, snatching off their hats and gazing at the mistress with longing eyes. If anything could be the essence of home and normality for them, it was the pretty, smiling, elegant little mistress on her dancing golden horse, courteous and benevolent and cheerful. She greeted them all and gave them the latest news she had of their families and asked them how they did.

'We are well enough, Mistress,' Jack said, 'Only we all want to come home.'

'Of course you do. And we want you home. Pray God this war will soon be over. But Dick, are you wounded?'

'Oh, it's nothing, Mistress,' Dick said awkwardly, looking down at the rags tied clumsily about his forearm.

'Let me look,' Mary Esther said, making to come forward. Kit had seen that wound, and did not think his mother ought to, and so he intervened quickly.

'We must get back to our troop. We have been gone too long. Mother, give us your blessing, and then ride home, and keep safe. As soon as the garrison arrives we shall march off.'

'When shall we see you again?' Mary Esther asked. Kit avoided her eyes. It was not a permissible question, and she saw her mistake at once. 'God keep you safe,' she said, 'all of you, and send you back to us soon. All our thoughts will be with you until then. Come girls, we must not keep them from their duties.'

The four men watched them ride away, with a soldier's hunger for the shape and texture and sound and smell of the civilization for which he is risking his life. When they reached the trees Mary Esther looked back once, and raised her hand to them, and then the three horses disappeared into the trees.

It was past four o'clock in the afternoon by the time Lord Eythin came up with the York garrison in good order, Newcastle's famous Lambs marching smartly in ranks, and it was six o'clock by the time they had settled into their positions on Marston Moor, with the road and a ditch between them and the enemy, who had had all day to consolidate their position and work out their plans of battle. The Parliamentarians had the slightly higher ground to the south of the road, while the royalists stood to the north, with Wilstrop Wood behind them, and a piece of enclosed land, called White Sike Close. Kit along with the rest of Rupert's own regiment of cavalry was on the right wing, under Lord Byron, for the Prince had decided to stay in the centre in command of his infantry, which was drawn up in three lines with the York garrison, the Whitecoats, Newcastle's Lambs, in the second line. To the right of Rupert's horse was the rest of Lord Byron's command, numbering about two and a half thousand altogether, there being a cavalry left wing of about the same number, commanded by Lord Goring. It was not long before word came that the enemy cavalry Kit could see drawn up opposite him was the newly formed and already famous regiment of Cromwell's Horse. One of Rupert's patrols had taken a prisoner, and the Prince had asked that specific question. Behind Cromwell's horse was an auxiliary of Scottish cavalry under David Leslie; in all, the enemy's left wing numbered about four thousand.

'So,' said Daniel, who brought the news, 'we shall have the pleasure of beating Master Cromwell's prodigies ourselves – if, that is,' he added drily, 'we ever get around to fighting at all. At the moment there is no sign of it. Whatever our Prince suggests, Eythin contradicts. There's no love lost between those two – Rupert still hasn't forgiven Eythin for getting him taken prisoner at Lemgo. That was after you left us, Hamil, at Breda.'

'And Eythin thinks our Prince is nothing but an impetuous boy,' Morton added. 'I should not be surprised if he had delayed in York all day on purpose to slight him.'

'At any rate,' Daniel said, 'it is sure they will not attack tonight. It lacks but an hour to sunset.'

'Two hours,' Hamil said, looking about him. 'It is the clouds that make it so dark. We shall have rain by and by.'

'It matters not,' Daniel said dismissively. 'The Prince has sent the order for the provision carts so we shall have our supper in a while. We may as well dismount the men, and rest the horses' backs. And let's hope they bring us something decent to eat. There's nothing makes me hungrier than doing nothing all day.'

*

Anne had managed, when they returned to the house, to bribe one of the stable boys to keep watch for the York garrison's passing on its way to the rendezvous.

'As soon as they come by, get word to me, but look you do it privily – no-one must know except you and me, do you understand?'

The boy understood all right. 'But how shall I come to you, Miss?' he said. 'I have no business in the house.'

'I will find some way to be outside. Perhaps I can help my sister to restore her garden – you can come to me there. Stand a little way off, call softly, and I will come to you. Do it, and I'll reward you well.'

The boy looked at her sympathetically. He had often been one of the servants who accompanied the hunts, and he knew more about her affairs than she realized.

'There's no need Miss,' he said. 'I'll do it for you anyway.'

But it was Anne's misfortune that the family was inside at dinner when the York garrison went past, and it was not until after six o'clock that Anne managed to slip out of the house again, and was at once accosted by the groom Simon. He placed a finger to his lips and went ahead of her into the stables. And then he said, 'They've gone, Miss. I couldn't get word to you. They've gone these two hours.'

Anne blanched. 'Gone?'

Simon nodded. 'They'll be at Marston now, Miss.'

'But I must speak to him,' she cried. 'I must see him before –'

'I have an idea,' Simon said. 'The provision carts will take supper to the army. I can easily catch them up on horseback. If you write me a letter, or give me a message that might be understood by him only, I can get one of the drivers to take it.'

'Him?' Anne questioned sharply. Simon looked kindly at her. 'Ensign Symonds, Miss,' he said. 'Don't worry, Miss, I know how to hold my tongue. But I've seen you and him

297

ride off together at the hunt, and come back with the horses barely warm.'

Anne bit her lip. 'I must see him,' she said, abandoning pretence. Simon shook his head.

'A message, Miss,' he said.

'No,' Anne cried. 'I have to see him.'

'It's too dangerous, Miss. What if you was to be found out?'

'It's too late to worry about that now,' she said. 'If I ride after them, maybe I can go with the provision carts.'

Simon said. 'There are women with the carts, but not the likes of you.'

She understood him. 'Nevertheless, I must go. Will you help me?'

'You'll need a cloak, to cover your dress.'

'I can't go back in. I might be seen and prevented.'

'Well, I could give you mine, but it isn't all that clean.'

'No matter. Fetch it, and saddle me a horse '

'Two horses,' Simon said firmly. 'I'll come with you.'

'But –' It would cost him his place, if he were found. He looked at her steadily.

'You can't go alone. Some of those followers are a rough lot.'

Anne gave a quivering sigh. 'Thank you,' she said, 'and bless you.'

He brought Anne his cloak of purplish plaid, much stained and smelly, and saddled two horses. Then they faced the problem of how to get past the gatekeeper. He was a trusted servant and would not be bribed, and it was equally impossible to slip past him unobserved; and so it was decided that Anne must brazen it out. Simon took back his cloak, and they mounted.

'Open the gate,' Anne commanded the gatekeeper in her most imperious manner. 'I must have a little air and exercise. I have been shut indoors for too long.'

'Well, Mistress,' the gatekeeper said doubtfully. 'I don't

know that you should – it isn't safe.'

'Nonsense,' Anne said sharply. 'I have a groom with me. Besides, I shall not go far. Once around the walls is all I need.'

'But it's getting dark, Mistress.'

'I shall be back long before dark, fool,' Anne said, and then, on an inspiration, 'don't you see I have no cloak? How could I go anywhere without a cloak. Come, open the gate, so that I may have my one turn around the walls. Hurry, man, or I shall not have time before it rains.'

This seemed to decide him, and painfully slowly he left his post in the guardhouse and opened the gate. Anne forced herself to sit still in the saddle, but at every moment she expected to hear an outcry behind her, the voice of Leah or Clement or her parents. But at last they were out, and in case the gatekeeper was watching they rode round the walls until they were out of his sight before they cut across country and put the horses into a canter. Once clear they stopped and Simon handed her the cloak, which he had bundled into his saddlebag, and they set off again at a fast gallop.

There were women with the provision carts, mostly the tough, hard-bitten little creatures who were the wives of professional soldiers, but also a fair number of whores, some permanent camp-followers, and some prostitutes from York and the neighbourhood who were going in the hope of some eve-of-battle profit. There was a deal of bawdy comment when Anne joined them, for despite the cloak she was conspicuous, and the horses even more so.

'Which one of the officers is it, dear?' one of them called out as she swayed and jounced on the back of a cart, and 'Does your father know you're out?' cried another.

A third came too close to the truth for comfort when she said, 'If he's not married you by now, Mrs, he never will, so its no use bringing the chaplain with you.'

Anne, her cheeks burning, rode silently behind, and

Simon kept close to her side. When they reached the lines, there was the problem of how to find the ensign. It was impossible for Anne to ride about amongst the soldiers, but equally Simon would not leave her alone while he went in search. They hovered near the provision carts, looking helplessly about them, until Anne by chance spotted a man she recognized amongst those collecting supper for their platoon. He had accompanied the officers as groom on some of the hunts and had a conspicuous scar down his cheek. Anne was not much in the habit of noticing servants, and would not have recognized him otherwise. She pointed him out to Simon, and the boy asked him where the ensign was.

'Away in the centre,' the man said in surprise. 'Where else should he be, but with his men?'

Anne and Simon exchanged a glance. It was impossible to ride into the centre of the army. Anne felt for her purse. There was not much in it, but enough, she hoped, to bribe a soldier.

'You are taking him his supper?' she asked. The man nodded, avoiding looking at her. He felt embarrassed by her presence in a place where she had no right to be. Ladies did not mix with followers. 'Here, good man,' she said, 'take this for your trouble, and tell Ensign Symonds that I am here, and that I must speak with him at once on a matter of great urgency.'

He looked doubtful, but at last reached out his hand for the purse, and having felt the weight of it said roughly, 'What name will I say?'

Anne exchanged a glance with Simon. The name Morland had better not be passed around. 'Tell him Mistress Anne.'

The man nodded. 'Go down by those bushes,' he said, sensing the need for secrecy. 'I'll bring him to you.'

They dismounted as instructed, and Simon hitched the horses to a branch. Beyond the bushes was a ditch and

300

beyond that the road, and on the other side, almost out of sight in the gathering murk, the enemy lines. In the sudden pause while their waited, Anne became aware for the first time of the danger of their position, and she looked nervously towards the enemy, and then at Simon. He shook his head and said, to comfort her, 'They would not be taking supper if there was any danger of an attack. Look, our men are all dismounted, resting on the ground.'

Anne shivered. 'I have never been so close to an army before. And it is getting so dark.'

'There's a storm coming,' Simon said, looking anxiously up at the lowering clouds. 'There will be rain soon – I'm afraid you'll catch an ague if you get wet. You should not have come.'

'Too late to worry about that now,' Anne said. 'Besides, an ague is nothing –' She stopped herself in time, and said no more.

At last Simon said quietly, 'Here he comes.'

Anne saw him coming towards her on foot, with the soldier she had bribed. She ran to him to fling herself into his arms, but he caught her by the arms and held her off with a little shake, and his face was dark with anger.

'Restrain yourself,' he hissed. 'There are people watching. For God's sake, Anne, what do you here? What could possess you to risk it? If ought should happen to you –'

'I came with Simon, he has looked after me,' Anne said quickly. 'I had to see you – Reynold, why did you not come to me, or even send a message? All this long time –'

'Hush!' he said, shaking her again, and then holding her ungently by one elbow, he hurried her a little to one side, out of the hearing of the servants.

'You're hurting me,' she complained when he halted and turned to face her.

He let go of her arm with a final little shake, and said, 'How stupid of you to come here! You must go back at once. And how could you expect me to come and see you from a besieged city? Did you think I could just walk out past the guards: "Excuse me, but Mistress Anne Morland wants to see me?"'

'I've been so worried,' Anne said. 'Reynold, I love you so –'

'There's no time for that now. You must go back –'

'Reynold, I must tell you,' Anne interrupted desperately. 'I am with child.'

In the silence that followed Anne watched the death of her hopes in his stony face. She was not sure what she had expected, but it was not this. Fear made him cruel, and he said, 'Are you indeed? And why tell me this?' Anne gasped, and her hand fluttered towards his arm.

'What – what do you mean? Reynold, don't you understand, I am to bear your child.' Her white face reproached him through the gathering gloom.

He shook her hand away impatiently. 'You must go home.'

'You must come with me,' she said, 'and tell my father we are to be married.'

'Don't be a fool,' he said roughly. 'I cannot leave the moor now.'

'I will not go without you,' she said. 'I cannot. Already they will know I am gone. If I go back alone, I will be shamed for ever. If you come not with me, I shall stay with you.'

'You can't stay,' he said impatiently.

'The army chaplain can marry us,' she said eagerly. 'I know you have a chaplain.'

'Who said I would marry you?' Reynold said.

She stared, seeing it at last. Shame and anger and bitter pain swept over her, and she felt as naked as if he had stripped her there and then in front of two armies. She saw everything, her own folly, his cruelty, her present situation, the black prospect of her future, and the child in her belly. In that moment she felt as utterly alone as if the rest of the world had died, leaving nothing but herself moving on the surface of the earth.

'I cannot go home,' she said at last, and her voice was as empty as a cold hearth. 'I can't ever go home. I am undone.'

And as she spoke, there was a noise from behind her, a confusion of cries and musket-shots, and as if it had been a signal, the heavens opened, and with a clap of thunder like cannon-fire, the storm broke and the rain came down in sheets. And then Simon and the soldier cried, almost in unison, 'The enemy! The enemy is coming!'

'It's an attack Sir! The Roundheads are attacking!'

Gasping with the suddenness of the rain, half-blinded, Anne felt herself swung around by the arm as Reynold put her behind him and stared through the downpour past the two men, and the horses pulling nervously at their reins, and saw a chilling sight: the whole Roundhead infantry, coming down the slight slope towards the road and ditch at a running march, pikes forward, muskets flickering like marsh-fire through the gloom and rain. They had been surprised. The enemy commanders must have seen them dismounting, lying down, sitting on the ground with their suppers, and ordered the attack. And he was away from his men, away from his horse, hampered with a woman and a groom. He ground his teeth in frustrated fury.

'Damn it!' he cried furiously, 'you must get away. You, boy, for God's sake bring those horses! Run Anne, pick up your skirts and run! This way –'

He whirled her round, half pulling, half shoving her away towards the provision carts. Anne stumbled, gasping, trying to wipe the rain and sodden hair from her eyes. Simon was struggling with the two horses, who were shying away from the yelling attackers, laying their ears back against the cold rain, too terrified to obey commands. Simon was terrified too, and hauled helplessly on their reins, casting his eyes again and again towards the line of infantry running down towards him. Soon they would be at the ditch.

'Come on,' he cried, pulling, and the horses pulled back perversely, rolling their eyes and flinging their heads up.

'I won't leave you,' Anne cried, realizing at last what was happening.

'You must – for God's sake, the Roundheads are coming,' Reynold screamed at her, as the rain rivered down his face. 'We're under attack!'

Somehow she broke away from him, and ran, as futilely as a panic-stricken rabbit, back towards the horses – towards the enemy. Reynold started after her just as the reins, made slippery by the rain, slipped from Simon's hands. The groom grabbed, caught one and managed to keep hold of it, but the other horse jumped away and galloped, stirrups flapping, away into the murk. Already the enemy were jumping the ditch behind them, and as Anne reached Simon there was a sharp crack of musket-fire, and he felt a violent thud in his back. He thought someone had struck him with their fist, but as he tried to turn his head to look, he found himself collapsing, and realized with a sickening swoop of terror, that it was a musket-ball that had hit him. His nerveless hand let go of the reins, his legs folded under him. He had been hit in the spine, and he felt nothing.

But Reynold was there, had caught the horse before it could bolt. 'Get Miss Anne to safety, Sir,' Simon wanted to cry, but he had no voice. No feeling, no voice, no sound, and now in the growing dark no sight. 'Get Miss Anne away,' he thought, 'get Miss Anne –'

Reynold saw the boy fall. 'Get up,' he screamed, and Anne, for wonder, obeyed him. He grabbed her leg and threw her into the saddle, but he could see she was in too much of a panic to help herself. He must get her out of the line of firing before he could get back to his own men. He was in a fever of anxiety – to be here with this damned burdensome stupid girl when his men were under attack!

He put his foot in the stirrup and swung behind her, and thumped the horse's flank just as the Roundheads came roaring and yelling over the ditch and round the clump of bushes. The horse screamed and leapt away from the pikes and lances, and Reynold, holding Anne tightly by the waist, drove it in an oblique flight away from the enemy, towards York. There was the sound of musket fire, and he felt the impact of a bullet hit his bridle arm, and at once lost all feeling, dropping the reins, knowing his arm was broken. A second thump was followed by a vicious burning in his back and lungs, and he sagged forward against Anne.

Unguided, the panicking horse swerved violently, cannoned into one of the provision-cart horses and swerved again round the tail of a cart, and Reynold slid helplessly off, dragging Anne with him. The two of them hit the ground while the horse, lightened of its burden, leapt away. One of the drivers was crouching under the cart, sheltering, and as the man and woman rolled on the ground he reached out and grabbed the woman's hand and pulled, and she wriggled under with him and with his help hauled Reynold too in under the cart's shelter.

He groaned, and Anne felt blindly over his face, whimpering with fright.

'Reynold, what is it, are you hurt?' she whispered. He groaned again, feeling the ball working its way inside him. Anne felt over his body, found his arm, dangling and folded the way an arm never should be, and felt sick. 'Your arm is broken,' she whispered. The driver clutched her arm and shook it.

'Hush!' he cried in terror, 'keep quiet, or the Roundheads will find us.'

Anne crouched down, her arms around Reynold, pressing with him against the earth in terror. Reynold thought despairingly of his plight, and his mouth formed the words, 'Damn you,' but he could make no sound that she could hear above the battle. A fresh searing of hot pain went through him. 'For God's sake,' he protested. Anne heard the breath of a whisper. 'What?' she asked him, pressing against him. 'What did you say?' But he was dead, and could not answer her.

CHAPTER SEVENTEEN

The provision carts from York brought little that was tempting by way of supper, and it was then that Kit remembered the food that the women had given him that morning. He was sitting with Jack and Dick and Con, and Daniel and Morton were not far off, so it was natural to call them over and share the good things with them.

'This is more like it, by St Mary,' Daniel cried when Kit broke a venison pasty in half and gave him the larger half. 'That cook of yours must be a genius, Kit me boy.'

'He is,' Kit laughed. 'My father always says that a man's cook is the most important person in his life – after his wife, I suppose.'

'Why suppose any such thing?' Daniel said. 'A man can live without a wife, but he can't live without food. Put the cook first, and be done with it. Don't you agree, Morton, you old sinner?'

'But of course, Danny, for a soldier. But if there were no men to take wives, there would be no more little cooks, eh?'

Kit laughed, and was suddenly aware of feeling strangely happy. It was good to sit at one's ease on the ground like this, the reins of one's horse slipped over an arm, chewing good venison pasties and listening to one's friends talking nonsense. Jack and Dick and Con were talking quietly amongst themselves, the horses were dozing or grazing fitfully at the tough moorland grass, and beyond on every side were friends, soldiers any one of whom could have changed places and been Kit's companion that night. He loved them all, and especially he loved rough, vulgar Daniel and little sharp, bee-sting Morton. He looked up at a flicker of movement and saw Hamil standing a little way off looking at them, and suddenly he loved Hamil too, and he held out his free hand in an expansive gesture and cried, 'Hamil, come and join us. We have eaten the pasties, but there are still the eggs, look. Come and share the good things.'

Hamil looked at him curiously, like an animal suspecting a trap, and then shook his head abruptly. 'I came only to tell you that we shall charge at first light tomorrow. The Prince will be with his Lifeguard – look to him for signals.' He glanced up at the sky, a canopy of purplish-black clouds. 'We shall have rain any moment. Better cover your saddles.'

He turned on his heel and went, and Daniel, with a sigh and a shrug, got up to follow him. Kit did not stir for a moment, feeling too comfortable and too happy, even in the prospect of heavy rain. Home and family and pain seemed very far away. This was reality for him, this easy, undemanding companionship of men and horses, united in one cause. Then a little cold wind lifted his hair, the wind that immediately precedes rain. Morton said, 'Here it comes,' and both of them began to rise simultaneously.

And then there was a terrible yelling and the sound of firing, the rumble of a cavalry charge, the screaming of horses. They whirled round on the spot and saw through the murk that the enemy lines were on the move, and the cavalry of the enemy's left wing under Master Cromwell was galloping towards their ditch.

'Attack! Mount up!' Morton yelled; and the rain broke over them, full and blinding. Thunder for a moment blotted out all other sounds. Kit struggled with Oberon, who was jerking backwards from him, hating the rain and the sudden smell of panic in the air, but he mastered him enough to mount, and once in the saddle it was easier.

'Mount up!' he cried, and jabbing Oberon into a trot he rounded up his platoon, who were milling in the confusion of not being able to see or hear clearly. But discipline prevailed, and once enough of them were mounted to be seen, the others followed suit.

Daniel was a little to Kit's right, and yelled to him, 'Watch for the signal. I'll relay it – you send it on. If we charge too soon we'll cross our own musket-fire.'

Musket-fire, Kit thought, in this rain? The slow-match would have been doused for sure. But there was too much noise to say it. He nodded, and then his head jerked round the other way, drawn by a familiar sound. Lord Byron with the main force of cavalry over to Kit's left had not waited for the signal, but had counter-charged, meeting Cromwell's horse in a head-on clash; but also cutting across the line of fire for Rupert's musketmen, and crossing the path of Kit's regiment. He could hear Daniel cursing volubly away to his right. It could be seen at once that Byron's horse were getting the worst of it, already beginning to fall back. Kit could sense the movement in the ranks of his own men, as they wondered whether to join the fight or run, and he turned his head to yell, 'Stand fast! Keep your ranks! Wait for the signal!'

The horses were shifting about in panic. Some of the men had not yet mounted up, others, taken unprepared by the attack, were already disheartened and trying to slip away. Then as Byron's ranks began to break, and some of his men began to flee, pressure on the waiting regiment grew to breaking-point, and the lines began to sag and waver. There was a regiment of horse under Lord Trevor between Kit's regiment and the front-line foot under Napier, and when they turned and ran, it was impossible to hold his own men. Oberon swung round and only by the force of his will did Kit keep the great stallion on the spot, turning tight circles, the great hooves skidding in the slippery mud, the horse snorting and whickering as others streamed past him.

'Hold your ranks!' Kit yelled desperately. 'Hold your ranks!' The rain ran into his eyes and he shook it out as a dog shakes water from his ears. But they were going all around him – and then, just as suddenly, it was halted, as if by magic.

Kit turned to look. The rain was passing now, as quickly as it had come, and as it grew lighter he saw the tall figure, the white horse, and the upraised sword of the Prince. His heart swelled in him. Rupert had come, Rupert was here! He saw his love mirrored in other faces around him, as he heard that familiar voice crying, 'What lads, do you run? To me, to me!'

And the next moment he was past them, galloping, scarlet-coated on a white horse, his dark hair rippling, and they were after him, charging, swords out, yelling, Rupert's own regiment, the best in the world, the invincible. This was where it had all begun, with this little band of brothers, proud in their belonging, who would follow Rupert anywhere, into the jaws of hell itself. They were the first and last, the core, the heart of the royal army. Kit was charging too, now, Oberon was galloping, his great stride eating up the ground, his ears pricked, his neck arched, pulling in his eagerness, and Kit yelled, not quite a battle-cry, but a paean of love and glory.

Now they were fighting. Cromwell's men were good, he thought in distant surprise. Not daunted by the charge, they held their ground and fought, and the lines swayed against each other, swords clashing, their brightness dulled. They fell back, reformed, and charged again. The ground was slippery with rain and blood; there were dead men and dead horses everywhere, and the many-tongued voice of battle clamoured in their ears. The rain and clouds had gone, and the clear pale evening light gave a sense of unreality to the scene. They charged again, following Rupert, but there were fewer of them now, so few, and the enemy seemed as numerous as ever, as if they were coming out of the ground like ants. Kit's heart failed him suddenly. They could fight forever, but they would only grow fewer, and the ant-like soldiers of the enemy, Cromwell's men, fighting like machines, would go on and on coming.

Then Oberon shrieked and went down, and Kit was thrown off sideways. He managed to keep his feet, but Oberon went on crying, his hindquarters collapsed, his forefeet digging the ground as he tried to rise again. He rolled a terrified eye towards his master, screaming in pitiful appeal. Kit could not bear it, he wanted to put his hands over his ears. Someone had slashed the stallion's hamstrings, crippling him; the horse dragged himself on his forelegs towards his master, his great quarters in the mud. Kit fumbled for his pistol, still in his sash. He must shoot the horse, end that terrible screaming.

Hamil, fighting grimly a little way off, saw Oberon down and Kit on the ground, apparently unable to free his pistol. He saw, also, the Scots reservist coming at Kit, unseen by him. Instinctively Hamil raised his pistol and aimed it at the Scot; one could not help saving a brother's life. And then he hesitated, and his hand went down again.

Kit looked up to see the Scot upon him, riding his little hairy pony, so small that the rider's feet grazed the grass, but tough and strong. The man was armed, unexpectedly, not with a broadsword, but with a rapier, a French duelling sword. Short of arms, perhaps – or perhaps the man fancied himself as a swordsman. There seemed time to notice these things, time for everything, time to see the wind-flayed, raw-looking, gingery face, the tufty, sandy-red hair under the little Scottish hat, pinned with a huge, vulgar brooch and two little grouse feathers. The feathers were absurdly small beside that enormous brooch.

Kit's sword was in his hand, and there was time to raise it and parry, slash the man's arm, time even to duck out of the way, get under his guard, hack him down. But suddenly he didn't want to. Everything was so unreal, and he was tired, tired to death of the fighting and the killing and the marching, and the pain of the horses, screaming in incomprehending fear. He wanted to lie down and sleep and never get up again, and his sword arm was too heavy to raise.

The rapier took him in the throat. The pain was astonishing, but he could not cry out, for he was choked with his own blood. He had no awareness of falling, but the ground was beneath him, he could feel it cold and wet under his back. His hat was gone, and the air was cool against his hair, and above him the greenish evening sky was clear and limpid as a pool. The storm had gone, and he was looking at one pale gold star, the first of the night, far, far above him. The sound of the battle faded, and there was just that one, indescribably beautiful star, floating away, receding ever further into darkness, until at last it winked out.

Anne did not know how long she lay there, pressed trembling against the earth, but at last it seemed to her that the noises had gone further away, and she dared to lift her head, and then to crawl an inch forward and look out from under the cart. The rain had stopped, and the fight was going on at some distance. She raised her head a little more, and could see that the men engaged in fighting appeared to be moving away from her, back towards the ditch. She felt at once a sense of safety, and realized that it was because movement in that direction meant that the enemy were being beaten back. Now was their chance. They must get away before the men came back again. She drew her head back and shook the driver who was crouched there.

'Come on,' she cried. 'We must get away. We must get this man to safety – he's wounded. His arm is broken. Come on, you fool, help me.'

The driver rolled over, pushed her away, and then reached over to look at Reynold. He opened his mouth to speak, looked at Anne consideringly, and closed it again.

'All right,' he said. 'Get out and hold the horse. I'll bring your master.'

Anne crawled out from under the cart and went to the

horse's head. It did not seem much alarmed, or much in danger of bolting. The reins were tied in a knot on its neck, and she unpicked the knot and climbed into the cart. The driver appeared, grunting and panting, dragging Reynold out backwards by the armpits.

'Be careful,' she cried sharply. 'Don't hurt him.'

The man grunted. Once they were clear of the cart, he stooped and managed to lift Reynold and heave him over the tail of the cart, and climbed up after. Anne would have changed places, but he prevented her.

'No, no, don't waste time, you drive. Flap the reins, Miss, get on. I'll hold your man, never you fear.'

'Which way?' Anne cried. The man rolled his eyes. 'Away from the fighting. That way.'

But 'that way' was towards home, and she did not want to go home. There was a farm, she knew, just beyond the wood. She would head for that – the woman there would dress Reynold's wounds. She shook the reins and sent the horse into a shambling trot, and the cart jounced and jolted, and the driver held on and gritted his teeth. They skirted the battlefield, and then Anne turned towards the wood.

'Where are you going?' the driver called.

'Wilstrop Farm,' Anne called.

'Nay, I want to go home. Turn towards the city,' the driver said.

'The farm's nearer. I must get help for the Ensign.'

Enough was enough, the driver thought, and besides, it was his cart.

'You can save your trouble, he's dead,' he said, and abandoning the body he climbed over the front of the cart and took hold of the reins. There was a short struggle, but Anne was not strong enough, and in a moment he pushed her ungently into the back of the cart and wrenched the horse around. Anne crawled over to Reynold. She did not believe he was dead; she thought the driver had said it to distract her. But when she took his head into her lap, she knew at once that it was so. The shock hit her only distantly; already she was a different creature from the girl who had ridden out to Marston – was it really less than an hour ago? Now she was a woman, and an animal bent on survival. She thought for a moment, and then began working Reynold's signet ring from his hand. It was too big for any of her fingers, so she slipped it over her thumb. Then she smoothed his face with her hand once, lovingly, kissed his forehead, and wriggled away to the tail of the cart.

The horse was old and undistinguished, and its trot was not much more than a brisk walking-pace. It was getting dark, and Anne had only to watch for a smooth place and slip over the tail of the cart. She fell to her knees, grazing the heels of her hands, but the cart went on and she was not much hurt. She stood up, got her bearings, and headed towards the wood. She could hide there until the battle was over, and then join Reynold's regiment. Francis would help her, or Lieutenant Symonds. At any rate, she certainly couldn't go home now.

In the centre, Francis had seen how most of the battle had gone. Their right wing had broken, but the cavalry under Goring on the left wing had broken Fairfax's horse and sent them to flight, and Goring could now be expected to lend them some assistance in the centre. Francis rode along his lines, encouraging them, when to his surprise Sam Symonds cantered up to him. What on earth could he be doing away from his own men?

'Frank!' Symonds' face was creased with anxiety. 'Something bad – your sister –'

'My sister?' Francis cried in astonishment. 'Sam, calm yourself – what is it?'

'One of the men just told me – he took Reynold to see your sister, down by the provision carts, just as the first attack was launched. She'd come to see him, God knows why. The man saw Reynold wounded, and then he had to run. It's taken all this time for him to get back to me – but Reynold hasn't come back, and God knows where your sister is! I must go in search of them.'

Francis had time for one despairing glance around. The enemy outnumbered them by at least two to one. 'Don't be a fool, man,' he shouted. 'Reynold will take care of her. What can you do?'

Sam opened his mouth the reply, but there was no time. The enemy kept on coming, and they were having to fall back. Francis wheeled his horse round. The close was behind them, and would give some protection in a defensive action. He began to fall his men back, carefully, section by section, so as not to give rise to a rout. There was no help coming from Goring – he was fighting for his life against Cromwell's horse, who, having broken the right wing, had swung right around the battle to attack the other wing.

They reached the close and took up position there. Francis's horse was killed under him, so he had to direct his men on foot, and could no longer see anything but the action immediately around him. He wondered briefly about Reynold and Sam and his sister – it must be Anne of course, Hetta would not do anything so mad. He took a wound in the arm and another in the face, but they were light and didn't trouble him.

It was growing dark, and they were fewer than before. The moon was up, a pale sickle in the velvet sky. They were surrounded by the enemy, including most of their cavalry, on every side. The enemy had greater reserves than they, and the Lambs were constantly fighting against fresh men. The Borderers were hand to hand against the Scots, the old enemy. It was too dark to see further than a few yards on each side. The white coats of the Borderers were red now. Francis pushed the sweat and blood out of his eyes with the sodden cuff of his coat. His arm was so tired that it was stabbed with pain when he lifted it. Then there was a pause.

The enemy held off. Could they be retreating? But no, it was only to give them a chance to surrender.

'Surrender!' came the demand on every side. 'You cannot win. Yield, and we will shew you mercy.'

Francis looked around at these men he had come to love, the tough little Borderers, and he saw in every face the same fury and scorn, the same determination. Surrender – to the Scots? Ask a Scot for quarter? They were the old enemy, hatred of them was in the blood of every whitecoat, bred into them through centuries of raids, murders, burnings, pillages. Surrender to a barbarian Scot? Never!

The attack was renewed. Where was Newcastle? Where were Rupert, Eythin, Goring, Byron, any of the commanders? Where was their cavalry? Gone, all gone, all but the Whitecoats. It was dark, it was finished, the battle was lost, England was lost, they were going down into the dark; but teeth bared in fury, the Lambs fought on, dying where they stood, dying in their ranks, their white jackets red with their own blood. Francis fell at the end, just before the Roundheads, sickened at last of the killing, stepped in and disarmed the last of the Lambs, taking them prisoner and so saving their lives. The regiment had numbered four thousand that morning; the prisoners numbered no more than forty.

Hetta at first kept silent when the gatekeeper reported that Anne and a groom had gone missing. If Anne came back soon, she would have some excuse at the ready, and Hetta did not want to betray her needlessly. But when the horses came in riderless, and the first reports of the battle sifted back, she could not keep the secret any longer. Her parents heard her in silence, and then Mary Esther, with a terrible heartbreaking cry, sat down, holding herself and rocking, her eyes wide with shock. Edmund strode to the door and called for Clement, and when he came, said, 'Saddle Titania and another horse and meet me in the yard.' Clement went, and Edmund crossed to the fireplace and took down the pair of pistols from the wall.

Mary Esther said, 'Edmund, what are you doing? You cannot go out – it's a battle, a terrible battle!'

'Would you have me do nothing?' he said. 'My daughter is out there.'

She knew it, and her eyes reproached him, but she said, 'You could be killed.'

'I have the best right. It is my own fault. I should have kept a firmer check on her.'

Mary Esther stood up and went to him, but the coldness between them prevented her from touching him. 'Take care,' she said. She did not see what good his going could do, and she feared to lose him as well, but she could not say these things. Since the horses had come back riderless Anne was probably already dead and beyond her father's help, and Edmund would risk his life in vain. Edmund flicked no more than a glance at her, and went out. The women were left alone to wait in silence for news of victory or defeat, life or death.

The first fugitives to come past were Roundhead cavalrymen, from Sir Thomas Fairfax's wing. Their news was that they had been routed by Goring. One or two paused for a drink of water or a bandage. Hetta, tending the wounded, asked in a quiet desperate voice if they knew anything of Ensign Hobart, but none did. Later Royalists came in, wounded or in flight. Richard ordered the servants to keep them out, and there was almost a rebellion on his hands until Mary Esther stepped in, calmed the furious servants, and told Richard in a quiet but firm voice that no-one was to be turned away. 'Do you dare to tell me what wounds I may dress, and not dress?' she said. 'I tended my enemies during the siege.' Richard looked ashamed and defiant, but he held his tongue.

The accounts of the battle were confused, and it was

impossible to tell what had happened. Each man knew only about that small section he had been in, and told his own story in a few broken words. Then Edmund came back, white-faced and weary and without Anne. Mary Esther had run down to meet him in the stable yard, and as he handed Titania to a groom he said, 'I went to all the houses round about, but I could find no-one who had seen her or heard of her. I could not get near to the battlefield. I think she must be there, under Symonds' protection, or –' He could not say the word. Mary Esther licked dry lips.

'How goes the battle?' she said. 'All accounts seem to be different.'

'It is hard to tell from a distance. They are fighting in the darkness, but it seems we have the more men.'

'*We?*' she said bitterly. He was too tired to react to her resentment.

'The Royalists are outnumbered,' he said, 'and the word is that Prince Rupert is fled, and all resistance is ended, but for Lord Newcastle's regiment.'

Their eyes met, and she was anguished enough to be cruel. 'And what of your sons?' she said, and held his eyes a moment longer before she went back to her tending of wounds.

A little while later some of Rupert's men came in, three of them riding one exhausted horse which threatened to collapse under them. They slid to the ground and begged for water, two of them supporting the third, whose arm was hacked nearly through at the shoulder. They carried him into the hallway, and Mary Esther knelt beside him to bind the wound as best she could, though knowing it would not help him. His face was waxy with loss of blood and approaching death. 'What news,' she asked softly. 'What news of my family?' The other two exchanged unwilling glances. 'For pity, tell me the truth. Have you seen them, Captain Hamilton and Lieutenant Morland?'

'Mistress, we know nought of Captain Hamilton, but we

318

saw Lieutenant Morland fall,' one said at last. The blow was less than she would have expected. The words did not seem to mean much to her. 'Tell me how it was,' she said.

'His horse fell under him, and while he was gaining his feet he was killed by a Scot,' the man said tonelessly. They had seen so many deaths that none of them could rouse much feeling. 'Not many of us got away. It's all up, Mistress. We want on'y a drink of water, and we'll be on our way.'

'This man cannot move,' Mary Esther said. 'Leave him with me, we will take care of him.'

The men exchanged glances. 'God bless you, Mistress,' they said. 'God keep you both,' she replied.

The news came in bit by bit, news of defeat. All were fled, wounded, or dead – thousands were dead. It was after eleven o'clock that they brought Francis in, two of the shepherds from the outlying fields, from that place where the dead lay heaped in the moonlight. They brought in Simon, too, but they could not find Master Kit, and there was no sign of Mistress Anne, dead or alive. But there was a story that Lieutenant Symonds had gone off to look for her, and had not come back, so there was hope that he might have her safe somewhere.

They carried Francis to the chapel and laid him down with the other dead. He was twenty-three years old. Mary Esther stood looking down at him, letting the pain have its way with her. She could not weep, but she felt his death and now, in seeing him, knew Kit's death too. Edmund came in and stood beside her. She looked up at him, seeing his face drawn with a pain worse than her own, and she wanted only to rend him, she had no pity for him.

'Francis, and Kit, perhaps Hamil, perhaps Anne too,' she said. He looked at her, and his eyes received the blows, and he made no move to avoid them.

It was impossible in such a battle to stay in one place, and before many minutes had gone, Hamil knew he was far from where Kit had fallen. He marked the place with his eye, but before long they were in flight, the Scots on their heels. Firefly was a big horse, and fast, and he had no trouble in outstripping the Scots on their little garrons. He saw others in flight, and headed like them for the wood, but unlike them went through it. He had no desire to be flushed out like a rabbit by stoats. He came out of the wood on the other side and circled back cautiously, and when he was as near as possible he hid his horse in a clump of blackthorn and crept back to look for Kit.

The battle had passed on from that place, and only the dead and wounded were left there. Some of the wounded cried out to him for help, others hunched, shivering, afraid that he had come to kill them, to rob the bodies. The ghouls were never far from the battlefield. He crept low to the earth like a dog, shivering himself with shock and revulsion. He didn't know why he was doing this, he only knew, with a strange lightheaded certainty, that he must find Kit and take him home. He had let him die, and he must atone. It was hard to tell one place from another under the wavering moonlight and with so many dead, but at last he saw Oberon, the big horse unmistakable, and close beside him was Kit.

His body was cold and damp from the earth or the dew. He felt very heavy, and Hamil was battle-weary, but he managed to get him up over his shoulder and began the long struggle back to his horse. Kit was a great deal taller than Hamil, and the dead are heavier than the living. After a while the lightheadedness was like a fever, and Hamil lost count of the time. When he finally got back to the bushes, Firefly was still there, head hanging, ears flopping; too tired to struggle or protest as Hamil, inch by inch, hoisted the body across his back, and at last unhitched the reins and led the horse forward.

He took a circuitous route to avoid what was left of the fighting. Firefly stumbled along, and Hamil stumbled with him, almost delirious, with Kit hung across the saddle, hands swinging with the movement of the horse. They circled the wood again and came down past Hessay to the Whin. There they stopped and found a beck unpolluted with blood, and man and horse drank thirstily and for a long time. From the Whin they went on more directly, and came at last, very late, to Shawes. Hamil led the horse up to the gate, and stood swaying, waiting to be let in. He did not call or knock; he knew he would have been seen. At last the gate was swung open, and a tall woman stood here. He looked at her blearily, not recognizing her, and said, 'Is she here?'

Ruth had known the moment she saw the man and the horse in the moonlight what it was that was hanging across the horse's saddle. He had come home in the only way he could have. She stepped back now and said tonelessly, 'Bring him in.'

Hamil led the horse forward, and said desperately, 'I let him die. I could have saved him, but I let him die. I hated him, because he had taken her away from me, and when I saw the enemy raise his sword I could have shot him, but I didn't. Where's Hero? Where is she? I must tell her.'

Ruth was tall and strong, and anger made her stronger. She seized Hamil by the throat, forcing him to meet her eyes. 'Be silent,' she hissed. 'You have brought him back, that is all. Say no more.'

'But I must tell her,' Hamil said.

'Why? To make her feel better? To comfort her? What do you think it will do to her, to know that? You want only to unburden your mean little soul at her expense. No, keep your guilt, and may it rot you! Keep it in silence, and let it eat away your life!'

She dropped her hold on him just as the door opened and Hero came out with Ellen and others of the servants, and came limping across, faster than Ruth would have thought she could move. In the darkness of the doorway another figure appeared, a small figure in a white nightgown. Ruth tried to put herself between Hero and the horse's burden, but it was a futile gesture. There was nothing to keep out the blow. Hero stopped still, her eyes huge, but she made no sound. Ruth gestured to Parry and another manservant, and they came forward to lift the body from the horse and carry it indoors.

They laid him down in the hall, and Hero knelt awkwardly beside him and smoothed his hair from his face. In the wavering candlelight he did not look so pale, though his face was as smooth as marble. He looked quiet – like a very beautiful statue. He was unmarked, but for the hole in his throat. Such a small hole, Ruth thought, to let out the life.

For a long time Hero stroked Kit's face and hair in silence, and then she held out a hand for someone to help her up, and Young Kit stepped forward automatically. She got to her feet, and stood with her hand on her son's shoulder, and they looked into each other's eyes. he was white, and trembling, but in control of himself, and they seemed in that glance to give and receive strength from each other.

'Let him be taken to the chapel,' Hero said, the first words that had been spoken in the house. Hamil made a move forward.

'Hero,' he said, and Ruth, standing beside him, twisted his arm viciously in warning. Hero looked, and for a moment did not recognize him, and then her face lit with amazement and the first gleam of joy.

'Hamil? Oh thank God, you've come home!' she cried. Hamil stood still, trembling, and said nothing. 'At least you're safe,' she said. 'At least we still have you.'

The sad little procession formed up and went towards the chapel, leaving Ruth and Hamil alone in the hall. He stared after them with eyes that just began to know the meaning of pain. Ruth let go his arm. 'Let *that* be your punishment,' she said.

Hero and Ellen washed him and combed his hair. Hero tried to tell herself that it was Kit, but he seemed not like Kit at all but like an effigy, a statue or a funeral mask, as if he was somewhere else still, and had sent this substitute for the ceremony. Round his neck was the oak apple on its leather thong. Hero removed it. There was a graze along the top of it, from the rapier. She looked at it for a long time, lying on her palm, and then she folded her fingers over it, and held her hands to her breast and rocked them, as if it was they that felt the pain.

Very late that night other horsemen came to the gate and hallooed softly. Ruth, gesturing Parry back, went close and called 'Who is it?'

'Madam, we are fugitives, seeking shelter. Will you take us in?'

She looked through the crack. From their clothes they could not be Roundheads, she thought. 'Royalists?' she asked. 'Aye Madam,' came the reply. She opened the gate. 'Dismount and enter,' she said. The men obeyed, and for a moment her heart stopped; for a terrifying moment she thought that it was Kit, that tall, dark-haired cavalier who led the way. There was a small, dark swarthy man, too, and three others who came behind them. The small man said, in a foreign voice, 'Madam, you are Mistress Morland, the wife of Kit Morland?'

'I am Ruth Morland, mistress of this house, and Kit Morland's cousin.'

The little dark man sighed with relief. 'We are friends of his, Madam, and needing shelter for the night, and knowing his house to be friendly to us –'

Ruth looked at the tall man – young, very handsome, broad in the shoulder, with a lean, sombre face and great

323

dark eyes – and she knew who he was.

'You are welcome here,' she said abruptly. 'Kit Morland's wife is within, and his son. And he himself –'

'God be thanked!' the little dark man said. Ruth shook her head.

'Do not thank Him. Kit lies in the chapel.'

The Prince spoke for the first time. 'Dead?'

'Dead, your Highness,' Ruth said. He gave a little shuddering sigh. 'So many,' he said. 'So many friends.'

Ruth saw they were all near to collapse. 'Come in, eat and rest. There is not much of the night left.' She led the way in, and remembered to say, 'Hamil Hamilton is here too, Kit's brother-in-law.' And the little dark man cried with pleasure.

She fed them in silence, and they ate in silence, after the first flurry of greetings with Hamil. They were worn out and leaned against each other, dropping asleep even while they ate. 'I will shew you where you may sleep,' Ruth said in a while. The Prince looked up, meeting her eyes with a straight and steady gaze as if they were of one kind and he knew she would understand him.

'We must go early in the morning, gather together those who are left and ride for the King.'

'I will have food ready for you, whatever we can spare. Come and sleep now.' She put the little dark man and Hamil together in the guest room, and the Prince she shewed up to her room while Parry settled the other three officers. Rupert looked around the small chamber as if dazed, and when she was about to withdraw he sat down on the bed and said abruptly, 'This is your chamber.'

'Yes.'

'But where will you sleep?'

'I shall not sleep tonight,' Ruth said. 'Kit lies dead in the chapel.'

Rupert looked at her. 'You loved him?' There seemed no reason to deny it, not to him.

324

'He and Malachi, my nephew, were all I loved. Now both are dead.' He nodded slowly, his great dark eyes wandering about the room as if in search of something on which to rest that would distract his thoughts.

'We should not have fought,' he said, 'but God knows I had no choice. So many friends – I was cut off from them. I had to hide in the wood, until it was safe. My horse was shot, I could not get back. And when at last I got to York, there were so few, so few –' He shuddered, and rubbed his hands over his face. 'Newcastle lost his whole regiment. All the whitecoats, all of them dead. He cried like a child.'

And now he was crying too. Ruth could see the great round tears running from under his fingers as he rubbed his face over and over with his hands, as if trying to reshape the things his mind saw. He looked so young – strong and young and vulnerable, like a colt. She moved nearer to him, instinctively, to comfort him.

'And then –' he said.

'Yes?' She was near enough now to touch him, and he looked up at her to see if she was to be trusted. She put her hand on his head, and the feeling of his hair under her fingers was like Young Kit's. She shuddered, and sat down on the bed beside him and stroked his hair. The tears still rolled from his eyes, as effortlessly as if he did not know he was crying.

'They told me – afterwards – that they had seen – my dog. He slipped his collar and followed me, when I went to join my regiment. They killed him – the enemy killed him. They said he was a demon in disguise. My poor Boye –' His last defence broke, and he put his head on her shoulder and sobbed. Ruth drew him against her, and held his head, and she cried too, but silently. She stroked his dark silken hair, and kissed his brow where her tears dropped, and in a while she lay down on the bed and drew him down beside her to comfort him the more easily. She kissed his brow and his wet eyes, and in a little while her lips found his mouth, and she kissed that too, and his hands came up and cupped her face. His mouth was sweet, sweet young curves to it like a child's, and the curve of his neck was tender, like a child's, and the fans of his lashes lay soft and silky against his cheek. But his body was strong and broad, a man's body, great shoulders and powerful legs. The contrast was heartbreaking, it moved her terribly, deeply.

She closed her eyes and held him and kissed him, and it was child and man she held, it was Kit as he had been when she had fallen in love with him, before bitterness and defeat had marked him. All the loneliness in her cried out for him, the love she had locked away poured out for him, and she lay with him in pain and in longing, and in the strange remote passion of two people who had always been distant from their world.

Afterwards he fell into an exhausted sleep, and she held him wonderingly in her arms, man and boy together, her lover and her child. He did not stir when she got up and left him. The next day at dawn they rode away, to collect together the rest of the surviving army, and take it southwards, and left the shattered north to reassemble its life as best it could.

CHAPTER EIGHTEEN

Anne hid in the woods for a long time, burrowing in deep under a thicket of holly which scratched her skin and tore her clothes but, she reasoned, would protect her from discovery. She heard the sounds of men and horses crashing about in the wood, and she lay low and waited for quiet. They might have been Royalist soldiers who would help her, but they might just as easily have been Roundheads; there was no way of telling. At last, when the woods were quiet, she crawled cautiously out. Whatever the dangers she must head for York, for whether victorious or defeated the survivors of the army would gather there. The only alternative was to go home, and death was preferable to the kind of disgrace which by now must attend her there.

She got her bearings by the moonlight filtering through the trees, and set off to the east. She hadn't gone far when she heard close behind her the sound of a heavy body crashing through the undergrowth. She was in a clearing, and there was nowhere to hide; all she could do was to press herself against a tree and hope the leafy shadows might hide her. The noise came nearer, and out of the bushes came a riderless horse, its broken reins trailing. Anne gave a cry of relief and stepped forward. The horse whickered a welcome to her and stood, lowering its head to her hand, glad to have found a master again after the terrors of the evening. Anne had never ridden cross-saddle, nor yet mounted unaided and without a block, and it took her a while to find the way of getting into the saddle, but the horse gave her no trouble, standing patiently until she got her foot into the stirrup and half-hopped, half-climbed aloft. She knotted the reins and kicked the horse into a walk, and they set off towards York.

Though they did not know it, Anne and Lieutenant Symonds had been close to each other for some time. He had ridden in search of her to the east wing of the battle, had been caught up in the cavalry fighting when Cromwell and Leslie attacked Goring, and had fled with the royalist cavalry when their force was broken to Wilstrop Wood. He had hidden up there, listening, like Anne, to the sounds of flight and pursuit, and as soon as he could he had slipped out and tried to get back to the battle. But even a distant view had told him the terrible story of the fate of his regiment, and there had been nothing for him to do but head for York and try to find the rest of the survivors.

York city had closed its gates to the enemy and the loyal soldiers both, no matter how they cried for food, water, and succour. Prince Rupert arrived there a little before midnight, and rallied those who were fit to fight on and sent them to spend the night in the old Scots camp to the north of the city. Symonds reported to him and was welcomed as an addition to the cavalry.

'Sir, I am an infantry officer,' he said. Rupert smiled grimly.

'You have a horse, Sir,' was all he said.

The next morning early, they marched off to the north, for though their objective was to get back to the King in the south, they must give the fugitives time to join them. Also, Montrose was in Richmond, and the Prince hoped to get help from him. Daniel O'Neil had come in during the night, and was reunited happily in the morning with Rupert, Morton and Hamil. He asked at once if Hamil was wounded, for he was so strange, moving as if in a dream, but Hamil only shook his head, and Daniel assumed he was grieving for Kit. The remainder of the baggage train assembled, and they set off northwards, stopping at Thirsk overnight and reaching Richmond the next day.

Anne travelled with the baggage train. The local whores had left it, and the women still with it were the professional wives and followers. They were kind to Anne in a rough and ready way, pitying her for her helplessness and her condition, and they allowed her to ride with them.

'You must be as strong as a horse,' one of them said approvingly, 'that you've not dropped that bairn.' Anne guessed that they would not have been so kind had she been a snivelling milk-and-water maiden, but toughness was a thing they understood and valued. One of them even gave her a cloak to cover her torn dress. It had come from a dead soldier, and was smelly and bloodstained, but it was better than nothing, and Anne accepted it gratefully. This, and the signet ring on her thumb, were her only possessions; besides the horse, and she did not keep that long. An officer, thinking her a follower who had had the luck to capture a stray horse, took it from her to supply his own need, and she dared not protest. So it was on the tail of a cart that she rode into Richmond, hugging her belly against the jolting of the cart and wondering what was to become of her.

In Richmond she learned of the presence of Symonds, for she saw him ride past in the market square. She called, but he was too far off to hear. The officers were billeted in the Kings Arms, and as soon as she could she went there and told the sentry on duty that she wanted to see Lieutenant Symonds.

'I doubt not,' he said indifferently,' but does he want to see you?'

Anne held her ground. 'He will, when he knows who I am. Send word to him,' she said with her best assumption of arrogance. Her voice made him look closer and see the prettiness under the dirt and dishevelment, the quality of the torn dress under the filthy cloak.

'Who are you?' he said suspiciously. 'What do you want?'

'I want to see Lieutenant Symonds,' Anne said, and shewed the ring. 'I have news of his brother.'

The guard made a grab for it, and she closed her hand around it as he caught at her arms. She was struggling fiercely when an ensign came by and said sharply, 'Guard, what's going on here?' Anne saw her chance.

'Sir, you are a gentleman – I must see Lieutenant Symonds. Take me to him – the guard takes me for a drab.'

The ensign looked at her doubtfully, and then said, 'Wait here, I'll tell him. Guard, let her inside the door but no further – and do not molest her again.'

The guard snarled at her, but let her by into the porchway of the inn, and Anne, shaking down her shoulders, stood inside the shelter and tried to smoothe her hair and clothes with her hands in a vain hope of improving her appearance. It was not necessary. As soon as Sam appeared in the doorway, he ran to her, taking her hands into his own, which trembled with relief.

'Anne! Thank God you are safe. I thought you must be dead. I looked for you everywhere when they told me you'd come to the battlefield looking for Reynold. But what are you doing here? Why have you left home?'

A glance at her would have told him the reason, but he was too agitated to notice. She turned her hand over and shewed him the ring.

'Reynold is dead,' she said bluntly, too tired and too afraid to seek for gentle words, 'and I am with child. I have no-one to turn to but you. Will you help me?'

Symonds stared at the ring, his face blanching, and then he turned from white to red as he could not stop himself from staring at her belly. He looked up at her, confused and distressed, hurt and angry. She had flirted with him, led him to believe she cared for him, but had lain with his brother – and long enough ago to have a sizable belly by now. But then he saw the delicate beauty of her face, and the strange, calm courage that had replaced its former expression of folly and vanity, and he was deeply moved. His brother's child in her belly, and her hands – those hands that had been so white and fine, now broken-nailed, grimed with dirt, scratched and bruised – resting trustingly in his, what could he do? He had loved her, vain and silly and proud, he could not love her less, distressed and afraid, but still proud.

'You should go home,' he said at last. 'It is not fitting that you should travel with the army. Let me find a way to send you home.'

She bared her teeth in desperation. 'If you try, I shall only run away again. I cannot go home. Will you help me – ?'

'Of course I will, but –'

'Black Tom Fairfax's wife travelled with his army,' she said, trying to smile. 'It is possible.'

He gave a sigh of consent, and drew her to him so that he could pass a protective arm about her shoulders. 'Very well, if it's what you wish. But in your condition – it is a wonder you have not miscarried before now.'

'Sam,' she said softly, 'it is your brother's child.' Their eyes met. 'I'm sorry,' she said. He pressed her hand and said slowly. 'If you will marry me, I will be the child's father, and no-one shall ever know that I was not always so.'

She was amazed at his generosity. 'Thank you,' she said, and each looked at the other with new respect. She opened her hand again and held out the ring to him. 'Take it,' she said. He shook his head. 'You must keep it, until I get a ring for you. It shall be your surety.'

'You are better surety than a ring,' she said. 'But I will keep it anyway.'

He led her towards the inner door. 'We must get you some food, and warmth, and better clothing, and I will send out for a priest, so that we may be wed as soon as possible. We must ask the Prince's permission, but he'll give it, I feel sure.'

On 7th July the Prince left Richmond again to work his way west and south through Lancashire to Cheshire, to recruit forces in Wales and the south-west. With him went a force of some seven thousand, amongst them Scots reinforcements brought by the loyal Montrose, and riding in the baggage train in borrowed clothes went Anne, the new Mistress Symonds.

On York plantation the numbers were slowly dwindling. In August Josiah, who had not been strong since the accident to his foot, took a fever from which he did not recover. Later that month Betty Hammond died, apparently of the same sickness. Her husband, Joe, was bewildered. He had never been apart from her for more than a few hours since they were married at the age of thirteen, and without her he did not know what to do with himself. He seemed simply to fade away, as if the wrenching away of his wife had left a wound which would not heal and was bleeding him to death. He died in the second week of September. The place behind the house where they had buried the dead child was becoming the regular graveyard.

Then in October, Pen Huster disappeared. No-one knew what had happened to him: Nell was sure he had run away, not liking the hard work and the prospect of winter in this bleak place. Ambrose thought he had met with an accident, and Rachel was sure he had been captured by Indians, of whom she had lived in mortal dread since hearing terrible stories in Maryland from other servants. In fact, they had never yet seen an Indian, although they had sometimes found evidence of their presence at some distance from the house. They seemed as cautious about approaching as anyone could wish.

The cold weather started in November, but it gave them no indication of what was to come. Nell's vegetables had grown and been eaten, all but the turnips she had insisted on holding back, but there were plenty of duck, and the wild geese had arrived, and there were still fish to be had, though their stock of grain had almost gone, other than the seed-corn for planting next spring. They were none of them as fit as they had been when they arrived, for the terrible hard work, the poor diet, and the continual low fevers had drained their strength. Nell was not properly recovered from her stillbirth, but was already pregnant again; Phoebe was frail; Ambrose was gaunt and haggard, though still indomitably cheerful; Austin and Rachel and the men were far too thin, and worn out with labour. Only the Goodmans, though they had lost their surplus flesh, were healthy. They had avoided the grueling labour, and they had avoided the fever-bearing mosquitoes, and somehow or other they appeared to be taking more nourishment from their food, or else taking more food.

But then the snow came. Nell awoke one night and was aware of an overwhelming silence outside, no sound of any sort, none of the usual night rustling, no movement of grass or twig, no sound of birds. Curious, she rose from the bed. It was breathtakingly cold. She went to the window and eased the shutter back just a crack, just enough to look out, and saw outside nothing but white, shining luminously in the starlight, and great soft flakes of snow like goose feathers drifting gently down and settling like a caress on the branches of the trees and on the earth. It was enchantingly beautiful, but Nell sensed that it spelled the beginning of hardship. Even she did not anticipate, however, the severity of that winter.

The river froze over, and the snow covered the ice until there was no knowing where water began and earth ended. One terrible day the ice at the edge gave under Will Brewer's weight and he went down into the river. He came up twice, terrifyingly blue in the face and unable even to call for help. They tried to reach him, but even when, lying down full length, John Hogg was able to touch his hand, no-one had the strength to pull his huge body from the water. Within minutes he disappeared through the ice once more, and did not surface again.

After three days of frozen whiteness a second storm

followed the first, and for a week it was impossible for them even to leave the house. They could do nothing but stay within and keep as warm as possible. And as long as they could not go out and hunt, they were using up their precious stores. Nell eked out the dried meat and the turnips as best she could, but it was not enough. When the storm ended and the men were able to get out again, hunting was difficult – even moving about was difficult in the deep drifts of snow. The goat died of the cold, and wolves came down from the hills and took away most of the chickens in the night, and then a third storm followed the second, and starvation stared them in the face.

Then one morning, very early, Nell woke to an unfamiliar sound, and for a moment could not think what it was. Then she realized that it was the sound of running water – a sound missing from her world for over a month. The thaw had come! Relief swept through her. As soon as it was light, they could move, get into the boat and sail down to the city for supplies. Or, if they passed some other settlement, ask for help there. She drifted back to sleep. They all slept a great deal now, partly from weakness, partly from hunger, and partly because the only place to stay warm was in bed. She woke once or twice, but it was warmer, and she could not drag herself from sleep until some time after dawn when she finally became aware that it was full light. Some noise had woken her, but she could not at first remember what it was. Then she remembered the thaw, and turned over to wake Ambrose and tell him the good news.

She sat up, and saw, at first with surprise, and then with apprehension, that the sleeping place usually occupied by the Goodmans was empty. She shook Ambrose awake, and then got up herself to wake the others. They were slow and stupid with sleep and weakness, and by the time they had dragged on their shoes and gone outside, it was already too late. The Goodmans had gone, and so had the boat. They had stolen off, taking what they could for trade, and left the inhabitants of York helpless. Without a boat, they were stranded.

To encourage the others, and to prevent despair and panic, Nell and Ambrose pretended that the carpenter and his wife had gone to get help for them all, but no-one believed it for very long. When the fourth storm closed in, the apathy of starvation prevented the worst of their fears. They huddled in their beds between waking and sleeping, stirring only to eat what little food Nell doled out to them. They ate the last of the chickens and the last pig, and finished the seed-corn, and then there was nothing more, and the snow still fell silently and relentlessly, smothering them, walling them in.

Rachel died, and then Robert Updike, and the survivors used up the last of their strength dragging the bodies outside. They buried them in the snow, but the wolves dug them up again, and the night was made hideous by the sound of the bodies being eaten. The wolves did not go away again. It was a lean winter for them too, and in the house were live human beings. At night they sang, and their wild music was eerily beautiful under the frozen stars.

Nell lost track of time. They no longer rose from the bed they all shared for the warmth – there was nothing to get up for. She woke and slept, and woke again, and in the stillness could not hear any breathing sounds at all. 'They have all died,' she thought. 'Now there is only me – and it will not be long until I die too.' Then she heard sounds outside – human sounds. The Goodmans had come back, against all the odds! She struggled to get up, but she was too weak. She shook Ambrose, but he did not stir. The noises were unfathomable, going round the house – why did the Goodmans not come in? Then she heard a voice under the window speaking in a strange language, and instantly she knew it was not the Goodmans. The people outside were Indians.

She was too weak to feel much fear and in any case there

335

was nothing she could do. After a long time there was a fumbling at the door, and then a pause, and then someone discovered how to work the latch, and the door was opened, and three figures clad in fur and skins came cautiously in, and stood just inside looking about. They were armed with spears and knives, and they called back to others behind them. Then one figure said something and detached itself and came over towards the sleeping-place. Nell closed her eyes briefly and prayed that it might be a quick death. Then she opened her eyes, and found herself looking into a pair of dark, curious eyes set in a brown, smooth, young face – a female face.

The Indian girl said something incomprehensible. Nell croaked, and very slowly managed to raise one hand and point to her mouth. The face went away and came back again, there was more foreign talk in the background, and then the Indian girl said slowly and quite distinctly, 'You – hungry?'

Nell thought she was dreaming. She croaked and nodded. The brown face smiled, and the girl said, 'Sleep. I get food.'

Nell drifted, remembering Mrs Colbert's words about the Indians. It was possible that they meant some direful harm, but she could not believe it of that face. There were sounds within the house, sounds of fire being kindled, food being prepared, and the smell of smoke and the smell of food pervaded her half-waking dreams until she could not be sure what was real and what was not. Then she was woken by an insistent hand, two insistent hands, which prised her up and supported her. There was a bowl with something in it that smelled so like food it made Nell feel sick, and the Indian girl said the one, wonderful word, 'Eat.'

She fed Nell a few spoonsful, and then shook her head; a little was enough for now. She laid Nell down and went around the bed to feed someone else, and then paused and smiled at Nell and patted her own stomach significantly.

'Baby,' she said, nodding. Nell smiled weakly. 'Baby,' she concurred, and fell asleep.

The girl and two others stayed for several days until the survivors had recovered enough to move about. Then the two men left, and the girl stayed; she was to look after them, while the two men would be back soon, with meat. They traded axes and tools with the Indians in exchange for the food they had brought and would bring, and the girl translated for them where signs would not do. She told them her name, but they could not pronounce it and so they called her Rose, which was something like the sound of it.

A fortnight after the battle on Marston Moor the city of York surrendered to the Parliamentary forces under Fairfax, and as far as York was concerned that was the end of the war. It brought no cessation for Edmund from his problem of balancing one side against the other, for there seemed little doubt now that the King would eventually have to come to terms with Parliament, and whatever those terms were, Edmund must be seen to have fallen within them. The savage reaction of some of the rebel soldiers over the chapel prompted him to modify it, lest another visitation did permanent damage. He stripped the altar and the lady-chapel, and hid the trappings, including the ancient wooden statue of the Virgin, in the secret panel behind the lady-chapel altar, where the family jewels were kept in time of trouble.

Mary Esther and Father Michael watched in sober silence. Edmund was master, and there was nothing either of them could do. The chapel, stripped of its ornaments, was still very beautiful, with its delicate fan-vaulting, stained-glass windows, and family monuments round the walls; but Edmund now ordered a modified form of the mass, and forbade the family and servants to genuflect or to cross themselves. It was a compromise, a straddling of the issue, and Mary Esther hated it, with all the fire of her straightforward soul. It should have pleased Richard, but he got little more pleasure out of the situation than his stepmother.

The side he had backed was winning, seemed likely in the end to win the whole war, and the King would then be forced to accept the new religion. Richard had, evidently, great influence over his father, and had already brought about changes in the house, and he ought to have been happy. But triumph had no savour for him: there was something unpleasant about pitting his strength against his father and winning. All his life his father had been the immovable rock against which he flung himself, and it disconcerted him to feel the rock shift under his attack. Katherine, who had had a miscarriage last year, was pregnant again, and that ought to please him, but he was growing tired of Katherine, and especially tired of her preaching and nagging. Pregnancy had made her bad-tempered; like him she found it difficult to reconcile marriage and childbearing with purity, and though it was she who had first insisted on their consummating the marriage, she tended now to blame him for her discomforts, and to hint that it was his lecherous nature that was to blame. As his infatuation with her faded, the luminous quality of clarity that had seemed to invest her ideas faded too. Richard began to perceive, very much against his will, inconsistencies in her philosophy; the crystal stream was beginning to look very much like any other muddy beck, and he began to notice that Katherine was really very plain indeed, and that there were several very pretty young maidservants in the household who looked upon him with a nervous respect that was cheering and refreshing after Katherine's strictures, complaints and criticisms.

One event only brought happiness to Morland Place: a letter arrived with the news that Anne, whom they had mourned as dead, was alive and well, was married to

Lieutenant Symonds and therefore, when the war was over, would be able to be received back into the house. Edmund was more relieved than he could tell anyone at the news, for he had blamed himself very bitterly for Anne's actions, and he could have wished that things were warmer between him and his wife so that he could share some of his joy at the news. But Mary Esther, though she hugged Hetta in her happiness at the news, only gave Edmund a cold look, as if to say, 'No thanks to *you* that things are not worse.'

Hetta, though naturally relieved that Anne was safe, was puzzled that she should have married Sam Symonds, when she had loved Reynold so much that she had risked lying with him and getting with child. She missed her sister exceedingly, and her life was now silent and without much laughter. She had, therefore, plenty of time for reflection. She compared her feelings for Charles Hobart, and wondered whether she, even if pregnant, could ever bring herself to marry Charles's brother. The question was beyond her. She could only hope that Anne loved Sam, that he was so like his brother she could not help loving him. For herself, her main worry was that her father would begin looking round for a match for her. She did not know whether Charles was alive or dead, and she might never know, but she wanted no-one else, and she did not know how she was to resist if her father found her a husband.

For the survivors at York settlement, life after the starving time had a strange and almost beautiful simplicity. All their ambitions, hopes, fears and desires were purified and clarified like metal that has passed through the refiner's fire. Morland Place and England they remembered still, but from a great distance; the starvation, the closeness to death, had placed more distance between them and their former lives than the great stretch of the ocean ever could. Now they were alone, with God and with His wilderness, and the

339

purpose of their lives was life itself, no more and no less.

There was hard work for them all ahead, but Rose was there to help them, Rose and the two Indians who often came down to visit. They learnt that the two men were her brothers. Through the winter they prepared for spring. The three York men, Ambrose, Austin, and John Hogg, went hunting with the Indian brothers, both for meat and for beaverskins, with which they could trade in St Mary's City for the things they would need. The younger of the Indians, Attqueho, shewed them how to build a boat, and when the weather was too bad to do anything else, they would sit out under the Goodmans' shelter and work on that, and on curing beaver and deerskins, a process which the older Indian, Natashek, taught them. As soon as they had enough skins, and the boat was ready and the weather mild enough, Ambrose, with Austin to help him, set out on his journey to the city to buy seed-corn, tobacco seed and livestock and anything else he could find that they needed. It was a mark of how much Ambrose had come to trust the Indians that he would leave Nell and Phoebe with only John Hogg to protect them.

While they were away, those remaining at York prepared the fields for planting, dragging the plough behind them like oxen. Nell worked on her vegetable garden, and on making a new feather-bed with all the goose- and duck-down they had collected, and on making shirts for the baby out of her own chemises. Rose was thrilled with the prospect of Nell's baby, and would often, as she passed her, put her hand on Nell's swollen belly and smile. 'My baby,' she would say, and Nell would laugh and agree. 'There would be no baby if you hadn't saved his mother's life, so, truly, you can say it is your baby.'

Ambrose was away a month, and when he returned he brought with him all he had gone to trade for, and more. John Hogg saw the boat coming, for he was working in the boat-shed on something secret, and he ran to the house.

'Mistress, the master's coming back, and there are two strangers with him.'

'Strangers?' Nell for one horrible moment thought it might be the Goodmans coming back, but she hastened with everyone else down to the jetty, and there was Ambrose grinning with delight, and in the boat with him were Austin and a man and a boy. The man was big and burly and bearded, and the boy was in his early teens, and skinny.

Once the greetings were over, Ambrose was able to explain. The planters in Virginia were very strict about runaways, and about enforcing indentures and upholding ownership of slaves – their lives depended on the labour that was owed them. Therefore, as soon as he reported the Goodmans' delinquency, he had great sympathy, and word was sent out that if discovered the carpenter and his wife were to be apprehended. He had only been a week in St Mary's City when the news came that the Goodmans were in Jamestown, living in considerable comfort, for Sam Goodman was a fine carpenter and Jamestown was now rich enough to require fine furniture for the houses of its leading citizens.

Ambrose confessed he had been very alarmed at the thought of having to take the Goodmans back, but in the event it was unnecessary. They had bought out their indentures, and with the money Ambrose had been able to buy two more, the man and the boy who now accompanied him. In addition, the Virginian council had imposed a mighty fine upon the Goodmans for theft, and had Ambrose not been too soft-hearted to tell of the dire consequences of their actions, they would have been proceeded against even more heavily. There was little love lost between old Virginians and Marylanders, but in matters such as this it was in each colony's interest to uphold the other.

Thus Ambrose came back with all their necessities, and a number of luxuries, and two more helpers. The bearded man, Henry Wood, was another such as Will Brewer, a man of muscle and simple brain, but he had great good humour, and a love of animals and small helpless things which made his size and strength seem unalarming. The boy's name was Ralph Enderby; he was thirteen and had lost both his parents on the voyage over from England. He was at first withdrawn and rather sullen, as might be expected, but he quickly came to look upon Nell and Ambrose as something more than Mistress and Master, and then he shewed his true nature, which was warm, loving, quick-witted, and energetic.

With this new help they planted the fields: corn for survival and tobacco for profit. Rose shewed them how to fertilize the cornfields with dead fish, an Indian trick which would double or treble the crop, and how to pinch out the top leaves of the tobacco plants so that the lower leaves would grow and remain tender. The vegetable garden flourished, and the new livestock settled in, chickens and a goat and kid and a fine black sow in pig; the Yorkshire trees came into blossom again, and the white rose budded strongly.

And in May, while Nell was out in her garden hoeing up weeds with a long-handled wooden implement that John Hogg had designed for her, to save her bending, her pains began. She dropped the hoe and clutched her hands to her sides with a little gasp, and then quietly walked back towards the house, calling for Rose. Something in the quality of her voice must have warned Rose, for the girl ran out, her long braids swinging, and her dark eyes wide.

'What is it, Missie? Is it my baby?' she cried. Nell put her hands into Rose's long brown hands and smiled through a mist of pain. 'Yes, I think it is,' she said.

Rose drew her into the house, and noticing her hands were damp with fear, said, 'Why afraid?'

Nell bit her lip. 'I lost my last baby,' she said, 'and that was with Rachel here, who knew about such things. I do not know how to deliver a baby, and nor does Phoebe.' Rose smiled.

'Not be afraid. *I* know. In our village, we learn such things.'

Nell sighed with quick relief. 'I don't know what we would do without you, Rose.'

The sleeping-place was curtained off, and behind the curtain Nell laboured while Rose and Phoebe mopped her brow and held her hands and encouraged her. The men found themselves jobs near the house – near enough to know when the baby had come, and far enough away not to have to hear anything. Ambrose chopped wood in a fury of anxiety, his face white as a sheet. Once in a pause in his chopping he heard Nell cry out, and he had to run away to a patch of weeds and throw up everything in his stomach. The other men when they passed him from time to time gave him looks of silent sympathy.

The baby was born in the middle of the afternoon, and when Rose appeared at the house door, smiling and beckoning, the men dropped their tools and came running, but they all slowed as they approached the doorway and became extremely polite in offering each other the first right to enter, after Ambrose. Nell was lying back on the bolster looking exhausted but radiantly happy, and the new baby was squirming beside her on a doeskin that had been cured by Attqueho to be as soft as its own.

'A girl, Ambrose,' Nell said. 'I hope you don't mind that the babe is not a boy.'

Ambrose knelt down and stared at the baby, enchanted. She was not red and wrinkled as babies usually are, but smooth and pearly and glowing like a fruit ripened to the perfect moment. She had a sheen of fine dark hair, and her eyes, open and wandering, were the astonishing blue of a kitten's. Ambrose put his finger to her palm, and looked up at Nell as the baby's fingers curled round it, and said, 'But she is *beautiful*!' His face was enraptured; how could anyone complain that this exquisite child was not a boy?

The other men came forward shyly to offer their congratulations and worship the little baby in their own way, and they were all struck with a kind of wondering awe that she was so perfect and so beautiful. Then John Hogg came forward, more shy than all the rest, and muttered incoherently that he had a present for the baby, if they would let him. He went out, crimson with embarrassment, and came back a little later carrying the thing he had been making in secret in Sam Goodman's boat-hut. It was a rocking-crib, lovingly made from sleek dark hickory, and the panels all around it were exquisitely carved. It had taken him many, many hours of painstaking labour. Nell asked to be propped up higher, and bid John bring the crib up beside her so that she could look.

'It's lovely, John, really beautiful,' she said. 'You have a great talent.'

'I really think it is even beautiful enough for my daughter,' Ambrose teased gently. They examined the carvings – John Hogg had decorated the crib with the things he knew best, and the panels were a riot of animals, a wonderful mixture of England and Maryland, the animals he had grown up with, and the new ones he had observed since he had been here. When they had looked all around, he pointed out a panel on the foot of the crib that had been left bare.

'Here,' he said, 'if you like, I'll carve the date, and the baby's name.'

And so, in a few weeks' time, it was done. The date was 5th May 1644, and the baby's name was Philadelphia.

CHAPTER NINETEEN

On the night after his return, Kit came to visit his wife, and brought with him a gift, wrapped in a scrap of cloth.

'What is it?' Anne asked as he held it out to her.

'Open it and see,' Sam said. He was smiling and flushing

It sometimes happens that when a man seeks out death, it avoids him. In every engagement and skirmish after Marston Moor, Hamil flung himself recklessly into the fray wherever the enemy was thickest, and his recklessness seemed like a charm over his life. He was, and remained, the only one of them never to have received a wound since they first joined the King at Nottingham. Just as he sought death, he sought oblivion in sleep and in drink from his memories and his guilt, and as death evaded him, so did oblivion. He drank twice as much as his friends when they sat around after an engagement or in camp at night, but he never got drunk; and when he lay down to sleep, he was wakeful for hours, watching the stars move across the sky in their courses; and when he did sleep, he would dream of Hero, and wake crying.

They wintered in Oxford, where the King and his principal advisers met commissioners from the Parliamentarians to discuss coming to terms. The discussions were long drawn out and futile, but it gave them all time to lick their wounds. So it was in Oxford, in Christchurch College where Kit had once studied, that Anne's baby was born late in October, though it was not until the beginning of November that Sam Symonds saw it, for at the time when Anne was giving birth he, along with the rest of Rupert's force, was still on campaign. The child was a boy, and the sight of it brought painful memories as well as pleasure to the parents. It was obviously necessary to find a neutral name for the boy – it would cause too much pain to name him after either of his fathers – so since he was born on 24th October, the feast of Crispian and the anniversary of the Battle of Agincourt, it seemed appropriate to call him Crispian.

On the night after his return, Sam came in to visit his wife, and brought with him a gift, wrapped in a tiny scrap of cloth.

'What is it?' Anne asked as he held it out to her.

'Open it and see,' Sam said. He was smiling and looking very pleased with himself. 'It's a charm for the baby, for luck. It's so appropriate, I couldn't resist it, though it cost – well, I won't tell you. Open it, Anne, see if you like it.'

Smiling indulgently she pulled away the scrap of cloth, and saw, cut from a curious dark-green stone, a tiny pair of shoes, joined at the heel by a gold link through which a chain or thong could be threaded. She looked up questioningly, and Sam said happily, 'Shoes, you see – St Crispian is the patron saint of shoemakers. Now you see why I couldn't resist it!'

'It's very pretty,' Anne said. 'What is this green stone?'

'It's jade – it comes all the way from Cathay, and the people there think it the luckiest stone of all. When people marry, or go on long journeys, or when a child is born, they give something made of jade, for luck.'

Anne held it up and shook it, looking at it critically. 'We can put it on a thong, to hang round his neck,' she said. 'You have learnt a lot about this jade very suddenly. Who sold it to you?'

'An old man in a little shop tucked away down New College Lane.' He went across to the crib where the baby was sleeping, and stared down with fascinated love. 'He's red and crumpled, and very sweet, like a crushed rose-petal. How good it is, after all the fighting and killing, to see something new and young! Life instead of death.' He looked up and met Anne's gaze. The change in her was more than he could comprehend. He had fallen in love with a silly, vain and capricious girl, but he had married a woman. Stripped by her experiences of her foolishness, she had a quality of directness and clearsightedness that

346

perhaps came from her mother, and an ability to assess people which shewed her that the man she had married, the quiet, reserved man whom she had despised as a poor contrast to his flamboyant, charming brother, had fine qualities of courage, generosity, and integrity that were worth all her devotion. And the directness in her would give that devotion completely and without hesitation.

'Nan,' he said now, a little shyly, 'I want you to know how happy you have made me, you, and now the boy. When the war is over, shall we go back to Northumberland, to my father's estate? You'll like it there, I'm sure. It's wild country, the Cheviots, sheep country, but very beautiful. And when my father dies, the estate will be mine, and we shall make a wonderful home for ourselves and our children –'

'Children?' she asked. Sam had taken her hand as he spoke, and she could see the dreams in his face, dreams of peace and growth and quiet and prosperity, the very antithesis of war and destruction and death.

'We shall have lots of children, shall we not?' he said.

And then the focus of his eyes changed as she said seriously, 'I should like to bear your children. But when you have other sons – what of this one?'

He looked across at the sleeping bairn, at its tiny perfect hand curled on the pillow beside the small red face. Reynold's child? But he and Reynold were of one blood, and he had loved him. He pressed Anne's hand and said, 'Nan, my wife, I love you. Your children are my children. If I have a hundred sons, Crispian will always be my firstborn.'

Anne lifted his hand to her face and pressed her cheek to it, for she could find no words to thank him.

Katherine's child was born in December, and was a girl. They named her Catherine; she was frail and sickly, and

347

seemed unlikely to survive, and Mary Esther was in a ferment of anxiety over it, for Richard would not have the little creature baptized, and she was afraid it would die unbaptized and therefore be exiled for eternity from heaven. There were other troubles, too, to plague her mind. Hetta was fretting over something, and it was affecting her health. She had always been such a plump, round, brown, cheerful little thing, and it hurt Mary Esther dreadfully to see her grown pale and thin and listless. She never sang now, while about her work, and when she played on the virginals or guitar, the songs she played were sad ones.

Mary Esther asked her what was wrong, but she would not tell; she asked Father Michael if Hetta had mentioned the cause of her sorrow in confession, but he said she had not. Mary Esther did her best to get Hetta out of the house, to keep her amused and occupied, but nothing seemed to help. She would have liked to send her away on a visit, hoping the change of scene would raise her spirits, but the only place possible in the present troubles was Shawes, and the atmosphere at Shawes would not be likely to help her.

That was another worrying thing – the scandal over Ruth's pregnancy. Such things could not be kept secret for long, and by Christmas it was known everywhere that Mistress Ruth Morland of Shawes, who was unmarried, was five months gone with child and would not say who the father was, nor did she seem to have any prospect of marrying before the bairn was born. After quarrelling violently with Ellen, Ruth had made friends with her again, and these two and Hero had drawn together, supporting each other and making a grim little fortress of the old house. There seemed little joy there, and Mary Esther worried about the effect it would have on Young Kit, to be brought up by two middle-aged women, one a crippled widow and one unmarried and pregnant, and a number of dour, elderly servants.

As often as she could find excuse, she rode over there to

visit, sometimes taking Hetta, but more often alone, though even she did not know what she could hope to achieve. If things had been normal, she could have tried to persuade Ruth and Hero to let Young Kit come to Morland Place for his upbringing, but as things were, with Richard and Edmund, it was impossible. Even Ralph was beginning to run wild, playing on the conflict of opinions between his father, his grandfather and his tutor, pitting one against the other. He was not a naturally vicious child, but he was high-spirited and intelligent, and the lack of discipline was having a bad effect on him. He was still respectful to Mary Esther, but he confused her with arguments compounded of scraps of three peoples' philosophies, and his quick wits always found some reason for doing what he wanted and she did not.

So in the circumstances she could not ask Hero for her son; and when she visited, Mary Esther could see that she would not have let him go anyway. Hero, in black mourning still, quite literally leaned on her son. He supported her as she walked, and when she sat, stood beside her ready to help her up or fetch things for her. He was a tall boy for his age, and very good-looking, but he was, to Mary Esther's mind, too quiet and solemn. It was obvious that he could not be merry and high-spirited, attending all the time on a mother who was still dazed with grief, and whose mind more than half the time seemed elsewhere. Mary Esther saw that there was an affection between Ruth and the 'Haltling's Bairn' as the servants referred to him, but it seemed to her not like a normal relationship between a woman of thirty and a boy not yet five. Ruth was a sharply-spoken, direct, unsmiling sort of person, and she treated the child like an adult of the same stamp.

Mary Esther could not get over her surprise at the look of Ruth, however. How could that downright plain child have grown into a beautiful woman? Ruth was tall and as thin as a workhorse, but she carried herself like a queen, and with that crown of soft red-brown hair and that porcelain-fair skin, she looked, even in her unadorned, dark-coloured clothes, both graceful and beautiful. Mary Esther did not wonder that she had had a lover. What puzzled her was that the man had not claimed her for a wife, for as well as being beautiful Ruth was a wealthy and unencumbered woman. Since Malachi's death, the Shawes estate had been undoubtedly hers. But no matter how Mary Esther cajoled or hinted or asked directly, Ruth would tell her nothing, and she would go away puzzled.

Ruth and Young Kit watched her riding away one day in the early spring of 1645, and the boy said in the abrupt way that was becoming habitual with him, 'What does grandmother want? She comes here and goes away again, but she never seems contented.'

Ruth never prevaricated with the boy. 'She thinks we are not happy, and she wants to do something about it,' she said.

'What?' Young Kit asked. Ruth turned away from the door and they went back inside. Ruth walked slowly, one hand supporting her belly, for she was large with child now.

'She doesn't know, but she thinks if she knew who was the father of my child it might help.'

Young Kit considered. 'And would it?'

'No, but she doesn't know how else to do.' She looked at the boy critically, seeing, as always, Kit and Rupert superimposed upon him. The duality of sight gave her pain, but she could not be rid of it. 'You are pale. You spend too much time indoors. She is right in that, at least. When this baby is born and I can ride again, we shall go out hunting.'

'Mother too?' Kit said.

'Of course. We'll ride out onto the moors, where the air is good.'

The word struck a chord with the child. 'Is that where my father died?' he asked. He had known his father too little to be unhappy at his death, but it fascinated him. Ruth winced inwardly, but she said only, 'There are more moors than one.'

The baby was born on 25th March – Lady Day, the day of the Annunciation.

'A week early,' Ruth said weakly when it was all over. 'Forty days and forty nights it should be – like Christ in the desert, a bairn should wander in the wilderness before it is born into this world of sin.'

She was half delirious with the pain and struggle, or she would not have given so much away. Ellen, who had birthed her, went away afterwards and counted backwards with the help of a pointed stick and the dust of the inner yard, and after some struggling with the awkward numbers she came to a very interesting conclusion which, being Ellen, she kept to herself.

The baby, a girl, was, by the time she was a week old, already very distinctive in looks, with eyes that would be dark and dark curly hair, and more individual features than new bairns generally have. 'She will look just like him,' Ruth said once with satisfaction. Hero admired the bairn, and wondered who Ruth meant, but refrained from asking.

'What shall you call her?' she asked instead. Ruth's sense of humour – rather dark and malicious it had grown in the last few years – asserted itself.

'In view of the times we live in, it should be a nice, plain, equivocal name. The sort of name my uncle Edmund would chose, to fit in with whatever side wins the war.'

Hero shook her head. 'I can't think of such a name,' she said.

Ruth smiled. 'She was born on Lady Day. I'll call her Annunciata.'

Ruth was too vigorous to stay long abed, and when Annunciata was three weeks old her mother went out for her first day's hunting, along with Hero and Young Kit. Young Kit supposed that Ruth would take the baby along as well, and was surprised when they set off without her.

'You are always staring at her,' he said. 'I didn't think you'd leave her behind.'

'I like to look at her,' Ruth said. 'Those big dark eyes – dear God, how she will haunt me.'

'What does that mean?' Young Kit asked. Ruth was brisk.

'Never mind. She's too young to come hunting. A pity really that she's a girl, too.'

'I'm glad she's a girl,' Young Kit said.

'Why, chuck?' Hero asked.

'Well, when I'm a man, she'll be a woman, and then I can marry her,' he said seriously. Hero and Ruth looked at each other for a moment, and then burst out laughing. It was the first time they had laughed happily and spontaneously since they had lived together, and it was like the lifting of a cloud; the passing of shadow and the coming of sunshine. 'We shall be merry, by and by,' Ruth thought. 'Maybe not merry enough for Mary Esther, but merry enough for us. Our men, our loves are gone, and won't come again, but we have each other, and the love of women is more enduring. Whatever comes, we shall get by.'

'It's so good to be out of doors again,' she said. 'Everything is so full of life and vigour, it does one good.' They were riding down to Ten Thorn Gap, to go up to Harewood Whin for rabbits. 'And look,' she said suddenly, pointing, 'how well advanced the spring is already.' The others followed the direction of her finger and saw that the hawthorns were in bloom, white with opening blossom like snow.

During the winter, while the inconclusive talks were going on with the King, Parliament had reorganized its armies into a single force along professional lines under one commander. The commander they chose was Sir Thomas Fairfax, and they called the force the New Model Army, and with it they hoped to push the war along to its conclusion. It became apparent to the leaders of the Royal forces that the commissioners they had sent to Oxford had merely been wasting time to allow for the reorganization.

In the early months of 1645 the King lost Shrewsbury, and the west was increasingly in danger. Prince Rupert urged that they should march north to relieve Yorkshire and Northumberland. Montrose was still winning victories for the King in Scotland with his Highlanders, and the Scottish army in the north of England was weakened by having to send reinforcements to Scotland to hold him down. If the Scots could be driven out of England, the King could join forces with Montrose and launch an attack on the New Model Army from a secure base.

May therefore found the Royal army marching northwards through Staffordshire towards Derbyshire; on the 22nd at Tutbury the news arrived that the New Model Army had taken the opportunity to besiege Oxford. The leaders were not much troubled – it was an expected move, and Oxford was well defended – but Sam Symonds was grateful that his wife had refused to be left behind and had insisted on travelling, as before, in the baggage train, with little Crispian and one small but enduring maidservant. He told her so when they arrived at Leicester on the 28th.

'I understand now,' he said, 'why Fairfax allowed his wife and daughter to travel around with him. I used to think him mad to risk it, but how much worse it would be to be in danger and apart.'

'The danger is yours, not mine,' Anne said serenely. 'I should have hated to be besieged. It was bad enough at home, though we were outside the city. Does the Prince think Oxford will fall?'

'Oh no, not at all. They are all very pleased that Fairfax should be kept busy by sitting outside a town that will never give in to him. The plan now is to draw them northwards by attacking their strongholds until we have them where we

353

want them, and then we can fall on them in a place of our own choosing. That's why we have come to Leicester.'

'Leicester is to be attacked?' Anne said thoughtfully. 'Poor Leicester.'

He touched her hand. 'Do not be too tender. It will come to nothing – Leicester is so poorly defended that they will surrender as soon as the Prince asks them, and there will be no bloodshed. We want only to draw the Roundheads away.'

But it did not turn out that way. Leicester defied the Prince, and so at midnight on the 30th an attack was launched, the royal army storming the walls on three sides. From a safe distance Anne watched and listened, but could make out nothing, and it was an anxious time. All that she could tell was that after some time the quality of the noises coming back was different. She, like the other women, was busy tending the wounded who were brought into the church in the little hamlet where they sheltered, and often enough all that she could hear was the groaning of the wounded men, the sharper cries as the surgeon got around to probing for bullets or straightening smashed limbs, but meanwhile there came like a distant surf, washing loud and then soft, the cheers and yells and howls and crashes and the sound of musket-fire, and then only a distant muted screaming. The women moved about silently, ignoring it all, only binding wounds and bringing water and holding the hands of the dying. Now and then Anne would get up from her knees and go to look at Crispian, but he slept peacefully through it all, tucked up in a reed-basket in a corner behind the altar on a nest of gleaned wool. She looked down at him sleeping, and thought of the boy whose hand she had just bandaged; he was not more than fifteen and his hand now lacked three fingers, and he was sitting with his back to a wall staring dazedly at the floor. He did not remember how it happened. It had been his first battle, and would be his last. That boy had once slept unaware like

Crispian, watched over by the tender eyes of the woman who bore him. Would her child grow only to be maimed in some battle fifteen years hence, or to die under the walls of a town far from his home?

She was turning back when a woman passing near said softly, 'Eh, mistress, isn't that thy master come in?' Anne's heart leapt in her chest very large and very cold, and then she saw, coming in through the patch of red light thrown by a smoking torch over the door two figures, both walking, one supporting the other. Relief flooded her. Not badly wounded, then – she knew by now the gait of the mortally hurt. She hurried over, knowing the supported one for Sam by his sash and his white waistcoat. The other, she soon saw, was Hamil.

'Over here,' she said. 'Set him down there. Where is it?'

Sam was white with pain, sweating. He had been holding his left leg clear of the ground, hopping on the right, and his left arm was thrust into his waistcoat and she saw there was something amiss with that, too. Hamil eased him down – with only one sound leg and one sound arm it was hard for him, and painful – and said, 'Broken – a wall fell on him. He'll keep. For God's sake, Anne, get me some bandages so I can get back – they're running mad in the town like crazy wolves.'

Anne gave a sharp cry, quickly stifled, as she saw the blood on him. He had a scalp wound that was pouring down his face, but she could see it was light – scalp wounds always bled profusely. The worse wound was in his arm, and when she pulled the torn cloth of his sleeve away she saw that the muscle was exposed, and that he must have lost a deal of blood that way too.

'Wrap something round my head,' Hamil said sharply, 'I cannot see with blood in my eyes. And bind up that arm tightly – I can still hold a sword in it. Hurry, for God's sake.'

He swayed as he spoke, and she said, 'Sit down while I do it.'

He obeyed, and she bandaged his head and bound his arm up tightly. 'Can you go back?' she asked.

'I must,' he said, and then grinned faintly. 'My first wounds – now we are all square.' He swayed again, and shivered. Anne got up silently and fetched a flask of wine. 'Take some,' she said. 'It will keep you going. You have lost much blood.'

He drank deeply and then got to his feet with difficulty. 'Look to your master,' he said, and then looked down at Sam with an odd expression, kindly, perhaps even longing. 'At least you'll be out of it now, Sam. Good thing too – you don't belong here. Go home to your farm, and take her with you.'

And then he was gone. Anne knelt down beside Sam to feel over his wounds with sensitive fingers. 'Take some wine,' she said abruptly. 'You look as though you would faint.' He lifted the bottle with his sound hand and gulped a little, and then set it down with a sigh. 'What happened?' Anne asked.

'It's terrible out there,' he said. 'We breached the walls quite soon and went in. The defenders put up a bit of a fight, but not much. And then our men went mad. They were rampaging through the town, looting and killing. Hamil commanded them to stop, but they were like mad beasts. I was down a narrow street and part of a wall fell on me. Hamil found me a few moments later and dug me out. Another bit of falling stone got him on the head.'

'And his arm?'

Sam shuddered. 'That was one of our men. He came along while Hamil was clearing the rubble off me, and just went for him with his sword, thinking he was one of the townspeople. Hamil nearly lost his arm. He took that wound, but he ran the other through before he dropped his sword.'

356

Anne's eyes were wide. 'He killed one of his own men?'

'Hardly a man,' Sam said. 'His arms were red with blood. They are butchering the citizens.'

'Hush now, don't speak of it,' Anne said. 'I must get the surgeon to set these bones. As Hamil says, at least you're out of it now.'

Their eyes met, and he said, 'Is it craven to say I am glad? Tonight has sickened me of war.'

'Not craven,' she said. 'There are other jobs to be done too. We must go home and breed sons to replace all those young men who have fallen. On Marston Moor they fell in their thousands, the Borderers. Who will farm the land and keep the cattle and the sheep?'

She had said the right words. She saw his own country in his eyes now, and with a sudden sympathy she saw it too, the silence of the wind-singing uplands, the lonely peace of purple distances and silver chiming becks. And their son – let Crispian grow up there, where violent death lay only between the deer and the eagle, the lamb and the crow. The blood of the Borderlands was in her, and the north called her as it called him and all its children.

'We'll go home,' he said softly. 'Of all the words in the language, *home* is the most beautiful.'

The surgeon came and looked at his wounds, and bound them. The arm was broken, but not badly. He might lose a little of the strength of it, but it would do. The leg was worse – the ankle-bone was broken, and some of the bones of the foot, and when they healed he would probably always limp. But he would walk and ride, perhaps even dance. He finished his job and went away, and then the sound came of a baby crying, a strangely clean, new sound after the noise of battle and wounded men.

'Our son,' Anne said, 'wants to be fed.'

Sam smiled and released her hand, and she stood up and went away, and as he watched her he knew that when she said 'our' son it had not been deliberate, but a slip of the

357

tongue, and it pleased him more than any compliment she could have paid him.

Rupert and his officers managed at last to halt the looting and murdering, but not before much damage had been done. 'At last the pamphleteers will have something true to write about,' Daniel muttered to Hamil afterwards. But the attack on Leicester had its desired effect too – Fairfax and the Parliamentary army left Oxford and came northwards. Rupert wanted to go on and tempt them further away, giving time for reinforcements to arrive in the shape of Goring's west country cavalry, but the King hesitated and other advisers contradicted the Prince, and in the end it was near Market Harborough, a little south of a village called Naseby, that the two armies met.

It was around ten o'clock on the morning of 14th June that the two armies were drawn up opposite each other across an open space called Broad Moor. Rupert's cavalry was on the right wing, and most of them were in good humour, for Rupert had for once decided to command them himself, instead of placing himself with the King in the centre in the command position. Hamil, however, was neither happy nor buoyant. He was tired, and the two-week-old wound in his sword arm ached abominably. It was not healing well – he knew the signs from long campaigns of old. When a man grew tired, and was undernourished, his wounds took long to heal, and sometimes never healed at all. Firefly, too, was weary: it would soon be time to retire him, and Hamil hated the thought of riding into battle without him.

But worse than the weariness of his body was the weariness of his spirit. He was, above all, lonely. There was still Danny, though little Morton was dead now, killed in a minor skirmish back in February, such a wasteful death; and there was still Rupert, the invincible, their inspiration.

But so many had gone, and Hamil's heart was empty. Kit, whom he had hated, he had yet loved in spite of himself, and he had killed Kit, as surely as if he had held the rapier that let out his life. And he had lost Hero, finally and for ever, and the guilt and pain of it ate away at his soul. He thought, often, of Ruth, and wondered if she was a witch, for the curse she had put upon him could not be shaken off. 'Keep it in silence, and let it eat away your life!'

And now there was another battle, and he had no stomach for it, no love of fighting, no glory in his heart. They would charge and kill and ride on elsewhere, and still the enemy would come on them. They were outnumbered again today, almost two to one: the enemy had something like fourteen thousand men, and the King's men numbered but seven thousand five hundred. It seemed that no matter how long they fought they could achieve nothing. Hamil was only glad that Anne and her Borderlanders infantry-officer-turned-cavalryman had gone, taking their baby with them. The more men like that that were out of it, the better. What good could it do for him to be killed? He was only a farmer, slow-witted, kind-hearted, and loyal; he was no soldier, like Hamil and Danny and the other tough, scarred men in Rupert's cavalry. Hamil looked about him at the dear, familiar faces of his companions, his brothers, and waited for the quickening of his heartbeat at the sense of his belonging. But there was none. He was lonely, alone, separate, despairing. His hopelessness ran like sluggish blood through him, weighting his arm, making it an effort to lift up his head, and he did not want to fight, not that day, not ever again.

Rupert wanted to keep the initiative, and before the enemy could make a move the trumpets ordered the *advance*. They kept tight order, trotting down the gentle slope at a brisk pace. Behind the hedges on their right the enemy had placed snipers, but the Prince, with Maurice at his side, kept them close to the hedges to cut down the field of fire, and there were no casualties. Then they reached the open ground, and the trumpets sounded the *gallop*. Hamil, aware of his men who looked to him, raised his sword and yelled the battle cry with all the old ferocity, but it was as if he could hear himself doing it, was a little way off watching himself. Firefly galloped, stretching his neck, excited by the other horses racing beside him and the enemy cavalry pounding down towards them.

They met, clashed, struggled, and broke through. The enemy cavalry line broke, wavered, and then turned and fled, and howling the triumphant cry, the Royal horse pursued them. At first, as fugitives always do, they kept together, but eventually they began to fan out, scattering away from each other, and at that point pursuit became pointless, and the officers hauled down their horses and began to try to stop and round up their own men. They had reached the enemy's baggage train, but for a wonder the train-drivers had not fled at their approach as was usual. The wagons were drawn up tight together in a square, and the drivers were inside this makeshift barricade, and most were armed with muskets or pistols or pikes.

Looting baggage trains was one of the cavalryman's unwritten privileges, and Rupert's horse, having broken the enemy, were not averse to claiming it, despite the vicious insect-whine of shot past their ears. Hamil and the other officers circled the milling horses, trying to restore order.

'Leave it, lads,' Hamil cried. 'Time for that when we've beaten the rest. Come on, you fools, drop it. Can't you see they've got muskets? To your ranks. Drop it, I say.'

Doing the work that had to be done; saying the words that had to be said. Being in command kept back loneliness, and Hamil felt himself watching himself being busy. Since Marston, since Kit, he had flung himself into the fighting they had had, seeking death as one might run to a lover's arms, but death had spurned him. Now, in this calmer, listless frame of mind, he just did what had to be done, out of old habit – what else was there? He could see, at the edge of the milling group, Rupert sitting like a rock on his new horse, a big black barbary, making, with his red coat and long silky hair, a rallying point to which they could send on the men, like huntsmen sending on the hounds. Hamil smacked one fool who was howling with demented greed at the baggage-drivers with the flat of his sword, and the man's babble was cut off in mid-stream with a yelp like a dog on whose paw he had trodden. Across the heads of the men, he caught Danny's eye, and they grinned at each other.

Hamil did not hear nor feel the musket-ball. It hit him in the side of the head just above the ear as he turned Firefly away, and he toppled sideways from the saddle. Firefly went a few steps and then stopped, puzzled, his reins trailing, waiting for directions. Hamil lay on the ground, face down, his dark curls spilling forward under his hat. One brown hand twitched, as though the fingers were grasping for the earth, and then relaxed, and was still.

By one o'clock the battle was irretrievably lost, and the King left the battlefield, fleeing with the remainder of his army towards Leicester, leaving perhaps a thousand dead on Naseby field. The enemy pursued them almost to the city, capturing the royal army's baggage train; and in revenge for the slaughter of the citizens of Leicester they murdered all the women and soldiers' wives, some hundred in all, whom they found in the train. Some of them were gentlewomen, too – Symonds had not been the only officer whose wife travelled with him.

CHAPTER TWENTY

Symonds and Anne had rested in Pontefract, and it was there that the news of Naseby caught up with them. After the battle, Rupert and Maurice had gone westwards towards Bristol, and some of the northerners in the cavalry had declined to go with them, and had slipped away quietly to head for home. These men passed on the news of Captain Hamilton's death, and of the capture of the baggage train and the massacre of the women. Symonds turned pale at the thought of what might have happened to Anne, but she was unmoved.

'It did not happen,' she said briskly, 'and could not have happened. These things do not happen by chance – God orders everything, even the fall of the sparrow. He gave you your wounds so that we might go home: had they been lighter, you would not have wanted to leave, and had they been heavier you might not have been able to leave.' Symonds was not comforted, and she smiled at him sadly. 'Lord, I would not have such a philosophy as yours, to think the world is a chaos and everything happens at random!' she said.

They decided to go on, instead of remaining longer to rest in Pontefract, for with the defeat at Naseby, Pontefract, recently won back from Parliament by Langdale's northern horse, would likely fall again.

'We must go to York,' Anne said. 'We must tell Hero about her brother, and ask for my father's blessing.'

'Will your father receive us?' Symonds asked tentatively.

'I do not know. I do not understand what he would be about, but we must try. And I want to see my mother again.'

Anne was unsure enough of her reception at home to go first to Shawes, meaning to send a message on from there. They arrived a little after noon one day at the beginning of August, and found not only Hero and Ruth and Young Kit and the new baby Annunciata to greet them, but also Mary Esther paying a visit along with Ralph and Edward. There was a joyful reunion between mother and daughter that even the underlying sadness could not mar. Leah wept openly, patting whatever part of Anne she could reach through the forest of embracing arms, and even Edward and Ralph viewed their sister with increased respect, on learning that she had been close to battle, before transferring their attention to Symonds and demanding the full story of how he got his wounds.

It was a story to interest the rest of the company too, and so he obliged, but when he came to mention Hamil's name, he faltered and looked at Anne, and her eyes went irresistibly to Hero. Hero was standing by the fireplace, leaning on Young Kit's shoulder. She looked, to Anne, strangely shrunken in her mourning clothes – though it was more than a year since Kit's death, she had not changed her black mourning for grey – though her delicate features seemed unmarked by age or grief, and her yellow curls framed her face as prettily as a girl's. Anne saw her hand tighten involuntarily on the boy's shoulder, and her eyes widened a little.

'You don't need to tell me,' she said in a faint voice, faint and flat and distant. 'Hamil is dead.'

'How did you know?' Anne asked. Hero's blue eyes looked through her at some inner landscape, and Anne saw how they were meshed round with fine lines that she had not noticed before. Here was the evidence of life in her, as if age had passed the rest of her by, to settle only in this one place; they were almost the eyes of an old woman.

'I have known for a long time. He was my twin,' she said. 'How did he die?' Anne and Sam exchanged a glance,

363

wondering if she should be told, and then Anne said, 'It was at Naseby, after we had left. Some of the men going home told us that he had fallen in the battle, but I do not know how.'

Hero nodded, and Anne saw the sigh go out of her in a relaxation of the shoulders. 'All gone now,' Hero said quietly. 'Mal and Kit and Frank and Hamil. Now we have no-one else to fear for.'

Ruth looked at her sharply, and then at Young Kit, and Ralph, and Edward. These were the new generation, and already Ralph and Edward were eager to be old enough to go to war. Were their lives doomed too?

Anne turned now to her mother and said, 'How is Hetta? Why is she not with you? And how are things at home?'

'She would have come if we had known you would be here,' Mary Esther said, avoiding the question. 'Things are quiet at home now, but not easy.' She lowered her voice so that only Anne could hear. 'Already there are changes – the Book of Common Prayer has been forbidden, and there are penalties for hearing mass. We have had to strip the chapel, and Richard says it is only his influence that protects us. I do not know – your father has already paid out large fines because of Kit and Francis fighting for the King. They do not call them fines – they are levies for provisioning the army, but they are fines all the same.'

'Then – will my father not accept us?' Anne asked.

'I do not know,' Mary Esther said. 'I do not know if it would be dangerous to admit you to the house, and if it were dangerous –'

'Then we should not come, of course,' Anne said quickly, to save her mother the pain of saying that she would be forbidden. 'We would not wish to endanger any of you.'

'Where are you going?' Mary Esther asked. 'To your husband's home?'

'Yes, to Coquetdale. He tells me it is very near to our own lands at Tod's Knowe. We shall stay there, Mother, and not

364

come back, so I would like to see my father once more at least, to ask his blessing.'

'I will ask him,' Mary Esther said, 'but I do not know what he will say.'

Anne looked at her carefully. 'Mother, how is it with you?' she asked very quietly. 'You are not looking well.'

'I am tired, that's all,' Mary Esther said evasively. 'It is hard to live all the time with fear and concealment and conflict.'

'It is more than that,' Anne said. She saw the marks in her mother's face of more than weariness, and it touched her with a sudden chill. Before she had always thought of her mother, in so far as she had thought of her at all, as immortal and forever young, the way mothers should be. 'You have been ill?'

'I have pains sometimes, in my side,' Mary Esther said, 'but they go away again.'

'Have you seen a doctor?' Anne asked. Mary Esther met her eyes squarely and said, 'It is not possible, as things are. Leah makes me up potions, and the pain goes away.' And her eyes forbade Anne to say any more on the subject.

Mary Esther raised her voice a little now and said more cheerfully, 'It seems so strange to think of you a mother yourself. It is hard to realize that one's bairns are growing up. And he's a bonny one, that Crispian of yours.'

Anne allowed the subject to be changed. 'He is not yet,' she said judiciously, 'but he will be when he is a little bigger. But Annunciata, now she really is beautiful. Such eyes!'

'It is good that there are babies again,' Mary Esther said. 'It makes us see that life goes on, in spite of everything. Even Richard's little Catherine is stronger now, though God knows she looks as though a breath of wind would blow her away. And Richard's wife is pregnant again. It is good to have babies in the house. It seems so long since I held one of my own in my arms.'

Her voice wavered, and for a moment Anne and Ruth saw

the stark loneliness staring out of her eyes. She was not old – not yet forty, though the last few years had aged her more than the previous decade – and she wanted to love, but one by one the objects of her love had been taken from her.

'I shall miss you, Nan,' she said abruptly, and for a moment it was on the tip of Anne's tongue to say, 'Come with us.' But she knew that if she said it, Mary Esther would have to refuse, and that it would be hard for her. She could not leave her husband, though loyalty to him alienated her from her family and her faith, and, worse still, staying with him she was yet shut out from his love.

'I shall miss you all,' Anne said lightly. 'One day, when the war is over –'

They all nodded. Yes, when the war was over –

Hetta rode out with her mother a week later to see Anne and Sam on their way. They had not been received in Morland Place, but Edmund had sent a letter, giving his blessing on their marriage and asking them, when they should reach home, to go to Tod's Knowe and see if Arabella and her child were safe, and give them any help that might be needed. No word had come from Tod's Knowe since Marston Moor, but it was not unlikely that Arabella was unable to send a message with the Scots still occupying the north of England.

Edmund also sent a present of money, all he could spare, he said, though he did not say from what. It was typical of the ambivalence of his position and his mind, that he would not see his daughter, but he would write to her; that he gave no dowry with her, but sent a gift of gold. If times had been normal he would probably have approved of the match. Sam was the eldest son, and the estate in Coquetdale, though small and, like Tod's Knowe, consisting largely of barren upland, would be his absolutely on his father's death. Moreover, since they had married without permission, he was not obliged to give a dowry commensurate with Anne's former position in society, which made the match better still. But times were not normal, and his approval was equivocal.

Anne was shocked at the change in Hetta, and wondered now, belatedly, if she had some secret that Anne ought to have found out. Hetta admired Anne's baby, and looked into her eyes with silent understanding, and kissed her new brother with sympathy and embarrassment, and to her Anne said, unable to resist the impulse, 'Hetta, come with us – come to Northumberland. You will be happy there, won't she, Sam?'

Hetta smiled gently and shook her head. 'I can't. Father would never let me. Besides –' she stopped. Besides, she meant, she must stay where Charles could find her again, if he was still alive. She finished the sentence, 'Besides, I *am* happy.' And Anne knew it was not what she was going to say, and that it was not true. A while later they started on their long journey north. Looking back from the crest of a rise, Anne saw her mother and her sister side by side, still watching, and they seemed at that distance absurdly alike, though there was twenty years between them.

The journey home was difficult, and sometimes dangerous, and it took them a long time, for Sam could not ride for long without resting, nor ride any faster than a walk; and even so, any slight jolt or jerk would make his face go white with pain. Anne saw it with concern. 'We should have waited until your leg was healed,' she said more than once, but Sam only shook his head. He was anxious to be home, and there was nowhere safe that they could remain.

They travelled light, and inconspicuously, accompanied only by Anne's maid and Sam's man. They wore stout, unadorned clothes and plain cloaks, and all their baggage

367

was in their saddlebags – they had little enough indeed, for Anne had run away from home with nothing but the clothes she wore, and Sam had lost all his baggage after Marston Moor. Their most precious possession Anne carried under her cloak: she supported the baby as country women sometimes did, with a sling of thick cloth passing round her back and over one shoulder, and she fed him herself, to the horror and consternation of her maid. Crispian was a very alert baby; and responded to his mother's voice and rarely cried, and the physical closeness that few gentlewomen had with their bairns made her love him far more deeply than she could have expected.

They travelled by an indirect route, avoiding the larger settlements where they might run foul of the Scottish army, passing from village to village and finding kindness wherever they went: for the people of the far north, hospitality was not merely a courtesy but a necessity, and everyone had sympathy for the wounded man with the gentle manners and the pretty young woman with the new baby. Besides, the Scots were everyone's enemy, and the people were glad to guide the travellers out of their way. They reached the Tyne towards the end of September, and circled to the west of Hexham to cross it just south of Acomb, for towns were likely to be dangerous; and then they struck northwards up the North Tyne valley, and Sam drew a great sigh of relief and said, 'Now we are on home ground. We are almost home, Anne, think of that!'

They could move more freely now, for these were the Borderlands, where the Scots still hardly dared to shew their faces. Just below Bellingham they struck off north-eastwards up the Redesdale, and now they began to climb higher, and the lands they rode through were wilder. At Otterburn the Rede valley turned away north and west towards Scotland, and Sam pointed up the valley and said, 'That's where your father's lands are – away and away, where the valley narrows and the hills are purple.'

Anne looked. 'My grandfather was born there, at Tod's Knowe.'

'Yes, I know,' Sam said. 'Even on our side of the hill, they sing about his mother; the Ballad of Mary Percy. Come, we ride this way. From now on, no roads, only tracks – and no more towns.'

They rode on east and north, and by evening came to the place where the River Coquet's deep valley ran away north-west, running parallel to the Rede; between the two valleys, and beyond Coquetdale, were the great bare hills, the Cheviots. Now they rode in a silence that Anne could taste and smell and feel as well as hear, that filled her like great breaths of fresh air until she felt drunk with it. Sam glanced at her from time to time, and saw the shining of her eyes, the exhilaration in her face that was almost an exultation. Autumn had come to the uplands, and on every side the sea of bracken stretched away bronze-gold and rippling like flame. The Coquet ran coldly chattering over the grey stones of its bed, making here and there pools that were mysteriously still, mysteriously quiet, where the rowans reflected their bosses of blazing scarlet.

They rode higher and higher, their horses' hooves silent now on turf, ringing sometimes on a granite stone gilded with lichen, and Anne heard the soft singing of the wind against her ears and the laughter of the innumerable little burns, and the shining sweetness of the air she breathed was almost more than she could bear. 'I have come home,' she thought, over and over, 'I have come home.' Her child slept against her breast, as if he needed to be watchful no more now that she had brought him to his own place, to the hills that had fathered him. Just ahead now were two great round flanks of hills, still green at their lowest, golden above, and grey-purple above that.

'Bell Hill, to the left,' Sam said, 'and the other is Loft Hill. We are home, Nan.' Here the river dipped low and ran between meadows, turning sharply from its source high up in the uplands to the south-west, and on the green space between the two great hills was the cluster of buildings where Sam had been born – the stout grey-stone house, its roof entirely golden with lichen, and the stone-and-wood outhouses and cottages, their roofs covered with turf like green wigs. They rode down to the settlement, and there were people running out to them, crying out with surprise and pleasure and doubt and joy. The singing silence fragmented into other sounds: voices, dogs barking, the ring of metal on metal from some workshop behind the house, the clucking of hens, the sound of wood being chopped, the gurgle of the river turning the paddles of the watermill; and there was a smell of peat-fires and cooking and cattle and humanity along with the smells of grass and earth.

Then Sam was being plucked from his horse, patted and embraced by these men and women who had known him from his childhood and never thought to see him again; and then the people grew quiet and parted, and a man came towards them from the house: a man old and gaunt, with sandy hair that had gone grey and a face so freckled with age and weather that he seemed dark brown. He was upright, and moved steadily with an appearance of ease, but Anne, from her vantage point, could see the effort it took him to appear so, could see the long fight against pain concealed in the lines of his face.

Sam bent his head – he could not kneel – and said, 'Father!'

The old man placed his hand on the head and it was a long time before he said, 'Bless you, my son.' The hand went down, and the other hand clasped it as if to comfort it or give it strength, and the old man and his son looked a long time into each other's faces, before the old man said, 'Reynold?'

Sam shook his head. 'He fell at Marston Moor, Father.' The old man did not brace himself against the blow, but received it openly, taking his time to absorb it as one who is used to pain. Sam went on, 'I am afraid the King's cause is lost. The rebels have limitless supplies, endless reserves, while our numbers and strength dwindle.' Anne could see that his father was not interested in this, and she guessed that Sam knew it, and was giving him time to adjust himself. The old man looked him over carefully, and said, 'You are wounded.'

Sam said, 'My leg and arm were broken. They will heal, but it was enough to put me out of the fighting, and so I came home.' The old eyes now travelled at last to Anne, sitting quietly on her horse, and Sam took half a step backwards towards her and said, 'Father, my wife, Anne Morland. And – our son.'

His father said nothing, and his expression did not change. He looked at her with still eyes, with that quiet immobility of the upland shepherd or herdsman who watches a kestrel hover ten miles away above some other man's flock on a distant hill. Sam nodded to his servant, and the man came to lift Anne down. She pushed the cloak back, and a breath moved round the watching servants like a murmur at the sight of the child in the crook of her arm: the young master's son, who would be master after him! Then she walked over to the old man, and with an easy movement went down on one knee to him, her eyes never leaving his face. After a long moment, though the impassivity of the face did not waver, she saw the quiet eyes smile, and he lifted his hand and placed it on her head in blessing. It felt as light as a bird's claw, but it did not tremble.

'Bless you, my daughter. You are welcome here.' She stood up. 'Give me my grandson,' he said. She slipped the bairn out of the sling and held him out, and the old man took him, handling him easily as a shepherd handles lambs. Crispian was awake now, but did not cry, looking with his unfocused gaze into the old man's face. The light caught the glint of gold in the shoe-charm, fastened round his neck with a thong. Sam was close beside Anne, and under cover of the folds of her dress and cloak, his right hand reached for hers and pressed it hard.

'You have come to your own place,' the old man said, and closing his eyes he kissed Crispian's forehead, and then setting him against his shoulder he turned towards the house. 'Come, come in,' he said. 'It is time to eat.'

Katherine was sitting alone at one end of the drawing room. She sat in one of the window-seats, her hands in her lap, staring out into the darkness. The room was lit only by fireglow, for she had been sitting there a long time and had not the energy to call for candles once it grew dark; besides, the darkness suited her mood of gloom. She was close to being unhappy, and it was only her resolve that kept her from despairing, for she knew despair was a sin, and that every problem could be resolved by hard work and by searching for guidance in the Bible. Well, she had thought and prayed and read the gospels, all without avail. She tried to think of her father and ask herself what he would have done in the circumstances, but it was impossible to imagine her father in the circumstances.

It had all seemed so luminously clear once, and now the light had gone out, the sense of mission and purpose had deserted her, and she was floundering in the darkness, unable any more to see her way or to hear God's voice. She had married Richard and come here to save his family, and that had been right: she knew it, because she felt the power flowing through her. Then came the difficult decision to consummate their marriage, and that was where things began to go wrong. It destroyed the singleness between her and Richard. She sensed from the beginning that the marriage act meant something different for him; she guessed that he got some ungodly pleasure from it, against which he had to struggle, and for that reason she restricted the commerce between them, ceasing altogether once she had conceived.

The death of their first child was a shock to her; then Cathy had been born, and though she had survived her first year, she was still sickly and weak and undersized. Was God punishing them for something? And now she was pregnant again, and feeling very unwell, sick and uncomfortable, and the light was more firmly doused than ever. Richard no longer heeded her; he avoided her company, and spoke slightingly to her; when she tried to speak of their mission he would cut her short and change the subject, or simply walk away.

And worst of all, despite the fact that she was pregnant and there was no reason for it, he insisted on trying to perform the marriage act with her. At first she had been too upset and embarrassed to do more than protest – she had not actually refused. But after a while, when her protests did not deter him, she was forced to refuse to have him, and she upbraided him for his carnality and tried to remind him of the purpose of marriage, and of their task in life together. But Richard had not heeded her, and last night, worst of all, when she had pushed him away, he had said roughly, in a voice so unlike his own that she had feared for a moment that he must be possessed, 'Have a care, Madam, that you do not push me too far. There are others who would welcome what you scorn.'

'What do you mean, Richard?' she had cried.

And he had said cruelly, 'If you push me from your bed, I shall go and find another, so be warned.'

For the first time in her life she had lost her temper, and cried out, 'Do so, and welcome, for you are no better than a beast of the field.'

Remembering it now, she began to cry again, and though she upbraided herself she could not stop. She felt so weak, so alone. Her childhood had been what others would have thought of as lonely, for she had no brothers and sisters, no mother, not even any friends of her own age – no-one but her father. But she had always, as long as she could remember, had the sense of Jesus's presence, invisible but close beside her, her perfect friend who understood her and guided her and was always patient with her stupidity, though He was sometimes obliged to reprimand it. With Him near her, she had never felt isolated. Now she felt Him no more, and when she called to Him, His voice was silent, and she was alone. Did He disapprove, she wondered, of her lapse from chastity? Even though it was done for the right reasons? Ah, her mind said, but was it for the right reasons? Perhaps, after all, she wanted her husband carnally, and pretended to herself that it was merely to further her cause? The tears rolled on weakly down her face, and she dabbed them away with her kerchief, but could not stop them.

She did not know how long she had been sitting there when the door at the far end opened cautiously, so cautiously that she expected to see one of the children, Ralph or Edward, peep round it, bent on some mischief. But it was two adult figures that came in, moving quickly and closing the door behind them so that she could not see in the firelight who they were. She started up, but aware that it would not be pleasant for her to be discovered weeping, she did not speak but pressed herself back in the shadows, hoping that they would go away again quickly, without seeing her.

It was not many moments before she realized that she had made a mistake. The two people were evidently a man and a woman, and by the little noises, rustlings, snufflings and murmurs that came to her they had not come into this dark room for any lawful purpose. Then she heard the woman laugh, soft and low, and it was a laugh filled with pleasure and excitement, and suddenly Katherine was hot all over with a mixture of shame and rage and misery – shame to witness such evil, rage that they should commit it, and misery at her loneliness and unwantedness that was emphasized by their behaviour.

'Stop, enough!' she cried abruptly, clenching her hands on her wet crumpled handkerchief. She took a few steps forward, trembling with rage. 'How dare you behave so in your master's house? Who are you?'

Then, faint but perfectly distinct, she heard a whisper in the darkness: 'Jesu, it's my wife.'

Katherine thought that she would fall, her legs trembled so, and her stomach seemed to fall inside her with a sickening swoop.

'Richard?' she whispered, terrified.

She heard him say, 'It's all up now.' And then the door opened, and the light from the staircase sconces fell inwards in a splash of yellow, and he said to his companion, 'You'd better get along. Say nothing of this.' The other dark figure scuttled out with a heavy swishing of a woollen skirt, and then Richard pushed the door all the way open and stood revealed in the stripe of light, facing Katherine with his hands on his hips. She came forward a little more, staring at him in a mixture of fear and anger, not knowing what he would do or say. From being her husband, whose actions and words she knew intimately, he had become as unpredictable as a wild wolf, and as potentially dangerous. His shirt, she saw, was undone almost to the waist, his hair was awry, and his undergarments were peeping through the fastenings of his breeches, and she felt sick at the thought of what he had been doing and at the sly sideways look one of the maids would give her by and by, when she passed her in the passage or was served by her at dinner.

'Well,' Richard said, 'what are you doing here?' He sounded amazingly cool and callous, as if he didn't care in the least that he had been found out.

'I have a perfect right to be here,' she said, and her voice sounded as faint and high as a bat's squeak.

375

'Spying on your husband, eh? Eavesdropping? Nice behaviour for a Christian woman.'

It outraged her that he should call her that in contempt.

'I don't need to ask what you were doing,' she said, her voice shaking with anger.

'You had better not,' he said casually, 'unless you want to feel the weight of my hand for your insolence.'

'You would not strike me!' she said in a fury.

'Wouldn't I though!'

'How dare you speak so to me! And how dare you – dally with a servant!'

'Dally?' He broke into harsh laughter at her choice of word, and the laughter made her flinch, as if each peal was a slap across her face. He stopped eventually, so abruptly that she could tell it had not been real laughter at all. 'You have only yourself to blame,' he said. 'I warned you what would happen if you pushed me away. Well, if you don't want it, there are others who do. There are others, my dear *wife*, who actually long for it, who do not find their husband's touch nauseating. Aye,' and his voice grew hard, 'I've felt you pulling away from me in distaste. Well, there's only so much of that a man will stand. You've got what you asked for – I'll leave you alone from now on, never fear, as much alone as even you could wish. I'll get my pleasure elsewhere, not that you were ever much pleasure. And you'd better hang onto that babe, because it's the last you'll catch by me.'

He turned away, while Katherine stood, trembling in her misery, sick with shame, watching him go. At the last minute she cried out, 'Who was it?'

'Find out,' he spat, and slammed the door behind him.

She knew that she would. She watched all the servants carefully, covertly, glancing out of the corner of her eye when she thought they would not be expecting it, trying to catch the end of a quickly hidden expression, but all that evening she watched, and there was nothing. The maids

376

had always treated her coldly – none of the Morland servants liked her – but there was no difference in their looks, no sly glances, no arrogance of one who has a secret.

Then on the next evening, as she had been feeling more than usually unwell, she decided to go up to bed early. She took her candle and climbed the' stairs, and walked along the passage shielding the flame with her hand. The door to her bedchamber was open, unexpectedly, and there was a light within, a thin rushlight – a servant then. She reached the door and saw that it was only her maid, Fear, turning down the bed. Relieved, she walked forward, about to speak, about to tell Fear of her backache – Fear, who had been with Katherine since she came to the Browne household at the age of ten, was always sympathetic, and was very helpful about rubbing her back to take away the ache – when she stopped, puzzled. Fear had turned down the bed, and now she had leaned forward and picked up the pillow from Richard's side and was holding it against her, cradling it against her cheek as one holds a baby or –

'Fear?' Katherine said quietly. 'What are you doing?'

The girl whipped round, dropping the pillow and giving a terrible little cry of guilty panic. Katherine stared at her, and her face reddened slowly, but there was just a hint of arrogance and defiance in the eyes that met hers. Sick horror swept through Katherine; there was a roaring in her ears, and a red-tinged blackness seemed to swell out of the corners of the room, blocking out the figure of the plump, pretty young maid. She heard Fear scream as she began to fall; the hardness of the floor as her head struck it was like a caress compared with the pain in her heart.

She travelled through a long, confusing dream of pain and sorrow, and when she woke it was dark, and she was in her bed, and there was a candle somewhere at a distance. Her body felt sore and battered and used up; she knew she had lost the baby, but it meant little to her. There was such darkness inside her that she felt as if all the blood and strength had been drained from her, and the space where it had been was filled up with cold shadows. She woke slowly and unwillingly; she knew that she did not want to wake, not ever, but she could not remember why. Then she remembered, and the knowledge settled like a stone in her chest.

Someone was beside her. A cool hand soothed her forehead, brushing away the hair, and a voice said, 'Do you want to sip a little wine?'

It was her mother-in-law. Katherine shook her head slightly. The dark eyes looked down at her with tenderness and pity, the dark curls, frosted with grey now, fell forward round a face lined with pain and sorrow but still filled with life and warmth, and she wondered suddenly why she had never liked Mary Esther, why she had hated her and fought against her. She was a woman, and she understood, and Katherine felt a feeble, sorrowful regret that she had wasted so much time in opposition. One tear rolled out of her eye, a tear of defeat, and she turned her head away. The kind hand stroked her again, and Mary Esther said gently, 'Do not grieve, child. There will be other bairns in time. You are with us again. We thought for a while that we had lost you, but you have come back,'

'I wish I had not,' Katherine whispered. Mary Esther was distressed.

'Child, don't say that. Everyone loves you. You are with friends. Richard has been beside himself with worry while you have been ill.'

'Richard —' she whispered. Mary Esther moved away, and her place was taken by the anxious face of Katherine's husband. He took the limp hand that rested on the counterpane and carried it to his lips, kissing it fervently, and pressing it against his face. He knelt by the bedhead, to be close to her.

'Katherine,' he whispered, 'forgive me.' She would not look at him. Her head turned away, she heard, but did not heed. He was dead to her; she had no feeling for him, not love nor hate, nothing. 'Katherine, I didn't mean it,' he said. 'I'm so sorry. I was angry, that's all, because you would not love me. I didn't mean any of it. I love you, Kate, I'll make it up to you, I swear. When you're better – we'll move away, if you like, and have a house of our own. Would you like that? Just you and me and Cathy and Ralph. And we'll have other children. Don't fret over the bairn, Kate. It was bad luck, but there'll be others. We could go back to Norwich, if you liked. We'll do anything you want.'

'All I want,' she said, so low he had to lean forward to catch the words, 'is never to see your face or hear your voice again.'

He blanched, and pressed her hand harder. 'But Katherine, I love you, I truly love you. The other thing – it was nothing, I swear it. I only wanted to make you jealous.'

But Katherine did not answer. Her head turned away on the pillow, she stared at the darkness that filled her soul, where once there had been light and certainty. Another tear rolled out of her eye, sideways onto the pillow. Mary Esther came around the bed and wiped it away, but as fast as she dabbed one tear away, another came, and another, silent and perpetual, as if Katherine were bleeding to death with tears.

Richard stayed beside her all night and all the next day, holding her hand, talking, always talking, apologizing, planning, telling her again and again how he loved her, but she would not look at him, nor give any sign that she heard him, nor speak, not to him or to anyone else. She lay still, utterly unmoving, except for the slow, seeping tears, and on the second night she closed her eyes and died.

379

The war was dying, but its death-throes went on interminably, despite the New Model Army, despite the military skill of General Cromwell. Prince Rupert, along with Maurice his brother, left England in 1646, four years after first taking up the King's cause at Nottingham, and by that time the situation was deeply confusing. The army no longer seemed to be the tool of Parliament, and instead of two sides in the war there were now three – the King, Parliament, and the army – or even four, if Scotland were counted separately. The King, having few resources left, played one of his enemies off against the other, being held captive first by Parliament and then by the army, while all sides struggled to come to some agreement. But agreement was impossible: the aims of each group were in direct conflict with the aims of the others.

As to the people, they settled down again as best they could and tried to live with the continually changing legislation. The Book of Common Prayer having been forbidden, the Anglican's position was as difficult as the Catholic's, for he could not hear mass without risking imprisonment. Worse, he could not marry, nor christen his child, nor bury his dead in the only way he considered lawful, unless he could find a priest willing to take the risk of performing the ceremony in secret. At Morland Place the chapel remained empty, and no services were said there, though the sanctuary lamp remained lit, and at any hour of the day or night one was likely to see a quiet figure slip in there to pray privately. Edmund continued to attempt the impossible compromise. He would not allow unlawful services to be held in the chapel, but on the other hand he did not dismiss Father Michael, even thought he knew Mary Esther and Hetta visited him privately in his room and, in all probability, took the sacrament there.

He would not go into the city on Sundays and feast days to attend an approved service, nor force or even encourage his household to do so; but on the other hand, he appeased the Puritan sector by forbidding the Sunday games, music and sport which had normally made that day so pleasantly different from the rest of the week. It was that rule which caused most discontent amongst the servants and tenants. Their lives were hard and stark, with few comforts, and starvation and disease were always only a pace behind, waiting to catch the laggard; but they were not unhappy. Life was made bearable by the pleasures they took from it: they loved to sing and play music, and to dance; to watch the jugglers and tumblers and morris dancers; to play games and wrestle and indulge in sport and boisterous horseplay; to drink in the taverns, to gamble on anything that moved, to hunt and poach and cock-fight and box and play football and fornicate. They were a cheerful, noisy people, and it was hard on them to have their pleasures forbidden by sour-faced, black-clad preachers, who had nothing to offer them in return but hell-fire, the threat of eternal punishment for their pleasures, and an eternity of a seemingly dull and dreary heaven for the few who managed to negotiate the thicket of rules.

Within the house things were a little easier for the family since poor Katherine had died, for Richard had been drifting gradually away from her religion and philosophy towards that comfortable indifference that was the hallmark of the Englishman. His servants, too, were no longer causing trouble, for the maidservant, Fear, mysteriously became pregnant, and the younger of the footmen, Wrastle, married her. It caused much mirth and derision in the Yorkshire servants that the proud Puritans had fallen so far from grace, but they forgot it soon enough, especially when Fear and Wrastle were transferred to the small staff that kept Twelvetrees: married couples were not kept on in the great house. If, the other servant, left the Morland service soon after Fear's lapse, and went back home to East Anglia, and the house seemed to sigh with relief as might a horse when three prickly burrs are removed from under its saddle.

Mary Esther guessed quickly enough that Richard had gone back to his old fornicating ways, but age and experience and marriage seemed at least to have taught him discretion, for she never discovered any of his affairs for certain. Her estrangement from Edmund continued, and her health was not good, but she comforted herself with the children. Cathy took up a lot of her time and her pity. The child had struggled through to her fourth year without ever appearing to have more than a tentative grip on life: she suffered from every ailment and a number of alarming accidents, and it seemed that she only lived at all because God could not decide with which disease to carry her off. At four she was thin and puny and her skin had a yellowish tinge, and she had no more than a thin wisp of hair on her head, for it had all fallen out during one of her illnesses and had never grown properly since. She was an unprepossessing sight, and the servants, who had a natural prejudice towards bonny, lusty bairns, neglected her as far as they dared. Richard regarded her with horror and would have nothing to do with her, and so, as with Ralph, Cathy grew up regarding Mary Esther as her mother; and Mary Esther discovered that despite her lamentable appearance and her physical weakness, she had a loving nature and a capacity for affection and for learning.

'One day,' Mary Esther would murmur when giving Cathy her goodnight kiss, 'one day we will surprise them all, chuck. We shall open a door and you will emerge beautiful and learned, like a butterfly emerging from its cocoon.' Even Mary Esther did not entirely believe it, but it made a pleasant fantasy, and when she gave Cathy her lessons she taught her to write at the top of her horn-book, where it was customary to dedicate the lesson: *Catalina Papilia Filia Christi* – Catherine the butterfly, daughter of Christ. But one day Father Michael came in and read the dedication, and roared with laughter, and taking Cathy's stylus he altered it to *Catalina Eruca Filia Dolorosa* – Catherine the caterpillar, daughter of sorrows. Mary Esther was angry, but she had to admit there was something appropriate in it, for Cathy, yellow and wrinkled and hairless, was very like a caterpillar. It was unfortunate, but the nickname stuck.

Katherine's death, and the departure of the Norfolk servants, eased relations with Shawes, and Young Kit now took lessons at Morland Place along with Edward. Edward at thirteen was a well grown, good-looking boy, much like his father in appearance and a general favourite with servants and family alike, but he was not clever at his lessons, and was lazy into the bargain, so Young Kit, who was eight, had no difficulty in keeping up with him. Kit was remarkably quick in everything, but he was also very sensitive, and having been brought up with nothing but love, he found Father Michael's fierce temper and loud voice upsetting. Edward's bold, fearless temper made him afraid of nothing, and he would often protect Kit by distracting the tutor's attention, while Kit would help Edward by explaining things he didn't understand and which Father Michael was too impatient to go over again. So a strong friendship grew between the two boys.

Ralph, at seventeen, was more of a worry to Mary Esther. He was a stunningly attractive boy, tall and broad-shouldered like his gradfather; a lot like Edmund in looks, in fact, for he had the same pale gold hair, classical features, and fine skin. His eyes were wide and grey, flecked with gold, and had the long impassive gaze of a great golden cat.

He was lithe and sensuous, too, like a cat, with a cat's love of comfort interspersed with sudden bursts of energy. He was a superb horseman, a fine athlete, and a sensitive musician; but underneath all this he was unhappy and restless and confused. It was not to be wondered at, considering his background. His early childhood had been spent regarding Mary Esther as his mother, being brought up in a devout Anglican household. Then his father had returned, and he had been subjected to a violent turn about, as Richard and Katherine had tried to make a Puritan of him. He had seen the family split, with Edmund siding with Richard against his erstwhile 'mother'; and then had come the long period of confusion and equivocation as Edmund tried to straddle every issue, and Richard once more ignored him.

Mary Esther felt deeply for him, more especially now when he was in a young man's most active years, yet, because of the situation both domestic and national, had not been sent away to school, or to university, nor been given any employment in his grandfather's estate or business. Mary Esther thought it was lucky that his natural good sense kept him out of trouble, for it was certain nothing else had. She did what she could in her small way to keep him occupied, and with that in mind she asked him to accompany her to Shawes one day at the end of July 1648.

'You could take Cathy up before you,' she said. 'Psyche shakes the poor child around so, and she has no flesh to pad her bones.'

'All right, if you like, Mam,' Ralph said good-naturedly. He had called her Mam for a long time, as a compromise between Mother and Madam. 'Only she had better wear a cloak, or she'll frighten my horse.'

'Oh Ralph, don't say so! It's cruel,' Mary Esther protested, and Ralph grinned.

'I was only joking Mam. Poor Caterpillar, I wouldn't hurt her feelings. Is Hetta coming too?'

384

'I asked her, but she said she wanted to finish a piece of work.'

'She ought to come, and get some fresh air. She stays at home too much,' Ralph said. 'Where is she? I'll fetch her. She won't refuse me.'

'She's in the bower, in the herb garden, I think,' Mary Esther said, and let him go. It was true that he could persuade Hetta where others could not, for being almost of an age and having been brought up together, they were closer than the other children. Sure enough Ralph soon came back with his young aunt. Hetta was nineteen now, and though she was well enough, and had recovered enough of her normal spirits not to worry her parents or servants, she was very different from the plump, merry child who had so deserved the nickname 'Sparrow'. She was still small and brown, but she was thinner and without her former liveliness, and her pleasant, sweet face had lost its sparkle. Where once she had loved nothing better than riding and singing and dancing, now she spent much time reading and in silent devotions, and often she could be caught staring at nothing, her hands idle in her lap and an expression of wistful sadness on her face that she was at pains most of the time to conceal.

The ride over the Shawes was pleasant, and Ralph earned Mary Esther's gratitude by chatting pleasantly to poor little Cathy, pointing out to her birds and trees and flowers and telling her their names. He was in a good mood, for he loved best of all to be out on horseback, and he liked visiting Shawes. There he found a sense of peace and of unity that was sadly lacking at home, and he had a great liking for Ruth, for he admired her bold, direct character and her plain speaking. When they arrived at the old house they found the family out of doors, in the small field just to one side of the path. It was barely more than a cattle-pen, a small paddock enclosed by moveable hurdles, and round its inner perimeter the grass had been worn away into a bare dusty track, for it was here that Ruth exercised and schooled her horses.

Hero was there, leaning on the fence, for she still found it more comfortable than sitting, and now that Kit was over at Morland Place for his lessons she had no shoulder to supply her need. She turned and smiled as they rode up, and said, 'Won't you tie up the horses and watch with me? Ruth won't be finished for another half hour, and I like to see what she's doing.'

'Of course we will,' Ralph said. 'We've even brought her another pupil, look. Down you get, little Caterpillar.' And he swung Cathy over the front of the saddle and lowered her gently until her feet touched the ground. Then he jumped down, handed his horse to a servant, and went to lift down Mary Esther and Hetta.

Cathy went to Hero, and Hero put her arm round the child and drew her in close and said, 'You stay with me, Cathy, and watch.' What Ralph had said could not have been more obviously a joke, for Ruth, in the centre of the paddock, was teaching Annunciata the finer points of horsemanship, and there could not have been more of a contrast between Ruth's daughter and Cathy. They were of an age – Annunciata was in fact a few months younger – but while Cathy was spindly and undergrown, Annunciata was big and strong for her age, and very beautiful. She had black, silky curls that seemed to spring with her mother's vigour from her head, and a haughty, beautiful face, with a long, sensitive mouth and enormous, dark, sparkling eyes. She was intelligent and quick-tempered, generous, and proud, and the servants adored her and spoiled her dreadfully. Young Kit was her willing slave, Hero petted her and was almost afraid of her, and only her mother ever countered her. Ruth adored her too, but she did not shew it in the same way. She treated Annunciata just as she treated everyone else – she spoke to her as she would speak to an adult, and spoke plainly, without flattery or deception or prevarication. The result was that though Annunciata flew into her worst rages with her mother, she respected her as she respected no-one else.

She loved an audience, and though Ruth did not by word or gesture interrupt the lesson to acknowledge that they had visitors, Annunciata at once began to play to the gallery. She was a fine rider, and handled her pony with expertise, but her pose became exaggeratedly elegant, and her gestures extravagant, and when Ruth finally called her in to a halt in the centre, she swung her pony round and halted him with a showy and quite unnecessary half-rear.

'That,' said Ruth sharply, 'is not the way to halt.' Annunciata's brows drew together at once. 'Your contact with your horse should always be delicate, as I've told you before. You have enough of everything, Annunciata, to be sparing with your effects. Aim for subtlety in everything.'

'Yes, Mother,' the girl said between her teeth, and Ruth forbore to argue further, not wishing to spoil a good lesson by a quarrel at the end.

'Very well, then,' she said, and they walked over to join the guests.

'What was it you were teaching her?' Ralph wanted to know when the greeting had been exchanged. 'It looked a little like sword-play.'

'It looked like what it was,' Ruth said. Mary Esther raised an eyebrow.

'Ruth, is it proper to teach a girl to handle a sword?' she said. 'I know the sword is only a stick in this case –'

'I remember you saying once,' Ruth interrupted, 'that nothing learnt is ever wasted.'

'I know, but –'

'When she goes hunting, she may carry a spear. Besides, the exercise makes her stronger and more supple in the saddle. Hero, have you ordered refreshments for our guests?' Ruth asked, changing the subject abruptly. Hero started.

387

'Why no, not yet. I was waiting for you to finish.'

'Do it now then. We shall come in as soon as we have dealt with the horses. Aunt Mary, will you take Cathy and Hetta in? And Ralph, will you help us with the horses?'

The party split, and Ralph accompanied Ruth and the servant to the stables, walking beside her and Annunciata's pony, and as soon as they were out of earshot of the others he said, 'It amuses me to watch you, Ruth. You and Hero and the children made a strange little household.'

'Why strange?' Ruth asked.

'Well it is strange for two women to live alone like this – without menfolk, I mean: I know you have a houseful of servants.'

'After the years of war, I should think it is not so strange any more. There must be many women whose men have not come back.'

Ralph nodded. 'Aye, I suppose so. But you and Hero – it's odd to see you. You are like the husband, and she is like the wife, and your two children are your two children. Nothing lacks. What were you teaching her, by the way?'

'As I said. I was teaching her sword-play. I would have her able to defend herself, if the need ever arose. When she is older I will teach her to use a pistol and musket, too.'

'You will make a boy of her,' Ralph said. Ruth laughed mirthlessly and gestured towards Annunciata, riding her pony a little ahead of them with a very obvious consciousness of what she looked like on horseback in her habit and soft little boots and her curls sweetly disordered.

'Make a boy of *that*?' she said. 'Of that little popinjay? Be assured, Ralph, that there was never a creature that walked this earth that was more sure of her sex than that one.'

'Then why –'

'The more reason to be able to defend herself. You know that the Scots have crossed the Border again?'

'No,' Ralph said, growing serious. 'I had not heard.'

'A Scottish army under Lord Hamilton, to fight for the

King. We heard of it yesterday. No doubt Fairfax or Cromwell will be marching north by this time to do battle. And so it goes on, and who knows when it will end, if it ever will? Annunciata is only four, but she seems like to grow up in a world where men go on and on fighting until none are left. I would not have her grow up dainty and timid in a world like that.'

'There will be more battles, you think?' Ralph said thoughtfully. Ruth looked at him speculatively. 'Already they are calling it the Second War,' she said.

Mary Esther was always up very early, for she liked to have an hour of silent prayer in the chapel before the house was astir. On the day after the visit to Shawes she came out of the chapel to find Edmund and Richard standing in the hall, their faces grave, with Clement hovering by looking anxious. Edmund was holding a piece of paper. The two men turned as Mary Esther approached and she stopped and said nervously, 'Something has happened. What is it?'

Edmund gestured with the piece of paper, but he could not speak. Richard said, 'It's Ralph. He left a note. He's run away to join the army.'

'Run away?' It took her a moment to absorb it; she remembered the talk at Shawes yesterday, of the Scottish army that had risen for the King. 'But why should he run away? Why did he not –'

Richard laughed harshly. 'Oh yes, you would have encouraged him, wouldn't you? Why did he not come to you? You would send anyone away to die for the King. It's the Morland tradition, isn't it? You and my father drummed it into me all my childhood – the precious Morland name.'

'Richard –' Edmund protested, but Richard stopped him with a strange, dismissive gesture of the hand.

'Well, it seems I've changed all that. He's run away to

join the army – to fight, but not for the King. He's gone to Cromwell's New Model.'

Richard swung around, and pushing Clement aside he left them. Edmund was still looking at the piece of paper. Mary Esther looked at him, hardly able to believe it, and at last, when her husband looked up, she said, 'Is it true, Edmund?'

'Oh yes,' he said. Mary Esther stared in horror.

'But he might be killed,' she said. 'Fighting for the wrong side. Dear God!'

Edmund seemed dazed, and despite her horror, she was moved towards him, seeing how deeply he cared. When Ralph was a baby, Edmund had slighted his mother's memory, but he was the first grandson, the heir. Mary Esther took a step nearer him, and though she did not reach out and touch him, the gesture was in her eyes.

'Edmund,' she said hesitantly. 'We must pray for him –'

Edmund seemed to come back to himself; she saw how deeply he was shocked. He licked dry lips, and said, 'He took Titania. Of all the horses in the stable, he took Titania.' Titania, the last foal of Queen Mab: she had died bringing her into the world, she was the last link with his youth. Mary Esther stared, her mouth turned wry, as if she had bitten a sloe, and she turned from him without a word.

The New Model had been in Wales when the crisis occurred, and under General Cromwell had begun a forced march northwards. Many of the army were barefoot, and they were all short of food, and they had not been paid for many months, but morale was good amongst the ranks, for they believed they were engaged in a holy war, a belief the officers encouraged. They would not have won so many victories, said the officers, if God was not on their side; and the men believed it, as did some of the newer recruits amongst the officers. The older ones, the veterans, were not so sure. What had seemed simple and straightforward back in '42 was intolerably complicated now, six years later, and those who lacked a blind religious faith in what they did went on more out of habit than conviction.

After Ralph had found the army, it took him a while to get himself passed to the right person to volunteer to, for the conditions of a forced march were not conducive to recruitment. When they camped at night, however, he managed to find a colonel with time to talk to him. The colonel had the strangely flat and nasal accent of Essex, which comforted Ralph. He would have been afraid a northerner would have heard of the name Morland.

'You've got a horse, have you? Good,' said the colonel. He stepped out to have a look. 'Pity she's so delicate-looking,' he said. 'Takes it out of a horse, army life. Still, anything with four legs is welcome. Can you handle a sword and pistol?'

'Yes, Sir,' Ralph said. 'Though I haven't got a pistol.'

'No matter. We'll find you one. Glad to have you, boy. No time for training now – we'll have to put you under someone reliable, hope he'll take care of you. Here, you, man, come here –' he called to a passing soldier. 'Take Mr Morland along to Major Daniel's platoon, give him my compliments, tell him Mr Morland is a new recruit.'

'Yessir,' the soldier said, and hurried away, and Ralph thanked the colonel and led Titania in the soldier's wake.

Ralph could smell as well as hear the cavalry lines before he saw them. The major greeted him kindly, had him shewn where to tie Titania, how to get food for her and for himself, and when that had been done and Ralph was back before the major again, the major said, 'I'd better find someone reliable to put you under for now. Let me see, perhaps Captain Hobart would be best. Jenkins, take Mr Morland along to Captain Hobart, will you?'

Hobart was a pleasant-faced young man, a couple of years older than Ralph, with a slight limp, and a long narrow scar down one weather-browned cheek. He greeted Ralph with a kind smile, and when he heard the name, he blanched a little, and said, 'From Yorkshire? It's a Yorkshire name, isn't it?'

'That's right Sir,' Ralph said nervously. This man was no Yorkshireman – had Ralph had the misfortune to be sent to the only foreigner who knew York? 'It's quite a common name in Yorkshire,' he added quickly. The captain seemed to recover himself a little at that.

'I was in Yorkshire myself, you know,' he said pleasantly, and Ralph's heart sank. 'During the siege of York. I was wounded, and I stayed at the house of some people called Morland – isn't that a coincidence? All the wounded were taken there. We were most kindly treated, though the family were royalists.'

Ralph nodded, his mouth dry. If they thought he was a spy, he would be in worse trouble than merely being discovered as a runaway. But the captain did not speak as if he was about to pounce. His voice was dreamy and rather sad. He said, 'Yes, the women of the house looked after us. Do you know them, by any chance? The Morlands of Morland Place? Are they relatives of yours?'

Ralph silently tried out several answers before saying, 'Distant relatives, Sir.'

Captain Hobart nodded vaguely, and went on, 'There was one young woman there – Henrietta was her name. The daughter of the house. She nursed me. We joked a little, about her name being Henrietta and mine Charles, like the King and Queen. She was so beautiful, and so kind. I fell in love with her.'

Ralph gawped. He had been thirteen at the time, not of an age to take notice of one adult out of so many, but he vaguely remembered Hetta sitting in the bower in the herb garden with one of the wounded Parliamentarians. Was this that man?

'I promised her I'd go back for her after the war, when it

wouldn't matter any longer that we'd been on different sides. Well, it was all a long time ago. It doesn't look now as though the war will ever end. And if it did – it's too late for me. She's dead, poor girl, and my hope with her.'

Ralph in his turn went white, and his voice failed him entirely. Was it possible that news had reached this man so quickly? Hetta had been well enough when he left home. Surely, surely – she could not have – was it possible? He managed at last to say, 'Dead, Sir?'

Captain Hobart looked at him, and gave a small smile, and patted his hand, touched that the young man was so moved. 'Yes, poor girl, long ago now. Did you not know? Perhaps, as they were only distant relatives of yours –'

'How did it happen?' Ralph asked faintly.

'It was at Marston Moor,' Hobart said. 'I heard afterwards from one of the captured soldiers – she had gone to the battlefield, I don't know why, in the company of a servant, and she was caught in our first surprise attack. Both were killed at once. It was terrible news to me. I wanted to look for her body, but of course it was not possible. I only hope someone from her family found her and gave her a proper burial. It grieves me horribly to think of her being tumbled with the rest into a common grave.'

'But – but –' Ralph hardly knew whether to speak or not; yet it seemed wrong to let this man, whose face was kind and pleasant, go on thinking that Hetta was dead. 'But it wasn't Hetta, it was Anne, and she wasn't killed either, though we all thought for some time that she was.'

'Hetta?' Hobert said. 'You know her then?'

'She's my aunt.'

Now it was the captain's turn to be confused. He stared with his jaw slack and his eyes a mixture of bewilderment and dawning hope, and Ralph said, 'I lied before because I thought you'd think me a spy if you knew I came from a royalist family. I ran away, you see, to join the army, and I didn't want to get sent home – or worse. But I'm Ralph

393

Morland of Morland Place, and Hetta is my father's younger sister. It was my aunt Anne who ran away to Marston Moor, and she wasn't killed there – she hid and then followed the army. She married a Lieutenant and went home with him to Northumberland.'

He seemed stunned.

'It was her sister at Marston Moor? It never occurred to me. I knew there was a sister of course, but I barely knew her. Hetta was so much in my thoughts you see, that I just assumed –' He paused, and Ralph waited in sympathetic silence.

'So Hetta's alive?' Hobart said, grasping this fact at last.

Ralph smiled now. 'As alive as you are, and safe at home.'

For a moment his face was radiant, and then a shadow passed across it.

'But she must be – nineteen? Twenty? She must be married by now, or betrothed.'

Now Ralph grinned openly. 'Not a bit. She's nineteen, and unwed. Not even a suitor. I wouldn't be surprised if she was still waiting for you.'

Captain Hobart grasped his hand and shook it in speechless joy.

'Will you go back for her, then?' Ralph asked.

'By God I will!' Hobart cried. 'Just as soon as I can honourably discharge myself. And you too – won't you go home with me?'

'I came to join the army, to fight,' Ralph said. Hobart looked at him sadly. 'I felt that way once,' he said. 'I can see it in your eyes – the longing for action, adventure, glory. It isn't like that. It's dirty and weary and dark, killing men who are no different from us, who believe in their cause as strongly and truthfully and faithfully. A civil war is a bloody war, and no-one can win. I went on because, with Henrietta dead – as I thought – I had nothing else to live for. It gave me, at least, a reason for waking each morning. But for you – you should not be here.'

Ralph shrugged. 'A man has to do something.'
'But not this.'

The next day they marched to Preston, and learnt that the allied army of the Royalists was close by, marching on the road south: a huge force of ten thousand Scots, four thousand of Langdale's northern horse, veterans of the now so-called first war, and about three thousand Irishmen. The Parliamentary army numbered only about nine thousand, and Cromwell decided to rely on surprise and attack at once before the Royalists could have warning of their presence.

It was not the time, therefore, for Captain Hobart to quit his post, and on that day, 17th August, Ralph had his first taste of battle as the New Model fell on the straggling line just outside Preston. Lord Hamilton's army was spread out in sections as the varying speed of march had separated it. The advance guard was fifteen miles ahead on the road, already at Wigan; the rearguard was a day's march behind, not even having reached Kendal yet. One battle followed another, as bit by bit the New Model attacked the sections of the allied army and killed and put to flight veterans and raw recruits together. It lasted through the month of August, and at the end of it the Royalist army was entirely destroyed, and the New Model was ready to march south again.

It was at that point that Charles Hobart resigned his commission. He had had little taste for his work, but honour had kept him to it until it was done. He had been in terror that he would be killed now, when at last he wanted to live, but he had come through unscathed. There had been nothing really to resemble a pitched battle, and he had been in little enough danger. So at the beginning of September he started for York, accompanied by his servant, and Ralph. It was not the fighting, the killing, or any moral scruple that enabled Charles to persuade Ralph to leave and go home –

it was the discomfort and the poor food. Ralph, for the sake of his pride, put up a good argument, but Charles, sensitive to that pride, painted a glowing picture of his family's grief at his absence and its joy at his return, and made it possible to do what he wanted to do for someone else's sake.

There was a joyful welcome when they rode through the barbican into the yard at Morland Place. The servants were wild with delight that the young master had come back, still in one piece, and with the mare Titania unmarked too, and at first no-one had any time to take notice of the stranger with the scarred cheek, who sat so quiet and pale on his horse, looking about him as if he were seeing ghosts. The family came running out, and cried their joy, Richard and Mary Esther and Edmund, and the Father Michael with the boys, Edward and Young Kit. Last of all came Hetta, summoned by the noise from whatever quiet corner she had been sitting in. She appeared in the doorway, blinking against the strong sunlight after the darkness of the house. She smiled at the sight of Ralph, and then her eye travelled to the stranger, and her smile disappeared.

Charles moved then, dismounted from his horse, dropped the reins, and walked through the group in the yard as if he did not see them. The babble of chatter faded as he passed between them and eyes followed him as he walked up the steps and stood in front of Hetta, gazing down into her face, devouring her with his eyes. Hetta stared up at him for what seemed like a long time, and then her hand came up and her fingers touched his scarred cheek wonderingly.

'It's all right,' he said. 'It's all over.' He reached up and caught the small fingers in his own and pressed them. 'I've come back for you, Hetta. I told you I'd come back.'

Tears spilled over from her eyes, but she was smiling too, though she had nothing to say. She put her other hand up to his shoulder, and he took that too, and they stood looking at each other, wordless, and laughed, while the tears still ran down Hetta's thin brown cheeks; and Mary Esther, watching, knew at last why her daughter had been grieving silently these four years.

The doctor went away, and Mary Esther slowly dressed herself, not wanting to call a maid, and when she had done, she stood for a long time at the window looking out. The great bedchamber faced south over the Italian garden and the rose garden, though neither could be seen at the moment. It was February, and everything lay under a blanket of snow that had fallen so recently it still looked thick and soft and warm, like a feather-bed. Even the moat had frozen over, and the swans were walking on the ice, looking bewildered, as they did every year, at this sudden betrayal by their element. The fields of snow stretched as far as the eye could see, broken only by the black skeletons of trees, to the metal-grey horizon. There was more snow to come in that leaden, heavy sky, and when it did, Morland Place would be cut off until the thaw.

The door opened and Leah came in. Mary Esther did not look at her, for she knew that Leah's face would be marked with grieving, and she did not want to see it. Leah came up behind her, and though she did not touch her, Mary Esther took comfort from her. The house was quiet, had been quiet since the terrible news that Cromwell and the other leaders of the army had put the King on trial at Westminster for treason. It had been at first impossible to believe, but reports had followed, one upon the other, confirming it. It was horrible, it was unthinkable, a blasphemy. The King was the Lord's Anointed, his person sacred, he was accountable only to God, and even those who had fought against him in the wars could not believe that Cromwell had done such a thing. At Morland Place, people moved quietly and carefully, and avoided each other's glance, as if to speak or look or touch each other would be to jolt a wound.

Edmund had told Mary Esther the news. He had called

her into the steward's room, and told her in a quiet unemotional voice; but she had seen his hands, holding the news-sheet, trembling. After a while he had said, 'I never could have thought it would come to this. It is a handful of fanatics who are doing it. General Cromwell – power has corrupted him. He is mad – or a devil, I don't know which. I never – could have thought – it would come to this.'

It was as near as he could come to an apology. It was not in his nature to explain himself, nor did the master of Morland Place ever need to stoop to account for his actions, but he was offering her what he could and she was not too proud to take it. She loved him still, had always loved him and always would love him, though they had been estranged from each other for so long that coldness had become a habit between them. But she accepted his words for what they were. She had said nothing, but when he had looked up at last their eyes had met, and he had seen the acceptance in hers.

Now they waited for news, and for the snow, wondering which would come first. She shivered suddenly, and Leah said, 'Better you should come downstairs, Mistress. One brazier does nothing in a room this size.'

Mary Esther turned unwillingly. Leah's eyes were red-rimmed, and she avoided her mistress's gaze like a guilty dog. 'You spoke to the doctor?' Mary Esther asked. Leah did not answer. 'Leah, old friend –'

Leah's constraint broke in one convulsive sob before she caught herself up again. 'He said –'

'Yes, I know,' Mary Esther said. She could not yet quite take it in.

Leah said, 'How long? Did – he – ?'

'He said – perhaps two months, or three, perhaps until summer. I should like –' she wanted to say, 'I should like to see summer once more,' but her voice was not yet under control. She shivered again, and Leah touched her lightly on the arm and then drew back.

'I will come down,' Mary Esther said. They moved

towards the door, and she stopped and caught Leah's arm, and said, 'No-one is to know, do you understand? No-one.'

'No, Madam,' Leah said, subdued. 'But the master –'

'I will tell the master, if I think fit. Leah, I depend on you. Keep my secret.'

Leah was crying again, and Mary Esther took her in her arms and hugged her and Leah leaned weakly against her.

'I'm an old woman,' she whimpered. 'I nursed you when you were a baby, and I nursed your babies. It isn't fair. It isn't fair.'

'Hush, no more,' Mary Esther begged. 'Leah, please, don't cry. I need you to be strong, for a little while longer. It was always you who comforted me.'

After a moment Leah straightened up, wiping the wetness from her face with the back of a wrinkled hand. 'Aye, well,' she said. 'We can only hope God knows what He's doing. Come down, my lamb, into the warm. I'll say nothing – you can rely on me.'

That evening, after dark, a messenger came to Morland Place, and it was surprising enough to cause a stir in the house. But when Mary Esther went downstairs to discover what it was, she saw the servants in the hall huddling together like sheep before a storm, looking frightened and shocked. One glance was enough. Without a word she hurried to the steward's room, where she knew Edmund had been sitting working before the messenger came. The door was open, the messenger was standing just inside, weeping. Mary Esther knew him – he was one of the gardeners at the school beside the Great South Road. She dismissed him with a flick of her head, and closed the door behind him.

Edmund was sitting in his chair behind his desk, and his head was bowed over his arms, and she thought at first that he was crying too. Her mouth was dry; she could only whisper, 'Edmund?'

He looked up slowly, a terrible grief in his face. He could

not speak, he could only hand her the paper the messenger had brought. It was a handbill, of the sort by which Parliament circulated news and edicts. But it was not issued by Parliament. It was issued by the Army Council. Mary Esther read it three times, unable to take it in at first.

The trial of the King was over. They had condemned the King as a tyrant, murderer, traitor, and public enemy of the good people of the land. On 30th January, at Westminster, they had cut off his head.

The house seemed as still as a tomb, but outside, beyond the doors, the muted sounds of grief rose and fell softly like the soughing of the wind. Outside the window it began to snow again, the great slow flakes falling relentlessly, a gentle oblivion hiding the earth, concealing the ugliness of man's works, smothering life and death alike. Edmund made a sound, as if he was drawing his breath to speak, and when she looked at him, he held his hand out to her.

She went around the table, and he stood up, slowly, like an old man, using his hands to push himself as an old man will. She stood in front of him, looking up, and he said, 'Oh Mary, I'm sorry.'

So little to say for everything, ridiculously inadequate to set beside all the years of loneliness, the deaths of so many unmourned, the mourning and sorrow unshared, the horrible murder of their anointed King. He stood alone, unloved, separated from all he valued by his own coldness, his own inability to reach out, but now in his extremity he cried out for help to her he had injured most. The very pity of the fact that it was she to whom he must call moved her. She shook her head, wordless.

'You know – I would not have – wanted this – countenanced it. God knows – Mary, I am as anguished as you –'

She knew, but what could she say?

'After all this – dear God, Kit, and Francis, and Malachi – it was never what I wanted. My children, Mary, my own children.'

She wanted to help him, to put a hand up to staunch the wound, but his wounds were beyond her healing. He was shaking, shuddering like a dying bull. She put her hands into his in a helpless gesture of pity, and he grasped them. He did not know his strength, and he gripped them so tightly that it hurt her; but he was looking at her, *at* her, not through her, and she bore it without wincing. 'Forgive me,' he said.

'There is nothing to forgive,' she said wearily. The flood was released in him now; he clutched her and poured out the words in a desperate torrent.

'It was never what I wanted, any of this. I did what I felt I had to. My duty – all through my childhood – my mother – it was always duty. I did not act to please myself, do you believe that? They brought me up to do my duty, and I did it, though it cost me everything I valued. But how could I do otherwise? I wanted to preserve all this, it was the one thing I knew about, the only thing I knew how to do. I held to that. Morland Place – the inheritance – if I could keep that whole – and I did, didn't I? But it gave me no pleasure. It cut me off from you, Mary. To be faithful to my duty, I had to break faith with you.' He broke off, and looked down at her with frightening longing, as a man on a scaffold with the rope already round his neck might look at the wisp of smoke on the horizon, rising from his own chimney.

'The choice was yours,' she said. He let go of her hands and walked to the window to stare out at the annihilating snow. There was a scratching sound at the door and then it swung open a little – the catch had not been fast – and Dog came in, looking for his mistress. He pushed his nose up under her hand, and she caressed his head absently. Edmund turned from the window and looked levelly into her eyes.

'You still think I was wrong, don't you?' he said.

'Yes,' she said. 'But you will have to live with that.'

'Yes,' he repeated dazedly. He looked down at the handbill on his table, picked it up and put it down again without seeming to know what he had done. He came to stand before Mary Esther again, and Dog sniffed at his hands, and then walked away to lie down with a sigh in front of the fire. The dog was old now, stiff and almost blind, and he spent long hours sleeping.

'Mary, my hinny, help me,' Edmund said at last. He held out his hands, palm upwards, in a gesture that seemed to shew her all his poverty, asking her to fill them with her own bounty. She looked at them, and at him, wondering how he could not know that she was as empty-handed as himself. 'Take me back,' he said.

'I love you,' she said at last, on a little downward cadence like the far-off cry of a marsh-bird. 'I never wanted to be apart from you. I had my duty too, like you. But always, always I loved you.'

He looked down at her, seeing the lines of age and sorrow that he had helped to put in her face, seeing the grey in her dark hair, and he wanted to cry out in rage and defiance at God, for it seemed so wrong that she should know age and suffering. He remembered her as she had been before the war, her round, smiling, sunny face. Now she was as thin as a starved bird. Hesitantly he put his arms round her, and she felt light and brittle, like a corn-stalk.

'I loved you, too – oh so much,' he said. 'You know – it is hard for me to say it – but I need you so much, Mary. I cannot face the future without you. Be near me now. Love me still, my hinny bird – I would be so lonely without your love.'

She leaned against him, feeling the undimmed strength of his great frame, glad of his arms round her, glad to rest in them near the end of her long journey. She could not tell him, not then – perhaps not ever. She closed her eyes, and he rested his cheek against her head and rocked her a little.

'Whatever comes,' he said quietly, 'we'll face it together.'

A log in the fireplace cracked, and Dog sighed and groaned softly in his sleep. It was so quiet in the room that the snowflakes made a sound like childrens' fingers tapping the panes as they struck the window. They stuck to the glass and gradually covered it, blocking out the day and bringing on the early February dusk.